Northern Girl

Northern Girl

FADETTE MARIE

teampublishing

First published in Great Britain
in 2010 by Team Publishing

A CIP catalogue record for this book
is available from the British Library.

ISBN 9780956770509

Typeset in 11/14pt Sabon by
Falcon Oast Graphic Art Ltd.
Printed and bound in Great Britain by
CPI Cox & Wyman, Reading, RG1 8EX

*For my lovely mum
Marie Therese*

Acknowledgements

Diane Pearson: without your expertise and constructive comments this book would never have happened. You were the first to read my manuscript, and on the day that I received your encouraging and complimentary letter my shock and joy was such that I could have been mistaken for a winner on *The X Factor*. Diane, I can't thank you enough for getting me going!

Janine Giovanni: without your help I wouldn't have contacted Diane Pearson in the first place, nor would I have had a clue how to go about getting a book ready for publishing. Having led me safely through the minefield of dos and don'ts of the publishing world, you are now about to introduce me to the mysteries of the marketing world. Thank you just isn't enough, Janine (but you know, don't you).

Claire Ward: I always have a smile on my face when I think of you, Claire. Whenever I've expected you to find me a pain because of my fussiness over the design of my book cover, you've always come back with a quip, or told me patiently that we'll get there in the end. Thank you for that, Claire, you are a pleasure to work with.

Alison Martin: as soon as I was told that my manuscript had almost completed its journey and was finally with you I experienced a huge sigh of relief. Knowing that it was in safe hands. For organizing the printing and production of my book I thank you, Alison so, so much.

Katrina Whone: although we haven't met, Katrina, I have been informed all the way about how you've given your precious time and how you've shared your expertise on the many aspects necessary to get my book out there. And on top of all that you introduced me to Lucy Pinney. Many thanks, and I hope that we do meet one day.

Lucy Pinney: what would I have done without you, Lucy? Your hands-on assistance has been invaluable to me, and the bonus is that I have gleaned so much from you in the process. I felt that we struck up a really good relationship via our emails, and I really look forward to working with you again in the future. Thank you, thank you, thank you.

My husband David: you've kept me nicely fed and watered (or should I say wined?) through the tears, tantrums and triumphs. Thanks, hon, it's been a trial, hasn't it?!

Angela Vernon: you have been encouraging through all the above processes, and more importantly you have listened when needed. Thanks, Angie.

Joanne Lidford: you knew that I would be particularly interested in an article in the Northern Echo depicting the village of Evenwood and very thoughtfully sent the article to me here in the south. To my amazement, there in the article, was a photograph of (the now long gone) Randolph Colliery just as portrayed in my story. Thanks you so, so much Joanne.

Chris Lloyd (deputy editor of The Northern Echo): thank you for taking the time out of your busy day to find the photograph of Randolph Colliery and for giving me permission to use the picture on the back cover of my book. I am so grateful for your help Chris, thank you.

Last and most definitely not least, *Jean* (our Jean): just like your character in the story, Jean, you always bring a smile, or more often a laugh, into our lives, and we, the family, love you for it. Thank you, just for being you.

Northern Girl

Chapter 1

Evenwood, Northern England
Saturday, 24 November 1945

Sitting on the top of the double-decker bus, Tom was suddenly aware of the pungent, sulphurous smell of his childhood: the coal mine. He shut his eyes and inhaled deeply. Perhaps, now, at last, he'd be safe. And all the terrible things that had been happening to him would finally stop.

'Evenwood Gate!' The yell from the conductress brought him back to the present with a jolt. He leapt to his feet, grabbed his kitbag, and raced for the stairs. He was too late. The clippie had already double-pinged the bell, and the bus was lurching forward.

'Whoops, sorry, luv, didn't see yer there!' she exclaimed as he jumped off the last stair, almost knocking her off her feet. She grabbed at the nearest seat to steady herself, then pressed the bell again, yelling at the driver, 'Hang on a sec, fer God's sake!'

And then, as the bus shuddered to a halt, she did a

double take, at this soldier standing before her, so tall and handsome in his uniform.

Tom caught her staring at him, straightened his shoulders, and smiled, revealing perfectly straight white teeth, while his blue eyes twinkled with mischief.

'Yer better hurry up, luv,' she said, motioning him off the bus. But at the same time wanting to delay him for a moment longer, she added: 'Haven't seen you around before. Do yer live round 'ere, like?'

Tom noticed how blatantly she was looking him up and down. 'Aye, I'm off home to see me family,' he said. He winked. The clippie was very pretty, with a mischievous face and wayward blonde curls, and he was about to ask her her name when he was distracted by the driver, who had swivelled round in his seat behind the glass panel of his cab, and was glaring at them both, tapping frantically on his pocket watch. 'Get a move on!' the driver mouthed soundlessly.

'Judging by your driver's face,' Tom said, 'I think he wants to get home as well. He looks right narked!'

Laughing, the clippie said, 'Don't you worry about 'im, lad. 'Ee's always moanin' about something. 'Ee's nowt but a pain in the arse, that one! But ah can deal with 'im, no problem!'

'I bet you can,' Tom said.

'See yer around, then,' the clippie said. She dinged the bell twice, but not before adding cheekily, 'If ever yer need a ride, mind, don't forget the number twelve bus!'

The driver pulled away so fast that the clippie had to

grab the safety pole on the platform not to fall off, and Tom found himself laughing out loud.

When the bus had gone he suddenly felt cold. There were dark grey clouds overhead, and he could tell it was going to rain. Not wanting to get wet, he broke into a run, and the sound of his boots on the road caused terrible images to flash in front of his eyes: falling men ... artillery shells exploding ... severed limbs. He stopped, and momentarily covered his ears with both hands, trying to push the memories from his mind.

As he continued the mile-long walk from Evenwood Gate to his home in the village of Evenwood itself, the grandeur of the pit loomed before him, filling him with awe, as it always had. He studied the tall, familiar brick chimney, flanked by slag heaps and wooden out-buildings, beyond which was the huge wheel at the shaft surface. He shuddered at the thought of the metal cages, more often than not crammed with miners, being reeled down to the coal face.

Tom shook his head. No man should have to do such a God-awful job, let alone his da! And yet he knew there was nothing else his da could have done. After all, he'd never been trained for owt else, had he? And it'd be too late, now, for him to learn anything new. He'd been down that bloody pit since he was ten years old! It just wasn't right!

Tom could understand why, before the war, his da had encouraged him to go into the building trade. He could hear him now, advising in his broad pit-man's dialect, 'Why, ye'll have a trade fer life, lad! People will always be needin' 'ouses. And, mind, there'll be money ter be made, yer nah!' He'd rubbed his forefingers and thumb together, to imply cash. Tom grinned at the memory, it was so typical of Da!

'But more than that, son,' Da had gone on, 'ye'll be outside, in t' fresh air.' He'd raised the palms of his hands heavenwards at this point, saying, 'Ye'll see the sky all day! Stick at it, lad, an' ye'll be all right!'

So Tom had stuck at it. Then the war had come along. He'd been called up, and that had been the end of that.

He looked again towards the chimney. It had thrown its gas flames so far into the sky that you could see the glow from at least ten miles away. And here it *still* was, still standing in all its glory. He leaned back to see the top of it, gazing in wonder, remembering how, as a child, he'd lain in bed watching the flames belt out of the top, and they'd lit up his whole bedroom with a fierce orange glow. He'd made up stories for himself about those flames, and they'd been so frightening he'd usually ended up going back downstairs, supposedly for a drink of water. His mam had never suggested he take a glass up with him before going to bed; she knew only too well that it would have taken away his excuse for coming down to be comforted.

Remembering how well his mam knew him gave Tom a warm feeling. It suddenly seemed like only yesterday that his imagination had run riot, making up stories about the dragon who'd so *obviously* lived inside that chimney. And probably still did, if that smell was anything to go by!

He sniffed at the air. Oh yes, that's a dragon smell all right, he thought, as he walked steadily home.

Fast approaching Bank Top now, he glanced up. 'Blimey! The bus shelter's still standing!' He was so amazed that he spoke out loud. He grinned, remembering its secrets. The shelter at the top of the bank, he thought. I suppose you'd call it the top of the *hill*, if you were posh. He was suddenly reminded of his upper-class army mates. He was wondering what the ones who were still alive would make of this quaint little mining village, when, all of a sudden, the heavens opened, and the rain came down in buckets.

Christ Almighty! He broke into a run. If I'd got on the right bus in Bishop Auckland, he thought, I'd have been home by now. But no, I had to get on the first bloody one I saw. I should have got the number eleven instead of the twelve. Then he reminded himself that he wouldn't have met the mischievous blonde clippie if he had.

In his haste to get under cover, he practically fell into the three-sided wooden shelter. After he'd wiped his wet face on the rough itchy sleeve of his coat, and once his eyes had adjusted to the gloom, he looked around. This place could tell some stories, he thought, remembering the brazen lasses who'd once shimmied around inside, displaying their naked breasts to an audience of eager village lads. For a brief moment he was back in the past, feeling a pang of embarrassment, and sitting on this very bench with his mates, staring in awe at those poor lasses, who'd do all kinds of mucky stuff in return for a fag, or even less.

It was all part of growing up, he supposed, and probably happened in most villages where there was nothing better to do. You could always go to the pictures instead, of course, but only if you had a tanner to spare for a ticket. Transported back to his teens, he sat on the damp bench a while longer. He noticed the musty smell of the shelter had got worse over the years, which he hadn't thought possible. He glanced at the rotting wooden walls. Apart from that, it was the same. Although it was comforting to find that things hadn't changed while he'd been away, it was also strangely disturbing, too. It was difficult to fathom how, after all that had happened in the world in the last six years, the pit chimney and the bus shelter could have remained untouched. Even the village looked intact. How the hell could that be? It just didn't seem right to him, this sameness, when, where he'd been, right in the thick of it, there had been so much destruction and death.

I'm getting all maudlin sitting here, it's time to move on, he thought, getting up. Outside, the rain was easing, so he decided to make a run for it. It was just as well he hadn't been able to let his mam know in his letter the exact time he'd be home. All he'd told her was the day, and that it would be some time in the afternoon.

He felt happy at the thought that he wasn't too far from her now. Oh, how he'd longed to see her! He wasn't afraid to admit that he'd missed her terribly. There'd been times, during the cold dark nights, when he'd actually cried. Not only out of fear, but because he craved her comforting embrace. Sometimes, his longing had been so intense that he had crouched in his dugout, oblivious to the mud, and wrapped his arms around himself like a child – in an attempt to alleviate the torture of his surroundings. But, invariably, he hadn't succeeded, and he'd broken down, doing his utmost to stifle the sobs over which he had no control. Even now, tears pricked his eyes, as he recalled that he'd not been alone in feeling like that.

More than once he'd come across the other lads in the same state, and they'd insisted that it was only the cold making them shiver and sniff. But he'd known better! There'd been no place for sentimentality in those bloody foxholes, so each and every one of them had had to find their own way of dealing with the homesickness and fear. They'd had orders to obey, they'd been there to fight. And by God, how they'd fought! He'd watched some of his closest mates fall at his side, and he'd had no choice but to keep on – running and stumbling over broken bodies where they lay, some so clogged with mud that he'd not have recognized them even if he could have stopped. And all the while, there'd been a never-ending fog, caused by the continuous bombardment.

How the hell *he'd* got out of it he didn't know, and he'd vowed to himself that if he ever got home, he was going to make the best of his life. No matter what!

Skirting puddles, he arrived outside his old school, which he remembered as being huge. He was shocked at how small it was. It was insignificant, he thought, as he stared at the tall narrow windows blending into the dull

7

grey stonework. I suppose our Jeannie must go there now. He smiled, visualizing his young niece. She'd been a funny little thing. She had to be ten by now, and he probably wouldn't recognize her.

Just ahead he could make out the red brick of *his* terraced street, where each house had its own back yard enclosed by high walls. Like the others in the village, his street was back to back with another, separated only by a narrow cobbled lane. So that on the rare occasions when washing wasn't strung out from one side of the lane to the other, causing the flapping sheets to blot everything else out, you could look straight from your own gate into the opposite yard. There was a hell of a lot of gas-bagging went on from one gate to another, he remembered. But that was the way in Evenwood.

He looked quickly at the church on his left as he walked by, but it was only a glance. Unlike his mother, he had never had much time for religion. He had even less now, since seeing what he had, in this world supposedly looked after by God. He just couldn't believe in an invisible and supposedly loving force that had allowed such things to happen, and more often than not to innocent folk.

Again, he had to give his head a little shake to rid himself of the visions, sounds and odours that crept into his mind unexpectedly: weeping children; tanks on fire with men screaming inside; the smell and sight of rotting flesh. They gave him so many nightmares that he was afraid to sleep.

He looked up, and saw that just above the downstairs

window of the end terrace house was the metal sign he'd visualized so many times, still clinging on to the red brick wall with its rusty old screws. Even the badly faded blue lettering couldn't obliterate the words he'd longed to read: GLAMIS TERRACE. Here it was, his street . . . the only one in the village with a strip of land along the front, which the proud residents had turned into gardens.

As he got closer he slowed right down. Only a few more steps to go, and even before he raised his eyes he knew she'd be there. Slowly, he looked up, and there she was, his mam . . . just as he'd pictured her so many times, waiting on the doorstep.

He cleared the lump from his throat and walked towards her, and before he could get there, her arms reached out to him. Without a word, Tom dropped his kitbag to the ground and fell into them. They clung together for a few moments, before Tom, in an attempt to stifle the emotion threatening to overwhelm him, held her at arms' length and questioned light-heartedly, 'Nice pinny, Mam. For something special, is it?'

She smiled through her tears, and, giving him a playful shove, answered, 'Yer know fine well that ah always wear me best pinny on special days, our Tom.'

'Aye, I do, Mam, but why you wear your best pinny over your best dress when you can't see the dress for the pinny, like, I'll never know.'

'Ay our Tom, yer still the same, pet, never serious.' She laughed. 'Anyway, what are we doin' out here talking about me pinny, when yer must be soaked ter the skin? Get yerself in here,' she said, pulling him none too gently towards the front room. 'And get in front of the fire while ah make us a nice cup of tea. That'll soon warm yer up. Then we'll have a good old chinwag, an yer can tell uz all about what yer've been up to. The bits yer didn't tell us in the letters, like!' she added with meaning.

It didn't escape him that, as she scuttled towards the scullery, she grabbed the bottom of her pinny and pulled it up to her eyes in a discreet attempt to wipe away the tears. Tom dropped his wet coat on the floor and flopped down into the armchair, looking around appreciatively.

The room gleamed, and a cheering blaze glowed red against the black-leaded fire-surround. There was a shining hob and oven, and a brass fender to catch any coals that fell. He called out, 'Are you all right in there, Mam?'

'Yes, pet, ah'll be there in just a minute,' she called back hurriedly.

Tom relaxed into the chair, relishing the cosiness of the house, which he felt was unique. He'd never come across anything like it anywhere else. Not even at Madeleine's, and that certainly hadn't been on account of her family, who he had gradually grown to . . . yes, love, he supposed. But French homes were much more sparsely furnished, and their tiled floors could be cold. Although at Madeleine's house there were rugs on the floor.

That thought prompted him to look down at the mat

under his feet. How many long winter nights had been spent making it? he wondered. He remembered how his mam – and sometimes the neighbours – had sat on high stools years ago, leaning over a large wooden frame. Sacking was stretched tightly across it, and with their 'prodders' they'd busily poke clippings – small strips of material – down through the hessian and back up again, the clippings being packed in tight against each other. Everyone had worked on their own little area, until, eventually, the whole of the sacking was hidden by brightly-coloured clippings. It had been a long laborious job, but they'd obviously made the best of it, because he remembered lots of laughter and chat.

Frustratingly, the grown-ups had never explained what they were laughing about, they'd said he was too young – but he certainly hadn't been too small to help cut the clippings! In fact, anybody who called at the house while the mat-making was going on got drawn in. Hannah, his mam would hand them a pair of scissors and some bits of fabric and old woollen clothes and set them to work. She said she liked woollen clippings best, because they were the warmest underfoot.

That must have been about sixteen years ago, he thought, as he bent forward and dug his fingers into the rug. 'Why it's still like new!' he said out loud, surprised.

'What's that? Were yer talking ter me, our Tom?' Hannah called from the scullery.

'No, Mam, just muttering to myself,' he called back.

'There's places fer people like you, yer know.' She laughed.

'I was just thinking about how you used to let me have a go with the prodder, when you were making all those mats in the old days,' he called.

'Aye, ah remember that all right. Yer were a right little bugger then. Hang on a sec, Tom, ah can't be doin' with shoutin' through the walls, ah won't be a minute. Just waitin fer the tea ter mash.'

Comforted by the familiarity of his mam having a go at him – and the promise of a sweet, warming mug of tea – he stretched his feet out. Poor Mam, he thought, I did lead her a bit of a song and dance when I was a nipper, I suppose. He could see why she'd sometimes lost her rag with him. Like that time when, feeling left out of the mat-making, he'd pestered her to let him use the prodder. She'd finally given in, but he'd soon got bored with pushing tiny bits of material through the sacking, and found it much more amusing to run around jabbing everything with the prodder, including the sideboard and the table. Worse, he'd accidentally jabbed someone's backside, which hadn't gone down too well with the neighbour concerned. Needless to say, he'd never been allowed to prod again!

Still unable to believe that he was really home, he stared into the blazing fire. It all seemed like a dream. He looked across the room at the old grandfather clock, standing where it always had in the corner, and listened to its non-stop pendulum swing back and forth. The sound always used to calm him, but today the 'tick tock, tick tock' suddenly grated. It was too loud and heavy in his head, so much so that when Hannah came into the sitting room with the tea he said, 'How on earth did that clock in there keep going through the war, Mam? I've come home to the same old pit chimney, same old bus shelter, same old clock. Why, the whole of the village is untouched, it's as if nothing's happened at all!'

Luckily, Hannah had talked to some of the other folks in the village whose lads had come back from the war, and was prepared for him to be unsettled and dis-orientated. Some of the lads had terrible physical injuries, and others had them in the mind – and these were, of course, far harder to assess. She was grateful that her Tom was sound in his body, but worried about what might be going on in his head. All she knew was that he, like so many others, had been through a torment that would make his old life seem abnormal; it was going to take time for him to calm down. She also knew that she had to be careful what she said.

So, as casually as she could, she answered, 'Like us all, lad, the clock kept on going, just as we've all had to, ah suppose. And we've had our moments, believe me!' She sighed. 'Anyway, let's not worry about that old clock just now. Yer must be shattered, and yer'll need ter get them damp clothes off before yer catch yer death of cold! Why don't yer go up ter yer room?' She added with a smile, 'That's still in the same place as well! And get some dry clothes on while yer there! But hurry up, because ah'm desperate ter have a good talk with yer before yer da gets in from work causin' his usual trouble!'

Tom grinned at the thought of his da, and got up and

hugged Hannah again. He said, 'OK, then, I'll not be a minute.' At the bottom of the stairs, he turned and looked at her. 'It's so good to be home, Mam. I can't tell you what it's been like out there.'

Close to tears, she replied lovingly, 'No need, lad, not till yer ready.' She made an effort to sound light-hearted, 'Now you get up them stairs, and you'll find all yer clothes where they always were an' all. Let's hope they still fit. Looks like yer've lost a bit of weight, mind! Then yer can come and sit by the fire while we have our cup of tea. So hurry up before it gets cold.' She playfully shoved Tom further towards the stairs, adding, 'Go on then, and be quick about it!'

'OK, OK! I'm going. Keep your hair on, Mam,' he teased.

'Get on with yer.' Hannah flapped the tea towel at him as he climbed the stairs. She headed back towards the fire, beaming with joy and thanking God for getting Tom home safely.

Tom rushed into his room and threw himself on the bed. He bounced on his backside, revelling in the comfort of the mattress, before laying himself down with a contented sigh, his head for once empty of anything as he folded his arms behind it and stared up at the ceiling. The promised mug of tea far from his mind, he just lay there staring blankly. Then, aware his eyes were becoming heavy, he told himself he wasn't to sleep, and sat up quickly, leaning against the headboard while he pulled himself together.

He put his hand into his pocket where the damp

Woodbines and matches were, and after several un-successful attempts to strike a match on the collapsed soggy box, cursed and gave up. Defeated, he wriggled himself down the bed until he was on his back again. This time his eyes rested on the old oak chest to his left, and for some reason he was gratified to see that it was still missing a handle on the bottom drawer. He felt panicky about his own thoughts. Why was he getting so upset about things that didn't matter: like clocks and handles? He'd only noticed this since arriving home; he was sure he hadn't felt like it in France or any of the other places he'd been. I've got to get this rubbish out of my head, he thought.

As he lay there, he found he had to open his eyes wider and wider to stop them feeling dry, and, realizing that he was losing the battle to stay awake, he made a move to get up, but he was suddenly as helpless as if he was drunk. The last thing he was aware of was smiling with pleasure at being home.

'Tom! Come on lad, wake up!' The voice seemed to be coming from some distant planet, until he felt a hand on his shoulder gently shaking him. He tried hard to resist coming round from what, for the first time for six years, had been a deep and peaceful sleep.

'Eee, yer've been out like a light this last hour or so, son! So ah left yer in peace, but ah thought yer'd want ter be awake afore yer da gets home.'

Tom sat up, squinted at his mam, then, after a loud and exaggerated yawn, said, 'Ay, Mam, I don't know what happened there! I was just having a lie on me bed, and the next minute there was you shaking me brains out!' He looked at his watch. 'I suppose the tea's gone cold, then?'

Laughing, she pushed him back on the bed. 'Get yersel' down stairs, and come and see all the bakin' ah did this mornin' ready fer yer homecoming!'

'It's funny, you know, Mam,' he said, getting up and following her downstairs, 'because whenever I used to think of you when I was away, you were always bakin', and sometimes if I tried really hard, I could smell the teacakes!'

Hannah turned at the bottom of the stairs to see his mischievous grin. 'Eee, yer daft, you are,' she said, giving him another shove. 'And yer must think ah'm as daft as a brush an' all. Anyway, come an' have a look!'

Tom followed her to the scullery, where she lifted the clean starched tea towels which covered her day's baking. Tom stood open-mouthed for a second or two. 'Blimey, Mam!' he said, staring at the array of cakes, jam tarts, iced buns, scones, meat pies, sausage rolls, and God knows what else.

'Mam! For goodness' sake! When are we going to eat this lot?' he said, picking up an iced bun.

'Well yer know what ah'm like, pet, ah like ter keep busy. And ah was so nervous this morning that ah couldn't stop. And ah'll be givin' some of it away more than likely ter old Missus Hurd next door.' She leaned towards him and whispered, as if divulging a great secret. 'She's never got any money, yer know!' Then, as if she needed to explain herself to Tom, she went on, 'Some of the other folk lent me their ration books ter get extra flour and sugar and butter, among other things. They all chipped in, so if there's anything left they can help themselves. Anyway, ah can't see you complainin', when it comes ter fillin' yer belly!' she joked. Then she laughed and added, 'Unless yer've changed, of course?'

Tom's eyes glazed for a moment, before he said, in all seriousness, 'Well, I think I have changed, Mam. Oh, not in the way you're talking about, but there's so much happened, I couldn't help but be altered by it . . .' He stopped abruptly, and remained deep in thought until he noticed the look of concern on her face. Quickly, he added, 'It's not *all* bad, mind!' Immediately he thought of Maddie, and shivered with excitement. He remembered how honoured he'd felt when she'd liked the way he had shortened her name, especially as no one else had called her that. And she was such a bonny lass! How he'd loved to show her off. He'd always noticed other chaps looking at her at the dances they'd gone to in Calais. Why, even officers had been queuing up to ask her for a dance, although, he reminded himself, he'd not been so keen on that!

He'd just put a freshly made mug of tea to his mouth when the clatter of the back door latch stopped him dead in his tracks. He turned, and there in front of him stood his da, his smiling face as black as coal. The whites of Jack Dawson's twinkling blue eyes and the pink of his lips stood out against the coal dust. Father and son stood face to face, both too overcome to speak. Without a word they moved towards each other, and for a split second faltered, before flinging their arms around each other so tightly that it was painful.

Tom, almost overcome by love for his da, said, his voice breaking, 'I've so much ter tell yer, Da.'

Jack glanced at Hannah for advice, and, picking up from the discreet shake of her head that now wasn't the right time, responded as casually as he could, 'All in good time, lad, all in good time. But fer now just let me get used ter havin' yer back home, eh? We never thought we'd see this day, son.' He patted Tom on the back.

Then, to avoid the danger of becoming emotional again, he pulled away and walked into the sitting room, where he began undressing. He climbed into the metal bath that was steaming before the fire and tactfully changed the subject with the comment, 'Ah see yer mam's been bakin' enough fer an army again. She must have thought yer were bringing them all back with yer!'

Tom laughed. 'Ay, Da, you haven't changed a bit,' he said.

Jack laughed loudly and said, 'Who are you talkin' to, lad, in that posh showin'-off accent? Is that from serving with all them army lads from down there in the South, like?'

'You'd better watch your P's and Q's now, Da, because I've P'd and Q'd with the best of them now, you know. And most especially I've peed!' Tom said teasingly.

Jack was really getting in to the banter now as he

winked at Tom and shouted to the kitchen, 'Here, Hannah Dawson! Come and scrub me back, will yer?'

'Get our Tom ter do it,' came the reply. 'Ah haven't got time fer your shenanigans. Ah'll be dishin' yer tea out in a minute, so get yer skates on!'

'Eee, lass, ah wuz just havin' a bit crack with yer, so yer didn't feel left out in the scullery there, all on yer own! Dinnet worry, ah'll be washed an' out a here before yer've got the kettle boiled, that's if yer ever get it put on, instead of yer mitherin'.'

A few seconds later Hannah came through into the living room, squeezing herself between the table and the bath tin, which as usual was taking up most of the space in the room. It hadn't struck Tom until that moment that his mam must have heated, on the fire, the endless pans of water required to fill up the bath all on her own. Damn it! How selfish of me to have fallen asleep like that, he thought angrily. I could have been helping her just like I used to in the old days. I used to love fetching that old bath tin through from the back yard. He stared at the rust on it. That's when I finally managed to get the thing off the bloody great nail that it was hanging on out there! Why had they always called it the 'bath tin', and not the tin bath? he wondered, for the first time. I remember the carry-on I had trying to drag it through the scullery into the living room, not that it was heavy, but I was only a bairn, and when I'd got it to the right position I'd just plonk it down there in front of the roaring fire, and me and Mam used to have a hell of a time filling the thing. I don't know how we lifted those heavy boiling pans off the fire. How on earth had Mam managed on her own all this time? he wondered.

'Hey, lad! When yer've finished yer day-dreamin' give us a hand here, will yer?'

'Sorry, Da, I keep doing that. My mind wanders,' Tom apologized, taking the huge bar of carbolic soap and rough flannel from Jack.

'It's all right, lad, it'll take time. We know that,' Jack answered.

Tom lathered the soap on the flannel and started to wash his dad's back with vigour. A pained shout brought him to a sudden halt.

'Ay, steady on, lad. You'll scrub me away if yer not careful!'

Tom had been so overcome by being at home with his mam and da at last, that in an effort to quell the tears he'd scrubbed too vigorously. His da's back was red.

Hannah pushed her way through once more, this time with an armful of crockery she'd collected from the sideboard under the window. As she passed, she squeezed Tom's arm to reassure him.

Tom was about to apologize to his da when Jack, drying himself, said, 'Come on, son, I think we're in need of a stiff drink while yer mam gets the dinner out. There's a drop of whisky in the sideboard, but don't tell anybody, mind!' He winked. 'Else they'll all be round expectin' their glasses ter be filled up!

Tom poured out two measures of whisky, *and* a sweet

sherry. He'd found half a bottle at the back of the cupboard. Jack hadn't mentioned that!

Seeing Tom hand the measure of sherry to Hannah, Jack grinned. 'Nobody knew about that, either, lad!' Then, glancing at his wife with an affectionate glint in his eye, he teased her, 'And don't you get yerself drunk before yer've seen ter our dinner, mind!'

Hannah answered indignantly, 'And when've you ever seen *me* the worse fer wear, Jack Dawson?'

'Never,' came the reply. 'But there's always a first time, just you remember that, Hannah Dawson!'

At that, she glanced towards Tom and sighed. 'Nowt changes, does it, lad?'

He reflected for a moment before answering, 'No, Mam, nowt changes.' And as he lifted the bucket to chuck more coal on the fire he added under his breath, 'Thank God!'

But whether he liked it or not, change was on its way.

Chapter 2

Marck, Northern France
Sunday, 2 December, 1945

'But, Maman! You *can't* send me to England, I don't even speak the language!' Madeleine stared at her mother in disbelief. It pained her to see that once-proud face looking so weary. She knew, too, that her whole family were equally devastated by what she'd done. The very thought of it made her stomach churn.

There was a moment or two of uncomfortable silence between the two of them, and then Madeleine asked, 'What do you think it will be like for me in England, when the furthest I've ever been from home is visiting my sisters in Boulogne, hardly an hour's train journey away? England might as well be on another planet!' She pleaded in vain. Her mother obviously had no idea just how distant it was.

Maman sighed and got up from the kitchen table, while Madeleine remained seated, consumed by a strange mixture of shame and fear; but more than that, she felt immense sadness because she'd let her mother down so badly.

Madeleine had had a problem looking Maman in the face lately. The hurt in her eyes had been almost more than she could bear. Now, when she slowly raised her head and glanced at her mother, she saw she was busying herself around the kitchen, opening the crock where the vegetables were kept, and looking sadly at the contents. For a second Madeleine felt she was glimpsing herself. She suddenly realized how similar Maman's facial expressions and mannerisms were to her own. It wasn't so strange, really, she supposed: after all, their likeness had been commented on many times before, but Madeleine hadn't really seen it until now, at the age of eighteen. We really *are* similar, she thought, except, that is, for Maman's hair, which unlike her own chestnut locks, had turned a beautiful silvery white. And Maman was still in her early fifties! No one had been very surprised when Maman's hair had gone white early, as it was a family trait, but Madeleine suspected that the war might have had something to do with the speed it had happened.

She hadn't really studied Maman closely before; Maman had always just been her mother. But now Madeleine realized that they had exactly the same large, thickly lashed brown eyes, neat noses, and delicately shaped lips. Even their wistful, sweet-natured expressions were identical. She was taken aback, and if she was honest, pleased. After all, Maman *was* considered to be very striking!

Oh, Maman, she thought despairingly, as she watched her peeling potatoes for the next meal. What on earth are you thinking, to suggest that I go and live in England? You must be feeling desperate to come up with an idea like that. She gradually slid further down into her wooden chair, causing it to wobble irritatingly on the uneven tiled floor.

She looked around, and although the room itself had changed little over the years, for her *everything* had changed. She could feel animosity right here in her own home, and it scared her even more than when their house had been occupied by the Germans. This was much worse, she decided: this was hostility from her own loving family. This was all the love and security that she had ever known crumbling around her.

She knew one thing for certain: she couldn't remain here the way things were, because, rightly or wrongly, she felt that everyone was now her enemy. She'd never have dreamed of arguing with her mother before, and couldn't believe that she was doing it now.

Why, even Papa – Papa who'd always been on her side – had taken to spending hours in his workshop doing carpentry, and only coming into the house to eat and sleep. Although she couldn't deny that financially it was good that he had so many orders, she also knew that, before, he would never have let work stop him from seeing his family. Before all this he would have found a way, even if it had meant going back to his workshop later on in the evening. But now he was obviously burying his head in the sand – or, in this case, sawdust. She thought this wryly, almost laughing out loud at the absurdity of it. How unrealistic of him to think that his problems would go away if he ignored them!

Some hope of *that*, she thought, folding her arms. She glanced at her mother again. 'And what about Papa? Is he still hiding?' She gestured towards the workshop, where she knew he was.

Maman turned sharply from the potatoes, dropped her knife on the table, and walked towards her daughter. Madeleine noticed that the colour had drained from her cheeks. 'I don't like your tone, Madeleine,' she said. 'You weren't brought up to talk about your parents like that.' Madeleine felt a stab of guilt as her mother continued, 'You have no idea, have you?'

'About what?' Madeleine was puzzled.

'No idea how you're Papa's treasured little girl, the baby of the family. Sometimes I think you're his favourite.' She said this with hesitation, aware it was disloyal to her other children, before continuing, 'He's always been so proud of you. Can't you see? He doesn't know how to react to his little girl being . . . being in this situation.'

'Being pregnant, you mean, Maman,' Madeleine broke in, 'You *can* say it, you know!'

Trying to avoid more argument, and realizing that Madeleine was being aggressive to cover her deep shame and embarrassment, Maman chose to ignore the remark. She went on, 'He needs time . . . we all do . . .

in order to deal with it in his own way. Right now your Papa is heartbroken.'

At this, Madeleine was suddenly overcome by grief. With a sob, she rushed from the kitchen and through the *bouanderie*, where they did their washing. Wrenching the back door open, she ran headlong into the garden. She ignored her mother's calls to come back, and instead threw herself down on the ground between the chicken coop and the fruit bushes, where she wept inconsolably.

Maman's words had hit a nerve, and made her realize that in the past few days Papa hadn't been hiding away so much as trying to protect himself from the painful truth. His favourite child was no longer an innocent virgin. He must be thinking all kinds of awful things about me, Madeleine fretted. Oh, Papa, if only you would talk to me about it! Her mind in turmoil, she imagined herself speaking to him. 'I wish you'd let me show you I'm not a common little tart.' She sobbed even more at that. 'How will you know, otherwise, that this is a terrible mistake, caused by something that happened only *once* in my *whole life*? How can you, when you won't let me explain? All you want is to get me away from here. If only we could sit down and talk about this as a family! You know our other problems have been solved like that.'

But even she knew this wasn't the usual kind of family problem. It was too new, too distressing; that was why none of the family could even look each other in the eye at the moment, let alone discuss it.

She sat up and peered over the fruit bushes, remembering watching Papa every night that week, and noticing how, after he'd locked the workshop, he still carefully put the keys into his overall pocket. It was the only one of his night-time habits that hadn't changed. There was no longer a spring in his step: he'd taken to trudging towards the house, his capped head bent so far forward that only the tips of his white moustache were visible. And this, along with the tufts of white hair poking out at the sides, had suddenly made him look like an old man, a shadow of what he used to be. Her heart had gone out to him.

Before, he would always pull up some lettuce from the garden as he walked from the workshop to the house, and the five rabbits would get up on their haunches in their hutch, their noses twitching in anticipation. Then he'd talk to them and push the leaves through the wire mesh as they hungrily devoured every last morsel. That done, he would stop off at the chicken run, enjoying the mayhem as he scattered handfuls of seed around. The resulting frantic fluttering and clucking had always been a great source of amusement to him, and as this noise could easily be heard from the house the family always knew that in a few minutes Papa would arrive for supper. But first, of course, he'd stop briefly in the *bouanderie*, to take off his well-worn blue overalls. By the time he came into the kitchen, the table would be set and a glass of wine poured ready for him, and his beaming, cheeky grin never failed to put a smile on Maman's face.

No more. Madeleine sighed. Papa's smile had gone. He now walked straight past the rabbits and the chickens, saying he was too tired to do anything else after working such long hours. But she knew how much he had loved feeding them, and how it had calmed him after a stressful day. And his work was stressful, because he never allowed himself to go over a client's deadline. This was commendable, she was sure, and benefited his business, but not his health.

For Papa was a perfectionist. No job was ever too big or small, and whatever he made – a small cabinet, a wardrobe, or a set of table and chairs – was always finished beautifully. Of course, this made him highly sought-after, and he always had work. He'd been busy all through the war, invariably giving each job his best, even if it was distasteful to him, like the time he'd been ordered to make desks and chairs for the occupying German officers.

Madeleine shuddered at the memory now, but she'd been so proud of Papa then, at the way he'd taken everything in his stride. But, she wondered: how could he have shown such calm then, and yet now, confronted with a problem with his own family, refuse to face up to it? It just didn't fit with what she knew of his character.

Maybe she could have coped better if her two sisters, Martine and Simone, had been around a bit more. Where were *they* when she needed their support? Although, to be fair to Martine, she at least had been there at the awful, shameful moment when Madeleine had had to tell Maman.

* * *

Even though it was a week ago now, Madeleine still felt nauseous when she thought of it. She shivered as she remembered how she and her sister – who was twelve years older – had walked hand in hand into the living room. Madeleine had almost crushed Martine's fingers as she'd tried to avoid approaching Maman, and she'd been trembling so violently that she'd found it hard to walk. As she'd clung on to Martine's hand with both of hers, what she'd been most aware of was a strong desire to rush from the room and vomit.

She hadn't been able to hear Martine's actual words to Maman, the blood was pounding so loudly in her head, and she'd been too ashamed to look up. That is until she heard the gasp of anguish that came from her mother: '*Oh non, oh non!*' She would *never* forget the look on Maman's face as the news of the pregnancy began to sink in. It would be etched on her heart for ever. The shock in Maman's brown eyes, and the way she'd clutched at her mouth to stop herself screaming, had been too much for Madeleine.

The room had seemed to spin, and she'd collapsed. She'd felt she was drifting away, and that everything was happening to someone else. As her body had slid down the door frame, she'd put her hand to her wet face. Tears had streamed down her cheeks, meeting under her chin, where they had trickled down her neck into the collar of her dress, drenching her. And there she'd lain, half propped up in the doorway, limp and motionless as a rag doll.

* * *

A thorn in her arm brought Madeleine's attention back to the gooseberry bush she was sitting next to. As she moved away, and tried to disentangle her cardigan from the gooseberry prickle, she thought about her other sister, Simone. At least Simone hadn't stayed long enough to gloat, she thought sourly. Where the hell was she, anyway? It was pretty obvious that she was deliberately keeping her distance, too. The six-year gap between Simone and herself wouldn't have mattered if Simone had acted like an older sister, instead of being on a never-ending quest for excitement. She was much more outgoing than either Madeleine or Martine, and made no attempt to disguise her liking for male company.

But, pretty as she was, her boyfriends never hung around for long. Martine had tried gently advising her to be a little less forward. But it hadn't worked. Madeleine rolled her eyes at the memory, as she coaxed a pulled thread back into her cardigan sleeve. She hadn't been any more successful with Simone, either. She'd been less tactful, and had told Simone straight out that if she wasn't such a tart her boyfriends might stick around longer. But did she listen? No. No one tells *Simone* how to behave.

The last straw with Simone, certainly as far as Maman was concerned, had been a month after the Germans had first occupied the house, in early 1940. Maman had walked into the *bouanderie* and found Simone pressed up against the wall in there with one of the German soldiers. Seeing her like that, all dishevelled and flustered, one thing had been obvious to Maman: Simone hadn't been forced into anything. The young soldier, the only decent one in the unit, had shrugged his shoulders and apologized to Maman as he'd backed off and walked away.

By then Maman had had enough, what with the whole house in turmoil, and *les monstres*, as the Germans were known in the Pas-de-Calais area, wandering freely about wherever they liked. She'd known that she had no chance of controlling Simone if she stayed at home: the only thing to do was to send her out of harm's way as quickly as possible.

Martine hadn't been best pleased when she'd heard about the plan for Simone to stay with her in Boulogne. 'Just until the war is over,' Maman had said, as a way of assuring her that it wouldn't be for long, because of course the war wouldn't last more than a couple of years. Martine had had a promotion that year, which meant moving from the bank where she worked in Calais to a different branch in Boulogne, and she'd been thrilled because there was a flat included. Madeleine had been pleased, too, as it had meant that she could get away from Marck for an occasional break in the school holidays.

There'd been nothing Madeleine liked more than getting on the train to Boulogne to visit her sisters. Though, of course, she could only be there for a few days each time, as it left only Maman and Dominic in the house to deal with the billeted Germans.

While Martine had thrived in her new independent life in Boulogne, Simone hadn't changed a bit. Maybe she had even got worse. Martine had been so busy that she hadn't had time to control what Simone was getting up to. And then, when the war had finally come to an end, and the sisters had arrived back home, the tension between them had been obvious to Madeleine. And, equally clearly, it was because of something Simone had done.

But Simone was Simone, Madeleine told herself now, and even if she had been around, she wouldn't have helped at all with the trouble over the pregnancy. Dominic was different. Madeleine's beloved brother Dominic had always been there to get her out of scrapes in the past. He'd done it ever since she'd learned to walk – even though he was only a year older than her. Because of the age gap between him and his two elder sisters, he'd always been closer to Madeleine. Especially once Martine and Simone had reached their teens, for, much as they loved their little brother and sister, having them hanging around all the time had become so annoying that they'd gone to great lengths to escape them.

Of course, when war broke out – and more so when the first German soldiers arrived from Belgium – their lives had suddenly become ruled by uncertainty, and fear of the terrible things that had happened to people they knew. And this had drawn all four Pelletier children closer. But even so, Martine and Simone had still been in Boulogne. Martine was almost like a second mother to her younger siblings, and there'd been so many times when Madeleine would have appreciated her reassurance and advice.

Dominic had been Madeleine's confidant and devoted protector right up until Tom came into her life. He and Tom had got on really well, and the two had become good friends. Such good friends that Dominic had finally relinquished his little sister, confident that she was in safe hands. Madeleine shivered as she thought how he must be kicking himself now, and wondering how he could have got it so wrong.

This news of Madeleine's must have hit Dominic really hard: she hadn't talked to him for nearly a week, or seen him for the last couple of days. It was as if he'd disappeared into thin air, right when she needed him most. She shivered again. It was getting cold in the garden, but she was in no mood to go back to the house. She pulled her cardigan more tightly around her, and crossed it over at the front, holding it together under her folded arms.

Mon Dieu! she thought, if he's not around who's going to convince Maman and Papa that I would rather *die* than leave my family to go and live with a new one *in England*? The amount I know about England, they might as well be sending me to the North Pole! Tom hardly told me anything about the place!

As upset and disillusioned as she was with Tom, she couldn't stop him from popping uninvited into her head, and playing havoc with her thoughts. If only she could stop thinking about him! She clasped her hands round her knees and dropped her head.

'MAD . . . E . . . LEINE!'

'Huh . . . ! What!' She looked up at the sound of Maman's voice.

'What on earth are you doing sitting out here in the cold?' Maman demanded, holding out her hand to pull Madeleine up.

Hesitantly, Madeleine took it. She followed Maman to the kitchen, and sat at the table. Maman put two cups of coffee down, sat opposite, and stared in pained silence at her.

'Madeleine, do you have a better idea than the one that we've come up with?' she asked. Madeleine didn't answer, so her mother continued, 'You're only eighteen! Think about your baby for a moment! In a few months you'll be a maman yourself, with no father for your child.'

'Oh, Maman, for goodness' sake! I'll manage somehow. Other girls do. After all, it's 1945, surely—'

Madeleine jumped, almost overturning her chair, as her mother shouted, 'DON'T! Don't be so silly, Madeleine! Of course you can't!'

Madeleine stood, breathing heavily, so emotional that she couldn't speak.

Maman said more quietly, 'We have no choice, and if it doesn't work out, we'll have to think again.' She reached over and took hold of Madeleine's hand, before saying hesitantly, 'It's too late, anyway. Dominic has already left for England, to see Tom and his family.'

Madeleine, still speechless, pulled her hand away, and stared open-mouthed at her mother. She struggled to control the indignation she felt, and the tears that she could feel welling up at the realization that this was why she hadn't seen Dominic lately. She burst out, 'Oh! How could you, Maman, when it's so obvious that Tom doesn't want me! Did he write? *Non!* Did he send any message? *Non!* And you expect me to go to him, just like that?' She snapped her fingers. Then, placing both hands on the table to steady herself, she leaned towards her mother, until their faces were only inches apart. Then she whispered harshly, '*Mon Dieu*, Maman, he doesn't even *know* I'm pregnant!'

'Well, he will soon enough,' Maman replied. 'Tom is a good man. He would want to know, I'm sure. And as we finally managed to obtain his address—'

'We . . . Who is we?' Madeleine interrupted. 'I suppose everyone knows about this perfect little plan except me!'

'We'll discuss that when you're in a better frame of mind, and prepared to listen,' Maman said. Then she added, 'What you need to know right now is that I've sent a letter to Tom's parents telling them Dominic is on his way, and why.'

'Well, you've certainly thought of everything,' Madeleine replied sarcastically, before pressing her hand tightly over her mouth. She knew she had gone too far.

Maman, knowing that her daughter was feeling angry at the whole world, didn't react. She just said mildly, 'Aren't you even *curious* about Tom's background, Madeleine? And his family? You know nothing about

35

them. Just imagine how you'd feel, if sometime in the future, your child asked about its Papa. What then? Would it be enough to say, "Oh, he was an English soldier who fought in the war, and that's all we know"? I think you'd be very sorry if we didn't try to do everything we could now.'

'Whatever you say makes no difference, because you've already made your decision.' Madeleine wiped a tear from her cheek. Then she said, 'And where, may I ask, does Papa come into all this? I notice *he's* staying well out of the way!'

'Papa knows what's going on, and as you should know by now, if we don't think things are right for you in England, then *of course* we won't send you there.'

Madeleine, unconvinced, thought of her brother, on his way to Tom's home, and felt betrayed that he hadn't discussed it with her first. She couldn't help remembering all the confidences the two of them had shared over the years. It was hard to believe that he would have kept such a huge secret from her. Papa and Maman must have applied huge pressure, else why would he have done it?

She sighed. 'How about Martine,' she asked, 'does she know?'

'About England? Yes, she does, and she agrees we have no option. You have to go.'

Madeleine raised her eyebrows. 'And Simone?'

'Yes,' replied Maman, more hesitantly.

Madeleine sat down. 'Huh! Well I suppose *she's* happy to get me out of the way!'

'That's enough!' Maman was exasperated. '*Mon Dieu*, Madeleine! Can't you see that we all just want what's best for you?'

'Are you sure it's not what's best for you?' Madeleine answered, so agitated that she couldn't keep still. Her chair clattered to the floor as she rushed upstairs to her room.

At the sound of her door slamming Maman's shoulders slumped in despair. Then she picked up a tea towel, covered her eyes with it, and cried as never before.

Madeleine's heart pounded wildly as she stood with her back against the bedroom door. Hearing a faint sound from downstairs, she pressed her ear to the wood, holding her breath to listen. Realizing that she could hear her mother sobbing, she crouched down, held her hands tightly over her ears to block out the sound, and whispered, 'I'm so sorry, Maman . . . So sorry, Papa!' She was tired . . . tired of crying . . . tired of worrying . . . and too weary to fight any more. She would just have to accept that she had no choice over what happened next. What was the point of feeling sorry for herself when her fate was sealed? Her family would be humiliated if she stayed – so she had to go to England. That is, if Tom would have her.

Chapter 3

Calais, France
Saturday, 1 December 1945

The cross-channel ferry loomed above the docks. Swept along by the bustling crowds in its shadow, Dominic thought he'd never seen Calais so busy. As he was buffeted towards the gates, he tried to stop and feel in his pockets for his ticket, and almost knocked over a screaming child. A few minutes earlier, when the queue had been stationary, the same child had been poking his tongue out at anyone who looked his way, and when Dominic had responded with equal rudeness, adding a vicious snarl for good measure, the boy had wailed, hoping to get sympathy from his harassed mother.

For some reason, Dominic had been infuriated by this spoiled little brat; even more so when his mother gave in to him. So when the boy's father appeared and took the situation in hand – giving him a resounding slap across the backside – and peace was restored, Dominic allowed himself a satisfied smile. And made a mental note to keep well out of the boy's way during the crossing.

Finding the ticket, he allowed himself to be jostled up the gangway. But all he could think about was Madeleine, and how she would feel when she discovered what he'd done behind her back. He knew how upset she'd be when Maman told her he was on his way to England, and he had no doubt she would have been told by now. He was the one person she really trusted and relied on, and his betrayal would hurt. But he'd felt he had to do it: his parents were so desperate.

He had been devastated, too, by what had happened to his little sister. And then the family had brought up the idea of a trip to England. After he'd got over his initial shock, he'd realized the alternative was worse. If Madeleine stayed in France, his parents would have to send her away. That was even more worrying. It was horrible to think of her going to a convent for un-married mothers; he knew the sort of women she'd end up with. He'd seen a group of them being taken into a forbidding stone building with bars on its windows on the outskirts of Calais. Some had walked in, dazed by misery, resigned to the fact that this was to be their life now, while others had had to be dragged there, viciously kicking and screaming. Tom, and his family in England, had to be better than that. And that was why he was at the docks now.

The hardest part, and the bit that had disgusted him most, had been keeping it all from Madeleine. But he'd known, like the rest of his family, that she would *never*

ever agree to it, because it would be so humiliating to have to ask for help from someone who had broken her heart. In fact, she would probably prefer to be sent to a convent, and they all knew it. And, because Dominic had come so close to telling her about the trip to England, he'd made himself scarce, terrified that otherwise his love for her would force him to confess. Martine and Simone had done the same, and he was sure that Madeleine must have been upset by this, too. It had been cruel of them, he knew. But what else could they have done, when Papa and Maman were so insistent that Tom had to be told?

Dominic knew his parents loved Madeleine, but they also felt the dishonour keenly. He'd been infuriated, that night in the kitchen a week ago, when Maman had said, 'Papa's business will be affected.'

'How the hell's that going to happen?' he'd shouted. 'I know carpentry isn't the best-paid work in the world, and, yes, I'm impressed by how Papa managed during the war, when so many didn't. But surely his clients, who are all friends, won't turn against him! After all, I know at least a couple of them have daughters who took money from the Germans during the occupation – and that's putting it politely. But they weren't the ones who got caught out, oh no! Not like poor Madeleine, who made one, only *one* mistake.' (He had no reason to doubt her story.) 'Where else would Papa's clients go, anyway? Why, there isn't another decent carpenter for miles!'

'Not everyone's like you,' Maman had said. 'When

something like this happens, it doesn't matter how respected the family is. People are narrow-minded and fickle. The family won't be seen in the same light. I know it'll ruin Papa's business. Then where will we be?'

Dominic had always thought Madeleine's upbringing had been too sheltered, and he probably hadn't helped by always rushing to protect her whenever he felt she was in danger. In fact, it was amazing that she'd turned out so kind and thoughtful. She could easily have taken advantage of the situation and been spoilt. The whole family had idolized her; and now that this had happened, she couldn't forgive herself for letting them all down.

'I've spoken with Papa,' Maman had said, 'and we both agree that Madeleine must get in touch with Tom. Let's hope that he still cares enough to marry her!' Then she'd added sadly, 'After all, she does love him, doesn't she?'

Dominic had said, 'You do know what you're suggesting, Maman? You do realize that Madeleine would have to *live* in England permanently? Because Tom wouldn't get work in France, that's for sure. He hardly speaks any French.' He'd looked pleadingly at his mother. 'Don't do this, Maman!' he'd said. 'Can't we just hide her away here somewhere?' Then, as if suddenly inspired, he'd cried, 'Tante Lucy! What about Tante Lucy? Madeleine could stay with her!'

He could tell by the set look on Maman's face that that wasn't an option. Her mind was made up.

He'd shouted petulantly, 'I don't believe this!'

41

She'd paused before saying, 'Papa and I want you to organize a passport – or a visitor's card if you can't get a passport quickly – and go to England at once to find Tom. You always got on so well.'

So angry he couldn't trust himself to speak, Dominic had rushed out of the back door, pushing past his father, who was coming in. He'd almost fallen into the garden, he was so desperate to avoid being press-ganged into going to England. And he knew he ought to discuss it with Madeleine first. Hands shaking, he'd rummaged in his pocket for a cigarette, and fumbled as he tried to light it. When the match had finally flared he'd inhaled deeply, and for a moment been aware of nothing but the smoke curling into the air.

Eventually, he'd turned to look through the kitchen window, where he'd seen his exhausted father walk across the room to his mother, and take her in his arms. Dominic couldn't hear what they said to each other, but he saw her press her head against Papa's chest and sob into his shirt. He'd realized then that he was going to have to go to England.

The crossing was rough. The ship lurched and tilted on the waves, spray hurled itself against the windows, and the decks and passageways were full of passengers being sick. Dominic sat in the almost-deserted café, clutching a cup of coffee, an overflowing ashtray sliding around the table in front of him. He was wondering, yet again, what he was going to say to Tom, when he heard voices singing, '*We'll meet again, don't know where, don't know when.*' Two bright-faced crewmen were bawling out the Vera Lynn song as they wove through the knots of queasy passengers, handing out brown paper bags.

They offered him one, but he waved them away. The song, though, struck him as pretty appropriate. He could still remember Tom's last words, as he'd gripped Dominic's hand feverishly.

'I'll see you again, mate. Not sure where or when, but I'll be in touch.'

They'd patted each other affectionately on the back, and Dominic was sure the same thought had crossed both their minds: even though they'd become so close, it was unlikely they'd ever see each other again.

Almost word for word that song is, thought Dominic, and I'll bet Tom would never have imagined in a million years that it would be *me* getting in touch with *him*, and so soon.

'*But I know we'll meet again, some sunny day.*' The two sailors swayed off to the next passenger, an Englishman, who showed his appreciation for his sick bag by immediately vomiting into it. Dominic, who'd been only vaguely aware of what was going on around him, was jolted back to the present by the Englishman saying, 'Thank God! Dover's in sight, mate, we'll be docking soon . . . half an hour at most, I reckon!' The poor man could barely contain his excitement at the thought of getting his feet on dry land.

Dominic smiled politely, but he had different feelings about stepping on to English soil. *Mon Dieu!* he thought. I just hope that Maman's letter has arrived. He wondered what kind of reception he'd get if it hadn't. Tom had probably already settled back happily into his old life. And here *he* was, about to arrive at his home and disrupt everything.

Dominic had learned a lot from Tom during the months that he'd been calling on Madeleine back at home in Marck, and the two of them had had some really good discussions, especially on the nights Tom and Madeleine went to dances at the town hall in Calais.

Dominic had always found it funny the way they'd rush in exactly on Madeleine's eleven o'clock curfew. And Maman or Papa would invariably be there to make sure that Madeleine and Tom said goodnight, and that she went off to bed alone.

Then, as soon as everyone else had gone to bed, Dominic would get the beer out and he and Tom would sit chatting in English, sometimes for hours, making Tom late getting back to his barracks. But, as he told Dominic, it wasn't a problem: he had ways. He always winked and tapped the side of his nose when he made that comment. Dominic smiled at the memory.

Disappointed to be too young to go to war himself, Dominic used to ask endless questions, and Tom, who didn't want to discuss the horrors that he'd witnessed, instead did everything he could to make soldiering sound dismal and dreary, and kept reiterating that Dominic was far more useful at home, protecting his parents and Madeleine from the Nazis. To an extent, Dominic had agreed with him. In order not to be sent away to work in a factory like most of his friends, he'd allowed himself to be treated like a servant by the Germans. He'd made himself indispensable – doing their errands and being at their beck and call – and he was never sure whether they were too dim to realize why he was doing it, or whether it was just that it suited them. Either way he hadn't cared. He hadn't even minded if others saw him as a collaborator. All that mattered was being able to watch over his family.

Invariably, those late-night conversations between him and Tom had ended on a light note, and they'd told each other a few jokes. Some didn't translate well from French, but Tom always laughed anyway.

Then, eventually, the day had come when Tom had called in to let them all know he'd been demobilized, and was going home at last. He'd talked about it for months, but once it actually happened it was obvious he was in no hurry to leave. He told Dominic he hadn't reckoned on *falling* for anyone, as he'd put it. The thought of leaving Maddie tore him apart, even though he'd known in his heart, right from the start, that it couldn't last. He'd always been aware that a relationship with a French girl could go nowhere. But, as he'd confessed to Dominic, Madeleine was so lovely she had got right under his skin. Sometimes at night, when he was lying in his bed back at the barracks, he imagined what it would be like when he had to go home. He'd decided that if he and Maddie promised to write to each other the parting would be easier. But what he hadn't said to Dominic was that, deep down, he had a feeling that the letter-writing would be short-lived, or simply wouldn't happen at all. Well, he couldn't just walk away, could he? He had to tell her – and himself – that they were going to keep in touch.

He'd also told Dominic how he'd hoped he'd get back to normal life quickly once he was home, because then maybe the nightmares would stop. And Dominic felt sad to think, 'Here I am bringing another nightmare right to his doorstep!'

Dover, England
Saturday, 1 December 1945

'Will all foot passengers please head for stairway C on the upper deck, and prepare to disembark!' The loudspeaker announcement made Dominic jump, and he looked up to see crowds of passengers pushing towards the stairs. He stayed where he was, marvelling at the mentality that made people fight other people to be first in line. He reached under the table for his case, and brushed the cigarette ash from the sleeve of his now-crumpled jacket. Then he stood up and glanced across to check the state of the queue. As he did so he caught the eye of an attractive dark-haired girl who seemed to be looking in his direction. He smiled, but she quickly turned away. I must have been mistaken, he decided. She wasn't looking at me at all. This business with Madeleine is playing havoc with my head. He walked towards the end of the queue.

Standing there, he found it impossible not to search through the bobbing heads in front of him to see if he could pick out the pretty stranger. There she was! As he stood on tiptoe, his stomach fluttered. Then she turned her head, their eyes locked again for a brief moment, and she smiled. He felt a pang of excitement. He wasn't sure if she'd blushed, or if the colour he'd seen had just been the deep red of her coat reflecting on her cheeks. Although she turned back to face the front of the queue, he could see she was shifting nervously from foot to foot. She was aware of his eyes on her, he knew.

Too soon, he lost sight of her. He ran his fingers through his dishevelled fair hair, allowing himself a wide smile, before addressing himself again to the job of finding Tom's family in . . . where was it? He fumbled in his pocket and pulled out the crumpled piece of paper, on which was written, in his mother's neat handwriting:

> *Mr and Mrs Jack Dawson*
> *9, Glamis Terrace*
> *Evenwood*
> *Near Bishop Auckland*
> *County Durham*

He pushed the paper back in his pocket, and concentrated on the queue, which was moving more quickly now. Standing on tiptoe again, he made a last attempt to see the mysterious girl, but to no avail. She was nowhere to be seen, and for a brief moment he felt an unreasonable sense of loss.

Chapter 4

Marck, France
Sunday, 2 December 1945

For Madeleine, *everything* had changed.

She pulled herself up from her bedroom floor, where she'd been sitting since her row with Maman, thoughts whirling in her head. She'd no idea how long she'd been there, fretting about the future. She went to the window and looked out at the back garden, with its neatly-trimmed grass, and rows of cabbages and root vegetables. She remembered how neglected it had been only recently. And, sad as she was, she couldn't help smiling as she recalled seeing both her papa *and* her maman out there, working to put it right after the mistreatment it had suffered at the hands of the occupying Germans.

She'd found the sight surprising, because before the war Maman had *never* had the time or the inclination to work outside. But once their unwelcome guests had left, she'd spent hours gardening with Papa, and seemed to enjoy it. It must have been something to do with her new-found freedom. Maman had taken on a fresh lease of life after those hostile bastards left.

And now, as Madeleine thought about the shame she had brought on the family, the cloud of sorrow hanging over her grew heavier. This war has changed us all, that's for sure, she thought, weeping as she looked at the neat rows of vegetables. Through her tears she couldn't help noticing how spectacularly the pale, filigreed carrot tops contrasted with the dark-green sturdiness of the round cabbages. They're just waiting to be cut and thrown into a pan, she thought, as a disturbing vision came into her head. She could still see the German soldiers laughing as they urinated over Papa's cabbages, and, not satisfied with that, kicked them off their stems and used them as footballs. She shuddered now, remembering how she'd put her whole family in danger. She'd been so enraged by their behaviour that, for one adrenalin-filled moment, she'd forgotten any fear she had of '*les monstres*'. She'd run outside, stopping only to grab a spade. Clutching it in both hands, she'd been about to take a swing at the two nearest soldiers, when Dominic, who knew only too well how they'd retaliate, had come up behind her and taken the spade before it did any damage. Everyone had stopped what they were doing, and there had been total silence as Madeleine was dragged back into the house by her trembling brother. Then the drunken Germans had laughed before resuming their game. They hadn't stopped until all the cabbages were smashed to pieces.

Madeleine hunched her shoulders. Dominic had gripped her arm tight. Once they were out of sight of the soldiers he had shaken her, shouting, 'Have you any idea what they'd have done to you? They're bad enough sober. Don't you see, they taunt us because they want us to react, and you . . . you played right into their hands!'

'You're hurting me, let go!' she'd shouted.

He'd released her and backed away, saying quietly, 'You're lucky they're only laughing about it.'

But that was no comfort to Madeleine, who knew the soldiers actively enjoyed her frustration. She was powerless, and they could do anything they wanted. Her biggest regret was that after that – after realizing how spirited she was – she had become a challenge to them for the rest of the occupation, and they had found her even more attractive. She'd drawn attention to herself, and wished she hadn't. 'Ugh!' She shivered at the memory as she wrapped her cardigan around herself for comfort. She refused to think about the Germans.

She was hungry now, and would have gone downstairs, but didn't want to face the family, so decided to stay in her room. She thought wistfully that if she'd been outside, and it had been summer, she could have picked blackcurrants, gooseberries and raspberries. It seemed a lifetime ago that she and Dominic had been little, and hidden behind those bushes stuffing their faces with as much fruit as possible. How they'd suffered afterwards! Maman and Papa hadn't been sympathetic about their stomach cramps and desperate visits to the toilet. They'd just ticked them off, and told them never to do it again. And of course they had taken no notice!

So many things had changed, and now here she was, eighteen and pregnant. She couldn't bear to think how distraught her Maman was, and as for Papa: she still adored him, but he'd changed completely. Gone were the times when she'd hug him every time he came in from work, her embrace releasing the subtle aroma of wood shavings still lingering on his clothes. That scent had always filled her with a sense of security, so much so that if she'd felt worried about anything, she'd just have to smell shavings to feel calm and safe. She'd lost count of the times she'd wandered into his workshop over the years, simply to be reassured by that powerful aroma, and to watch him plane wood, running a hand over it to check the smoothness until the surface shone like silk. The look of pride on his serene, kindly face had often brought tears to her eyes. But she'd always left him alone if he was concentrating very hard, because she knew he took his work so seriously. Madeleine pulled a face similar to Papa's now as she remembered his expression at those times. She would watch him quietly, not daring to utter a word, scarcely even breathing. And she wouldn't relax until the dovetail joints were fitted perfectly, followed by a triumphant, '*Et voilà!*' as Papa set down his mallet and chisel.

Now, with the war over, Papa was taking on jobs that weren't remotely connected with carpentry or cabinet-making, but he was his usual considered self about it: he simply did what he could. So *why*, she wondered, can't he cope with my situation now? How can he have altered so much? she thought, recalling her eleventh birthday. That day, feeling particularly happy, she'd crept into the workshop while Papa was out, and, seeing the giant heap of curly wood shavings against the wall, she had, as usual, longed to jump into them, even though it was forbidden.

But this time she'd been unable to resist, and taken an enormous leap on to the top. It was as soft as landing on a cloud, and there she lay in ecstasy, allowing that aromatic scent she loved so much to fill her whole being. She'd been there for some time when, to her dismay, Papa walked in.

She sat up quickly, stuttering an apology for the mess, 'S-sorry Papa—'

He looked at her, laughing, and said, 'I'll tell you a secret, *ma fille*, I've always longed to do that myself, but never had the courage.'

She gazed at him in surprise. 'Well, come on then, Papa, you must do it now!' When he hesitated she pleaded, 'Just think how awful it would be to wish you had done it, when it was too late!'

He smiled at this, and as she held out her hand he hesitated. So she stuck out her hand even further while he looked around furtively to check if anyone else was around. She seized the opportunity to grab his hand, and with a sharp tug he was in. 'Come on, Papa, get into the middle where you can *drown* in ecstasy!' she said.

'Shush!' Papa answered. 'If Maman sees us she will think I've lost my mind!'

'Well, you can tell her you were looking for it in the wood shavings, then!' Madeleine said, throwing a handful at him.

'If I didn't know you better, *ma fille*, I'd think you'd been at my wine bottle,' Papa said. Then, seemingly without a care in the world, they'd thrown shavings at each other, and for a short time Madeleine had glimpsed what her papa must have been like as a boy.

She'd treasured their special closeness. Thinking of it now made her heart fill with love; and sadness, because it had gone.

As she turned away from the window, she caught sight of the pretty blue dress in a crumpled heap on the bed, and, feeling ashamed at how childishly she'd stormed off to her room after the confrontation with Maman, she picked it up and held it against herself. Before the argument, she'd thought, stupidly, that she could bring a little joy into Maman's day by wearing it. She'd rushed down into the kitchen to show it to her, and even though she'd been unable to look her mother in the eye, her arms had been outstretched to show all the hard work she'd done. And she'd asked with a twirl, trying to provoke the smallest sign of approval, 'Well, what do you think?' After all, she'd sewn every stitch herself, and it *was* something that Maman had been nagging her to do, ever since Tante Lucy had given her the material. Madeleine had hoped that maybe Maman would start believing in her again, once she saw that she could apply herself to a difficult task, and wasn't a complete failure.

But her mother hadn't given the dress a second glance, telling her to sit down.

There was something much more urgent to discuss: the plan to send her to England.

It had been six months since the daisy-printed material in cornflower blue had been brought to the house by Tante Lucy, and Madeleine had fallen in love with it at once. Tante Lucy was great fun. She was Maman's sister, and the whole family loved her. She owned a farm just a few kilometres from their home in Marck. As a result she was able to stop off quite frequently and visit them whenever she went to Calais, which was only a few kilometres further on. She'd deliver her farm produce to outlets in and around that town, and if she had time, call in again on her return journey. It was on one of these trips, after she'd been given it by one of her regular customers (who was short of cash that week), that Tante Lucy had turned up with the roll of fabric on her shoulder. The material had been no good to Tante Lucy, who couldn't even sew a button on without pricking her finger. She'd only accepted it because she knew that Madeleine would put it to good use. And Madeleine, who was always delighted to hear the clip clop of Tante Lucy's pony, Horace, along with the squeaking wheels of the trap he pulled, had hardly been able to contain herself when her aunt had given her such a lovely present. She couldn't remember the last time she'd had a new dress. She usually made do with altered hand-me-downs from one or other of her sisters. But that day, she'd hugged her aunt delightedly, and danced around with the fabric draped over her shoulders, while Tante Lucy sat her stout little self down at the kitchen table with a satisfied look on her face. As always, Tante Lucy drained the red wine from her glass fast before banging it down on the table to be refilled by Maman. Tante Lucy always managed to cheer everyone up with her funny stories – which became more and more exaggerated after a few glasses of wine. There were days when it was pure luck that she got home at all. When Madeleine once voiced her concern about this, Tante Lucy had answered blithely, 'Don't worry, Horace could do the journey with his eyes shut!' This was reassuring, because Madeleine was sure that Tante Lucy drove him home with her eyes closed, too!

Although Madeleine had never especially wanted to be good at needlework, she had to admit it made her very popular with her friends. Especially the ones with older sisters who passed on their cast-offs. Madeleine had the knack of reworking these into chic outfits, and her friends loved her for it. Once she had left school, Madeleine regretted that she hadn't been more appreciative of the nuns, particularly the ones who'd guided her into sewing, and shown her how to do it professionally. The Catholic school, which both of her sisters had attended before her, had been within easy walking distance of the three Pelletier girls' house. (Unlike Dominic's school, which was in the centre of Calais and had to be cycled to.)

When Madeleine had first been told she had a gift for sewing she'd rebelled, and tried to convince her parents that a course in typing would be much more useful. She'd often bashed away at Martine's rickety old typewriter, and fancied herself as a secretary. She'd only ever seen secretaries at the cinema, where they looked glamorous and led exciting lives. But her parents had seen how naturally sewing came to her, and after a discussion with Sister Thérèse, Madeleine's needlework instructress at school, Maman had become convinced that Madeleine's future lay with this gift of hers. Madeleine had only agreed reluctantly, until, months later, she'd begun to feel a sense of pride and interest in her work, and this had drawn her into studying harder, on her own.

As it turned out, this was just as well, because, as far as she could see, most of the nuns, except for Sister Thérèse, were far too distracted during the last two years of the war to pay any great attention to the pupils. If they weren't rushing around looking flustered, they were praying. The girls in Madeleine's class discussed this frequently, but no one had a clue as to why the nuns were suddenly so panicky, and there were all kinds of rumours flying around. The most ridiculous was that they were hiding someone from the Germans – in the cellars. Why on earth would they do that, when it would endanger not only themselves, but the whole school? Yet this particular rumour surfaced time and again. And yes, Madeleine had known at the time that there were plenty of hiding places in the maze of passages that ran off the main corridor in the cellar.

The girls usually craned their necks in that direction, straining to look along the candlelit passageways, whenever there was an air raid and they had to go down the stone steps. But the nuns always rushed them past so quickly that all they saw were the many huge, heavy, forbidding locked doors. They were given no opportunity to dawdle, and it was impossible to work out whether the rooms there were being used.

Madeleine smiled with affection now, as she remembered how efficiently the nuns used to spring into action during air raids, determined to save the girls from the bombs. As soon as the sirens sounded, there would be an almighty clatter of feet as nuns ran along the concrete floor of the corridor to collect the girls from their classrooms. Then the florid-faced sisters would burst in, flustering and flurrying around, but in a strange floaty manner. And the girls, scared as they were, would struggle to stifle their giggles as they were hurriedly gathered together and pushed down the corridor towards the cellar door. Once the girls had arrived, and were crowded up by the entrance to the cellar, the flustered nuns would do a quick head count before shoving them down the steep stone steps into the darkness. Madeleine had often thought it a miracle that none of them were killed *before* the bombs fell!

Sometimes, after school, she, along with her four closest friends – Sophie, Hélène, Elise and Fréderique – would spend hours trying to think of a way to sneak down into the cellars and investigate. In fact, for a while they were completely obsessed by it, but when it came to action, none of them were brave enough to try. Not only were they afraid of what they might find, but if any of them had been caught by the nuns, who were extremely vigilant, they'd have been punished by having to sit in an empty classroom for hours and hours, praying continuously. It was a powerful deterrent.

Remembering those times in the cellar never failed to make Madeleine shiver. Even though she was never alone down there, she'd still sometimes be so afraid that she couldn't bring herself to close her eyes in prayer. Instead she'd distract herself by looking at the nuns, who always knelt facing their pupils, giving her a perfect opportunity to study their faces.

There was pretty Sister Thérèse, who was far too kind for her own good. She was Madeleine's favourite, and being good at needlework herself, was delighted by Madeleine's progress and enthusiasm. She helped, too, with all the sewing Madeleine undertook for her friends and fellow pupils. Granted, it wasn't much more than a few alterations, but Sister Thérèse hadn't minded that at all, and thought it good practice for Madeleine. Especially as the shortage of money meant that most people couldn't buy new clothes. So, whenever Madeleine's friends had a special occasion, they went straight to her with old cast-offs, and expected her to work miracles. Occasionally, she did. And dear Sister Thérèse always downplayed her role in this. She was just happy that Madeleine was doing so well. She and Madeleine had even wondered sometimes whether

Madeleine would end up running her own sewing business. Or a fashion house! It had been good to dream.

Sister Beatrice was one of the other nuns in the cellar. She had a sharp-nosed, gingery face and always listed slightly to one side, so she looked like an inquisitive fox peering around a corner. Sister Bee – as she was known by her pupils, though never to her face – taught English. But, because she was so woolly-minded, she was unable to hold the girls' attention for long. Consequently not much English was learnt. Madeleine hadn't cared at the time: why on *earth* would anyone need to speak English anyway? She had no way of knowing that her lack of attention in Sister Bee's English classes was going to be one of the major regrets of her life.

The remaining four nuns in the cellar were Sisters Trudi, Matilde, Emmanuel and Céleste, whom Madeleine, much to the amusement of her friends, had nicknamed 'the gargoyles'. All four of the gargoyles prayed frantically with their eyes half-open, so they could watch the girls. And as they'd peered out from under their wimples, the candlelight had exaggerated the whiteness of their wrinkly faces, so that they really did look as if they were carved from stone.

Madeleine winced now, remembering how un-comfortable it had been, kneeling on that hard floor. They hadn't dared fidget, either, as the wrath of the nuns, especially the gargoyles, was as terrifying as the bombs. Aware how tightly she was holding the crumpled blue dress, she laid it neatly on the bed, and tried to smooth out the creases. She suddenly felt desperately sad about those dead – and as she now knew – heroic, nuns.

Bewildered by her sudden changes of mood, she looked around her comfortable, sparse bedroom. Despite all its problems, this was the place she loved best, the house where she'd been born in 1928. It was the only home she knew, and very soon, one way or another, she'd be leaving it for good.

Chapter 5

Marck, France
Sunday, 2 December 1945

The village of Marck was separated from Calais by a huge cemetery hidden behind a high wall. And when Madeleine was six, she'd had an irresistible urge to climb that wall, even though it terrified her. Tom had laughed when she asked him to help her. It had been easy for him to climb it, of course, because he was taller. Her stomach fluttered now as she remembered how he'd lifted her so that she could grip the stones on the top, and pull herself up to look over. She'd gazed down, shivering, at the gruesome headstones – many of which had figures on them that looked like the Devil – and been half scared to death. The villagers walking past had been amused but not surprised. Most of them had known Madeleine all her life, and knew how mischievous she was. They thought it endearing.

Madeleine sighed, remembering the good reputation she'd enjoyed locally. It had been obvious from the way that people had treated her – but now it had become an extra burden. In fact, only recently she'd cringed on overhearing a conversation between her mother and a villager, who'd complimented Maman on how well all her children had turned out. According to this woman, Madeleine was not only beautiful but possessed that rare gift, common sense, too. And poor Maman, not knowing about the pregnancy then, had responded with such pride, 'Yes, we are very lucky with our youngest.'

Common sense? Madeleine thought now. Well, they'll discover soon enough that I've none at all! No wonder Maman is so hurt and ashamed. She flopped back on the bed and dabbed at her tears with the blue dress, crumpling it even more. A few moments of madness had changed her whole life. And Dominic? What did he think he was doing? She pressed her face to the pillow in frustration. Why wasn't he here with her, instead of going on this . . . this fool's errand? His entire journey was a waste of time. After all, there'd been no word from Tom since that warm autumn afternoon three months ago when he'd said goodbye.

Tom, a corporal in the Durham Light Infantry, had come into her life like a breath of fresh air. He'd even made her forget the war. Visualizing his dark hair, bright blue eyes, and melting smile, she almost shrieked into the pillow, 'Oh, *what in God's name* does Dominic hope to achieve in England?'

To her, Tom's silence said it all. He clearly didn't want her any more – so how could she go over to England and live with him? Madeleine almost laughed at the idea. What makes my parents think that Tom is going to welcome me with open arms? He just wants to get on with his life. He certainly doesn't want to be burdened with me and a baby. Why can't the others see that? I'd rather take my chances in a convent than be forced by both our families to live with Tom.

As she thought this, she glanced up at the suitcase balanced on top of her wardrobe, and for a fleeting moment it entered her head that she could run away. Shocked at her own thoughts, she rolled on her back, her mind wearily going over her options, and for the first time since discovering she was pregnant, she began to think that everything could be all right again, if only the baby wasn't there.

She started day-dreaming, and it wasn't long before Tom rode in and out of her thoughts, just as he had on the carousel where they'd first met.

In the closing weeks of the war, a unit of British troops, tired and weary from fighting in Belgium, marched through the village to billets just outside Marck, where they waited to be demobilized. Then the war finally ended, and the villagers, who wanted their children to have some fun, too, when they all celebrated their long-awaited freedom from the Nazis, decided to have a fair. It was to be a new beginning; Madeleine didn't realize quite how new a beginning it was going to be for her.

When the fair eventually opened, the excitement was almost tangible, particularly in Madeleine's house, because that was the day her two sisters were expected back from Boulogne. Madeleine was on tenterhooks waiting for them, and kept rushing to the window each time she heard the slightest sound, restlessly anticipating their arrival. This was a great source of amusement to Dominic. Well, even she had to admit he had a point when he said sarcastically, 'I can't think why you're so excited. All the three of you ever seem to do is argue and slam doors when you're together, anyway!'

'For your information, Dominic, I do love my sisters.'

He raised his eyebrows in response.

She screwed up her face, sighed, and said, 'Yes . . . even Simone!'

Much as she was looking forward to seeing them, she was also desperately hoping they'd take her to the fair, because she knew that Papa wouldn't let her go on her own. Dominic had already made arrangements to meet up with his friends elsewhere, so there was no point in plaguing him. The alternative – to wait until the weekend, when her old school friends wouldn't be working, so she could go with them – didn't appeal. She really wanted to be there on that first day.

Madeleine could always find the time to do things she wanted in the daytime; it was a perk of working from home that she'd grown to appreciate. She'd forgotten how much she'd once envied Sophie and Elise: they'd been the first of their gang to start work, and wildly enthusiastic about leading a proper, grown-up life.

Ever since the five close friends had gleefully walked out of the school gates for the last time, they had kept their promise to meet up every two weeks. And as they no longer spoke every day, they always had so much to tell each other!

It had been at Sophie's house – after they'd all piled excitedly into her bedroom, armed with make-up and a bottle of wine that Elise had managed to sneak from her papa's cellar – that Fréderique had taken issue with Madeleine saying: 'Well, I think the nuns at school were all right, really.'

Fréderique had thrown herself on the bed next to Madeleine and exclaimed crossly, 'What do you mean? All we ever did was complain about them the *whole* time we were there!'

'Well, *I* agree with Madeleine,' Sophie had butted in, lifting the lid of her mother's powder compact, and sneezing violently, so fine beige dust flew everywhere. 'I think we were really cruel sometimes.'

And Hélène, transfixed by the sight of Elise pursing her lips in the mirror and coating them thickly with bright red lipstick, had said, 'I think the pair of you must have gone soft in the head! Have you forgotten how much we longed to leave school? And all the praying, and the sore knees?' She'd rubbed her own to emphasize her point. 'We couldn't wait to get away, and never have to think about those stupid nuns again! Yet here you are, feeling sorry for them! *Mon Dieu!* Let's talk about something more interesting like . . . men, or sex or . . . *chocolate*! Anything but those bloody nuns!'

'Men and sex will do for me,' Elise had said, turning

from the mirror and striking a sophisticated pose – unaware that her badly-applied lipstick made her look remarkably like a clown.

'We'll need some experience before we can talk about those!' Madeleine had reminded her.

'What do you need to know?' Elise had countered, in all seriousness.

No one was sure how much Elise knew. But, out of all of them, she was the most likely to have had some experience.

Hélène had laughingly thrown a pillow at Elise, saying 'OK, Mademoiselle Sexpot, tell us everything!' At this they'd all ended up in a giggling heap on the bed, and spent the next hour or so inventing ridiculous stories about their sex-lives. All talk of nuns and school had been forgotten. Now, whenever Madeleine thought about that conversation she was filled with sadness. The next time the nuns were discussed everything was different, and Madeleine couldn't help feeling upset at the way the five of them had poked fun at the poor sisters, when they had turned out to be such heroines.

Madeleine, along with her family and all the villagers, had been – and always would be – consumed with hatred and disgust whenever she thought of those Nazi bastards and their despicable final insult to the village. The fact that the war had been almost over at the time only served to make that disastrous night more horrific.

The Pelletier family, like others in the village, had gone to bed early that night. Maman, Papa and

Madeleine in the attic, and Dominic in the little pantry at the back of the *bouanderie*; Madeleine had refused to sleep there again after the incident with the German soldier.

As usual the billeted Germans were left downstairs playing cards and drinking, propping their feet on the table, which was sticky with spilt beer and cigarette ash. Whenever they drank, which was often, neither Madeleine nor her mother dared go near the table to clean it, for fear of being ridiculed. Or, in Madeleine's case, constantly fondled on the bottom, to the childish amusement of the soldiers. Any cleaning was always left till the following morning, when the Germans went out.

Madeleine, who was still awake, was lying there that night, listening to Papa's snoring and wondering how Maman could sleep through it, when she was nearly thrown out of bed by the explosion. It was so powerful that she heard the windows at the back of the house shatter.

She shot out of bed and ran downstairs barefoot, where she found Dominic struggling into his coat shouting, 'They've gone! The bastards have gone!' Then, pointing to the glass on the floor, he called to Madeleine over his shoulder while bolting for the front door, 'Mind where you put your feet!'

'Gone . . . ? Gone where?' Madeleine was confused. 'What's happened?' she asked, but Dominic had already disappeared.

Maman and Papa arrived downstairs, both with their coats on over their nightclothes, Maman demanding,

'What's going on? What was that noise?' Her voice trembled with fear.

But Papa guessed what had happened, and placed a reassuring hand on her shoulder before going outside to join Dominic.

Madeleine and Maman stood holding each other and shivering, not only with cold, but fear, and Maman asked, of no one in particular, 'Where are they . . . where are the Germans?'

'I don't know, Maman,' Dominic said from outside. 'They've gone.'

The second explosion knocked them all off their feet. Madeleine and Maman fell to the floor, still entwined. They called out to Dominic and Papa, who were now nowhere to be seen. And the front door swung open, revealing a sky red from billowing flames rising from a pall of smoke and dust near the church.

'*Oh non! Oh non!*' Maman sobbed. 'The church . . . they've blown up the church!'

'No, Maman, it can't be. Who would do that?' Madeleine reassured her.

Maman said with unconcealed venom, '*They* would . . . that's who!'

Madeleine shook her head in disbelief. 'They wouldn't . . . Surely, Maman, even the Germans wouldn't do that!'

Papa and Dominic were gone for at least twenty minutes. Then they suddenly appeared in the doorway, their silhouettes black against the glow, staring at the flames. Madeleine, shivering, went up to her papa, and he turned and put his arm around her, saying gently, 'Those explosions . . . it was the church and . . .' He looked at Madeleine, sadness in his eyes, before adding, 'and the school.'

A sick feeling rising in her throat, Madeleine immediately turned to Maman, begging her with her eyes to say it wasn't true.

Maman, unable to speak, took her hand and said nothing.

'But the nuns! *The nuns are there . . .! Sister Thérèse!*'

Madeleine made as if to run to the school, but Dominic grabbed her and held her back, saying, 'There is nothing we can do. The gendarmes are dealing with it. They asked us to leave.'

Madeleine ran upstairs, and opened all the bedroom doors, one after another. She needed proof: proof that the Germans had left. And when she realized that all their equipment had disappeared, she gripped her head in both hands and screamed through her tears. 'Their stuff! It's gone! The bastards have gone!'

They never found out whether the soldiers who set the charges had known that the nuns were still in the school. But Sister Matilde lived long enough after the explosion to tell the village priest about the family who'd been hidden there. The family had gone to the nuns after one of their cousins had been arrested by the Gestapo: he was suspected of being in the Resistance. This family of five, including three children, had apparently been at great risk from the Nazis, and unable to go to the gendarmes for help, as there was rumoured to be at least one collaborator at their headquarters in Calais. So, with nowhere else to go, they had turned to the nuns in desperation, and been taken into the cellars below the school. And now that family was dead, along with the nuns. Once this news reached Madeleine and her friends, all their past suspicions about the nuns had suddenly made sense.

It took weeks for the village to come to terms with this devastating final act by the Germans. Morale had been low, and meetings had taken place to decide what could be done to help rebuild confidence. Nearly everyone had said they wanted music, and even the older villagers had admitted they yearned for a bit of fun. And so they had decided to have a fair on the village green.

With renewed energy all the adults, and most of the children, worked to clear the area of rubble. And it soon became clear that this new project was having the desired effect. People began smiling again as they worked together with a sense of pride and purpose.

The opening day of the fair seemed never-ending to Madeleine. She waited and waited for her sisters to arrive, and when at last she heard the front door burst open, and the sound of their familiar voices calling out, 'We're here! We're home!' she almost fell over herself in her haste to greet them. Dominic held back, not wanting to look too eager, and Maman came rushing from the kitchen to hug her two girls. She'd missed them terribly, even if she had sent Simone off in disgrace. But she had trusted Martine to keep an eye on her, and hadn't questioned her behaviour since then.

Most important of all, her two oldest daughters had survived the air raids. And here they were, home at last! There were hugs and kisses all round, and everyone talked at once, including Dominic, who'd supposedly been so unimpressed by his sisters' return.

After the two girls dumped their cases in their rooms, Martine, along with Madeleine and Dominic, set about helping Maman get lunch ready, while Simone told stories about their lives in Boulogne. It's just like the old days, Madeleine thought, like the days before the war.

It seemed Martine and Simone had enjoyed their time away, even though they'd sometimes been frightened by bombs. Running to shelters had become part of their life, but according to Simone it hadn't always been scary or tiresome, sometimes it was fascinating. 'After all, you never knew who you were going to meet down there.' She winked at Madeleine as she'd said this, and Martine immediately threw her a warning look, as if she'd gone too far. Fortunately, Maman was preoccupied by looking for an oven glove, and didn't notice. But Madeleine's curiosity was aroused. Sensing it would be a mistake to do it right then, she made a mental note to find out more later.

Even though the two girls had managed to come home a few times in the last few years, it had been a good while since their last visit. While Maman was getting a ragout out of the oven, Martine cornered

Madeleine in the *bouanderie* and said she was worried about how tired Maman looked. Madeleine whispered that, though she and Dominic had done their best to shield their mother from problems during the occupation, they'd each had their own personal difficulties to deal with, which had been hard to conceal. Maman had often sensed something was amiss, and though they'd always reassured her that everything was fine, knowing she couldn't help, she wasn't stupid. She'd worked out for herself what one problem had to be, and begged Dominic to protect his sister.

That was when Madeleine and Dominic had swapped beds, Madeleine moving to the relative safety of the attic. And the worry had taken its toll on Maman, who in turn had kept everything from Papa. She'd been afraid he might get angry and confront the German soldiers, exacerbating the situation.

'But what happened, exactly?' Martine asked, just as Maman walked into the *bouanderie*.

'Come on, girls, what's all this whispering about?' Maman was smiling at last.

'Oh, just girls' stuff, Maman, nothing very important,' Madeleine reassured her.

'Come then, let's eat!' Maman beckoned them into the kitchen, while Madeleine grabbed her sister's arm, and whispered with some urgency, 'We'll talk about it later, OK?'

Martine squeezed her hand in response.

Madeleine planned to ambush Papa once he'd got home from work and had a rest, and beg him for permission to go to the fair. In the meantime, her sisters were harder to persuade than she'd anticipated. They weren't anywhere near as interested in going as she was. All they wanted to do was unpack and relax. Eventually, however, she won them over by offering to do any sewing they wanted for a month. All they had to do was accompany her to the fair for two hours. And even then, only if Papa agreed!

She'd have promised anything at the time, she so badly needed excitement and noise to distract her from traumatic memories. Even though the Germans were long gone, she still woke every night in a cold sweat, imagining she could hear the sound of one particular soldier's boots clanking across the tiled kitchen floor towards her bedroom.

Chapter 6

The day his daughters came back from Boulogne, Papa hurried to finish his work early. He was late for lunch, and, tantalized by the aroma of coffee, he headed straight for the kitchen, where Martine was grinding a batch of coffee beans so vigorously that she didn't hear him come in.

Smiling to himself, he playfully crept up on her. When he tapped her on the shoulder her shriek of surprise was so loud that it brought the whole family in from the garden, where they were waiting in the warm sunshine in wondrous anticipation of Martine's promised cup of *real* coffee, made with *proper* coffee beans! It was a luxury they had all missed badly during the war years. Simone had somehow managed to get hold of the beans in Boulogne, and no one asked too many questions about how she'd done it.

Maman, Simone and Madeleine rushed into the

kitchen, only to find Martine and Papa laughing and embracing. Simone squealed with delight at the sight of Papa and rushed to hug him, too. With unashamed pride, he pulled both daughters in close, and joked, 'At last! Maybe Maman will let me sleep again, now that we're all safely back together.' Then, as if resigned to the situation, he shrugged and added, 'Until she finds something else to worry about, of course!'

Madeleine, watching, couldn't help thinking how lucky she and her family were to have come through the war alive. They all ought to make the most of their lives now, she thought. And, seeing Papa in such a good mood, she decided to start on her own behalf at once. 'Papa, there is something I want to ask you,' she said.

Hearing her pleading tone, Papa realized she was going to beg for something she had less chance of getting from Maman. 'Yes, *ma fille*?'

'Can we three girls go to the fair this afternoon?'

Papa glanced at his other two daughters and, seeing the reluctance on their faces, said, 'Do your sisters really want to go, or have you talked them into it?'

Madeleine was about to protest, but Papa held up his hand, and continued, 'After all, they've only just got home, and I'm sure they have lots of other things they want to do.'

Madeleine looked at her sisters for help.

Martine said, 'Well, you're right, Papa, we do have other plans, but we told Madeleine that if you agreed to it we would take her to the fair for two hours.'

'See, Papa, it's fine,' Madeleine said with undisguised

excitement. Then, looking encouragingly at Simone she said, 'You want to go, too, don't you, Simone?' Before Simone could answer, Madeleine, her eyebrows raised in mock anticipation, leaned towards her and confided in a whisper, 'I'm sure there'll be lots of interesting *new* people there!'

Papa, realizing they'd already planned the whole thing, said, 'Well, that's exactly what I'm concerned about, Madeleine!'

'Oh, come on, Papa, I'm almost eighteen. You can't protect me for ever, and I need to have some fun before I go mad! It's been so dull around here lately. We've got to celebrate our freedom, haven't we? No more Nazis to order us around, no more shutters closed because of the blackout. We can laugh if we feel like it now, we can sing . . .' She started dancing round the kitchen.

'All right, all right,' Papa interrupted. 'You've made your point.' He glanced at Maman, but she just shrugged and said nothing, her expression saying that she was tired of making decisions, and more than happy to leave this one to him. Papa continued to look at Maman while talking to Madeleine, 'I had planned on all of us going together to have some *fun*, as you put it, at the weekend, but as usual you can't wait.'

Madeleine was quiet for a moment. She looked pleadingly from Papa to her sisters and back again, knowing he always melted at the sight of her big brown eyes, and, true to form, he relented. 'But,' he added warningly, 'if I allow you to go, you must stay with your sisters the whole time.'

'I will, I promise. Thank you, Papa! I'll go and change my clothes.' She immediately ran up the stairs, looking back at her sisters and calling, 'Well, come on, you two, what are you waiting for?'

Before they could move, Papa grabbed Martine's sleeve, holding her back. He whispered, 'Look, there are British troops billeted just a few miles away from the village, waiting to be demobilized, and some of them will be at the fair. After all, what else is there for them to do around here, unless they go into Calais? So I'm trusting you girls to behave sensibly, and keep a tight hold on Madeleine.'

Simone, her eyes lighting up at the thought of troops, replied, 'Of course we'll stick together, Papa. Don't worry. After all, Martine and I looked after ourselves for five years and never came to any harm!' She chose to ignore Martine's disdainful expression.

Papa, his hands outstretched and palms towards the ceiling, shrugged again, saying, 'I know! But I still can't help thinking of you as my little girls.'

'Oh, Papa!' Martine and Simone both laughed.

He looked a little hurt as he said, 'You can laugh. But one day, when you have your own children, you'll understand what a worry they are. And I don't need to tell you the war hasn't helped at all. It's made all of us over-protective.'

The two girls kissed him on the cheek, and Martine said, 'Papa, we're not laughing at you, not really. And, yes, we'll stick together at the fair. You don't need to worry about us. The war is over now, and I'm sure we can deal with a few soldiers.' Catching Simone's eye, she added meaningfully, '*If* we need to, that is!'

Papa looked at his daughters: Martine with her striking auburn hair and classic good looks, and Simone, the only blonde in the family, her usual pretty and frivolous self. He felt compelled to labour his point. 'Well, I hope so, because you are the kind of girls who get noticed. Especially by soldiers who've been confined to barracks for months.' He studied them appreciatively. 'Just look at you! And as for Madeleine, so beautiful but still so childish, can you blame me for being worried?'

At times like this, he regretted the way the whole family had cosseted Madeleine far more than was good for her. But then, she was the baby of the family. He was always going to fret about his daughters, but he also knew that he had to let them go, and this was as good a time as any to show his faith in them. So he patted them playfully, saying, 'Off with the pair of you, then. Go get Madeleine and have some fun.'

They ran upstairs to change out of their travelling clothes, and had barely finished before Madeleine dragged them out of the door, afraid her parents might change their minds. Once out of sight of the house, she breathed a sigh of relief. She'd run a little way ahead of the other two, but now she slowed down to allow her sisters to catch up.

'For goodness' sake, Madeleine! What's the rush?' Simone demanded.

And with a breathless Martine following close behind

they stopped for a moment. Martine warned, 'If you two are going to get ahead of me like this once we're in there, you can forget the whole thing. We've made a promise to stick together. Remember?'

Madeleine was only half listening. She flapped her hand and said, 'Shush! Can you hear it?' The atmospheric, slightly muffled sounds coming from two streets away were already making Madeleine's heart beat faster. The sound of stallholders shouting, the music of the rides, and the hustle and bustle of the crowds filled her with such excitement that she grabbed her sisters' hands. They all ran to the fair together.

At the entrance Madeleine glanced at her sisters and saw even they were looking round in awe. There were so many people! 'See, aren't you glad you came now?' she said. Without waiting for an answer she let go of their hands and dodged through the crowds, coming to a sudden halt in front of the carousel. 'Come on, let's go on this.'

Martine, feeling reluctant, glanced round for Simone, hoping to persuade her to go on with Madeleine, only to see that she'd wandered on ahead and started chatting and laughing with a boy selling balloons.

Frustrated, she turned back to Madeleine. 'Look,' she said. 'You go on it. I'll get Simone, and we'll meet you back here in five minutes.' Madeleine didn't have to be told twice.

Everyone was scrambling on to the ride, and not wanting to be left behind, she hurriedly reached for the supporting pole of one of the vacant wooden horses.

But as soon as she touched it, a hand slapped on top of hers. Both she and someone else had grabbed for the same pole. She turned around indignantly, ready to argue, and found herself greeted by the most disarming smile.

'So sorry, *please*, you take the horse,' the stranger offered apologetically, in English. Madeleine was so disconcerted by dazzling good looks, dark hair, and the dimples in his cheeks, that for once she was lost for words. Assuming she hadn't understood him, he backed away and half bowed, stretching his hand out towards the horse in a chivalrous gesture that could have come from a fairy tale.

At this, she managed to muster a crooked smile, and, with a slight nod of her head, climbed on the waiting wooden horse. The ride started, and she loved every second, but she couldn't stop thinking about the charming English stranger, who was very obviously a soldier.

The carousel ended too soon for Madeleine, and as it slowed she looked around for her sisters, who were nowhere in sight. What she could see, though, was the stranger, gazing in her direction. Oh, *mon Dieu*! she wondered. Was he watching her, or just waiting to get on the ride?

When the carousel finally came to a standstill he stepped up and offered to help her down. Madeleine's stomach fluttered, and she knew that it was nothing to do with the ride. She took his hand and jumped down, then smiled and thanked him. '*Merci*, monsieur!' She straightened her dress, and glanced at him, noticing that he seemed to be feeling equally awkward.

Laughing nervously, he said something she couldn't understand, and then he added, 'Tom Dawson,' which was obviously his name. He was introducing himself. His eyes twinkled as he offered his hand.

'Monsieur Dawson,' she said, shaking it. She tried to conceal her amusement at this very English custom by quickly saying, '*Je m'appelle* Madeleine.' She pressed a finger to her chest for emphasis, furious with herself for not having paid more attention to Sister Bee's English classes.

Tom looked at her blankly. His French was worse than Madeleine's English, and he was beginning to fear he wouldn't be able to talk to this lovely girl at all when she suddenly said, 'My Engleesh . . . it is very bad. I try . . .' She continued awkwardly, struggling to make her voice heard against the noise of the fairground, 'My . . . name . . . it is Madeleine . . . Madeleine Pelletier.'

There was no way Tom could even attempt to respond in French. He looked at this gorgeous girl and knew that he had to at least try to communicate, so very slowly and carefully in his own language he made an attempt, 'I . . . was . . . transfixed,' he began slowly, aware that he was likely to make a fool of himself yet somehow unable to prevent it. He went on, 'Transfixed . . . by . . . the shine of your . . . lovely . . . chestnut hair.' Then he pointed at her hair, feeling like a complete idiot.

Confused, she put her hand to her hair.

This made him feel he had to continue. ' I . . . I was trying to say . . . that your hair . . .' By now he was feeling so stupid that he finished hurriedly, 'Anyway, your hair is very nice.'

With a puzzled expression Madeleine shrugged her shoulders.

This suggested, to Tom's relief, that she hadn't much idea what he'd just said. And ashamed of making such a lame remark, he changed the subject. 'You like nougat?' he asked, raising his eyebrows in anticipation of a favourable answer.

'Ah, nougaah,' Madeleine responded, recognizing the word. '*Où?*' she'd questioned, looking around eagerly.

Tom, relieved that they were now on the same wavelength, confidently pointed beyond the pink and white hoopla stall they could both see in the distance. Then, in a voice that had risen an octave or two, he asked, 'Shall I show you?'

And Madeleine, all thought of her sisters gone, readily agreed.

So, with Tom leading the way, they headed off towards the hoopla. There were hordes of people, and they weren't just locals or soldiers. Madeleine thought they must have come from Calais and the towns and villages around. It was so crowded that they had to push their way through, and to avoid getting separated, Tom turned and held out his hand. At first she hesitated. But then, trustingly, she took it.

As Tom felt her fingers curl around his he allowed himself a secret smile.

The harder they pushed through the crowds the more Madeleine clung to him, sometimes even grabbing his sleeve with her free hand. She was mesmerized by this soldier with the cheeky grin, and she couldn't wait to get to the nougat stall, because then they'd talk again. Or at least try to.

When they finally got there, she stared in awe at the huge selection of nougat. She had no idea what to choose, and looked at Tom, and he, seizing the opportunity to try and impress her, asked the plump stallholder if they could try a little of everything, indicating this by using clumsy sign language.

The stallholder laughed, understanding at once. He said in English, 'What? You want to look like me?' rubbing his hand over his ample stomach.

'What do you recommend, then?' Tom asked, hugely relieved that the bloke could speak the same language.

'I choose for you,' the stallholder said, rapidly filling up a paper bag and handing it over.

'Is the ones you want,' he said convincingly. 'Is good, and your lady, she will like!'

Tom glanced towards Madeleine, who burst into laughter at his bewildered expression, even though she wasn't completely sure what had just been said.

With a comical shrug of his shoulders Tom responded light-heartedly, 'I guess we'll take them, then.' After he'd paid the man he ushered Madeleine to the side of the stall, where they sat on a pile of stones. And Madeleine decided that, just for this one day, she wasn't going to think about the fact that they had once been part of someone's home.

Tom handed the nougat bag to her and she gratefully picked out a chunk. She watched Tom select a piece, and was guessing that he must be in his early twenties when he looked up. 'I guess you want to know something about me?' he said.

Allowing her no time to convey that she was unsure what he'd said, he continued, aided by many hand gestures, 'Well . . . my camp is a few kilometres from Marck.' He pointed in the general direction. 'But my home, my real home is in England, in the north-east.' Madeleine appeared to be listening intently, and he stopped for a moment, before asking, 'And you? Do you live close by?'

Madeleine had been concentrating so hard, trying to make out what he was saying, that she wasn't immediately aware that she'd been asked a question, until, with a smile, he repeated it: 'Do you live close by?'

'Oh *merde*!' Madeleine exclaimed, frustrated by how little she could understand.

Tom, very familiar with this popular French swear word, laughed, then suggested, with the aid of more hand gestures than were probably necessary, 'Look, we will . . . speak . . . very slowly . . . until we . . . understand . . . each other.'

Madeleine, with a serious look, said, 'OK . . . You smile . . . You Tom. *Je suis* Madeleine. *Je vis ici* . . . in Marck.' She waved her hand in front of her face, relieved that she'd managed to convey even that much, and, feeling pleased with herself, added slightly more confidently, 'I live with my parents . . . also my brozer, and . . . my two seesters.'

But before Tom could answer, she had jumped up from the stones, her hand clasped over her mouth in horror exclaiming, '*Oh, non!* My seesters! . . . I forget . . . my seesters . . . I go! Continuing to mumble to herself in what, to Tom, was the fastest and definitely the most incomprehensible French he'd ever heard, she started running back to the carousel.

Tom chased after her and caught her hand. 'Wait, I'll come with you.'

This time it was Madeleine leading the way through the crowds and shouting desperately to anyone in her path, '*Excuse-moi!*'

In the meantime, Martine, with a chastened Simone, had returned to the carousel only to discover that Madeleine had disappeared. They'd been there as the carousel came to a standstill, but there was such a huge crush of people trying to climb on the horses before the previous riders had got off, that they hadn't noticed Madeleine going off with Tom. So they'd wandered around, anxiously looking behind every stall, until Simone saw Madame Renaude, a notorious old woman from the village who had nothing better to do with her time but spread malicious gossip. Simone nudged Martine, who exclaimed, 'Oh no! I can't believe she's still alive, she was old when *we* were children . . . Don't let her see us, for God's sake!'

And as they tried to edge past her inconspicuously,

her shrill voice, brimming with undisguised glee, brought them to a sudden halt: 'She's gone off with an English soldier!' There wasn't just pleasure in her voice: they could clearly make out disapproval, and a breathless anticipation of scandal, too. She was the only woman they knew who could somehow express three different emotions at the same time.

Simone, unable to resist it, asked, 'Who has gone off with an English soldier, Madame Renaude?'

'Why, Madeleine, of course. Who else?' came the reply, accompanied by a disdainful sniff.

Although Martine was as desperate as Simone to find out what Madame Renaude knew, she thought the old hag might just have made up the whole thing to amuse herself. So, sensing that Simone was about to become abusive, she nudged her in warning, before forcing herself to smile at Madame Renaude. 'Thank you so much, Madame,' she said graciously. 'We'll go and find her.'

Madame Renaude, obviously disappointed that her scandalous titbit had been received so calmly, flounced off, muttering something uncomplimentary about the youth of today.

Really scared now, and with the promises she'd made to Papa echoing in her head, Martine began searching frantically through the crowds.

Madeleine, in a panic, with Tom in close pursuit, had almost reached the carousel when Martine suddenly gripped her by the arm. 'Where have you been?' she said furiously. 'We've been looking for you everywhere.'

Tom, guessing this was one of Madeleine's sisters, said, 'I'm so sorry . . . it's all my fault.'

Martine and Simone stared at him, and before they could say another word, Madeleine burst out, 'This is Tom, and we were at the nougat stall. I'm so sorry, I just got carried away and I forgot what I was supposed to be doing.' Her sisters glared at her, and, in an effort to dispel the tension, Madeleine turned to Tom. 'My seesters, Martine *et* Simone . . . not . . . happy.'

Then she glared at her sisters and continued in her own language, 'This is ridiculous, I'm almost eighteen, after all!'

At this Martine pulled her to one side. 'Just what do you think you are playing at, Madeleine?' she demanded. 'We trusted you, and you repay us by wandering off with a soldier you've never met before! I can't believe you could be so stupid.' She pulled Madeleine even further away from the other two, and whispered through gritted teeth, 'It's the kind of thing I'd expect from Simone, but not you. I think it's best if we go home now. I'm not staying here to nanny the two of you!'

'But Martine, you don't understand, I did nothing wrong. We only went to buy nougat. I just got carried away for a moment – but I came back as soon as I realized you'd be looking for me. After all, I'm hardly likely to get lost in my own village!'

Tom, who was watching Madeleine and Martine intently, glanced at Simone, conscious that she was weighing him up. 'I meant no harm, you know,' he felt obliged to explain. 'We were only buying nougat. Look!' He opened the bag and offered it to her.

Simone was not sure what he'd said, but guessed it was an apology. Always ready to oblige an attractive man, she'd just put some nougat in her mouth when Martine returned with Madeleine, who, in Simone's view, looked suitably reprimanded.

Simone had never quite managed to disguise the jealousy she sometimes felt towards her two sisters. There were times when she loved them, but mostly she found herself unable to handle the envy she felt in their presence. She had never really accepted that her main problem was her unsubtle attitude towards the opposite sex, and instead thought all her troubles stemmed from her sisters' 'meddling'. She was never short of attention from men, but keeping them interested was another matter entirely.

She found it very irritating that whenever she had a boyfriend he quickly preferred the company of her more modest sisters. It made her flirt even more desperately. So she couldn't help feeling pleased that Madeleine was the one in trouble for a change.

Tom, following the sisters as they started to walk away, caught up with them and courteously handed the bag of nougat to Martine, who stopped to look at him. After staring into his eyes unflinchingly she declined with a curt, '*Non, merci,*' before strolling on.

Madeleine was already feeling humiliated by being ticked off in front of Tom. Seeing Martine shun his offer of nougat so rudely infuriated her. So she turned to Tom defiantly, making sure that her words were loud enough for Martine to hear. 'No . . . be . . . offend . . . by my seester . . .' Giving up the struggle, she finished in French, 'I liked the nougat, Tom.'

Tom, slightly bemused, offered her the bag again and apologized once more. 'I'm so sorry to get you in trouble, Madeleine.'

She waved her hand carelessly, making light of the situation. 'Forgive me.' She tried to explain further: '*Ce ne pas normal. La guerre nous a fait peur. Tu comprends?*'

What Tom did comprehend was how warmly he was feeling towards this lively girl. He took her hand, and forgetting to speak slowly, blurted out, 'Look, if it will help, I will come home with you to explain.'

The genuine concern on his face made Madeleine smile. But having understood the word 'home', she exclaimed in a panic, '*Non!*' She knew how her parents would react if she arrived home with a soldier. *Mon Dieu*, they'd be angry! '*Crayon?* Er . . . pen?' she asked Tom. He took a broken pencil from his pocket, and after searching in vain for paper, handed her the nougat bag, which she wrote her address on with some difficulty.

She gave him back the bag, saying hopefully, 'Anozer day, no?'

Tom smiled widely, and, imitating her glorious accent, answered, 'Anozer day! Maddie, yes, *definitely* anozer day!'

Noticing how he'd shortened her name, she looked at

him questioningly before repeating, 'Maddie? I like.' Then she added in rapid French. 'I'll warn Maman, because otherwise when you call she'll slam the door in your face and say, "There's no one called that here!"' She laughed at the idea, and Tom, enchanted but uncomprehending, laughed too. Then he let go of her hand and she began walking towards her sisters, but couldn't resist one last glance back at Tom. Her heart skipped a beat when she saw him still standing there watching her. '*A bientôt!*' she called through the crowds.

This was another expression that Tom had often heard, so he was able to call back confidently, '*A bientôt!*' He stood watching her a few moments longer, hands deep in his pockets, and when he finally turned he walked with a spring in his step, whistling the first tune that came into his head: 'It's a Long Way to Tipperary'.

Madeleine broke into a run and caught up with her sisters. Simone, unhappy because they'd had to leave the fair early, had lagged behind Martine a little, and when Madeleine arrived breathlessly at her side, she gave her a sideways glance and said, 'Well, if that had been me who'd gone off with a stranger like that, there is no way that Martine would have let me linger to say goodbye.'

'Well, I suppose that even though Martine was cross, she sensed Tom wasn't a bad person. Anyway,' Madeleine said, changing the subject, 'he's going to call at the house to see me. That way the family can see how nice he is.' She added happily, 'Did you notice he called me "Maddie"?'

Simon was about to reply when Martine butted in, horrified, 'Well, if you think Maman and Papa will let him visit, you're more stupid than I thought,' she said. Martine knew that Madeleine must be wondering why she was being so disapproving. She also knew that she was being unfair, assuming that Madeleine would turn out like Simone, but recent events had made her cynical. They were why she'd left Boulogne earlier than she'd wanted to.

What had happened there was still so raw that she couldn't even face discussing it with Simone, so instead she'd just endlessly fretted about it, knowing that one day her frustration was bound to come to a head. To be honest, today she was as cross with herself as she was with Madeleine for allowing the incident with the soldier to happen. It was just like Boulogne! Would she ever learn? she wondered. She really resented being the eldest, and always having to watch over her sisters. How she longed not to have to be so responsible all the time. When was she going to have any freedom?

As they reached the exit, Martine looked over at Madeleine and felt a pang of guilt at having been so hard on her. 'Look, I'm sorry, Madeleine, but I don't know what's come over you since I've been away. You used to be so sensible.'

'Well, maybe I'm tired of being sensible. And maybe, *just maybe*, I've grown up!'

Martine said, 'Oh, so you think you behaved like a

grown-up today, do you? I think not!' She gave a wry little laugh. 'It's OK to call you Maddie now, is it? After you made it so clear to us just how much you disliked your name being shortened!'

'That was then! Anyway, it sounds different in English, and I like it!'

Madeleine walked ahead of the other two on the way home, wanting to get there first, and thinking it would be better if she spoke to Maman before her sisters did, to give her own version of events. Just in case everything got distorted in the telling, particularly by Simone, who'd said very little so far.

Madeleine rushed into the house, only to find a note from Maman saying that she'd taken the opportunity to pop over to see Tante Lucy, and that Papa was in his workshop. Relieved, and preferring not to have any further discussion with her sisters, Madeleine ran upstairs to her room. There, still upset at having been treated like a child in front of Tom, she flopped down on her bed and wondered why Martine, who'd always been so understanding, had reacted like that. Something serious had happened in Boulogne, she decided, and she wouldn't mind betting Simone was responsible! The tension between the two sisters was obvious, and they'd both changed. Martine was jumpier and crosser than before. And as for Simone: Madeleine had never seen her flighty sister so quiet.

Chapter 7

Marck, France
Friday, 22 June 1945

'Are you coming down?' Martine called from the bottom of the stairs.

Madeleine had been sitting in the same position for so long, sewing, that she hadn't realized she'd become numb. She didn't answer straight away, because she was rubbing her legs to try and get the pins and needles to go away. The next time she heard Martine's voice it was outside her bedroom. 'Madeleine?' Martine tapped on the door. 'Madeleine, are you asleep?'

'No. I'm just freezing,' Madeleine said.

Martine smiled. 'Well, it's warm downstairs. Come on down, and we'll have a coffee before Maman gets back from Tante Lucy's.'

'OK.'

Martine added hopefully, 'I'll go and make the coffee, shall I?'

'If you like.' Madeleine carried on rubbing her feet,

pleased that Martine seemed to have forgiven her. Madeleine knew she'd behaved thoughtlessly at the fair, and that she couldn't really blame her for being angry with her, but she also knew that Martine had over-reacted. In the past Martine might have been strict, but she'd always been fair, and very tolerant. Except, that is, for that last trip Madeleine had taken to Boulogne a year ago. She'd felt she hadn't been treated fairly then, either: over a simple friendship she'd formed with a local girl called Nicole. Madeleine hadn't even been allowed to say goodbye to Nicole before Martine had whisked her back to Marck so quickly that her feet had scarcely touched the ground.

She could still remember the delicious smell of baking bread that had first drawn her to the curious little *boulangerie* just down the street from Martine's apartment. The café inside was warm and cosy. It only had four tables, but they were covered with fresh red cotton tablecloths. Even better, and despite the shortage of eggs, flour and butter, there was a chocolate gateau displayed smack in the centre of the glass-fronted counter on that first visit, and her mouth fell open at the sight of it.

Nicole, who worked there, was kind to her right from the start, and they'd both been so grateful to have some-one of their own age to talk to that they'd soon become friends. From then on, whenever Madeleine was in Boulogne visiting her sisters, she would drop in on Nicole at the *boulangerie*, and they'd chat and giggle their way through portions of gateau that Nicole saved specially. They'd both revelled in the friendship, loving the way it made them oblivious to the depressing, rubble-strewn streets – and even the war itself.

More often than not, these meetings were made even more fun by three old locals who frequented the place. These women, who always wore their headscarves pulled forward, were dressed from head to toe in black – which went well with their equally dark conversation. Madeleine and Nicole got to hear who'd died, which street had been bombed, who had been caught fraternizing with the Germans, and how no one seemed to care that Boulogne had been reduced to nothing more than a pile of burnt stones.

Listening to these dismal conversations brought out Madeleine's natural mischievousness, and on one occasion, unable to resist winding the old ladies up, she nudged Nicole before eating her slice of chocolate gateau with loud cries and gasps of ecstasy. The resulting disapproval made the two girls collapse with laughter.

Madeleine and Nicole talked endlessly, about many things, but Nicole never said much about her family, and Madeleine didn't ask. All she knew was that Nicole lived nearby with her mother, Ginette Jobert.

They did, however, discuss their schools, and tell each other stories about their childhoods – another source of much hilarity. So it was an uncharacteristically solemn moment when Madeleine discovered that Nicole's father had left her mother some time ago, for another woman. But Nicole didn't dwell on the subject, and

Madeleine didn't press her, sensing that her friend didn't want to discuss it in any detail.

Madeleine had such warm memories of Nicole, and whenever she thought about how quickly their friendship had ended she felt a confused anger towards Martine which saddened her.

Martine had never said why she'd done it, nor had she explained why she'd reacted so violently at the very mention of the *boulangerie*. It still irked and puzzled Madeleine. 'Why do you need to go there?' Martine had snapped, after finding out about Madeleine's visits. 'It's easy enough to make coffee here in the apartment. And besides, what about all this studying you're supposed to be doing?' She'd gestured at the books and papers lying around the flat. 'Surely the best time to do it is while Simone and I are out at work?'

Madeleine, shocked and hurt, had said, 'So you want me to study *all* day?

'Of course I don't expect you to stay in all the time. But I don't want you sitting in that café, either.' Then she'd added, almost as an afterthought, 'And, besides, the *boulangerie* is too far from the bomb shelter. What if the sirens go off? Where would you go?'

'I'd just follow the others to their shelter, of course!' Madeleine had retorted, finding it hard to believe that Martine would say anything so ridiculous.

Madeleine decided that she was going to go on seeing Nicole. And so she continued to do so, not caring whether there was an air raid or not. Things were quiet for a while after that, so Madeleine assumed that

Martine thought she'd successfully put her off going to the *boulangerie*. Martine didn't bring up the subject again, which made it easier for Madeleine to go on dropping in there: she didn't have to lie.

On later trips to Boulogne, Madeleine always visited Nicole in the mornings, making a special effort to concentrate on her studies and her sewing in the afternoons; and because Martine saw Madeleine's work progressing, she became relaxed and even-tempered. At least until a little later, when Madeleine – convinced that if Martine met Nicole she would like her – plucked up the courage to ask if she could invite her friend to dinner one evening.

Madeleine nearly jumped through the ceiling when Martine turned, with a look like thunder, and shouted – actually shouted – in disbelief, 'You mean the girl from the *boulangerie*?'

'Yes,' Madeleine answered.

Martine yelled, 'No, she can't come here!' And refused to explain why.

Totally dumbfounded, Madeleine was about to speak when Martine said, 'Are you telling me that you've been going there all this time, behind my back?'

Madeleine's stunned silence answered the question.

'Well, it's obvious that I can't trust you!' Martine said. ' I asked you not to go there for your own good.' Then, after hesitating, she asked, never taking her eyes from Madeleine's face, 'Have you been to her house?'

'No, I have not!' said Madeleine, feeling really agitated by now. 'But what if I had?'

'That's enough!' Martine warned, holding up her hand to stop her confused younger sister from saying another word. Then she grabbed her coat, telling Madeleine, 'I'll have to talk to you about this later. I need to go out now.'

'OK, if you won't tell me,' Madeleine said indignantly, 'I'll just have to ask Simone when she comes back. I'm sure *she* will be only too happy to explain!'

That had been the end of the conversation, and later, to Madeleine's astonishment, the reason for Martine *needing* to go out had become abundantly clear. She'd bought a train ticket, so Madeleine could go home the very next morning.

When Simone came home later that night, Madeleine was still so upset that she stayed in her bedroom and didn't bother to ask her about Nicole. She thought she probably wouldn't get an honest answer while Martine was there, anyway.

She'd agonized about it all the way home on the train, and been unable to imagine what the problem could possibly be. But she made up her mind that she was going to get an explanation; she wasn't going to let it go. Unfortunately she didn't have Nicole's home address, so couldn't let her know what had happened. She wrote to the *boulangerie*, just in case, but never got an answer.

What *must* Nicole have thought of her leaving without saying goodbye? she wondered now. She knew her sisters were expecting her downstairs, but she wasn't sure she wanted to join them just yet. The events at the fair, on top of all this unresolved stuff about Nicole, had made her determined to force an explanation from Martine as soon as possible. She was jolly well going to find out what was going on!

On this positive thought, she picked up the little jacket she'd been remodelling and tried it on in the mirror. One sleeve was set into the shoulder completely wrong. As she ripped out the stitches she listened for the sound of Maman's footsteps outside on the road. Although, if she knew Tante Lucy, she'd be filling Maman in on all the local gossip, which meant Maman could be gone for ages. She hoped not; she wanted to talk to her before Papa came in from his workshop.

Even though she had no doubt that Maman and Papa loved them all, and had done everything they could for them, Madeleine couldn't help feeling that if only she was allowed a little more independence – and came up against fewer secrets – she'd be able to cope with things better, the way her friends did.

The reason for the awkwardness between Martine and Simone was yet another secret that was being kept from her. Well, she wasn't a child, and she wasn't putting up with it any more. She was going to let them know that there were to be no more secrets in this family.

At least Dominic confided in her. She smiled at the thought of her brother, only to realize with a jolt that she was guilty of exactly the same thing her family was doing. When the soldiers had been billeted in their house during the occupation, hadn't she lied to Dominic to protect him?

'Why are you suddenly so jumpy and irritable?' he'd asked.

And she'd said, 'No reason. Everything is fine. Really.' At the time she was terrified that, if he knew, he'd kill the soldier who was tormenting her. Everything had certainly not been fine. But she'd lied to protect him.

She cringed at the thought of those slimy Nazi hands, and the way they'd touched her at every opportunity. She'd been so terrified that she hadn't even dared confide in her friends, in case it got back to her parents via theirs. What could Papa and Maman have done, anyway? What could anyone have done?

It had happened after the German soldiers had taken over the bedrooms. Madeleine had been adamant that she wanted a private place to herself, so she had ended up on a folding bed in the tiny room next to the *bouanderie*, which was normally used for storing odd bits of furniture. This had left poor Dominic, much to his chagrin, with no alternative but to share the attic with his parents. The family had been given no choice about it; they'd just had to cope as best they could.

The first few months of the occupation were nothing short of hell. The soldiers expected their clothes to be washed, dried and ironed for them – and there was endless cleaning to be done, the soldiers delighting in walking in muddy boots across freshly scrubbed floors.

There were two sittings for every meal: the soldiers provided luxuries for themselves like meatballs and sausages, and after they'd been fed, and started drinking by the fire, the family would sit down to the sparse left-overs, padded out with potatoes from the vandalized garden, and, very occasionally, vegetables and eggs from Tante Lucy.

As a result Madeleine gradually became so tired and debilitated that she could hardly put one foot in front of the other. And one night, with Maman's help, she managed to get to bed early. Once there, she didn't do her usual thing, and lie awake worrying, but fell into a deep sleep.

In the depths of her dreams she became vaguely aware of a presence, and sensed movement, but her eyes were so heavy she was unable to open them. Her dreams, though, became troubled and uncomfortable. In an unconscious bid to stay asleep, she wriggled around before turning on to her stomach. But, still semi-conscious, she became increasingly uneasy. And with her eyes still tight closed, but unable to hold on to her desperately needed sleep any longer, she lifted her head to push her pillow into shape, and, to her horror, felt a hand under her body!

As she tried to leap away, and scream, the nauseating smell of alcohol filled her nostrils. A hand was clapped over her mouth, and the stale-cigarette odour that oozed from it made her retch. The soldier it belonged to tried to rip her nightdress off with his free hand, and she struggled and fought with a viciousness that she had no idea she possessed. But his strength was greater, and he managed to push her back down on the folding bed. Holding her down with both hands gave him the opportunity to straddle her, his full weight pressing down on her writhing body.

Once astride, he reached behind with one hand to lift her nightdress, while with the other he covered her mouth. Hearing the cotton fabric rip, she desperately bit into the hand covering her mouth. Salty blood filled her mouth, and the soldier snatched his hand away cursing with rage.

At that moment, her disgust far outweighed her fear. She struggled like a wild animal, biting and tearing at the soldier with her nails, and she managed to push him away, using not only her hands but her knees. Then she screeched, 'Get off me, you bastard! *You . . . monstre!*'

And the way he laughed drunkenly at that somehow gave her the strength of another creature altogether, so that with one, final, almighty shove she pushed him on to the floor. Adrenalin took over, and, for one brief moment, as she stood over him, hands on hips, she was the one in charge. She looked down at his prone body in the darkness, and through gritted teeth said, '*Get out!*'

Her moment of triumph was over almost as soon as it began. He stood up, looming above her in the tiny darkened room, and, gripping both of her arms tightly, he said, 'I'll be back.' Then, to make sure she understood, he repeated in bad French, '*Je reviens.*'

He let go of her and she stood there shaking, listening

to the sound of his boots clanking across the tiles. The thought struck her that the idiot hadn't even had the sense to remove his boots before attacking her. But what had struck her more fiercely was that he intended to come back. And there she was, in the darkness, with no idea which soldier he was. The fact that he'd have a bite on his hand wouldn't help her identify him, either, as the German soldiers wore black leather gloves most of the time.

Terrified, and with no chance of getting back to sleep, she sat rigidly on the bed, staring at the door, as if anticipating his return. And then she suddenly stood up, shocked. *Mon Dieu!* she thought. Why are you sitting here like an idiot? He's going to come back! Get out of here – quick!

Panicking, she jumped off the bed, grabbed her coat and peered through the open door, not knowing whether he'd gone back up the stairs. Feeling strangely out of control of her shaking body, she paced back and forth across the tiny room. What to do? What to do? She was too afraid to go out of the door in case he was still there, lurking in the shadows. And her parents were sleeping right at the top of the house, in the attic, so she was unable to get to them without passing the floor where the Germans were sleeping.

Why on earth hadn't anyone – including herself – guessed that this might happen? Her annoyance at her own stupidity stirred her into action, and made her think more clearly. She moved quickly to the window, where she placed her shoes and coat on the inner sill. That done, she hoisted herself up on to her knees on the windowsill, and taking hold of the brass hooks each side of the sash frame, strained to push it up. At first there was a slight judder. Then nothing: the window wouldn't budge.

Oh, merde alors! Madeleine's instinct at this point told her to smash the glass and forget about the consequences. But first she gave it one more try, and in desperation shook the window, praying that somehow it would loosen up. She looked over her shoulder nervously, thinking that she must be making enough noise to bring the whole household downstairs. Scared as she was, she didn't want to waken everyone. After all, the German soldiers wouldn't believe her, or care, even. She'd seen how they all sniggered and joked whenever she was in the same room. They might all be aware of what this bastard had done, anyway. Perhaps they'd put him up to it. And she knew exactly how her parents and Dominic would react, and that was reason enough not to wake them. Her family would jeopardize their own safety to stand up to these *monstres*.

She'd just given the window another shake when she heard a creak from the *bouanderie* next to her room, and her heart thumped so hard that she almost fell off the sill. Determinedly, she heaved with all her might, and the window moved a little way before sticking again.

Seeing that the gap was now big enough to squeeze through, she dropped to the floor, thinking that she might be able to pull herself through head first if she lay on her back. She shuffled into position, managed to get her head out, then, holding on to the bottom of the window frame, she heaved and wriggled until she was on her knees on the outside sill, and while she was still facing that way she grabbed her coat and shoes and jumped down to the ground. By standing on her toes she could just reach the bottom of the frame of the newly loosened window, and she jiggled it back shut, covering her tracks in case the soldier came back into her room.

She wasted no time getting into her coat, and when she turned to walk into the darkness of the garden, realized she had no idea where to go. She'd thought no further than getting out of the room. She stood there for a moment, pressed to the wall, shivering until her teeth chattered. She knew she would have to get back into the house in the morning without the family knowing, but decided to worry about that later.

Dominic is going to have to swap beds with me after this, she thought tearfully, because there is no way I am sleeping in that room again. But now she had to find somewhere to hide, so, with her shoes wedged under her arm she ran towards the chicken coop. She opened the rickety wire netting door of the run, causing the chickens to cluck indignantly at the intrusion. 'Shh, shh,' she whispered as she fluffed up the straw in a corner of the coop before crouching down in it. And there she stayed for the remainder of the night, wedged into a corner and unable to sleep, with the family totally oblivious. And that's how she planned to keep them, for all their sakes.

Next morning, having managed to sneak back into the house when her Papa had come out to visit the toilet, she'd been busy at the range, checking on the boiling saucepans, when she'd suddenly shuddered at the clank clank of boots approaching across the tiled floor. Her body stiffened with panic, but she purposely didn't turn round. Instead, as the soldier's hand slid across her bottom she lifted the heavy saucepan of boiling potatoes and turned abruptly to face him. Then she looked him straight in the eyes while holding the pan perilously close to his groin.

She knew she'd unnerved him when she saw him hesitate. He didn't want to lose face in front of his comrades, though, so he'd smirked openly, while she'd continued to stare straight into his eyes. No words were spoken; he just gazed unblinkingly back, and for a second the tension was all-consuming, until, with a mocking grin, he turned and walked away. The grin told her that that wasn't going to be the end of it.

Her only consolation was that he'd now identified himself. She still had no idea what his name was, but to her, from then on, he would be 'Hanz', a word derived from the English for 'hands'. Fitting for a pervert with no control over his, she thought.

Unknown to her, Dominic had witnessed part of the confrontation on his return from an errand for Papa. He was pushing his bicycle towards the shed in the back garden when he stopped to glance through the window, wanting to let Madeleine know that he was back. What he witnessed filled him with such fury that he threw the bike to the ground, and, flinging the back door open, charged into the house, where Hanz – with his sickening smirk – had just left the kitchen.

'What was all that about?' he asked Madeleine, trying to catch his breath.

'All what?' she replied calmly. She had no intention of telling him what had happened, knowing how he would risk his life rather than let anything harm her.

'Come on, Madeleine, I saw him through the window!'

Madeleine turned to her brother. 'Dominic,' she said. 'You can't do anything about it.'

'That's where you are wrong,' he'd answered, heading towards the door through which the German soldier had just left.

Madeleine rushed to restrain him, saying, 'Look, I can manage him. You saw how I got rid of him. I think he's as scared as we are,' she lied. 'But you mustn't forget that they have the upper hand, and we just have to put up with things until the war is over.' Hoping to pacify her brother, she added lightly, 'Anyway, because of his wandering hands, I have named him Hanz.' She smiled at Dominic. 'Don't you think that's funny?'

Dominic looked back at her grimly. 'He *has* been pestering you, then.'

'Dominic, please,' she pleaded. 'We have to get through this somehow.'

'He has no right to touch you, we could report him.'

'Oh, Dominic, you know that would be a total waste

of time. Who'd believe us, and even worse, who would care?'

Dominic stood there looking hopeless. 'You *must* promise to tell me if it . . . when it happens again,' he hissed. His fury scared her. She'd rarely seen him like that.

'Yes, Dominic. I promise,' she lied.

Chapter 8

Evenwood, England
Saturday, 1 December 1945

Tom had miraculously managed to avoid Jessie since arriving home. So far, anyway! God knows how I've managed that when she lives in the same village, he thought, as he glanced at himself in the only bit of mirror still unmarked by the mottled black spots gradually eating away at the whole thing.

He picked up his shaving brush from behind the cracked but spotless ceramic sink, and splashed it around in tepid water before rubbing it vigorously over the shaving soap. Then, lifting his chin, and casting his eyes down at the mirror, he briefly ran his hand over the stubble to check the whisker growth, before, with the soapy brush, making rapid circular movements. Once his chin and cheeks were white with lather, he stood with razor poised, then leaned in towards the mirror until he was close enough to see what he was doing in the dim light of the scullery, gripped his nose and pulled his head to one side. It had always been a bit dark in there, the only daylight coming through the tiny window overlooking the backyard.

While he shaved, his mind wandered back to Jessie, but he only felt the slightest tinge of guilt. He wasn't ready to meet her yet. In fact, he wasn't sure if he ever would be. Trouble is, he thought, I'm nothing like the same bloke who left the village all that time ago.

'*Shit!*' he suddenly exclaimed, as he nicked his chin with the razor. '*Bloody hell!*' he cursed, grabbing the first thing he could find, which was a dish cloth. He pressed it firmly to his chin while cursing himself for not concentrating. It never ceased to amaze him how much blood leaked from such a small wound. He finished shaving quickly, then picked up the *Northern Echo*, and tore a small triangular piece from the bottom corner before slapping it on to the wound, trusting it would act like blotting paper on the continuous trickle running down his chin.

He pushed the kettle further into the flames of the coal fire, his mind all the while on Jessie, and he found himself becoming increasingly agitated, knowing that he was going to have to deal with her at some point.

He'd known Jessie, a friend of his sister Rene's, since their early teens, when she'd become his girlfriend. And though she'd not been one of the brazen hussies from the bus shelter, she hadn't exactly been an introvert, either. He must have found that appealing at one time, he supposed, and what with her being a friend of Rene's, she was always around his house. Realizing he wasn't being fair, he reminded himself that he had found her attractive. She was a grand-looking lass. But he knew that somehow, over time, their relationship had just become a habit.

Much to the envy of his mates, Tom had never had any trouble getting girls. Why, according to them, they fell at his feet! He grinned now at this gross exaggeration. But he was aware that if he didn't handle the situation with Jessie right, he would end up saddled with her.

He knew it was cruel keeping her in the dark, and he'd have much preferred to do nothing and just hope the problem went away. But he also knew that it wouldn't. He knew her well enough to realize she'd automatically assume he'd marry her now he was home – even though he'd always avoided mentioning the subject. The best he could hope for, he supposed, was that during the last few years she, too, might have changed her mind.

He'd thought about her very little while he'd been in the army, but there'd never been anything in her letters to make him think *she* might have cooled off. Admittedly at first he'd been only too pleased to get those letters. In the early days, when being away from home in such hostile circumstances had scared him shit-less most of the time, he'd found the trivial gossip in them very comforting.

Over time, though, as he and the other squaddies in his division had become closer and more reliant on each other, he'd ceased to be interested in her ramblings.

What was the point of learning who'd said what, and who wasn't speaking to someone else in Evenwood? But then, how could she, or anybody else back home, be expected to know what it was like for him? How could they imagine the heat of the desert in Egypt, or the struggle to survive the bloody battle on Brittany's Gold Beach? Why, I was actually in Jerusalem, and even *I* can't really believe that now! He'd *never* forget it, though. Or Bethlehem ... He shook his head, still amazed that he'd actually been there. I remember imagining how my mam would be beside herself when she got to hear about that! he thought. Not that *he* was particularly religious, of course. But as far as his mam was concerned, for her son to have been to Christ's birthplace was a miracle. He knew that she'd never be able to fully grasp that her Tom had written to her from the holy places she'd listened and learned about when she was a bairn in Sunday school, and then at the Wesleyan chapel she still attended every Sunday.

He'd had a real strong sense of his mam while he'd been there, too. Being in places like that, so exotic and far from home, had felt like a fairy tale to him. He smiled now, remembering how happy he'd been on the day he'd picked wild flowers in Bethlehem. And how, when he'd got back to base, he'd been teased by his mates about it. But he'd taken it all in good part, and carefully placed the flowers between neatly torn squares of old newspaper. They only ever had out of date newspapers there. Then he'd placed the bits of newspaper containing the flowers between the pages of the small Bible that he carried around, but never read.

They'd been expecting a post run the following day, and he'd cheekily managed to cadge some brown paper to wrap the Bible in from Sergeant Jacobs, who got sent writing paper and other stationery by his family. Every now and then, the Sarge would sell a few bits and pieces to the lads for a pittance, or maybe exchange an envelope and writing paper for a couple of cigarettes, but mostly he gave it to them for nothing, as he did that day with Tom, because he knew Tom wanted to make his mother happy. Tom remembered the sigh of mock-despair that came from the Sarge as he'd handed over the paper .

He was a good lad, was the Sarge. They'd all agreed on that. Tom had said, 'Thanks, Sarge!' Then continued awkwardly, 'Er, I know a letter costs a penny ha'penny to post in England, Sarge, but you wouldn't happen to know what it'd cost to send a parcel, would you?'

The Sarge had answered absentmindedly, 'Never mind that for now, Dawson, we'll sort it out later.' Then, smiling, he'd added, 'Let's just hope that the parcel gets to your mother before you do, eh, the way the post is over here!'

'Yes, Sarge!' Tom had saluted with a grin, because the cost didn't matter a toss. Just knowing how over the moon his mam was going to be was enough to put a grin on his face for the rest of that day.

Startled by the kettle boiling frantically and spurting water from its spout into the hissing fire, Tom rushed into the living room. He stood for a second, uncertain

113

how to tackle it, until, remembering that he'd seen Hannah put a pile of newly ironed tea towels into the sideboard the day before, he yanked the door open and grabbed one. Folding it as thickly as possible he wrapped it around the handle of the iron kettle, before running like the clappers towards the scullery with the still-boiling water spurting from the spout. He swiftly dropped it into the sink and ran cold water from the tap over the handle, then, after wrapping the tea towel around the handle again, he poured the boiling water into the sink.

'Good heavens, what's goin' on, lad? There's more steam in 'ere than on a station platform!' Hannah, just back from shopping, had come straight into the living room, where, having dumped her basket on the dinner table, she was busily flapping a cloth around to disperse the steam.

Tom shouted through to her, 'Keep your hair on, Mam, it's all under control.' Then he added, laughing, 'Anyway, give us a bit of peace, will you? I'm trying to have a wash, *in private*, if you don't mind!'

'In private, indeed, ah'll give 'im in private!' she said. Then she called through the gap in the door, 'Ah've seen it all before, yer know, yer can't embarrass me, lad!'

Tom called back, 'Well, it's me that's embarrassed! Anyway you get on with unloading your shopping, and let me get finished here – before the water goes cold, and I have to make the house into a steaming station platform again to warm it up.'

'Cheeky monkey!' he heard her mutter.

He remembered Jessie calling him that. And now here he was, back home and trying to avoid her. Hannah had kept her promise not to tell Jessie exactly what day he was coming home, but nevertheless she'd hinted several times that he should go round to see her, warning him that most of the village would know that he was back by now, anyway, so she was sure to find out.

'After all, lad,' she reminded him, 'she did pop round every now and then to see how we were while you were away, yer know.'

'I know,' he answered. He knew Jessie had her good points, but he couldn't help wondering if her reasons for 'popping round' were as pure as Hannah believed. More like she was calling to make sure there was nowt going on that she didn't know about, he thought.

But despite all that, he would have to go to see her, and soon. He hadn't even been in touch with his mates yet, either. For the past week he'd just enjoyed the peace of mooching around the house and catching up on family news. And he knew Hannah had loved having him all to herself for a while, too.

'When's our Rene coming to see us then, Mam? And where's the towel, for goodness' sake?' Tom called from the scullery, where he was stripped to the waist shivering after what had turned out to be a tepid sink wash, because he'd put too much cold water in.

He heard his mam 'tut tut' as she took a towel from in front of the fire, then, making a big thing of turning her head away, she threw it in to him, saying, 'Ay lad, get that round yer. Yer never did think of getting the towel *before* yer got washed. And ter answer yer first question, our Rene should be back from Darlington sometime tomorrow. She really wanted ter be here when yer arrived home, yer know, but she had this course ter attend fer work, like. Anyway she said she'd written ter yer plenty, so you'll know all her news already, I expect.'

'Aye, well I do I suppose, but it'll still be nice to see her . . . And the bairn, is she coming an' all?'

'Yes, our Jeannie's been stayin' with one of our Rene's friends in Darlington, while her mam's been on the course. It wasn't very long, she only missed two or three days of school, like. Eee, Jeannie'll be that pleased ter see yer, lad! Yer 'er favourite, you are, and she'll be ten this year, yer know.'

'God, she must've only been about four or five when I went away. And I'll bet she's a right little madam now.'

'Well, she can be, if she doesn't get 'er own way, like, but she's got a good heart, has our Jeannie.'

Tom smiled. 'Well, she was always willing to share her sweets, even gave us her last one when I was going away. Brought a tear to my eye, as I remember.'

'Ay well, our Jeannie would've given *you* 'er last anything. There was nobody like you, as far as she was concerned.'

'Well, I'll reserve my judgement till I see what she's like now that she's ten.'

Hannah looked serious for a moment. 'If our Rene's back tomorrow, yer'd better get yerself over ter Jessie's beforehand, otherwise there'll be ructions. Cause yer can be sure that she'll get ter know that yer back home, that's if she doesn't already. Yer goin' ter have ter sort this out, lad. Don't keep her hangin' on if yer not interested, pet. It's not right.'

'Oh, I know that, Mam, but it's not as simple as that. I think she's assumed we're going to get engaged, like.'

Seeing Hannah's face light up, he raised his hand to stop her. 'Before you say anything, Mam, I never said a word. She just got it into her head. I've hardly written to her, either, since I realized that she might be thinking that way. She started talking about rings and stuff.'

'Well, yer better put her straight now, and get it done with.' Hannah looked concerned.

'All right, Mother, don't go on. I'll see to it tonight, right?'

It was easy to tell when Tom was annoyed. He always addressed his mam and da as Mother or Father. And he was especially irritated to be faced with what might be a very awkward situation. Tom hated rows, and always avoided them, in the hope that they'd prove unnecessary. Which rarely happened, of course. So, having finally realized that this particular problem had to be faced, he resented being reminded of the fact; especially since it was going to be *bloody* awkward to sort out.

He'd heard there was a dance on tonight at the village hall, or 'Scout hut', as it was known. He supposed it must have been built originally for Scout meetings. Anyway, it had been used for all manner of things since, village dances being one. The dances had been popular

117

before the war. And the first one since 1939 was being held tonight, and promised to be a special event.

After much deliberation, he decided his tactic would be to drop a note in at Jessie's while she was at work, telling her that he was back, but omitting to tell her just when that had been. She was sure to ask, but he'd get round it somehow, and make out he'd not been back long. He'd say he'd been shattered and needed to rest and get his mind together, which wasn't a lie really, and now that he was feeling better would she like to meet up at the dance tonight? He'd tell her that he would like to see her, and he'd warn her that there was something he needed to talk to her about.

Then, after thinking about it carefully, he decided not to say that he wanted to talk to her. She might assume I'm going to propose, he thought, and if she gets that into her head things will be even more difficult than they are already. Absolute disaster, in fact!

Right then, here goes. Best do it while Mam's popped next door to take Mrs Hurd's bit of shopping round, then she can't interfere, he thought, getting the pen and paper from the sideboard drawer.

Dear Jessie,
Sorry no letters for while, circumstances you
know! Anyway I'm home at last, and have rested
now, after a tiring journey home.
Hear there's a dance on in the Scout hut
tonight, wondered if you fancy going?
If you're not there by about half past seven,

I'll call round yours to see you anyway.
   See you later on, then?
Love Tom x

He folded the piece of paper neatly, and after hunting high and low for an envelope he gave up and just folded it over again, making a square. He pulled the front door closed, then headed straight over to Jessie's house, which was in Ramshaw, a village which would have adjoined Evenwood if it hadn't been for the cemetery and a field or two in-between. It was a similar set-up, in fact, to the way Marck and Calais were separated in France, and he felt a bit of a pang as he strolled past the cemetery with the note to Jessie in his pocket. But it was Maddie he was thinking about, and the way she used to get him to bunk her up the cemetery wall, so she could peer wide-eyed over the top at the huge, sinister-looking ornamental gravestones.

I've never even looked over this one, he thought, as he came up alongside the old grey stone wall, which was about two feet taller than he was. Suddenly curious, he jumped and managed to dig his fingers into a crevice on the top, which enabled him to pull himself up. Maddie would be disappointed, he thought, scuffing the toes of his newly polished shoes in an effort to keep balanced. It's nowhere near as impressive as that one over there in France. Why, these gravestones are puny in comparison. No, this wouldn't do for Maddie at all, he decided, as he jumped down. Then, turning swiftly around, he brushed the palms of his hands together, to rid them of crumbling bits of mortar, and walked on, lost in thought.

He hadn't mentioned his relationship with Maddie at home, partly because he felt inexplicably protective about it, and partly because he was sure he'd never see her again. He had great respect for her, but her life was so far from his here, and from the way in which he'd been brought up, that he felt they were simply too different. His time with her in France seemed so distant now, that sometimes it was as though it had all been a dream, a lovely dream. But he only had to remind himself of their painful goodbye in France to know that she had been real. He'd got so close both to Maddie and her family, and especially her brother Dominic, that he'd almost become assimilated into their way of life. If only it hadn't been for the language barrier, he thought.

God, it was so different here! It was neither better nor worse, he told himself, just very different. He looked around, taking it all in. I should have written to Maddie, he thought. I can't imagine what she must think of me. He'd convinced himself that the reason he hadn't was because – since he'd arrived home and seen the realities of his way of life and his situation – he couldn't see the benefit of prolonging something that couldn't survive.

He supposed that he'd realized all this early on, as he was sure she herself must have done. But then he'd fallen madly in love with Maddie, something he'd not banked on, and just wanted to spend every spare minute with her, and at that point of time living in the moment had seemed more desirable than planning for the future.

It *had* crossed his mind that he should write at least once to let her know what he was thinking. But not really knowing what to say, he'd kept procrastinating, telling himself that he needed more time. He didn't feel very proud of himself now. As he walked, he wondered what she was up to, how she was feeling – even worse, if she hated him.

His thoughts were soon interrupted. Even before he reached Jessie's house he could hear her mother's rough cackle. There was no mistaking it, even after all this time. He knew she'd be out on the doorstep where she spent most of her time, and had ever since he'd known her. He rounded the corner at the bottom of the road, and there she was, nattering away fifty to the dozen. The sound was so familiar that he could easily have imitated her.

Suddenly her voice stopped, and for a split second all was quiet. He didn't glance at her at once, but then she boomed out, 'Well, well, well, look who it isn't!' He looked straight into her eyes and she stared back with obvious distaste. She continued without taking a breath, 'Yer've lowered yersel' at last ter come ter see our Jessie, then? Well, ah've got news fer yer. She isn't 'ere. She's got better things ter do, than ter 'ang around all day waitin' fer the likes of you.' Stopping to take a breath now, she looked him up and down.

'Well, that might be,' replied Tom patiently, 'but I've not been long back, and this is the first chance I've had to get here.'

'Oh aye, well, pull the other one, it's got bells on it! Cause ah 'appen ter know that yer've been back a while, an ah've not let on ter our Jessie fer fear of breakin' 'er 'art.'

Tom tried to interrupt but couldn't get a word in edgeways as she went on with the tirade. 'An' what about the bloody letters? *You* didn't 'ave ter see 'er disappointment every day when there was no letters in t' bloody postbox. Why the 'ell she hangs around waitin' fer the likes of you, Tom Dawson, ah'll never know.'

Tom, determined to rise above it and stay calm, said quietly, 'Look, Mrs Parkin, I know you don't think much of me, but will you please pass on this note to Jessie? I'll explain everything when I see her.' He couldn't resist adding mockingly, 'And yes, I'm safe and well, thanks for asking!'

Saying nothing more, Jessie's mother snatched the note from his hand, then went inside, slamming the door behind her, leaving the neighbour she'd been talking to standing awkwardly on her doorstep.

Tom stood there for a moment face to face with the door, which was no more than an inch away from his face. Bloody hell, he thought, this is going to be worse than I thought. He mouthed to the slammed door, 'Bloody nutter!' He turned to leave, but not before bowing politely to the neighbour, who, mouth open, was still standing there, as if frozen in time.

On seeing the twitching curtains of the invisible audience behind them, Tom took a second bow – then left. Jessie's mam had never really taken to Tom, or his family for that matter. It was plain jealousy, he knew that. Because, even though his mam and da weren't very well off, and his da in particular spoke in broad north eastern miners' talk, as did all the pit families round about, what they did have was plenty of common sense and graft. Jack Dawson was a fountain of knowledge, and Hannah kept a spotless house. In fact, when he thought about it, everything the two of them did was for the good of the family. Jack had always worked hard, and mostly they'd had a happy family life.

But Jessie's mam, now, that was a different matter. Tom had never seen her look anything but scruffy. What with her dirty pinnies, and the fag hanging out the side of her gob, its smoke billowing up into the scarf she always had tied on her head, covering hair that she never washed, she was a dirty bitch.

He headed swiftly back towards home, all the time turning the encounter over in his mind. And as for the house . . . ! Well, if Jessie hadn't tidied and cleaned a bit now and then, you'd have called it a hovel. He'd known when he'd first called on her there that Jessie was ashamed of the house and her mother. But he'd purposely not mentioned it, and anyway he'd been warned about it by their Rene, who was friendly with Jess, and went there often. And he remembered thinking at the time: well, if our Rene can ignore it, so can I.

Anyway, he hadn't had to call there too much. They'd usually arranged to meet somewhere easy for both of them, somewhere away from her mother. But, regardless of her mother and the house, to give her her due,

Jessie had always looked clean, and worn nice clothes, at least since she'd earned her own money as a clerk at Doggarts department store in Bishop Auckland. And, he thought, their Rene probably gets clothes at a discount for her, too.

Suddenly feeling painfully sympathetic towards Jessie, he pushed the thought aside, telling himself, Oh no! don't go down that path for God's sake, or you'll never finish with her!

Meanwhile, inside the house, Mrs Parkin had thrown herself down into the only chair free of a pile of clothes waiting to be ironed, and after several attempts at lighting a match she shakily lit another fag, all the time muttering in anger, 'Bloody upstart, comin' round 'ere as if 'ee was God's gift! Huh, the whole bloody family think their shite don't stink.'

As she leaned forward to flick the cigarette ash into the fire, she glanced at the note that she'd chucked on to the cluttered mantlepiece, realizing for the first time that it wasn't in an envelope. She picked it up and turned it over, examining it closely. Well, our Jess'll never know, she thought, with the note already half open in her hands. She quickly scanned it before, without a second thought, screwing it up and chucking it in the fire.

There, that'll teach the little git, she thought. Let 'im hang around waitin' fer her fer a change. It never crossed her mind for a moment that maybe all this anger was nothing to do with how she thought Tom had treated Jessie. Or that maybe it was more to do with *her* fear that if they did eventually marry she'd be left on her own now that Jessie's da had run off with that daft lass half his age.

Tom arrived back home just after Hannah, who was busily checking what was left in her ration book. As he walked in she glanced up at him. 'If ah didn't know any better, lad, with a face on yer like that, ah'd think yer'd lost a five pound note and found a tanner! But ah know yer didn't have a five pound note in the first place, so come on, what's up?'

'Well, for your information, Mam, I've been over to Jessie's, and had a right to-do with her mam. She's not right in the head, that one!' He paced around in frustration.

'Eee, lad, she's had problems, yer know. Yer have ter be a bit lenient, pet.'

'Oh, give over, Mam! She's nowt but a lazy old cow. She's filthy! The house is filthy! And she just sits on her arse all day . . . gossiping old hag!'

'Well, she never used ter be as bad as all that when our Rene first started knocking around with their Jessie,' Hannah said, coming up closer to him and discreetly pointing a thumb over her shoulder, as if what she had to say was too awful to be heard by anyone else. 'It'll be since 'er husband left 'er, yer know,' she whispered. 'It's probably sent 'er a bit doolally.'

'Well, I'm not surprised he bloody left her. Slammed the door in my face, she did! And all the bloody nosey parkers across the road were lapping it up, hiding behind their filthy nets. So I gave them all a gracious bow before I left.'

'Eeee, yer never did, our Tom!' Hannah laughed. 'Yer only make things worse fer yerself, yer know.'

'Well, I've left her a note to give to Jessie about the dance tonight, so if she comes I'll do my best to break it gently. But seeing her mam like that today hasn't helped one bit. *Christ!* Jessie could turn out to be just like her. In fact when I think about it, she wasn't that far off when I last saw her!'

'There's only you can sort it out, lad, and the sooner the better, fer both yer sakes,' Hannah advised. Then she added, 'Mind you, she'll probably think yer've asked 'er ter the dance because yer want ter be with 'er.

'That's as may be, but I can't sit her down in the house and do it face to face, so I'll choose me time and try not to make too big a thing of it.'

If this had been any other lad she'd been listening to, Hannah would have thought he was taking the cowardly option, and selfishly finding the way that best suited him. But this was *her* lad, who in her eyes could do no wrong, and he was certainly no coward. After all, he'd fought in the war, hadn't he! So closing her mind to any thoughts that might spoil that image, she suggested, 'Just try not ter go at it like a bull in a china shop, eh? She's got feelings, yer know. And don't forget she's Rene's friend, an' all. We don't want ructions as soon as *she* gets back tomorrer.'

He laughed now as he remarked, 'No, we wouldn't want to upset our Rene now, would we!'

Hannah, lightening up a bit, responded, 'Well, ah hope you two are goin' ter get on better than yer did before yer went away, cause yer used ter fight like cats an dogs.'

'Well, only because she had to have her own way all the time,' Tom joked.

'As ah remember it, yer were as bad as each other. Stubborn as mules, the pair of yer!'

'Aye, well a lot's happened since then, Mam. Maybe we'll have both grown up by now, eh?'

'We'll find out soon enough,' Hannah said with a sigh of resignation.

'Aye, we will that,' said Tom, as he made for the stairs. 'I thought I'd go and get myself changed and ready for tonight's episode, if you don't mind, Mam!'

'Get on with yer,' Hannah grinned.

Chapter 9

Evenwood, England
Saturday, 1 December 1945

As Tom approached the Scout hut, not even the band could drown out the sound of clattering feet on the wooden floor. 'Sounds more like a herd of elephants than the Gay Gordons,' he said to a stranger, who, hands in his pockets, was pacing around outside the hut.

The chap nodded without replying as Tom walked past. Inside the hut, the sound was deafening as Tom dodged between the youngsters who were stomping around with little idea of the right steps. Checking his watch, he edged through to the far end of the dance floor in an endeavour to find Jessie, who was nowhere to be seen.

He stood on tiptoe to see above the bobbing heads, and was pleasantly surprised to spot two of his mates, George and Harry. He made a beeline across the room towards them. George, his mate since school days, had joined the navy at about the time that Tom had gone into the army, so they'd not seen each other since the outbreak of the war. And as for Harry, he'd been a conscientious objector – and had taken plenty of stick for it according to his da.

George, seeing Tom, raised his hand excitedly above the bouncing throng to beckon him over. Tom acknowledged him just as eagerly, waving as he pushed his way through. As he made his way across the hut he not only had to dodge the dancers, but the bairns, who squealed with delight as they slid haphazardly across the floor. It didn't seem a very good idea to let youngsters in, but perhaps if they weren't allowed, then parents who had no one to mind their bairns couldn't go, either.

Tom, George and Harry greeted each other with clumsy bear hugs and over-enthusiastic back-slapping.

'Welcome home, mate!' shouted George over the din.

'Have a pint, lad?' questioned Harry, gesturing to make himself understood.

'Aye, I could do with a pint, thanks, Harry. I'm parched,' Tom shouted.

Tom and George watched the dancers while Harry went to the bar. 'When did yer get back, like?' George asked suddenly, trying to make himself heard above the band, who were now well into a barn dance.

Before Tom could answer, Harry arrived with the drinks, and Tom gratefully gulped his pint, exclaiming, 'I needed that!' At a lull in the music he said, 'You haven't seen Jessie on your travels, have yer?'

George shook his head. 'No, mate, ah haven't.'

Harry shook his head, too, then asked, surprised, 'You two still on then, are yer?'

Tom shrugged his shoulders. 'Who knows, mate?' The band started up again before he could elaborate. 'Look, it's impossible to talk in here,' he yelled. 'How about we all meet up in the working men's club through the week, and have a proper catch-up, eh?'

'Aye, mate, that'll be grand,' both George and Harry shouted in unison.

Then Tom, looking around again, mouthed, 'Better go and see if Jessie's outside. See you later, lads, and thanks for the pint.'

When he'd gone, George and Harry looked at each other and shrugged. 'Nowt changes with Tom and his women, then,' Harry shouted to George.

'Nah, yer right there! Lucky bugger!' George raised his glass, grinning his approval.

As Tom made his way back towards the exit to look outside, the five-piece band stopped momentarily, before going into their own version of 'The White Cliffs of Dover', which cleared the dance floor immediately. Tom noticed with amusement how all the single youngsters scuttled to opposite sides of the room, with the boys standing on one side, and the girls seated on the other, each one hoping that she'd be approached to do the slow dance.

God, he remembered it so well! First off, there'd been the sheer embarrassment of wandering over to a bonny lass, more often than not seated next to one that you'd not look at twice, even on a dark night. But the plain one would have her backside off the seat almost before you got there, and she'd be ready and willing, until you took the hand of the bonny one, leaving the other looking embarrassed.

How God-awful cruel it all is, he thought. And here it is still going on with the next lot! He was relieved when he got to the door. 'Hell, I couldn't hear myself think in there!' he said to the girl behind the counter at the cloakroom.

He stepped outside, and was just about to light a cigarette, when he heard what sounded like a squeak coming from the side of the Scout hut. He stood still for a moment, listening. When there was nothing, he struck the match. Then, on hearing a scuffle, followed by a familiar female voice yelling, 'Get yer 'ands off me yer bloody bastard, or ah'll ave yer guts fer garters.' Tom threw the match down and ran round the side of the hut, straight into the lass whose voice he'd have recognized anywhere. She flung her arms around him without even looking up to see who he was, so keen was she to escape from the bloke following close behind.

Tom, having taken in the situation, held the lass tightly, pressed himself to the side of the hut, and stuck his foot out, bringing the bloke to the ground with a crash. Cursing repeatedly, the fallen man tried to get up, only for Tom to push him back to the ground. Meanwhile the girl, released by Tom, jumped inside the doorway.

Tom had the bloke pinned down under one knee now,

and said furiously, 'What the hell do you think you're playing at?'

His victim spluttered, 'Sh . . . she's me girlfriend, man! An' she thinks she can chuck uz just like that! No bloody explanation. "Just 'ad enough," she said, an' that's it!'

Tom loosened his grip slightly, recognizing the silent, pacing bloke he'd spoken to on the way in. He said through gritted teeth, 'Ah thought you were up to no good when ah saw you earlier, you bastard. Well, no matter what the situation is, there's no excuse for acting like a bully. I'm not surprised she wants to chuck you. Best thing you can do is bugger off home, before I really show you what's what.'

The man scrambled to his feet, and bolted.

Tom looked round to where the lass was standing shivering. He brushed his hands over his jacket and trousers and smiled at the pretty blonde clippie from the bus. 'Well, well, well, fancy seeing you here, then!' He smiled broadly.

In a mocking tone she answered, 'Bloody 'ell! Ah know ah said ah hoped ter see yer sometime, but this is the limit!' Then, with genuine gratitude, she added, 'But ta fer getting me out of trouble like that.'

Tom laughed as he questioned, '*Was* he your feller, then?'

'Well ah'd been out with 'im a couple of times, so 'ee thought 'ee was. And look at me dress now, all crumpled! And it's brand new, first time ah've worn it.'

Tom, glanced at the dress, which showed a bit of

petticoat just beneath the hem, either because of the scuffle, or maybe because it was the fashion, who knew? 'It's lovely,' he said, 'and I'm sure it'll come up like new when you iron it. Anyway, never mind the dress, I think you could do with a drink. I know I could. There's a bar up the top end of the hut, if you want to make your way across the dance floor.' He looked at her. 'We've met twice now, and I haven't even asked your name yet.'

Feeling a bit calmer now, she smiled. 'Well, ah'm Maisie, and who might you be? Apart from me knight in shinin' armour?

Tom took a bow. 'Sir Tom at your service, madam.'

Giggling, she took his hand, and he led her through the throng of dancers now making an effort to do the Saint Bernard's Waltz. As he crossed the room, he couldn't resist joining in the stamping.

By the time they reached the bar, Maisie was giggling uncontrollably. She asked for a dry sherry.

'A brandy would do you more good in the circumstances, but you can't get hold of the stuff,' he complained, handing her the glass with one hand, and picking up his beer with the other. Then, seizing the opportunity while most people were up dancing, they grabbed two empty seats by the makeshift bar, where it was just possible to hear each other speak.

Tom gave a cursory look round, and Maisie, noticing this, asked intuitively, 'Were yer meetin' somebody?'

'Well, yes, sort of. It's a bit complicated, like.'

'Must be a girlfriend, then?' Maisie answered.

'Yes and no,' Tom said. Then seeing Maisie's puzzled look, he explained. 'I have something to do, and I'm not looking forward to it one bit.'

'Is it anything like what ah've just done?'

'Aye, it's exactly like what you've just done.'

'Well, it might be better if ah'm not around when yer do it, then. Ah think ah should go. Ah'm not really up fer dancing now, anyhow. So, look, ah can't thank yer enough fer what yer did, *Sir Tom*,' she said with a smile. 'But ah'm gonna go now, an leave yer ter yer deed.'

'Will you be all right for getting home, then?' Tom asked.

'Oh aye, ah'm not far from 'ere. So don't worry about me! Ah'm just grateful yer were around when yer were.'

Tom looked at her, impressed by her classiness, and answered, 'Any time, Maisie, any time.' Then he added regretfully, 'Another time, another place, eh?'

'Yes, another time, another place, Tom.' She understood his meaning, and was still gripping his hand in readiness to say goodbye, when, from nowhere, a profusion of red and purple taffeta landed in front of them. The dishevelled dress flounced into place, revealing a slim body with hands placed firmly on hips. From somewhere behind the mass of dark curls came a loud, venomous voice, 'Well, Mister Tom bloody Dawson! Let's see how yer get yersel' out a this one, then!'

'Jessie!' he exclaimed.

Chapter 10

As the train pulled into Victoria station, Dominic, who'd been struggling to pull his case out of the luggage rack, bent down and peered through the window, only to find his view obscured by steam billowing from the engine. Reaching up to the rack again, he yanked at the case until it fell to the floor with a thud. Bending down to pick it up, he took another look through the window, and for a fleeting moment, between the wafts of steam and the silhouetted people rushing along the platform, imagined he saw a red coat, the red coat! Feeling a pang of excitement now, and with eyes squinting against the steam, he was certain he saw a flash of red disappearing out of view. He leapt off the train.

He was weaving through the passengers as they dispersed in different directions, when there ahead, and there was no mistaking her, was the girl from the boat, struggling with her valise. As his pace quickened he wondered if she was English. Even though she had the look of a French girl it wasn't always easy to tell these days. Panting, he caught up with her, and decided to try English first, asking between laboured breaths, 'May I help you with your valise, mademoiselle?'

Still walking quickly, she glanced sideways and smiled in recognition, before answering in French, 'Your English is very good, monsieur, but no thank you. I am heading over there.' She nodded towards a café. 'I have half an hour to wait for my connecting train.' She glanced at him again and asked, 'Are you catching another train too?'

Dominic, relieved she was a compatriot, answered in rapid French, 'Oh yes, possibly more than one. I'm not altogether sure, to be honest. All I know is I have to get a taxi to take me to King's Cross station, because I'm travelling north.'

'It sounds as though you need a coffee more than me! You are welcome to join me if you wish.'

'I would like that very much, er . . . ?'

'Oh, pardon, I am Yvette.' She paused momentarily, then added, 'Yvette Marchant.'

'Dominic Pelletier at your service,' he replied, holding the door to the café open for her. Once inside he led the way to a table by the window and asked, 'Is this OK?'

'Oh yes, I don't care where it is, as long as I can sit down,' she said with a sigh, then, as if talking to herself, she went on, 'I always take too much with me when I travel. Why do I do that? I never learn.'

'Ah, you travel frequently, then?' Dominic

questioned, while trying not to stare at her too much. He thought her incredibly beautiful.

'Not really, but I have been to England a few times now.'

Dominic raised his eyebrows in surprise. 'Oh?'

'Yes,' she answered, 'To visit a friend.'

Fleetingly he wondered if it was a girl or a boyfriend that she was visiting. He glanced towards the counter, and seeing a cake on display, he asked her, 'Would you like a piece of gateau with your coffee?'

'Oh, certainly I would,' she replied as if the very question was ridiculous. As he approached the counter, he turned to look at her, and she smiled.

Dominic came back with the two coffees, and then returned to the sullen-looking woman behind the counter, and tried to charm her into cutting two large pieces of the cake. At first, the woman wasn't amenable. But for some reason, when she saw Yvette at the table looking on so eagerly, she relented, and in a strong cockney accent said, 'Oh, go on with yer then, me duck, but don't blame me if yer feel a bit tom after it. It's very sweet.'

He glanced at her enquiringly. She was about to explain when she thought better of it, and instead said, with a crooked smile, 'Look here, yer'd better get this cake over ter yer girl there, she's looking a bit desperate, if you ask me!'

They both looked over at Yvette and smiled, and as Dominic handed over a shilling he said, 'You are right, madame. Thank you, and keep the change.' As Dominic walked back to the table, Yvette almost leapt up with pleasure at the sight of the cake. He laughed and said, 'My younger sister would be just the same!'

'Oh, I apologize if I act like a little girl,' Yvette said, looking slightly embarrassed, 'but it's so good to buy gateau again.' She took a mouthful, and after swallowing it, declared, 'I think you will find that most girls are happy to eat gateau. How old is she . . . your little sister?'

'Oh, sorry,' Dominic apologized. 'You misunderstood. She's not a child, she's eighteen.'

'Oh!'

'But you are right. Most girls do love gateau. Well, not just girls, you know!' he added, plunging his fork into his portion.

Yvette continued, 'You are very fond of your sister?'

'Yes, I have two older sisters too. But Madeleine . . . well, she is the reason I'm in England right now. I am here to help her. I hope!'

There was silence between them for a second, then he suddenly changed the subject by asking, 'And you?'

'Oh, my home is in Amiens, and I am also here to help someone. My friend who lives in Southampton.' Seeing the puzzlement on his face she explained, 'It's on the south coast, not too far. Anyway, she married an Englishman, a sailor. She was sure it was the right thing to do at the time. But a year later, it's all gone wrong. He drinks heavily, and she spends too much time alone. Her English isn't good, so she finds it hard to make friends, and she's very low right now. So I try to cheer her up.' Then she added with a shrug, 'But I can't make the problem go away, there is only so much I can do.'

'I'm sorry,' Dominic sympathized, alarmed by the similarities between their two situations. What if Madeleine ended up as unhappy as Yvette's friend? He was sure that Tom wouldn't be as selfish as this southern chap, but there was still the huge problem of the language barrier. He felt slightly nauseous, and was unable to finish his gateau.

Yvette, seeing the same distant look on his face that she'd noticed on the boat, slid her hand across the table towards his. 'And you? I think you have a lot on your mind, too, and I really hope that everything works out for you. I have to go and catch my train now, but if you like I will leave you my address, and maybe we can let each other know what happens?'

'I'd like that,' said Dominic, feeling the same odd sense of loss at their parting as he had on the boat. As they exchanged addresses it was all he could do to stop himself from pleading, 'You will write, won't you?'

He picked up her valise, and they walked together to the next platform, where her train was already waiting. The hissing and billowing steam, and the slamming of carriage doors made for a hectic goodbye. As the final whistle blew, they looked at each other as if words were needed. But neither spoke. The train began to rattle and shudder as it moved, and Dominic walked down the platform beside it, while Yvette seated herself at a window. When he raised his hand to give a final wave, she smiled in response. Then he walked back to the café, where he'd left his case with the woman behind the counter.

'Cutting it a bit fine, aren't yer?' she commented, assuming that he was catching the train standing at the platform near the café.

'No, I'm OK, I need to get a taxi now,' he said, hunting in his pockets for loose change. Not finding anything smaller, he handed her half a crown.

'Wow, two and six! Ta very much!' she exclaimed, before telling him where to go for a taxi.

Thankfully, there were plenty of free seats on the train he took from King's Cross, and after placing his valise on the rack, and hearing the slamming of the carriage doors, followed by a loud whistle, he stood up to take his jacket off. But the train, jerking as it moved off, hurled him back into his seat. Feeling embarrassed, Dominic had to stand up again to remove his jacket, which he did quickly, before pushing it up into the rack.

The only other person in the compartment was hidden behind a newspaper, for which Dominic was grateful as he stumbled again. He stared out of the window to avoid any eye contact. It was going to be a long journey. About eight hours, the stationmaster had told him. He looked at his watch. It was two thirty in the afternoon, English time, so he decided he'd have to find accommodation for the night when he arrived in Darlington. It would be far too late to go to *anyone*'s house, never mind that of a family he wasn't even sure was expecting him. And anyway, he'd still have to get a train from Darlington to Bishop Auckland after this, which, according to his map, was a further twelve miles. Then a bus from Bishop Auckland to Evenwood, which was another five miles, and after that he had to find the house, Tom's house. No, he definitely wouldn't be able to do it that day. He'd speak to the ticket collector, maybe he could recommend a hotel. At least, Dominic thought, it means I'll arrive at Tom's house early, and I won't be tired.

That decided, he laid his head back and attempted to relax. He gazed through the window. The steam had thinned now, and he could see endless tiny terraced houses and back gardens, where people were busying themselves earnestly, preoccupied by their own little problems. Like me, he thought. Remembering his meeting with Yvette, he wondered anxiously if they really would meet again, or if it had just been a pleasant little interlude.

He studied the other passenger in the compartment. It was an elderly man, whose head was already rocking sleepily from side to side with the motion of the train while his newspaper dangled loosely from his hand. Dominic was relieved that he wouldn't need to make conversation. It meant he could allow himself to daydream about Yvette. He conjured up her deep brown eyes, so sincere and warm, and the angular cut of her straight black hair, which framed her pretty elfin face so exquisitely. With a sigh, he remembered her full lips, painted in a deep red lipstick that matched her coat perfectly. He smiled, only vaguely aware of the hypnotic clickety-click, clickety-click as the train made its way along the lines, taking him closer and closer to Evenwood.

Chapter 11

Evenwood, England
Saturday, 1 December 1945

At the Scout hut dance, Jessie's eyes didn't leave Maisie for a second as she demanded, 'Who's this whore that yer've picked up, then? Yer don't hang around, ah'll give yer that! Now ah see why yer didn't bother ter let uz know yer were back.' Tom had no opportunity to answer before, in the brief moment of comparative quiet at the end of the band's first set, Jessie yelled, her words booming out across the hut, 'Cat got yer tongue, then? Yer selfish git!'

The band lurched straight into a Glenn Miller routine, which never failed to get everyone on the dance floor. Tom, with an apologetic glance at Maisie, seized on the opportunity to get Jessie out of there. Grabbing her hand, he practically dragged her across the hut towards the exit. He was so angry that he ignored her protests that he was gripping her wrist too tight.

When they were near the cloakroom he said in a

dangerously calm tone, 'You don't change, do you? Bite first, ask questions after!'

'What was ah supposed ter think? Yer didn't even let uz know yer were back, then ah walk in ter find yer cosyin' up to that . . . that whore!'

'For your information, she's no whore, she's a clippie that I met on the bus bringing me from Bishop. And if you must know, I helped her out of a bit of trouble she'd gotten herself into, and that's all it was. And d'you know what? I don't care whether you believe us or not. *And*, what d'you mean I never let you know I was back? What about the note I left at your house?'

Jessie pushed a mass of curls away from her eyes and glared at Tom. 'Oh aye, left me a note, did yer, and where exactly would that be, then?' She leaned towards him for full impact. 'Yer a bloody liar, Tom Dawson! Yer'll say owt that comes inter yer head, ter get yerself out of trouble. '

'Ask your mam where the note is, then,' Tom interrupted calmly.

'Me mam?' Jessie looked confused. 'What's she got ter do with it?'

'Ah,' exclaimed Tom. The penny had suddenly dropped. 'You didn't get the note! That explains this warm greeting of yours, then.'

Jessie, impatient now, demanded, 'What note? Ah don't know what yer on about.'

'The note telling you I was home, and asking you if you'd meet us here tonight! That's what note.'

Jessie slumped down on a chair by the cloakroom,

fumbled in her bag and pulled out a ticket, which she gave to the girl in charge of the coats. Then, lighting one cigarette, she absentmindedly handed another to Tom. Tom helped her into her coat before asking, 'What are you gonner do now, then?'

Jessie, buttoning her coat, answered, 'Ah'm goin' ter see me mam, that's what ah'm goin' ter do. See what *she's* got ter say about all this!'

At that she disappeared into the darkness, and Tom was left wondering whether he should follow her.

His dilemma was short-lived, though, as his old mate George turned up, pushing his way through the revellers and calling out, 'Come on, man! What yer playin' at with these lasses? Yer must be ready fer another pint be now. Get yersel' in 'ere, some of the other lads are here now, and they're keen ter see yer.'

So Tom, having briefly considered the alternative, went back in with George, who, noticing Tom glance around the hut said, 'She left, mate. She must've gone out behind yer, when yer were occupied with Jessie, like.'

Punching George playfully on the arm, Tom answered, 'Bloody hell, you don't miss a thing!'

'Well, we always did foller yer love life wi' interest, and it seems nowt's changed. We had a little bet on, like, as to which one ye'd be leavin' with. An' we all lost, cause they've both gone!'

'Aw, man!' Tom answered, just as they were reaching the other chaps. 'It was neither nowt nor summat, all a bloody misunderstanding. You know what women are like.'

'Ay, come on, Tom,' his mates sympathized as he joined the group.

Harry said, 'Ah thought the little blonde was all right, mind! 'Avn't seen 'er around 'ere afore. Is she local, like?'

Tom grinned. 'Ay, you talk about me! And you haven't changed yourself, mind! Always were a one for the lasses, if I remember right, Harry.'

Harry laughed, but he was still waiting for an answer to his question, and gave Tom a nudge. 'Well?' he said.

'She's a clippie. I met her on the bus, but it's a long story and I'd like to forget it for now, if you don't mind. So come on, lads, what are you drinking? We might as well get stuck in, cause you can't have a decent conversation with this din going on.' Nodding with enthusiasm they followed him to the bar, where he bought the next round.

Meantime, Jessie, beside herself with anger and embarrassment, cursed as she struggled to fit her key in the front door. The house was in darkness, but she knew her mother wasn't asleep, because she'd seen the bedroom light go out as she'd turned into the street. And anyway, she thought, what the hell was she going to bed at this time for? It could only be about nine or so. Unless, of course, she was keeping out of the way for some reason!

At that thought she ran up the stairs, barged into her mother's room, switched on the stark light bulb, and stared at what appeared to be a pile of rags on the bed.

Seeing a slight movement under the pile, she marched over and yanked at it, and said, 'Ah know yer there, Ma!'

Her mother, eyes wide open, sat bolt upright holding the bedclothes tightly against her. 'Ah know what yer gonner say, our Jessie,' she said, 'but ah did it fer yer own good.'

'Did what, Ma?' Jessie questioned. 'Just what *did* yer do, Ma? Or, more ter the point, have yer any *idea* of what yer've done?' she yelled, yanking the bedclothes from her and chucking them across the floor. 'Call yerself a mother! All yer care about is yerself!' Jessie held out her hand, thinking how pathetic her mother looked at this moment. 'Show uz the note, then,' she said.

'Ah can't show yer the note,' her mother muttered.

'Just tell uz where it is,' Jessie said impatiently.

'It's on t' fire,' her mother shouted, and, seeing Jessie's shock, she talked rapidly, hoping to extricate herself. ''Eee came round 'ere brazen as brass, 'ee did. Tellin uz ter give yer the note as if nowt was wrong. Huh! well ah knew different, and ah thought if ah got rid of it, yer'd be saved the 'artache.'

'Saved the heartache, my arse! All you bloody want, is ter keep uz here at your beck an' call. An' yer have the gall ter call Tom a selfish git! Huh! Well ahve 'ad it with yer!' Seeing her mother sitting shivering on the bed she felt nothing but disgust. She threw the bedclothes back. Then she ran down the stairs, stopping only to grab her bag before slamming out of the door.

When she looked across the road and saw the twitching curtains, it brought home to her, and not for the first time, how grim her life was. It was going to be like that for evermore, too. 'Piss off, yer nosey bloody parkers, and get back ter yer own hovels behind yer filthy net curtains!' she shouted in frustration. And then she stomped off down the street without a clue where she was headed. Having humiliated herself at the dance, she couldn't face going there. So she kept on walking, pushing her way through the lines of damp washing still hanging across the darkened back streets.

She stopped momentarily to strike a match, then cursed when she realized that she'd got coal dust all down the sleeve of her coat, from brushing against a coal-house door. Taking a deep drag on her cigarette, she glanced down the street, irritated by the high brick walls enclosing the back yards of all the houses at Tom's end of the village. The only real difference between these streets and ours, she thought, are the people who live in them. Cleaner curtains and scrubbed steps apart, they look exactly the same. Bloody snobs! she said to herself, throwing the cigarette stub on the ground and stubbing it out with a twist of her foot. She stood there, trying to decide what to do next.

'I know the first place ah'll go,' she said, setting off at a faster pace now. Five minutes later she found herself in the Dawsons' back yard. She reckoned it must be about a quarter to ten by now, so Hannah would likely still be up. Taking a deep breath, she knocked tentatively on the back door.

She heard Hannah scurry through the scullery, lift the latch and call, 'Who is it?'

'It's only me . . . Jessie!'

'Oh, Jessie, what on earth's the matter?'

'Ah'm sorry, Hannah, but ah've 'ad such a row with me mother, ah've walked out, and ah didn't know where else to go.'

'Come on in then, pet, have yer seen our Tom, then?' Hannah asked carefully.

'Oh aye, ah've seen him all right. That's how the trouble started.'

Hannah was at a bit of a loss as to what to do or say next, when Jessie reassured her, 'Oh don't worry, Hannah, ah know ah can't stay 'ere, what with Tom back, and your Rene and young Jeannie due ter come back termorrer. Ah just need ter catch me breath a bit.'

Relieved to hear that, Hannah relaxed a little, and Jessie added, 'Ah just couldn't stay in the house with Ma. Ah'm sorry ter put yer out like.' Then, thumbing over her shoulder towards the stairs, she whispered, 'Is Jack in bed then?'

'Oh aye,' whispered Hannah in response. 'Eee's got an early start in the morning, so he thought he'd go up and get his beauty sleep while he had a chance.' She added with a laugh, 'Beauty sleep, indeed!'

'Well, ah won't keep yer any longer, Hannah. Ah'll let meself out, but will yer let Rene know that ah called, and ah'll see 'er termorrer? Apart from that, ah need ter explain somethin' ter Tom.' She was careful not to say that she wanted to apologize to him. She still felt that he was the one who should apologize, because he hadn't written her any letters. She felt that was unforgivable. None of this would have happened if he'd kept in touch, she told herself. But she was willing to hear his side, now that she knew he'd at least told her the truth about the note.

She bade Hannah goodnight, and let herself out.

Chapter 12

Evenwood, England
Sunday, 2 December 1945

'Ah'll be glad ter get 'ome, mam, won't you?' Jeannie said, as she skipped along the pavement with one foot on the kerb, and the other in the gutter.

Rene looked at her daughter in despair. 'Jeannie!' she corrected, 'How many times must I tell you it's "home", not "'ome".'

'Aw, mam, ah keep fergettin'. Anyway why der yer want uz ter talk all proper? Nobody else does round 'ere.'

'I want you to talk *all proper*, as you so eloquently put it, because one day, when it helps you to get a really good job away from here, you'll thank me for it.' Jeannie was looking puzzled, so Rene smiled sympathetically before adding, 'Oh, pet! I don't expect you to understand right now, but when you grow up, if you speak nicely and go to the right kind of places you will meet the right people, and hopefully it will lead to a better life than you can expect if you stay here.'

'But ah like me life 'ow it is right now,' Jeannie protested, as she hopped along the footpath – on one foot.

Rene sighed with frustration. How was she ever going to teach this girl of hers the finer things in life while they still lived here? She looked around at the rows of terraced houses, and felt sick. Her affection for them had waned long before she'd gone to work in Bella's, the new fashion shop in Bishop Auckland. But this new managerial post that she had just taken on had brought home to her just how much hung on how you acted and spoke. Not that she didn't slip up herself, from time to time, much to the amusement of her friends – and sometimes even her family. They were all for her being ambitious, but couldn't help finding her struggle to be posh a little comic. Even so, they all admired her for working hard, and even for going to elocution class. She had grit, and didn't care who thought she was getting above herself.

What was she going to do about Jessie? she wondered. Right from the start, Jessie hadn't wanted her to go on this managerial course in Darlington. What had she said? 'Why, yer getting too big fer yer boots, man! Yer'll be too good fer the likes of me be the time yer get back.'

Rene had to admit that that remark was prescient.

'Mam?' Jeannie broke her train of thought.

'Yes, Jeannie? What is it?'

'Will our Tom be back when we get 'ome? Er, ah mean *home*.'

151

Rene sighed again, but this time she smiled as she looked down on Jeannie's dark bouncing ringlets, which had finally freed themselves from the restraint of the pink ribbon that had kept them in check during the bus and train journey from Darlington to Evenwood.

Jeannie, waiting for an answer, lifted her pretty face towards her mother.

'Yes, pet, Tom should be back by now.'

'Ah can't wait ter see him. Can you?' Jeannie questioned excitedly.

Rene turned to face Jeannie, put her case down, and took both small hands in hers as she answered, 'No, I can't, pet. Let's hurry and get home, shall we?'

Tom, his hand pressed to his forehead, was wandering around the house looking for headache pills to stem his hangover. He'd drunk far too much with his mates at the Scout hut dance the night before. Suddenly the back door flew open with a bang, and in barged Jeannie, who jumped straight into his arms shouting, 'Yer back, our Tom! Yer back!'

Tom didn't know whether to laugh at her, or cry at the increased throbbing in his head. Holding her at arms' length, he said with a grin, 'Hold on, lass, give us a chance!' He put her down and crouched down beside her, exclaiming in genuine surprise, 'Eee, just look at you, all grown up since I last saw you!'

'Ah know! Ah'm ten now, yer know,' she confided, wriggling coyly. Rene, following behind, was hardly through the door before Jeannie was calling to her for confirmation, 'Aren't ah, Mam?'

Tom looked up to see his sister lugging her case in through the door. 'Rene!' he called, grabbing her case with one hand and enfolding her with the other. 'Aw, don't cry, lass, else you'll set me off,' he said teasingly. He held her away from him. 'Let's have a look at you, too.' Studying her pale-grey jacket and matching pencil skirt, he said, 'Ay, aren't you looking smart, our Rene! But how the hell you can walk in shoes with heels as high as that I don't know!' She smiled, and before she could answer he went on, 'I've been hearing all about your new job, you know!' He added with a sly grin, 'I always knew you weren't cut out for round here, like!' Letting go of her now, and with an exaggerated bow, he beckoned her towards the living room. 'Your ladyship!'

'Aw, come on, Tom. You make me feel like a right snob. I do care about the people around here . . . well, some of them, anyhow, but I want more, both for me *and* our Jeannie, and it's never going to happen if I stay here.' Although she was trying hard, there was still a Northern softness to her speech, giving it a gentle charm.

'Well, I'm glad to hear you've not lost *all* your local accent anyhow,' Tom said. 'It'll always be there, our Rene, you know. Just mind you keep your feet on the ground, and you'll be all right,' he advised.

Giving him a shove she joked, 'Aye, ah'll do that all right, our Tom. Anyway, there'll be no chance of doin' otherwise, with you keeping yer beady eye on uz.'

'Well, I've got better things to do than keep a beady eye on you, like looking for something to get rid of this bloody headache, for a start. Where's me mam keep all the medicines and stuff, anyhow?' he complained, opening and closing one drawer after another.

Rene went straight to the relevant drawer, and as she handed him the headache pills she asked, 'You will try to watch your language in front of our Jeannie, won't you?' Then, realizing that what she'd just said might have sounded snooty, she added, 'The cursing, I mean. Your accent's gone a bit with the war, hasn't it? I like it.' And without waiting for a response she asked, 'Where's Mam and Da, anyhow?'

'They've gone to church,' he rolled his eyes. 'Can you believe Da's gone with her?'

'Well, yes, I can,' she replied. 'He started going when you were away fighting in the blessed war, when he knew you must be in the thick of it. He needed the comfort of the church then, and I guess he thinks it would look bad if he stopped going now that he's got what he prayed for, and you're home safe.'

'Oh no!' Tom laughed, touched by his dad's dilemma. 'I suppose he's saddled himself with it now, and can't see a way out, poor sod!'

'Oh! Knowing our Da, he'll make his excuses when he thinks the time's right,' Rene said confidently.

'Aye, I suppose he will. It beats me why they've got to walk all the way down to the Methodist Church anyway, when the Pentecostal Church is just over the road there! Surely one place of worship is as good as the next?'

At this Rene warned, 'Well, I wouldn't let Mam hear you say that, you know she's Methodist through and through, and *nothing* would induce her to go to the church over the road. Even if it meant walking to the next village, she'd do it.'

Tom responded with resignation, 'Aye, I know you're right, lass. Each to their own, eh? And in the meantime, should we be doing something about the dinner?'

'Well, in case you hadn't noticed, *I* put the beef in the oven while you were putting the world to rights . . . Did Mam tell you that Grandda Elliott is coming for dinner?'

'Well, no. I haven't seen her this morning. I had a bit of a skinful last night, and they'd gone to church by the time I got up. Eee, Grandda Ellott! I haven't seen him since God knows when,' Tom said, just as Jeannie came hurrying back in from the outside lavvy with her skirt half-tucked into her knickers.

She exclaimed, 'Oooh, Grandda Elliott! Does that mean that ah can have me Yorkshire puddin' before me dinner, with milk and sugar on, like he does, Mam?'

Tom picked her up and lifted her up over his head laughing, 'Well, that depends, young lady!'

'Depends on what?' she giggled, while he shook her around. 'Ah'll be sick on yer head if yer don't put uz down, our Tom,' she squealed.

'Ugh! Disgusting!' Tom pulled a face. 'Tell you what,' he said, setting her down on the floor. 'You lay the table nicely, and I'll make sure they let you have your Yorkshire puds with milk and sugar just like your great grandda.'

Rene, who was busily putting the potatoes in the roasting tin alongside the beef, gave Tom a look, reminding him that there would be no hope of ever getting their Jeannie to appreciate the advantages of etiquette as long as he encouraged her like that. But it was their first day together since she couldn't remember when, and there was no way she was about to spoil it over something like Yorkshire pudding, of all things.

Jeannie had just managed to get the last of the plates she'd been balancing precariously on her arms on to the table as her gran and grandda came in, followed by Great-Grandda Elliott.

'Well, this is a sight fer sore eyes,' Jack commented, with a satisfied grin, as he walked into the living room. 'Ah never thought ah'd see the day . . . The whole family together, at last!'

Hannah, having hugged Jeannie several times, looked over at Rene and exclaimed, 'Eee, pet! Well done! Yer a manager now, then?'

'Yes, Mam, a fully fledged manager.'

'That's grand! Aw, come here, lass.' Hannah held out her arms.

Rene, feeling really pleased with herself, stepped over to her mother and they hugged.

Hannah looked at Tom. 'What de yer think of yer big sister, then, lad? Passin' all them exams on fashion and buyin' and accountin' and all that? She'll be runnin' the shop in Bishop now, yer know!'

But before Tom, who was still enfolded in the arms of his granddad, could answer, Rene told Hannah the other bit of good news she had. 'I'll soon be out from under your feet, Mam, because the rooms above the shop in Bishop are being converted into living accommodation, and they'll give me a good rate on the rent—' She stopped mid-sentence at the concerned look on Hannah's face. 'Oh, Mam, be pleased for us!' She glanced at Jeannie, who was busily pestering her great-grandda while he struggled to light his pipe, and said quietly, 'We need to get away from the village, Mam. It's stifling us.'

'Oh, ah know, pet. It's just me bein' selfish.'

'Mam, you are the least selfish person I know.' Then, making sure they were well out of Jeannie's earshot, she whispered, 'I've asked about the local schools for our Jeannie, but I haven't told her yet. The living accommodation won't be ready for a few weeks, so I'll do it nearer the time.'

Hannah gave her a hug. 'Well, ah'm that pleased fer yer, pet. It'll be a step in the right direction, that's fer sure. But ah'll miss yer, and the house'll be dead without our Jeannie runnin' around.'

Jack, having overheard some of this, added his twopenn'orth now. 'Fer God's sake, woman, they'll only be five miles down t' road, half an hour on the bus!' He added with a wink, 'We could do with a bit more space round 'ere, anyhow, now that our Tom's back ter clutter the place up!'

'Aye, well, you've got me for a while yet, and all,' said Tom. 'Because when I was chatting to the lads at the dance last night, they were telling us that brickies are needed down the pit, so I thought I might go and see, like!'

'Yer don't want ter be workin down t' pit!' Grandda Elliott interrupted, without looking up from the armchair where he'd settled himself.

No one was ever sure just how much Grandda could hear. But he'd heard this all right, and, seemingly, had a strong opinion on it.

Tom laughed affectionately. 'You're right, Grandda, I don't want to work down the pit. But it won't be being a miner, it'll be building, like, and it'd probably only be for a month or two, till I get on me feet.'

Jack joined in now. 'I have ter agree with yer Grandda, lad, the whole point of goin' into the building trade was ter be outside in the fresh air. Yer don't want ter be stuck down there fer long, ah'm telling yer, lad. The only fresh air ah get is when ah'm on the allotment digging up carrots and potatoes, and such like.' He added proudly, pointing to the vegetables in the pans, 'Ah grew all those meself, ye know!'

To which Hannah, who could be heard in the scullery vigorously beating the mixture for the Yorkshire puddings, shouted in response, 'Not half as much fresh air as yer get walking to and from the club nearly every night, mind!'

Grandda Elliott, totally oblivious to the conversation in hand, suddenly called out, 'Don't ferget, ah'll 'ave mine afore me dinner, with milk and sugar on. Can't stand that bloody gravy on me Yorkshire puddin's!'

'Me an' all!' shouted Jeannie.

'All right, Da, ah think ah know that be now,' Mam called back, while the rest of the family fell about with laughter.

An hour or so later, with the joint of beef cooked, and the Yorkshire puddings nicely risen, the family gathered around the table, where they ate heartily. Grandda Elliott and Jeannie sat together, their Yorkshires covered in milk and sugar, while Rene looked on disapprovingly, eating hers with gravy.

Eventually, Grandda Elliott looked at Jeannie, and said, in a voice louder than it needed to be, 'Ay, that was good, wasn't it, pet? Ye'll be ready fer yer roast dinner now, won't yer?'

'All right, Da, ah get the hint. Yer proper dinners are on a plate all ready for yer in the oven,' Mam said, wiping her hands on the tea cloth, about to get up from the chair.

'Sit still, Mam, I'll get them,' said Rene.

'Mind yer get the oven cloth to open the oven door, the knob'll be mighty hot be now,' Hannah warned.

'Yes, Mam, I'm not about to make that mistake again, my fingers still tingle sometimes, even now, after that last time.'

Once everyone was sorted out, the family settled down to catching up on each other's news. They all had so much to tell, animated chatter and laughter competing with the clattering cutlery – but it all came to a sudden halt when there was a loud knock on the back door.

They glanced at each other, and Hannah asked no one in particular, 'Who on earth could that be at dinner time on a Sunday?'

She was about to get up when Tom, who was already on his feet, held up his hand to stop her, saying, 'You sit still, Mam, I'll get it!'

Chapter 13

'Oh my goodness!' cried Madeleine with a start. She put down the jacket, whose sleeves now fitted perfectly, wondering how long she'd been there. This is ridiculous, I must go downstairs, she thought, feeling on the floor for her shoes.

She hesitated for a moment on the bottom stair, wondering what kind of reception she'd get from her sisters.

'Ah! There you are!' Martine said, appearing not to notice how long she'd been gone. 'The coffee is made, if you want to join us,' she offered, as Madeleine walked sheepishly across the kitchen to where her two older sisters were sitting facing each other at the table.

'Still no sign of Maman, then?' Madeleine asked.

'No. So you're still safe. Maman doesn't know yet about you disappearing at the fair,' Simone said, not bothering to hide her sarcasm.

'That's enough, Simone,' Martine retorted angrily. '*You* have no right to criticize your sister – or anyone else, for that matter! And don't you forget it!'

'Oh, I can see you're *never* going to let me forget it!' Simone blurted out angrily. Then, losing her temper completely, she added, 'You and that Louis bloody Lamont! I wish neither of us had ever set eyes on him . . . Oh!' She clapped her hand tightly over her mouth, looking remarkably like a naughty schoolgirl.

Martine just sat there, saying nothing for a moment. But there was no mistaking the look of defeat in her eyes as she looked up at Madeleine. 'Well, now you know,' she said. 'You wondered why we came home earlier than expected. That's the reason.'

'But I don't!' Madeleine held her arms out in exasperation. 'Don't you think it's time you explained things?'

Simone looked at them both in panic. She said, 'Does this mean the whole family has to know?'

'I think we can spare the rest of them!' Martine said, glaring at her.

Madeleine poured herself the coffee she'd been offered, sure she was going to need it. Sitting back at the table, she looked at her two sisters, waiting for them to speak. '*Well?*' she asked.

Simone immediately got up. 'I'm not going to sit here, taking the blame for something that wasn't entirely my fault.'

'*Sit . . . down . . . Simone!*' Martine hissed. At that, though Madeleine was anxious what she might hear, a smile involuntarily twitched her lips. She'd sometimes

162

had the same urge to laugh in the school cellars during air raids. Serious situations often made her giggle. It was probably a kind of hysteria, she thought.

Martine poured herself another coffee, still without speaking, so that when she finally did say something, Madeleine jumped.

'It was shortly after your last visit to us in Boulogne—'

'You mean the time you sent me home early, without explaining why?' Madeleine interrupted.

'Yes, that time,' Martine answered. 'But please don't ask me any questions about that just now. This will be easier and quicker if you don't interrupt.'

Madeleine shrugged her shoulders. 'OK. Sorry.'

Martine began again. 'Shortly after your last visit about a year ago, I met a man, Louis Lamont.' She could see that she had Madeleine's full attention as she continued, 'He was a customer at the bank where I worked, and he'd had an account there long before I moved to Boulogne. He was handsome *and* he knew it.' Martine looked wistful, and paused before adding, 'Anyway, it was obvious that the girls in the bank liked him, and he was well aware of it. He made a point of flirting with them, but he never came to my window. That is, until the day he asked me if I would like to have a drink with him when I finished work.' She stopped again before adding, 'I was very surprised, because I wasn't even aware he had noticed me. He was charming and *very* persuasive, and, after some hesitation, I agreed. We talked a lot that day, and met quite frequently afterwards. It turned out that he knew lots of people, many of them working in the nightclubs still being run in cellars below the rubble-strewn streets and deserted buildings. And as Simone was busy with her studies in the evenings . . .' Martine glanced at Simone, who was looking decidedly uncomfortable, but continued, nonetheless, 'Sometimes I went with him to the clubs, which was an exciting escape from day-to-day routine and the depressing sights on the streets. It was like another world down there. And, yes, he used to gamble a little – but he made no secret of it.' Martine was answering a question that hadn't even been asked.

'Anyway, I didn't mind,' she continued, 'Because I was having a good time. After a few months, I knew that I really liked Louis, loved him, even. And he told me he loved me.' At this point, Martine flashed her eyes at Simone, who looked away immediately.

'We became much closer after that.' Martine glanced at Madeleine. 'If you know what I mean?'

'Of course I know what you mean!' Madeleine said.

'Anyway,' Martine continued, 'One day when we were out together, Louis became really worried and upset, telling me that the friend he'd been sharing a flat with had died. The flat was going to be sold, and he had to move out. I didn't even have to think about it before saying he could move in with me. And your sister . . .' She nodded towards Simone, '. . . had already met him by then, so everything was fine. Huh! That is, until a few months later, when I came home earlier than usual and decided to organise dinner ready, as a surprise.'

Simone had been fiddling nervously with her coffee

cup, but now, suddenly, she pushed her chair back as if she was going to leave.

'*Sit still!*' Martine ordered. 'You're listening to this whether you like it or not.' Then, glancing briefly at Madeleine, she said, 'I think you can guess who got a surprise.'

Madeleine put her hand to her mouth and looked at Simone, horrified, while Martine continued, 'I walked through the hall, where I picked up one of Simone's shoes. Nothing unusual in that, as she was never very tidy. Then, when I went to put it away, I heard sounds – giggling, coming from her bedroom. I opened the door and there she was, cavorting on the bed . . . naked.' Martine looked directly at Madeleine now, and asked, 'And who do you think she was with, Madeleine?'

Madeleine whispered incredulously, 'Louis. She was with Louis.'

'Yes, she was with Louis.' Martine glared at Simone, who was sobbing.

'I'm so sorry, Martine,' she said. 'How many times can I say it? I'm sorry, I'm sorry, I'm sorry.' She jumped up, scraping the chair back across the tiles, and ran upstairs. Martine let her go. She'd said what she wanted. Accidentally triggered by Simone's earlier outburst, this had been an opportunity for Martine to release her pent-up feelings at last.

Madeleine felt pity, not just for Martine, but for Simone, too, who was obviously suffering because she'd hurt her sister so badly. Maybe this would be a turning point for Simone, and in the future she would be more thoughtful.

Madeleine and Martine lingered at the table. Martine was staring blankly out of the window when Madeleine reached out and took her hand. 'I'm sorry that you've had such heartache,' she said gently. 'I realize now why you've seemed so different since you've come home.'

Martine smiled weakly, gripping Madeleine's hand. 'Don't be too distressed on my behalf,' she said. 'Because, in a roundabout way, Simone did me a favour.'

'A favour?' Madeleine looked puzzled.

'Louis wasn't just a womanizer. I discovered that after I'd thrown him out of the apartment, because only two days later, he was arrested.'

'Arrested?' Madeleine questioned in horror, 'Arrested for what?'

'Oh, wait till you hear *this*, my dear sister,' Martine said, with a wry smile. 'Then see what kind of man your elder – and supposedly sensible – sister fell in love with! Maybe then you'll understand why I was so hard on you when you went off with this Tom at the fair today.'

'Go on,' Madeleine urged, fascinated.

'He was arrested when he was caught passing information to a German officer. It was a few months before the end of the war, and this particular officer had been a frequent visitor at one of the nightclubs, which was obviously where Louis used to meet him. Anyway, apparently he had been paying Louis handsomely for information. Apparently, a close friend of Louis's, who was in the Resistance, suspected him, and planted false information about a plan to blow up a particular railway bridge. When the Germans lay in wait at the bridge and nothing had happened, Louis realized he'd been set up. So, panicking, and fearing reprisals from the Germans, he went to the gendarmes, hoping for protection.' Martine added quietly, 'Of course he was arrested, but, you see, there are gendarmes who are sympathetic to the Resistance. So I know I will never see Louis again. No one will . . . '

Madeleine kept quiet, waiting for Martine to continue. 'The sums of money Louis had paid in to his account, and the dates he'd done it, were checked after his arrest. And because I knew the details, I was interviewed too.'

'Oh, Martine!' Madeleine exclaimed. 'Weren't you afraid they'd think you were involved? When they discovered he lived with you?'

'At first, yes, I was. But fortunately they believed me. They'd been watching him for some time, and of course they knew he'd started doing it long before he met me. But they did check me out, too.'

Both girls were quiet for a few seconds, each dwelling on the situation in their own way. Then, abruptly, and with an obvious desire to finish the conversation, Martine got up, saying, 'Anyway, that is how I spent my last year in Boulogne. But it's over now. I've got to move on.'

'It does explain an awful lot,' said Madeleine.

Martine gave her sister a warm smile and said, 'I know, and I should have told you before. I *will* try to remember that you're not a child any more.'

'Thank you,' said Madeleine, pleased by this turn of events.

'Now I'm going to see if I can help Simone put this behind her. I'm hoping that when I tell her Louis collaborated with the Germans for money, and that maybe she did me a favour after all, she will realize I'm willing to try to forgive her.'

'You mean you haven't told her about that?' Madeleine was shocked.

'No.' Martine looked pensive. 'But I'm starting to think that maybe she's been punished enough for her selfishness. I just hope she's learned something.'

Madeleine sat there a while longer, as her sister headed for the stairs and Simone's room. What she had just learned about her two sisters had been a real revelation. And as she listened to the muted voices coming from the bedroom, she really hoped that this episode would clear the air between Martine and Simone once and for all.

Madeleine reminded herself that she still needed Martine to explain why she had sent her home from Boulogne so abruptly on that last visit. But she would have to choose the right time for that – and this certainly wasn't it.

She'd just started to clear the coffee cups away when Maman opened the front door. 'Hello, Maman,' Madeleine called. 'How was Tante Lucy?'

'Oh, you know Tante Lucy, always the same,' Maman replied in an amused voice. Hanging her coat on the hook behind the back door, she asked, 'And how was your visit to the fair? Did you girls have fun?'

'Yes, we had fun, Maman.' Martine, coming down

the stairs, answered the question before Madeleine could. 'It was lovely.'

Madeleine looked over at her and mouthed the word, '*Merci.*' Then she turned back to Maman. ' I rode on the carousel for the first time since I was tiny, and it was fantastic!'

'I can't remember the last time I had a fairground ride,' Maman mused.

'Well, you really should go this weekend, Maman. It will do you good.'

'Oh, I think I'm past all that now,' Maman answered, laughing.

'Never, never, Maman. You need fun as much as the rest of us, if not more,' Madeleine urged.

'We'll see,' Maman said, more encouragingly. 'Where is Simone?' she asked. 'Not still at the fair, surely?'

'Oh no, Maman, she's upstairs unpacking. After all, I didn't give my sisters much of a chance to do it before dragging them off to the fair, did I?' Madeleine said.

Maman, satisfied with this answer, went to get the vegetables out of the pantry.

Martine had wandered down the garden to the toilet, and Madeleine, guessing that she'd gone there to give her, Madeleine, time to talk to her mother, said cautiously, as she helped carry some carrots back to the kitchen, 'We met an English soldier at the fair today, Maman. He was very nice.'

Maman stopped what she was doing, and turned to look at her daughter. 'Who is "we?"' she asked.

' "We" is all of us,' Madeleine put in quickly. 'Oh,

you needn't worry, Maman. It was all above board.' Well, that wasn't a lie really, she thought. She felt slightly guilty, all the same.

Maman, looking reassured, asked, 'And who is he, this English soldier?'

Madeleine, braver now, because Maman was being so reasonable, said enthusiastically, 'He's called Tom, and he's billeted just outside the village, and he said that he would like to call on me—' She corrected herself quickly, 'On *us*. With your and Papa's permission, of course! You will make it all right with Papa, won't you, Maman?'

'Just give me time to think, will you, Madeleine?' Maman answered, sounding harassed, before changing the subject. 'Is Papa still working down there?' She glanced through the kitchen window towards the bottom of the garden.

Madeleine had forgotten about Papa working in his workshop, what with all the dramatic revelations since getting home. 'Oh, Maman, he is, and I forgot all about him! I didn't even take him a coffee, or go to tell him about the fair! And after I forced him to let me go, too!'

'Don't worry. Papa would have come in if he'd been desperate,' Maman said consolingly. Then she added, 'Come on, help me with the dinner before he finishes. No doubt he'll be starving after being out there all day.'

And so there'd been no more talk about the fair, or soldiers.

Chapter 14

Martine was feeling strangely liberated. She knew that what she'd said would remain between her and her sisters. She could see no reason to worry her parents – or anyone else – about something that was over; even though Louis's betrayal, not just of her, but of her country, still hurt.

Simone, on the other hand, was sitting in her bedroom, trying to take in what Martine had just told her. She clenched her hands into fists, feeling a confused mixture of fury and gratitude. She was furious with Martine for leaving her to suffer and repent all this time, when her fling with Louis, although wrong, had had a positive side. But then she was also grateful to know why he'd suddenly disappeared. She'd thought that he'd lost interest in them both, and that that was why he'd vanished without a word.

Anyway, she'd saved her sister from a life of hell.

After all, he was a complete bastard! Well, what else would you expect from someone called 'Louis Lamont'? She laughed mirthlessly. It probably wasn't even his real name.

She remembered how gullible she'd been, from the very first moment she'd set eyes on Louis. It was an evening in the autumn of 1943, and he'd come to take Martine to a nightclub. Simone had been envious, not just because her sister was going to have fun while she stayed in to study, but because Louis was a stunner: blond, debonair, impeccably dressed.

She flinched even now, remembering how – because Martine was still excitedly getting ready – she'd opened the door of the flat to Louis. He'd insisted on kissing her hand, and she'd blushed. Once inside, he'd prowled around, picking up ornaments and examining them minutely, opening doors, and glancing up at paintings.

'Martine won't be long,' she'd said.

He'd just smiled, answering her with a question, 'What are you going to do, Simone, while we are dancing the night away without a care in the world?'

'Me! Oh, I will be studying,' she'd answered. 'It's all I ever seem to do these days.'

He'd smiled widely. 'And what wonderful job are you studying for, if I may ask?'

'I want to be a pharmacist, but I sometimes wonder why.'

'That's a good profession, but life is too short for a dazzling girl like you to spend your time studying, especially now. After all, who knows what the future holds?' Then, after gazing at her with a smile on his lips, he'd added, 'You look like you need some fun.'

Martine had walked into the room at that point, looking gorgeous in her one and only best dress. The red fabric had set off her auburn hair amazingly, and Louis had devoured her with his eyes; he'd looked at Simone in much the same way earlier.

Simone's heart had ached with jealousy as she'd heard them laughing in the street. Once they'd slammed the car doors and driven off she sat on the settee miserably. She glanced over at the small dining table and two dining chairs heaped with her papers and textbooks.

The apartment was comfortable enough, but that evening it felt empty and dismal. With a sigh, she got to her feet and made a decision. She walked over and gathered up her papers and books, shoving them in the deep drawer at the bottom of her bedside cabinet. She'd had enough of studying, she decided. Louis was right. Who knew what would happen in the future? She could be dead tomorrow.

She had to continue with her daytime job assisting at the local pharmacy, if only because she needed the money. Anyway, she'd probably learn a bit while she was there. It beats going to evening classes twice a week, she thought. She was going to enjoy herself instead. She reasoned that there would be plenty of time to study after the wretched war was over. It couldn't go on much longer, could it?

She was very nervous the first few times she missed her classes; she went to the cinema instead with her friend Nadine – who worked with her at the pharmacy – and hoped no one would see them. Nadine had no career plans of her own, so was happy enough to tag along wherever Simone went. Nadine's dream was to marry her boyfriend, Philippe, and have as many babies with him as possible.

As Martine became more and more entranced with Louis, Simone found it easier to skip her classes. She told her tutors that she had to go home to Calais for a while to see her family. And after a few weeks she became confident enough to stop hiding away in the cinema, and instead frequented one of the most popular cafés in the *centre ville*, where she and Nadine met all kinds of interesting people.

Simone tried her first cigarette there. Well, everyone else seemed to be smoking, so why not? And anyway, it made her feel sophisticated. She and Nadine spent very little money on these outings, sometimes making two cups of coffee or a beer last all evening.

Nadine, like Simone, didn't want to sit around while life passed her by; or, even worse, wait for a bomb to 'drop on her head', as she put it – to Simone's amusement. Both girls really looked forward to the free time they spent together, and Simone convinced herself that it was doing her much more good than studying. She told herself she had enrolled in the school of life. Even Martine, engrossed in her work and the ubiquitous Louis, commented on how much more easygoing and contented her sister was. Simone didn't know it – but she was about to have a new experience. And one that, at the time, she foolishly imagined would make her happier.

Feeling hot and flushed by that particular memory, Simone got up from the bed and walked to the window, where she cooled her face against the glass, hoping that if she gazed at the garden for long enough, she would think about something else. But her mind was brimming with memories; there wasn't any way to avoid them.

That night was still so vivid that it could have happened yesterday. She remembered saying goodbye to Nadine outside the café before setting off for her bus stop. And a car drawing up beside her, and slowing down to walking pace. She tried not to look at the driver, and walked with her head down. But then she heard a familiar voice call out, 'Hey, Simone, no night class tonight, then?'

Oh *merde*, she thought, I'm in trouble now. He knows I've been playing truant. But she held her nerve, and said casually, 'Oh, hello, Louis. No, I didn't have any classes tonight.'

'Hey, slow down, Simone. What's your hurry?' he asked, as it started to rain. 'Look, get in and I'll run you home.'

She had no umbrella, so with only the slightest hesitation she jumped in, and when he turned his roguish smile on her she felt she'd melt.

'So Martine doesn't know your little secret?' he'd said, laughing, obviously knowing the answer.

'I am going to study. Just not now,' Simone said, feeling strangely confident.

'I guess some lucky man is pleased by your decision,' Louis said playfully.

'Oh no! I haven't been meeting a man,' Simone answered quickly. 'I've been with a girlfriend.' For some odd reason she wanted to make that clear to him, and she knew it wasn't because she was scared he'd tell Martine. In fact, she'd known for sure that he wouldn't. She simply wanted him to know there were no men in her life.

When they arrived at the end of her street he stopped the car, suggesting that it might be safer to get out there than in front of the apartment. She agreed, and he leaned over to open the door for her, just as she turned her head to give him a peck on the cheek. Whether by accident or design she still wasn't sure, but their lips met and she didn't object. In fact, she was so overcome by desire that she pulled him tightly towards her. She sensed he was fully aware how much he excited her, but she didn't care. He gripped the back of her hair and kissed her lips so fiercely that their soreness caused her, reluctantly, to pull away.

'Can we meet?' he asked with urgency.

'Soon, very soon,' she answered, and two days later they were in the apartment alone, frantically undressing each other.

And that was when they'd been caught by Martine, who had walked out of the bedroom without a word, banging the door behind her.

Chapter 15

Evenwood, England
Sunday, 2 December 1945

The clattering of cutlery and animated chatter came to a sudden halt as Tom walked back into the room. His face was ashen, and he was holding a letter in one hand and an envelope in the other.

'What is it, Tom?' asked Hannah, getting up from the table and rushing over to him.

Tom didn't speak. He simply stared ahead and handed her the letter Norah Atkins from No. 1 Glamis Terrace had brought round.

'The nine must 'ave been mistook for a one on the address, there's only a small loop at t' top – look,' Norah had said, pointing to the number on the envelope. 'But you'd think the bloody postman would've known our names by now,' she'd added, handing the letter to Tom at the back door. She'd gone on to explain that she'd been out when it had arrived yesterday, and only got home about five minutes ago.

'So ah thought ah'd better hurry and get it round to you,' she'd said. 'It looks like it might be from France, lad!'

'Aye it does,' he'd answered. Then, thanking her, he'd torn the letter open and scanned its contents before closing the door. And, seeing his expression, Norah had walked away, knowing better than to ask any more questions.

Seeing the looks on their faces, Rene jumped up from the table, saying to Tom and Hannah, 'Well, what is it? Has someone died?'

Hannah, having read the short letter twice, dropped her arm until it was hanging limply by her side. Then, looking searchingly into Tom's eyes, she begged, 'Tell me this isn't true, lad!'

She had her answer when Tom flopped down on the couch. Gently, Rene took the letter from Hannah's hand, and could see immediately that although it was in English it hadn't been written by a native.

Wednesday, 28 Novembre 1945
Cher Monsieur et Madame Dawson,
We think that this letter will be a shock for you.
But we do not know what else to do.

We have to tell you that your son Tom and our daughter Madeleine are going to have a baby.

We are sending our son Dominic to talk with you and Tom. He will be travelling to England on Saturday, 1 Decembre, and we hope that it will be OK with you to see him. We very much regret

this shock, but as you will understand, we are
very worried, and as Madeleine's maman et papa
we think that Tom should be told about this.
With regards, Monsieur et Madame Pelletier

Written on behalf of her parents by Martine, the
older sister of Madeleine.
  And we very much hope that this letter arrives
with you before Dominic, as everything has been
arranged very quickly.

Having read it through, Rene looked from Tom to
her mother, who'd now also flopped down on the
couch.

'Well, it's not the end of the world,' she said gently.

When there was no answer to her remark, she looked
at her brother, and with eyebrows raised she asked, 'Is
it, Tom?' There was still no answer, so, without taking
her eyes off Tom, she handed the letter to her dad, who,
while turning it the right way up to read it was saying,
'Whatever it is, it can't be that bad.'

Mam suddenly sat forward and asked Tom, 'When
did it say her brother was comin'?'

Tom got up and started pacing the floor. 'He's already
in England now, according to the letter. He could be
here any time.'

'Good God!' Mam exclaimed. 'He could arrive terday!'

'Is there a sweet after dinner, lass?' Grandda Elliott
suddenly piped up, while wiping his mouth, seemingly
oblivious to anything but the food.

'Yes, there'll be some apple pie in a minute, Da,' Hannah replied absent-mindedly, getting up from the couch.

Tom followed her into the scullery while Rene and Da sat back down at the table. Jeannie, who'd been playing with some of her grandda's collection of pipes, looked from one to the other. 'What's goin' on, why has everybody got long faces?' she asked, and then had a coughing fit because she'd been sucking on one of the empty pipes.

'For goodness' sake, Jeannie, what on earth possessed you to do that?' Rene scolded, patting her on the back, while Jack, who'd made no comment so far on the letter, smiled reassuringly at Jeannie and poured her some fizzy pop to take away the taste of the stale old pipe.

'Well, Great-Grandda Elliott looks happy enough when he's smoking a pipe,' Jeannie said, in all seriousness, 'and you lot have all got long faces, so ah thought ah'd give it a go and be 'appy like me great-grandda.'

' "Happy", Jeannie, not " 'appy",' Rene implored.

'Oh, Mam!' Jeannie sighed.

Rene ignored Jeannie's protest and turned to her father, placing her hand over his, and saying, 'It will be all right, you know, Da. It's just a bit of a shock, that's all.'

'Aye, it's a bit of a shock, all right,' Jack answered. He shook his head, feeling sympathy for his son, before adding quietly, 'Bah, ah thought 'ee had more sense than that, like. He'll have ter marry her, don't yer think, lass?'

'I don't know, Da. He'll need time, no doubt, to get used to the idea.'

In the scullery Mam was flustered, busying herself cutting the apple pie, when Tom said, 'I had no idea, Mam.'

'Well, *we* had no idea that you'd even taken up with a lass over there, Tom. Yer kept that one quiet enough. Yer can't bury yer head in the sand over this one, lad, yer'll have ter face up to it one way or the other, yer know.'

'I didn't tell you about her, Mam, because I thought that was the end of it, like. What with me coming back to England and her living in France—'

'Do yer love 'er?' Hannah interrupted.

'Aw, Mam, how can you ask us a question like that?' he shook his head.

'Well, it's simple enough, lad. Yer either love 'er or yer don't,' she said abruptly.

He'd never seen his mother in this mood before. 'Look, Mam, I loved her when I was over there, and I even got to love her family. But I knew all the time that I had to come back to England and my own family. She . . . Maddie, I mean, doesn't speak much English, and, well, you know what my French is like! So there was no future as far as I could see. You must see that yourself, Mam.'

'All ah can see at the moment, lad, is that you've got a bairn on the way.' She carefully didn't mention the word 'marriage'. The thought of her beloved son

181

marrying a stranger from another country was hard for her even to think about. As she walked past him to take the pie to the table, she said crossly, 'Whatever were yer thinking of, lad!'

She placed the pie on the table none too gently, and looked around at her family, at a loss as to what to say to them.

Rene put a hand on her arm. 'It'll all be sorted somehow, Mam. Try not to worry too much. Let's just wait and see what this girl's brother has to say, eh?'

'Well, more ter the point, what are we goin' ter say ter 'im, when 'ee gets 'ere?' Hannah said, looking anxious. 'And I hope he can speak English, an' all!'

'Even if 'ee can 'ee's goin' ter have a job ter understand us, lass!' Jack put in.

Tom came back to the table and glanced towards his father as he sat down. Jack looked at him, sympathy in his eyes, but didn't say anything.

'What *is* up with you lot? Yer look as if yer've lost five bob, and not even *found* a tanner!' Jeannie observed between gulps of fizzy pop and pie.

'Get on with your pie,' Rene said. 'And don't talk with your mouth full.' Her scolding was only half-hearted.

'The custard's got a skin on it!' Grandda Elliott complained loudly, as he picked up the heavy white jug.

'Oh, give uz it 'ere,' Hannah said quickly. She scraped the skin off the top, before pouring the custard on to his piece of pie.

Jeannie, swallowing the last mouthful of hers, said,

'Will yer come and play tiddlywinks with uz, our Tom?'

Tom, feeling a desperate need to get away from the table and out of the room to think things through, answered, 'Of course I will, lass. Go and get them, and we'll put them on a stool out in the yard.'

'What do you say before you leave the table, Jeannie?' Rene warned, seeing that she was about to leap up.

'Oh, can ah leave the table?' Jeannie said. Rene, still not satisfied, prompted her with a nod of the head and waited.

Jeannie sighed, '*Pleeeese!*'

'You may.'

Hannah caught hold of Tom's arm as he carried the stool towards the back door. 'How can yer think about playin' tiddlywinks at a time like this, lad?' she asked, with more than a touch of annoyance.

'I can't hear myself think in here, Mam. I need to get outside for a while.'

'Well, yer'll not get ter think much with our Jeannie talking fifty ter the dozen,' Hannah answered sharply.

'Just give us a bit of space, Mam, will you? I'll be all right in a bit.' He said this gently, while setting the stool down in the yard.

Monday, 3 December 1945

Thankfully, Dominic didn't arrive that Sunday, and the next morning Rene went off to work early, about

183

the same time as Jack. Mam was getting Jeannie ready for school, while Tom was still upstairs – on orders from Hannah to get his bedroom organized for an extra guest before he went for his interview at the building site in Bishop.

He had filled the family in as much as he could with regard to Madeleine and her family. They'd all been wide eyed with fascination, and were now looking forward to meeting Dominic, albeit a little warily. He himself was at sixes and sevens, with no idea what he was going to do. It still seemed possible, in a hazy way, that he might not have to get married, that things could be sorted out differently. He was half-hoping Dominic would have the answer.

Once he gets here he'll be able to see for himself how impossible it would be for her to live here in this house; or for me to go to France, for that matter, Tom thought. And why do I keep referring to Maddie as 'her'? She has a name, for God's sake! It's because using her name makes her too real. But this *is* real! He'd reminded himself of that over and over throughout the night. He couldn't even think properly now. He didn't *want* to think, he'd decided, by the time he came clattering down the stairs and shot straight out of the front door.

Jeannie came rushing in from the scullery, where she'd been having a wash, shouting, 'Gran! Was that our Tom goin' out in a mood? Cause ah nearly jumped out of me skin, 'ee made so much racket!'

'Take no notice, pet,' Hannah answered. 'He's got things on his mind at the moment.'

''Ee wants ter think himself lucky 'ee hasn't got ter go ter school like me,' Jeannie answered.

Hannah put her arm around her granddaughter and smiled. 'Eee, yer brighten the place up, yer do, our Jeannie.'

'Gran, did ah tell yer ah had ter write a composition all about my hero, at school?'

'No, yer didn't, pet. And who did yer write about?'

'Well, ah wrote about me dad, and about how brave he was goin' on all those bombing raids in his aeroplane. And then how he was shot down in France, and how he might still be tryin' ter get 'ome . . . *home*.' She corrected herself. 'Nobody ever seems to talk about him any more. Ah won't cry if they do, yer know, Gran.'

'Oh pet! Ah know yer wouldn't. You're a brave girl yerself, you know, just like yer dad. But if he was comin' home he'd have been back be now. The war ended a while back. But ah'll tell yer what! If ever yer want ter talk about yer dad, yer can always talk ter me, yer know, pet.'

'But what about me mam? What if she wants ter talk about him?'

'Well, ah think for the time bein' she likes to talk about him in her own mind, because she still misses him, pet, and it's still too painful for her ter talk out loud about him. That's why she's occupyin' herself with her new job now. And ah think it'll be good for her, you'll see.'

Jeannie suddenly flung her arms round Hannah's soft and reassuring form, while Hannah, who was discreetly wiping a tear from her eye with the bottom of her pinny, said more brusquely than she intended, 'Now, come on, lass, we've school ter get to.'

Chapter 16

England
Sunday, 2 December 1945

The chap sitting opposite Dominic on the train turned out to be pretty friendly. In fact he even recommended a guesthouse. The journey was delayed by a suicide on the line. In fact, they were stuck in a siding for so long that it was impossible *not* to converse. And even though Dominic hadn't wanted to get involved in small talk, they struck up a conversation – as much to alleviate the boredom as anything else. Dominic was quite pleased with his mastery of the English language, and his fellow traveller – Donald Henderson – was good company.

The guesthouse was only a stone's throw from Darlington Station, and when Tom finally arrived there at five in the morning – and mentioned Donald Henderson's name to the landlady – she gave him a very warm welcome. Apologizing for its lack of space, she showed him to a small but clean attic room. 'Mind you, you're lucky to get a room at all on a Sunder, lad,' she said. 'In fact, ah wouldn't normally have let yer in, but if yer good enough fer Don Henderson, yer good enough fer me!'

Although Dominic couldn't understand everything she said, he couldn't help smiling at his prim and proper landlady. She had a peculiar falsetto voice, and held her head high, looking disapprovingly down her nose at him. One thing his school English lessons hadn't prepared him for was her strange dialect. Donald Henderson had been much easier to understand, but then he was a well-travelled businessman, living in London. Dominic really hoped that Tom's family weren't going to speak like the landlady; things were bad enough without having to suffer the embarrassment of a language barrier. He took some comfort from the fact that he'd been able to talk to Tom. Even though their conversations had been strained at times, they'd mostly understood each other. But there'd been times when even Tom had come out with words or phrases that bore no resemblance to anything Dominic had been taught. They'd had some good laughs over that, but it had been different, then. He and Tom had shared the same sense of humour, and that had got them through the language problems. He wasn't sure a shared sense of humour was going to help now.

Monday, 3 December 1945

To Dominic's horror, there had been no trains running to Bishop Auckland on Sunday. He'd had a whole day to kill. Shattered and anxious, he'd lain on top of the bed in fitful sleep, emerging only for dinner late in the afternoon.

At 7 a.m. he was woken by the sound of a long piercing whistle. Bleary-eyed, half-asleep, he sat up, and for a moment had no clue where he was. Then there was another whistle, and he realized the sound came from the station across the road.

What did today have in store for him? he wondered. He guessed that Tom's family – if they'd received Maman's letter, of course – would be just as curious about him as he was about them. What would they be expecting?

Seized by a sudden panic, he got up, washed, and went down to the small dining room, where he was served, as on the previous day, by a plump teenager who looked as if she'd prefer to be somewhere else. He picked at his porridge and reconstituted scrambled egg, and, relieved the teenager had drifted off and he didn't have to apologize to her for eating so little, hurriedly went back to his room to pack.

When he got downstairs the landlady was hanging around waiting for him in the hall.

'Yer off then, are yer.' It was more of a statement than a question.

'Yes, I am off as you say, and thank you again, madame, for taking me in yesterday.'

With a limp flap of her hand she answered, 'Oh, go on with yer, it was a pleasure, I'm sure.' She laughed girlishly, pleased to be referred to as 'madame' by this handsome young man with the foreign accent.

Dominic took his wallet from inside his jacket pocket and asked, 'How much, please?'

The landlady, snapping to attention at the mention of money, said, 'Well, ah'll have ter charge yer full price ah'm afraid, even though yer didn't eat yer breakfasts. Was they not ter yer liking?' she asked.

Dominic stood frozen for a moment, trying to work out exactly what she'd asked.

Seeing his puzzlement she explained, 'Breakfast not good?'

'Oh, *le petit dejeuner*!' Dominic laughed. He answered as diplomatically as he could, 'Yes, good. But I was not hungry for the porridge and eggs. I eat little at home. Maybe just a croissant, *avec confiture de fraises*. And a cup of coffee, of course!' Madame's face was a picture when he teasingly used a little French. After all, it couldn't do any harm to let people know just how puzzling a different language was.

She chose to ignore the French, and in a slightly indignant tone now, she said, 'Well, it's not right ter waste food! It's difficult to come by, with rationin' and all that. So yer see, ah'll have ter charge yer for it, lad.'

'I understand very well, madame. It is the same at home, also,' Dominic answered.

'Yes, well, that'll be two pounds two and sixpence, please,' she said, looking slightly embarrassed.

Dominic pressed the money into her hand and closed her fingers around it, saying, 'Thank you very much again, madame.'

'Ay, lad, yer can stay here any time you have a mind ter,' she said with a smile. 'And good luck with whatever it is that yer've got on yer mind.'

Dominic, catching her meaning more from her concerned expression than her actual words, looked at her in surprise.

She went on, 'Ah can see that yer burdened with something, lad. So let's hope yer get it sorted, eh?'

'Thank you,' was all he could think to say, as he headed for the station.

He stopped to ask an old railwayman for directions as he entered the booking hall. 'Train for Bishop should be on platform five,' the man answered. 'Yer'll be in Bishop in half an hour or so. But make sure yer get on the right train, mind,' he cautioned. 'Then yer just need ter get on the number eleven bus to Evenwood, and anybody'll tell yer where ter get that, lad! Yer lucky yer can speak such good English, so yer'll have no bother,' he said confidently.

But Dominic wasn't confident at all. And, as for being lucky with the English language, huh! Little did the old boy know just how hard he'd had to work at it over the years.

Having taken a right turn, platform five was now looming before him, and he experienced a moment's apprehension, before thinking, Right, this is it! Just get on with it, Dominic.

Tom's meeting with the builder at Bishop Auckland had gone well, and he was going to start the job in a week's time. He felt extremely pleased with himself. He'd even got on the right bus this time – the number eleven heading directly for Evenwood village – not wanting to make the same mistake as when he'd first arrived, and had to walk all that way. It was a shame he wouldn't see Maisie, of course, with her being on the number twelve. But it was for the best; he wouldn't be good company for her while Maddie was on his mind. He was well aware that his family could only do so much: it was down to him alone to sort out the problem.

He sat upstairs in the double-decker and stared out at the countryside, lost in thought, until a sudden light tap on his shoulder made him look up sharply. He was so shocked you could have knocked him down with a feather.

'*Dominic!*' he exclaimed, jumping up from his seat. 'Bloody hell! Fancy you being on the same bus as me! Sit yourself down, man!' He laughed at how unreal it was: Dominic sitting right next to him on the number eleven! He'd been so certain Dominic was a world away, securely in the past – and yet here he was! 'Eee, man, I can't believe it's you!' Tom, in his excitement, spoke fast, with a strong local accent, forgetting how clearly he used to have to enunciate so Dominic could understand him.

But Dominic, seemingly unfazed, laughed for the first time since he'd left France, and said, 'I was sitting at the back of the bus, and I recognize the shape of your head! It was a shock for me, also.'

Tom ran his hand over the back of his head,

exclaiming, 'Well, I never! I've been called a big head before, but I hadn't realized that it was an unusual shape an' all, like!' Tom smiled, then, taking in Dominic's tired face, he said more seriously, 'Ay, you look done in, man! You must have had one hell of a journey!'

Dominic's puzzled look made Tom realize he hadn't made himself clear enough.

'Sorry. I mean, you look tired.'

'Ah!' Dominic expressed his understanding. 'I am not too tired, because I sleep yesterday in a . . . Oh, how do you call it?

'A bed and breakfast?' Tom smiled.

'Yes,' said Dominic. 'It was very close to Darlington station, so I was here quickly, and now that I am here I am more worried than tired.'

'You and me both,' Tom replied.

'You received the letter from Maman, then?' Dominic asked the obvious.

'Aye, we received the letter all right,' Tom said before adding, 'I'm so sorry, Dominic.' He looked directly at Dominic, asking tentatively, 'How is she?'

'She is not good, Tom,' said Dominic.

Tom ventured very cautiously now, 'There's no doubt, I suppose . . . I mean, about me being the father, like?'

Dominic couldn't have looked more shocked if someone had held a gun to his head. His expression changed, and his right hand curled into a fist.

Tom immediately realized his mistake and said quickly, 'Aw, I'm sorry, man! I should never have

193

said that, but, you see, I only went with her the once!'

Dominic said stiffly, 'I understand that you are in shock, Tom, and it saddens me that you would even think that of Madeleine. There is no doubt that you are the father.'

'In my heart I knew that,' Tom responded. 'God knows what made me say such a thing—'

He started to apologize again but Dominic interrupted. 'Shh, *mon ami*, let us forget "sorry" now, and concentrate on today, and your family, who I still have to meet.'

'Aw, man! You've no need to worry about them. They'll love you, all right!' Tom said confidently.

'But what do they say to this news?' Dominic questioned, not at all reassured.

'They're shocked.'

Dominic said nothing, just looked out of the window, not really seeing the village they were passing through.

'West Auckland,' Tom informed him half-heartedly. 'It's where I went to school after I was eleven. Only another couple of miles and we'll be home.'

They both sat quietly looking at the passing countryside, lost in their own thoughts.

Dominic couldn't think beyond the impending meeting with the family, and Tom was back on that lovely warm day early last September. In his mind's eye he was following Maddie along the footpath in Marck. He was admiring her swaying hips, as he'd done so many times before. She stopped to pet a passing dog, and he crept up behind her and put his hand over her eyes. She squealed, but he knew she'd guessed who it was. He smiled now, remembering how she giggled at first, before, in mock-anger, pushing him, 'Oh, you . . . you Tom, I have fright. I thought you are at the camp today?' she said, but she was obviously pleased he was there.

'I'm here because I have something to tell you,' he answered hesitantly.

Seeing the seriousness in his face she stopped walking. 'What, Tom? You are going away?' Her eyes were full of fear, guessing the answer.

'You read me too well, Maddie,' Tom answered sadly.

'I expect it,' she said bravely, carrying on walking, but not raising her eyes from the pavement.

Tom pulled her round to face him, and tenderly lifted her chin. 'Look, Maddie, we can write to each other,' he said encouragingly, trying to hide his own unhappiness.

'Oh, Tom!'

Tom remembered being touched at the way despair made her French accent stronger.

'When?' she asked, not really wanting an answer.

'We demob the day after tomorrow. But we won't be allowed off camp after today.'

'Oh, *mon Dieu*! So soon!' she exclaimed.

'Yes, *mon cheri*.' Tom used the expression he'd heard so often from her own lips. He took her hand and cajoled, 'Come on, Maddie, this is our last day together. Let's make it a good one!'

When she looked up at him with tears in those big brown eyes he thought his heart would break there and then.

'OK,' she said, wiping her tears with the back of her hand. 'Come with me to give this dress.' She held out the parcel she was carrying. 'I have sew it for Madame Declemy. Then maybe we walk . . . no? It is a beautiful day.'

'Let's do that!' he answered enthusiastically, before taking both of her hands in his. He leaned forward, and, without another word, they'd kissed gently, before moving on together hand in hand, making brave attempts at their usual light-heartedness; both equally miserable about the imminent parting.

Madame Declemy saw them approach – she was working in her garden. Tom and Maddie smiled at the sight of her head bobbing up and down in the middle of her raspberry cage.

'*Bonjour*, madame!' Maddie called, trying to stifle her amusement as she opened the wooden gate into the garden.

'Ah! *Bonjour*, Madeleine, *et bonjour*, monsieur,' Madame Declemy answered, looking at Tom appreciatively.

'Madame Declemy, this is Tom, my friend, and he is going back to England very soon,' Madeleine said, in rapid French.

'Oh, well, you won't be wanting to hang around here for too long, then, Madeleine,' Madame Declemy replied, equally rapidly. She winked. 'I will get your money, and thank you for doing the work for me so quickly.' She took the parcel before disappearing off into the comparative darkness of her house.

While they waited in the bright sunshine, on impulse, Tom bent forward and kissed Maddie full on the lips, as he'd done so many times before. Except this time, it was different. The kiss was deeply passionate, and he knew that Maddie felt it. They pulled away slightly, still wrapped in each other's arms. Their eyes locked, and both of them knew what was going to happen next.

As the bus jogged along, Tom allowed himself a wry smile, remembering how they had sprung apart like two naughty children when Madame Declemy came out with the money. And how, aware of their embarrassment, she had immediately said, 'Now run along, *mes enfants*, and make the most of the time you have left together.'

She'd turned to look at Tom, who'd smiled in response to her cheeky wink, even though he hadn't been sure what she'd said. But he'd seen that she approved of him, and was maybe even a little envious of their love for each other. I'll bet *she* was a right lass! he'd mused at the time.

'Come on,' Maddie'd nudged him, 'Let's walk! We walk to Tante Lucy's farm, and she gives us a ride. Horace pulls us in the cart. It will be funny, and I think we need . . . to be happy?' She looked up into his face her eyes aching with sadness.

Tom enfolded her in his arms, and their kiss was even deeper.

'That sounds like a good idea,' he said, reluctant to release her, and fighting the urge to have her there and then. 'I would like to see your family before I leave, anyway,' he said gently, though he wanted to yell, 'God, Maddie! I don't care where we go, as long as we can be alone together!'

Maddie led the way over a stile and into a field, explaining, as she hit at the long grass in front of her with a stick, how it was a short cut to Tante Lucy's. They worked their way along the path, which they could just about see. It meandered round the ragged remains of previous crops, and was so narrow that, in parts, they had to walk in single file. Tom, who was walking behind, became increasingly dizzy with desire. And as he watched Madeleine beat back the grass, he was unable to think of anything but her bare, suntanned arms and legs, her lithe body in the thin summer dress, or the way her hair curled damply in the heat. Sensing a change in his mood, she stopped and turned to him, asking, 'Tom, you are OK?'

He didn't answer, but took her in his arms again, and her heart pounded so heavily against his chest that it felt like his own. He had to clear his throat to answer, 'Yes, I'm fine, but . . .'

Before he could say any more she had pulled his head down to her mouth and kissed him full and hard. They kissed, and kissed again, until they could breathe no longer. He moved away to kiss her forehead, her nose, her chin – and the only word he was capable of uttering at that moment was her name, over and over again. It was when she responded by repeating *his* name that he lost the little control he had left. And when he fumbled with the tiny buttons at the front of her dress, she brushed his hand away and did it for him, allowing him to slide one side of the dress from her shoulder. He felt her shiver as, with the palm of his hand, he caressed her skin. Then, hearing her moan as his fingers ran the length of her spine, he kissed her again, full on the mouth.

When he thought about the way he'd felt at that moment, he realized it had been strangely like the violent fever he'd had after contracting malaria in the Middle East. Then Madeleine sank down into the long grass, and he fell on top of her. He remembered how firm her body felt, and how lush the green grass was beneath her. Her chestnut hair tumbled in a mass of waves around her face, and the bright autumn sunlight threading through it momentarily made him think of a painting he'd seen in church as a child. How mesmerized he'd been by that painting, in which the girl's hair had spread out behind her, so full of light that she'd appeared to be flying! In a dreamlike state he took up a handful of Madeleine's hair, and it felt like silk as he held it against his cheek.

When Maddie turned her head slightly to face him her expression changed: she no longer looked like a young girl, but like a woman. A woman who knew what she wanted. And when she lifted her hands to cup his face her touch made him tremble.

'I love you, Tom,' she said softly.

It was then that he'd lifted himself on his arms, releasing the pressure of his body on hers, and looked into her pleading brown eyes. He hadn't the courage to tell her that he loved her. How could he, when he knew that he had to leave? Instead, his voice hoarse with desire, he said, 'Maddie. Are you sure you are ready for this?'

'Shh, Tom. Yes, I am sure,' she answered with undisguised urgency.

Tom hesitated, but Maddie seemed to have lost all trace of her usual modesty, and begged him, 'Please, Tom!' And by that time, with her there in front of him, writhing in the grass, wild horses couldn't have stopped him.

He couldn't say how long they lay there afterwards, naked, abandoned – and totally content. All he remembered was a strange feeling of completeness. It was then that he realized that this hadn't been just sex; for the first time in his life he had made love. This knowledge was almost frightening, and for a split second his sense of self-preservation made him want to run from it – but his heart wouldn't allow that; and as he held Madeleine close in his arms his mind had been in turmoil.

Even though there had been many other, earlier opportunities to make love, they hadn't taken them. They'd managed to curb their desire, as much out of respect for Maddie's parents as anything else. But this time had been different. Tom wasn't sure whether it was because he was about to leave, or whether it was simply that they had resisted for so long that they couldn't fight it any more. When the euphoria of the moment subsided a little, he lay there with an overwhelming feeling that he'd betrayed someone, but he wasn't sure who.

Thinking about it now, he realized that it was her family's trust that he had betrayed: they had treated him as one of their own. He hadn't dared ask Maddie how she was feeling, because he'd been afraid of the answer. Although, when he'd helped her do up all the tiny buttons on her dress, which a little earlier she'd so urgently opened for him, she'd sensed his concern and assured him, 'Is OK, Tom. I am OK.' And before Tom could answer, she'd gripped his hand tightly, and looking straight into his eyes, reiterated, 'I am!'

But this time when she'd smiled, Tom had been aghast to feel a tear sting his eye, and silently said to himself: For God's sake not *now*, don't bloody cry *now*! He'd quickly got to his feet and held out his hands towards her, pulling her up from the ground and into his arms, where she'd stood on her toes and kissed him gently on the lips.

They hadn't spoken again, and they'd walked off, not in the direction of Tante Lucy's farm, but towards Maddie's home . . .

'EVENWOOD! BANK TOP!' The bus jerked to a halt, and the shrill yell of the conductress penetrated Tom's thoughts so sharply that he jumped, almost knocking Dominic off his seat. He glanced at Dominic, who looked scared, as if he'd been shaken awake. 'Ay, come on, man, we're here,' Tom said, grabbing Dominic's arm while Dominic quickly picked up his valise. As they ran towards the stairs at the back of the bus Tom said, 'Eee, I'm sorry, mate! I wasn't concentrating. Got lost in me thoughts, like.'

'Me too,' Dominic said, looking more than slightly flustered.

With a grin, Tom slapped him on the back. They clattered down the stairs, and as soon as they'd jumped off, the bell dinged and the bus disappeared off into the distance. Tom and Dominic glanced at each other in mutual understanding of what lay ahead, before setting off on the short walk to Glamis Terrace.

Chapter 17

Evenwood, England
Monday, 3 December 1945

'Mam!' Tom called as he entered the house just ahead of Dominic, 'Mam! Are you there?'

'Eee, lad, ah wuz on the lav, and ah wasn't goin ter shout from there now, was ah?' Hannah rushed in through the back door, and came to a sudden halt. 'Oh . . . !' She clapped her hand over her mouth at the sight of the nicely dressed fair-haired lad standing in the middle of her front room.

'Mam, this is Dominic. And Dominic . . .' Tom smiled, extending his arm towards his obviously embarrassed mother '. . . meet me mam.'

Hannah quickly collected herself and walked towards Dominic. 'Come 'ere, lad,' she said, holding her arms out towards him.

Dominic, feeling slightly bewildered by this strange greeting, nervously put his case down while glancing uncertainly towards Tom. Tom nodded and

Dominic walked into Hannah's outstretched arms.

'Ay, this is a right to-do. What are we goin' ter do, lad?' she questioned, as she hugged him. 'Yer mam and dad must be beside themselves an' all,' she added – more as a comment than a question – before releasing him.

Dominic answered the bit that he'd understood. 'Yes, Madame Dawson, not only Maman *et* Papa, but the whole family is worried. And no one has an answer.' He bent to pick up his case – he'd no idea why.

Hannah, noticing his agitation, implored, 'You put that down, lad.' She looked at Tom and asked, 'Will yer take it upstairs for 'im, Tom, please?'

Tom did as he was bid, while Hannah rushed to build the fire up ready for boiling the kettle. She said to Dominic, 'You'll have a cup of tea, won't yer, lad?'

He understood 'cup of tea' very well from Tom's constant desire for one when he'd been in France, and he could tell that she wouldn't be expecting no for an answer, so he said, 'Yes, madame, thank you.'

'Good, well, you sit yerself down here,' she said, ushering him to a chair beside the now roaring fire. Then, with a smile, she added, 'And as nice as it sounds, there's no need ter call me madam, me name's Hannah.'

'Oh, sorry, Madame Hannah,' Dominic replied, looking concerned, 'but in France it is a sign of respect to address our elders as madame or monsieur.'

Hannah looked up, aware of Tom coming down the stairs, and said, 'Well, it's very polite, I'm sure! It's a shame we don't have the same custom here. A few good manners wouldn't go amiss sometimes—'

'Aw, come on, Mam!' Tom interrupted, 'No one's got more respect for their mam and da than me and our Rene!'

'Ah know, pet. Ah was only tryin' ter make light of the difficult situation we're in here,' she answered, with concern.

There was no response to that, either from Tom or Dominic.

But once supplied with a cup of tea and a very strange gateau, which Madame Hannah called an 'iced bun', Dominic did begin to relax a little. He felt comfortable enough to describe his family to Tom's mother, and the thought of meeting Monsieur Dawson, and Tom's sister, Rene, began to seem slightly less daunting.

While he talked he studied Tom in his home surroundings: he fitted in there so well that it was hard to imagine him living in France. That thought reminded Dominic that he had promised to send a telegram to his parents when he got to Glamis Terrace, but it was too soon to be able to tell them anything other than that he'd arrived. And he didn't think there'd be any significant discussion until the whole family were assembled, anyway.

What a mess! he thought. Here were two families from totally different worlds, who would never have known of each other's existence if it hadn't been for the war. But they were going to be forced together, and it seemed that Tom's kindly mother thought that everything could be solved over a cup of tea! Or maybe that was just her way of coping.

He realized that he was going to have to develop a taste for tea, as the famous English drink seemed to be served at *any* time of the day. Aware that his mind was wandering, he made himself listen more closely to what Hannah was saying. She was talking about how her friends and neighbours had all clubbed together to provide food when they'd known Tom was coming home.

'Well, Mam, I should think so, too, after all the running around you do for that lot,' Tom butted in. 'I expect it's their way of repaying you.' Then, looking at Dominic, he added, 'You should have seen the spread she put on for us on the day I arrived home! We're still wading through it now!'

'Stop yer exaggeratin', our Tom.' Hannah glanced kindly at Dominic, adding, 'Anyway, if ah'd known which day you were comin', ah would have put on a spread for you, an' all!'

'A spread?' Dominic assumed a puzzled expression. It had hardly been off his face since he'd arrived.

Tom smiled. 'It means loads of grub, mate!'

Not much wiser for the explanation, Dominic couldn't help wondering how on earth Madeleine would manage here, with her limited knowledge of the language. He had been pleasantly surprised at the way her English had improved after meeting Tom, but *this*! This bore little relation to what they'd been taught in school. His mind was churning. *Mon Dieu*, Madeleine! he thought. I pity you. He stared through the front window into the neat little front gardens, noticing how different this view was from the one at the back, which simply looked out on to an identical row of houses.

While the kettle had come to the boil, Tom had taken him out into the small concrete backyard and shown him the outside toilet and the coal house. This last had a small, waist-high door, called a hatch, which opened on to the back street. Tom had explained how the coal was delivered by a man with a horse and cart. He'd tip the coal outside in the street, where it formed a gleaming black heap. Then each householder would open up the hatch door and shovel the coal through into the shed. On delivery days, by the time everything was safely shovelled inside, not only was the coalman covered from head to toe in coal dust, but so were the inhabitants of each street.

Tom had explained that the family took it in turns to fill up a bucket with coal from the shed, as and when it was needed. '*And* it's all free, cause me da's a miner,' he'd said. Dominic had sensed bitterness in his voice at that last remark. He assumed it was because Tom felt free coal was the least the mine could do for his father. But, not really understanding the coal mines himself and how they worked, Dominic had said nothing. If he was honest, all he could think about at the moment was this very different lifestyle. He simply couldn't picture his sister living here.

He was brought back to earth by Hannah suddenly getting up and putting her coat on. 'Ah won't be long, ah've ter go collect our Jeannie from school,' she said.

'That's our Rene's girl,' Tom explained to Dominic.

'Yes, I remember you talking about her with Madeleine,' Dominic answered.

Tom looked from one to the other, and said to Hannah, 'I think we'd better pretend that Dominic is a friend from France who is over here on business when our Jeannie gets in, eh?' Hannah nodded her head in agreement before closing the back door behind her.

Noticing the loud ticking of the grandfather clock, Dominic walked over to look at it. Fascinated, he opened the small door on the front, which housed the pendulum and the chain, and after watching the pendulum for some time, as it swung hypnotically with each tick, he suddenly turned to Tom and asked, 'Do you mind if I wash, and maybe shave, Tom, before the rest of the family arrive?'

'Of course not, mate. Sorry, I didn't think of offering,' answered Tom, momentarily distracted from his own painful thoughts. 'I'll put the pan on to heat the water up. It won't take long with a fire like that.' He gave the blaze another poke. He filled the pan before showing Dominic into the small scullery behind the kitchen. 'There's a bit of a mirror over the sink, for your shave,' he said. 'And, look!' There's even a drop of warm water left in the kettle.' He poured the tepid water into the sink. 'There, lad, how about that?' he exclaimed, well satisfied.

Dominic did his best to hide his horror at the primitive arrangements, and thanked Tom. How strange this family were, not to clean themselves at washstands in the privacy of their own bedrooms!

Madeleine had always been so fastidious and discreet, and this – this cold scullery with no locks on the doors – was where she would have to wash if she lived here. And he knew that she *would* have to live in this house if she came over, because it would probably be a long time before Tom could afford a place of his own.

'Here you are, lad!' Tom said brightly, bringing in the pan of heated water, and pouring it into the sink. 'Mind you run plenty of cold water into it, cause it's boiling hot!' he warned. He went out to the kitchen with the empty pan, then, remembering Jeannie would be home soon, popped his head round the scullery door to warn Dominic, 'And you'd best hurry up, because I can guarantee that our Jeannie will come rushing through there to the toilet as soon as she gets in.'

At this Dominic hurriedly finished washing, and was just drying his underarms when he heard the front door open, followed by an excited young voice calling out, 'Where's the Frenchman, Tom?'

'Well, hello, Tom! And how are you this afternoon?' Tom joked.

'Oh, never mind all that! Where is he?'

Tom laughed. 'Be patient, young missy. You'll see him soon enough.' Jeannie gave a little squeal of pleasure, and Dominic guessed Tom had swung her playfully off her feet.

He smiled to himself in the scullery as he heard her ask, 'Can he talk French, then?'

'Of course he can talk French!' Tom said. '*And* he can talk English, and all. How about that?'

'Well, ah can talk English, there's nowt special about that!' Jeannie replied, moving towards the scullery.

When the door suddenly opened she visibly jumped, and Dominic, smiling widely, headed straight for her. 'Bonjour, mademoiselle!' he said, crouching in front of her. *'Je suis Dominic . . . et vous?'*

'Eee, is that French talk?' she asked with unusual shyness.

'Yes, and it means, "Hello, young miss, I am Dominic, and you?"'

'Hello, Dominic. I am Jeannie, and your English sounds daft.'

'Jeannie!' Hannah scolded. 'That's very rude! Apologize!'

'I didn't mean it awful . . . I meant it nice!' Jeannie protested as she ran out into the backyard, embarrassed.

Hannah shrugged her shoulders as she apologized to Dominic on Jeannie's behalf. 'Sorry, lad, but she's never come across a Frenchman before. Anyway, we're the last ones to criticize. What must we sound like to you? You learned your English all proper at school, then you're confronted with the likes of us!'

Dominic, not wanting to say the wrong thing, answered, 'I am not offended by Jeannie. She is just a child, and I'm sure she didn't mean it badly. I will go bring her in . . . no?' He raised his eyebrows in question.

'Aye, you go talk some sense into her, mate,' Tom agreed.

As Dominic walked through the scullery to the backyard, he called out, 'Hey, Jeannie! Come climb on my back, and I will carry you back in the house.'

He couldn't see her, but he crouched down all the same. Suddenly, she appeared from behind the toilet door, and, giggling, jumped on his back. She brandished an imaginary whip, and was just calling out 'Gee up!' when the back gate swung open, and there stood Jack Dawson, as black as soot, a bucket of vegetables in his hand.

With Jeannie still clinging to his back, Dominic froze in shock.

'Ay, what's goin' on here, lass?' Jack asked, looking at Jeannie on this stranger's back.

'Grandda, this is Dominic, and he talks French,' Jeannie said, hardly able to contain herself. She went on, without pausing for breath, 'Gran told uz that 'ee's here on business, but 'ee's stayin' with us. Wait till ah tell them all at school.' She spoke as if Dominic staying was the most exciting thing that could have happened.

Dominic lowered Jeannie to the ground, and straightened up, before holding out his hand towards this stranger, whose bright blue eyes shone out from the blackness of his face.

'I am Dominic Pelletier. You must be Monsieur Dawson, no?'

'Monsieur Dawson, eh? Ah've been called a few things in me time, but monsieur! That's a new one on me, lad!' He smiled, shaking Dominic's hand.

The three of them walked into the house together,

Jeannie completely forgetting her previous upset. Jack, seeing the empty space in front of the sitting room fire, asked Hannah, with a discreet wink at Jeannie, 'Where's me bath, then, lass?'

'Eee, Jack, there's been that much goin' on ah forgot all about it. Ah've never done that before, *ever*!' Hannah said to no one in particular as she rushed around.

'Don't fret, lass. Ah wuz only pullin' yer leg. Ah can see that ye've got yer hands full,' Jack said kindly. 'Ah'll see to it meself fer once. Then ah'll have a bit crack with young Dominic here,' he said, giving Dominic a pat on the back.

Hannah gratefully accepted the offer. 'That would be grand, then ah can see ter gettin' the vegetables washed and peeled, ready fer yer tea. And judgin' by the amount of muck on them tatties, yer must have brought the whole allotment home with yer.'

'Ay, yer never happy unless yer complainin', lass. Yer want ter think yerself lucky that we've any tatties at all, the way things are with the rationin', mind!'

'Oh, ah know all that. It's just that it's the devil of a job cleanin' them in that small sink.'

A couple of seconds later she popped her head around the door to check the clock.

'Our Rene'll be home soon, so be sharp with yer bath, won't yer!' she said, before retreating to the kitchen. She ignored Jack's mumblings as he went out to the backyard to unhook the bath tin from the wall.

Tom went to the front door and beckoned Dominic to follow him. 'It's gonner be bedlam in here for a while. D'yer fancy a pint?'

'A pint?' questioned Dominic.

'Beer!' Tom explained.

'Oh, yes,' Dominic answered with relish, 'a *bière* I would like.'

'Come on, then!' Tom grabbed his and Dominic's jackets from the back of the chair. 'We'll go up to the working men's club.'

'Club?'

'Oh, come on, lad. I'll explain on the way. You'll learn,' Tom said, before calling out over his shoulder, 'Be back in about an hour, Mam!' He didn't wait for an answer, knowing that she'd be only too pleased to get them out of the way for a while.

'Ah s'ppose *ah'll* have ter find somewhere ter go, while me grandda 'as 'ees bath, an' all,' sighed Jeannie, fully resigned to the situation.

'There's some bits of crayons upstairs in yer room, pet. Ah got them from the school cheap, like, and yer'll find some old rolled-up wallpaper cut-offs in the bottom of the airing cupboard at the top of the stairs. Yer could draw something nice on the back fer yer mam when she gets back,' Hannah said.

'OK, Gran.' Jeannie sighed again. 'Ah get the hint. Ah wouldn't want the shock of seeing me grandda with no clothes on now, would ah?'

'Get yerself upstairs, yer cheeky monkey,' Hannah chided.

Jeannie ran upstairs giggling, while Jack rattled about with pans of water on the stove.

Dominic and Tom sat across from each other at a table in the working men's club. The club, which had been frequented by miners for as many years as anyone could remember, was at Bank Top, across the road from the bus shelter.

Once inside, both Tom and Dominic had to wait for their eyes to adjust to the gloom, and Dominic experienced a moment's embarrassment when, as they entered, the only other occupants, a group of old miners, fell silent. But after Tom nodded to them they quickly resumed their conversation.

Listening in to what they were saying, Dominic concluded that they might as well have come from another planet, for all the sense they made to him.

Tom grinned. 'You've no idea what they're talking about, have you, lad?'

Dominic smiled, and shook his head. The way the miners talked was yet another worry. Even if Madeleine somehow managed to master the English language, she'd still have a terrible struggle coming to grips with this unusual way of speaking in the North. And, lovable though Tom's family obviously were, he wasn't sure that their kindness would compensate for having to live in that small house, with no privacy at all, not even when you *bathed*! He was still trying to come to terms with Tom's papa washing in a bath in the front room, as they called it.

And what about when Madeleine had the baby? Oh, this whole situation was impossible! He felt as if his head was going to explode, and his hands automatically clutched at it.

'What is it, Dominic?' Tom asked.

'It's Madeleine,' Dominic blurted out. 'We need to talk about Madeleine.'

'I know, but what am I to do?' Tom answered looking crestfallen and hopeless, as he stretched his arms out emphasising the question. 'I've no money, no house, no nothing! You've seen how it is, Dominic! Tell us, what can ah do?' There was a moment's silence between them before Tom went on awkwardly, 'She does definitely want the bairn, I suppose – er, the baby, I mean?'

Although Dominic was aghast, he tried not to show it. He choked down his feelings, and struggled to answer reasonably. 'Even if she did not want the baby she has no choice. The Catholic religion does not allow otherwise, as you know.'

Tom, sensing Dominic's horror, tried to explain. 'I'm sorry, mate, but I need to ask these questions. We need to explore all the avenues. You must see that.'

With a sudden surge of confidence, and without warning, Dominic blurted out, 'Do you love my sister, or not? If you don't there is no point in trying to – as you say – explore anything!' After all, he reasoned, there was no point worrying about how his sister was going to cope here if Tom didn't want her. He felt Tom just wanted to avoid discussing the issue for as long as possible. But Madeleine's baby was not going to go away, so Tom had to be given a push. He was angry with himself now: he'd been so nervous about meeting this English family that he hadn't insisted on talking about the problem with Tom's mother that afternoon. She'd deliberately steered clear of the subject.

It seemed to him that everyone here was afraid of saying the wrong thing, and so they said nothing. All the conversations so far had been small talk, or flippant, even. Well, maybe it was their way of dealing with things, but it wasn't his family's way. It was wrong, too, when he knew that his maman and papa were waiting, and wondering anxiously what was going on.

Tom, not answering Dominic's question about whether or not he loved Madeleine, instead asked lightly, 'Another one, mate?'

Dominic finished what was in his glass and nodded as he handed it to Tom, who'd been caught off guard by Dominic's question, and needed time to think how to answer it.

'Same again, please,' he said to the barman.

'Comin' up!' the barman answered, pulling the pints. Then, with a quizzical look, he asked Tom, 'Are you Jack's lad, be any chance?'

'I am that!' Tom answered absent-mindedly.

''Ave these on me, then,' the barman offered.

Seeing Tom's dumbfounded look, he went on to explain, 'After what yer must have been through in t' war, lad, it's small compensation. Ah just wish that ah could 'ave been there alongside yer, shootin' the buggers. But *this* . . .' he said, looking down at his foot,

'. . . this bloody leg stopped me. Bloody thing's about an inch shorter than t'other one, yer know!'

Tom winked at him and said, 'Well, thanks for the drinks, mate.' Then, after a moment's thought, he added on a much more serious note, 'I'll tell you what I told my mate over there,' he nodded towards Dominic. 'Cause he thought he'd missed out, and all. "Well, you missed nowt, and I wouldn't have wished that purgatory on anybody. If we weren't roasting in the desert we were half-starved and freezing in a foxhole. And we were shot to bits by the Krauts. I still have the nightmares now, man!"' He stopped for a second before adding with a wry smile, 'So just think yourself lucky!'

He picked up the two glasses of beer and hurriedly slurped the froth off one before raising it to the barman in thanks, and leaving him to contemplate his luck at having a gammy leg.

Even before Tom put the drinks down on to the table he could see that Dominic needed some answers. 'Look, mate!' he said. 'I did . . . well, I still do,' he corrected himself, 'love Maddie. You must know that, man. But all I can offer is for her to come and live here with me and my family.'

There was silence between them, before he continued, showing a little more optimism, 'Mind you, our Rene and the bairn will be moving out soon, so we'll have an extra room then, and it's a bigger one than mine.'

'Tom, I know that you mean well, but can you imagine Madeleine and her baby—'

'*Our* baby!' Tom interrupted quickly.

'Pardon! *Your* baby,' Dominic apologized, encouraged by the nature of Tom's interruption. 'But what about your parents, also, Tom? It will not be easy having a small child in the house, for *any* of you.'

'Well, if our Jeannie's going, it might be the very thing me mam needs,' Tom answered pensively. He added, as if to himself, 'Aye, a new baby to dote on might do her a power of good.'

Dominic couldn't help feeling Tom wasn't thinking this through properly. Nearly all the alternatives were worse. But, on the other hand, if only he could convince his parents to let Madeleine stay at home, maybe Tom could marry her, and then come and visit from time to time, just until he could afford a house. Why couldn't that work?

'Come on. Sup up!' Tom said, looking at Dominic's troubled face. 'It should be safe to go home now, my da's had plenty of time to have his bath. We'll have a proper talk tonight when the family are all there. See what they have to say, eh?'

Tom got up from the table, and Dominic, seeing that it would be hopeless to try and talk any more until Tom had the security of his family around him, 'supped up' and got up from the table.

As they left Tom raised his hand to the barman and called, 'Thanks again, mate!' Dominic followed suit by raising his hand and calling, '*Merci*, monsieur, *et au revoir*!' Which created another sudden hush as they left the club.

Tom had to laugh in spite of himself. 'Ay man! That shut them up! Did you see their faces?'

Dominic smiled politely in reply. More pressing right now was his need to contact his parents. 'Is there a place where I can send a telegram to my family?' he asked.

'Aye, there's a post office in the village, but what are you going to say?' Tom looked concerned.

'I promised my parents that I would let them know when I arrived. What else can I say right now?'

'OK, let's call in on the way home,' Tom suggested.

Once in the post office Tom asked Dominic, 'Now, what exactly do you want to tell them?'

Dominic thought for a moment. 'I will write it on a paper, so madame can copy it, no?'

The postmistress behind the counter handed him a form, and Dominic had no idea what to put, so made it short.

> *J'arrive chez Dawson.*
> *Tout va bien.*
> *A bientôt!*
> *Baisers, Dominic*

That will have to do, he thought as he handed over the form to the postmistress, who looked on curiously. As she took the paper, he hesitated, wondering if maybe he shouldn't have included '*tout va bien*' it could be misleading. Reading that all was going well, they might think a solution had already been found.

The postmistress glanced at the alien words. 'I hope this is not a hoax, young man!' she said sternly.

'A hoax?' Dominic bemused, looked at Tom, who

immediately turned to the woman demanding, 'Just get it sent. You can hear that he's French, can't you? Well, that writing is in French.'

'Huh!' was her reply as she looked disdainfully down her nose at the pair, who, in her opinion, smelled suspiciously strongly of alcohol.

'Take no notice of 'er,' said the young assistant behind the counter, as the postmistress retreated to a back room. 'Always got 'er knickers in a twist over somethin', that one! She's an old spinster, yer see.' Then, leaning towards them over the counter, she added in a whisper, 'If yer ask me she's in need of a good—'

'There'll be no takers here!' Tom interrupted sharply, before grabbing his change and leaving the post office. 'Feeling better now, mate?' he asked Dominic, who only shrugged in reply.

Tom put an arm around his shoulder, and that's how they walked down the road back to Glamis Terrace.

'Ah, Rene!' Tom called as he walked through the door, followed closely by Dominic. 'Meet Dominic! Dominic, this is my sister, Rene!' Rene stepped forward, uncertain whether she should hold out her hand, or offer her cheek for a kiss.

Dominic, sensitive to her dilemma, placed his hands gently on her shoulders before kissing first her left cheek, then her right. She couldn't help thinking how much more civilized this was, compared to 'How now!' or 'Hoo noo!', which was the usual greeting around here.

As Dominic let her go, he said, 'I have heard so much about you, Rene.'

'And likewise,' Rene responded with a smile. 'It's so nice to meet you, I just wish it was under other . . .' The moment was spoiled as Hannah came through from the scullery, telling them all that they could go and wash their hands because tea was nearly ready.

Jack chirped in, 'Wash me hands! Ah've just washed me whole body, how much cleaner der yer want uz, lass?'

'Get on with yer, yer daft ha'porth,' she said, dismissing him with her usual flap of the tea towel.

'Where's our Jeannie, anyway?' Jack asked.

'She went out with a couple of the lasses from down the road ter play at skipping. They called round for 'er when yer were in the bath.'

'Aw, yer didn't let a couple of lasses in while ah wuz in the bath, did yer?'

'What, and frighten them off men fer the rest of their lives, poor lasses!' Hannah winked at the others, who just raised their eyebrows as they went through to wash their hands.

There they go, joking again, thought Dominic. And yet, even after knowing them for a short time, he was aware that under all this teasing they were deeply troubled by the change about to come into their lives. They needed time to come to terms with it, and giving themselves this space – and filling it with trivialities and jokes – was obviously how they coped with unpleasant situations. And although he didn't really understand their behaviour, there was something warming and comforting about it, too. He was suddenly sure that when they did finally settle down to talk properly, all the joshing would stop.

Tom watched as Rene dished out the potatoes, carrots, cabbage *and* a chicken, which Hannah had somehow miraculously got hold of since Dominic's arrival. It never ceased to amaze him how his mam got decent meals together when rationing was so stringent.

'Come and sit yersel next ter me, lad,' Jack said to Dominic, patting the seat to his right.

Dominic sat down willingly. He felt so drawn to this family that it was as if he'd known them for years, not just a single day.

'Tom, run out and fetch our Jeannie in, will yer!' Hannah called from the kitchen, where she was vigorously stirring the gravy. 'And be sharp about it, else yer tea'll get cold!'

Outside, Tom could hear Jeannie and her pals chanting a skipping song further up the back street. My God, nowt changes, he thought in amazement. Why, they were chanting that old verse when *I* was a kid!

'Ah wish ternight was Satder night,
termorra would be Sunder
and ah'd be dressed in all me best ter go out with . . .
Molly!'

He arrived just as Molly jumped in.

'Molly likes whisky, Molly likes rum,
Molly likes ter kiss the boys, eee by gum!'

And Jeannie jumped out from the rope straight into Tom's arms. 'Steady on, lass,' he said, as he caught her. 'Your tea's ready, and Gran'll be spitting blood if we're not there double quick.' At that he grabbed her hand, and before she had the chance to object – before she even knew it – they were down the street and into the backyard.

'Get yourself in there and get your hands washed,' he said, shoving her unceremoniously towards the sink.

'What about your 'ands, then, ower Tom?'

' "Hands",' Rene called out in exasperation.

'Ah washed them before I came out to get you, you cheeky monkey. Just hurry up and get yourself to the table. We're all starving, here!'

'Starvin' indeed!' Hannah retorted. 'That'll be the day.'

Everyone tucked into their tea, and they continued to try to keep the mood light, mostly for Jeannie's sake, because Jeannie had no idea about the problem hanging over them, and that's how they wanted to keep it – for the time being, anyway.

But when Tom glanced across the table towards Dominic, his stomach churned. There were times when Tom despised the weaker side of his character: the way he buried his head in the sand whenever he found himself in a tricky situation. He was weak because he couldn't fight this tendency; and yet he could fight with

223

his fists if he had to. It wasn't so long since he'd helped that lass Maisie out at the dance, he reminded himself. But give him anything emotional to sort out, and he couldn't cope. His only defence was humour. Trouble with that was, it made everyone else think he didn't care.

Dominic was being regaled by one of Jack's stories, and Tom, watching, wondered: What can I say to him? What kind of a message shall I send Maddie, when I don't have the means to take care of her? He wondered why he had been so bloody selfish and taken her on that warm September day. But then he reminded himself how they'd *both* felt then. There was no doubt she'd wanted him as much as he'd wanted her.

He thought of some of his mates, who went with lasses all the time and got away with it. Then he thought of poor Maddie, the last lass on earth to be too free with her favours. And the one time she let herself go, look what bloody happened . . .

'*Tom! Tom!* Are yer deaf or what?' Jeannie's voice brought him back with a start.

'Oh! Sorry, Jeannie, I was enjoying me tea so much that I went off to paradise, and I couldn't hear you mortals down here,' Tom answered with a grin.

'Oh, you, Tom. Yer always foolin' around.' Jeannie gave him a gentle push.

He looked around the table, and everyone was busily chatting and tucking in, so he hadn't been missed while he'd been day-dreaming about France. And it really *had* been paradise there, particularly during those last few months. Oh yes, he'd loved Maddie all right, he'd adored everything about her. Looking at Jeannie now, he asked, half-heartedly, 'Well, what was so important, that you had to bring me back from paradise for, then, missy?'

'Ah want yer ter teach me to play "itchy bays"!' she announced, in no doubt that Tom would know how to play. After all, he knew everything, didn't he?

Tom's initial reaction was to say not now, but the part of him that still needed more time to think seized on the opportunity to delay a little longer. So he answered, 'I think you mean hopscotch, don't you? Well, we'll need some chalk, and a "dabber" to throw.'

'What, yer mean like a piece of slate, or something?' Jeannie was asking, as Hannah, hearing the tail end of the conversation, butted in.

'Well, yer not ter be chalkin' in my backyard. Ah've got enough ter do without havin' ter wash "itchy bays" off the yard.'

'Nooo, Gran! We'll do it in the back street,' Jeannie explained.

'Yer'll do no such thing,' said Hannah, in no uncertain terms.

'Where *can* we do it, then?' Jeannie asked.

'Aw, come on, Mam,' said Tom. 'I'll clean it up after I've shown her how to play.'

'Come on, Gran!' Jeannie pleaded, putting on her best anguished look.

'Oh, just this once, then,' Hannah relented. 'After that yer'll have ter chalk it out in the school yard at playtime.'

'Well, ah *will*, Gran, once ah know how ter play it.'

'You weren't being a bit cheeky to your gran there, were you, Jeannie?' said Rene, catching her daughter's tone of voice. Rene had broken off the conversation she'd been having with Jack and Dominic.

'Nooo, Mam. Ah wuz just tellin' her that ah'll only mess up the yard once, that's all it'll take. Cause ah'm such a fast learner, aren't ah, Tom?'

This comment made the whole family laugh. Even Rene concealed a smile – and ignored her daughter's terrible grammar for once.

'Aye, you're a fast learner, all right,' Tom answered. Too fast for my liking, he thought, as he glanced at Hannah, who he could see was thinking along the same lines as him. Maybe it was just as well that she and Rene would be moving out of the village, because otherwise Jeannie might end up like the brazen lasses at Bank Top. After all, there wasn't much else for youngsters to do. Nowt's likely to change there either, he mused, as he put a last forkful of food in his mouth.

He looked around the table. Dominic and Jack were talking about the coal mine, and it was obvious from Dominic's expression that he was horrified by Jack's stories. And Hannah and Rene, having thoroughly discussed tonight's supper, were planning tomorrow's tea. He smiled warmly at Hannah and said, 'I'll clear the table.'

Hannah, trying not to look too surprised at this unusual offer, answered, 'All right. Will yer put the dishes in the sink? And put the kettle on while yer up, we'll be needin' some hot water fer the pans, if nothing else!'

Jeannie helped Tom clear the dishes, then immediately grabbed his hand in an attempt to drag him to the back door. 'Come on, Tom! Itchy bays, remember?'

Tom glanced at Hannah. 'Oh go on,' she said, 'Get yerself out there and show the bairn how ter play the game. That's if you can see in the dark.'

And Dominic, with Jeannie's encouragement, and after thanking Madame Hannah for his tea, agreed to go outside, too, and see this mysterious game of itchy bays.

'All right,' Tom said to Jeannie. 'But we'll just do a quick one tonight, cause by the look on your mam's face I would say it's close to your bedtime, and us grown-ups need some time on our own. We've got talking to do.'

He and Dominic exchanged a pained glance at this. Though Dominic was heartened by Tom's remark, both men wondered what they could realistically hope to achieve through talk alone.

Back in the scullery, Ma and Rene were busy washing up, and fretting over much the same subject. 'He seems really nice,' Rene was saying. 'Obviously well brought up, and his manners! You don't see manners like that around here. I wonder what his sisters are like,' she mused.

Mam pulled the plug out of the sink and dried her hands. 'Well, this Madeleine'll be pretty, that's for sure. Our Tom always gets the pretty ones.' She made it sound like a curse.

'From what Tom's told me about the family, they are all very close. A bit like us, I suppose—'

'But not like us, Rene!' Hannah interrupted. 'Not like us at all. Close, maybe, yes, but there's the end of it. She's been livin' a different life to us.' Then she added, almost in awe, 'Why they even have a different way of showin' their feelings, them French . . . all emotional, like! Someone like that would never settle here. Never.' She looked around at the little house she'd always been so proud of, then, glancing at Rene, she gestured, 'Just look around! Can you imagine the poor lass – and her bairn, don't forget! – havin' space enough here?'

'Well, Mam! Tom can't live in France, either. For a start he'd never get a job over there without the language, now would he?'

'Well, he managed all right when he was over there! Enough ter get ter know some lass well enough to get her pregnant!' Hannah retorted, totally out of character.

Rene, seeing that Hannah was upset, stopped drying the dishes and put down the tea towel. 'Aw, Mam, I know he's your blue-eyed boy, but he's going to have to face up to reality some time. I love our Tom too, you know, but he does bury his head in the sand hoping things will sort themselves out. Well this . . . this is different, Mam. He *can't* ignore it. All we can do is stand by him, but he has to make the decisions. And I think he's going to have to marry her.' She looked at Hannah.

'Oh, ah know that yer right, pet, and ah know yer love him and want the best for him. But it breaks me heart ter see him pretendin' that all's well when ah know that he's churnin' up inside. It's all bravado, yer know, lass!' Hannah very carefully did not use the word 'marry'. She'd always dreamed of Tom marrying a nice northern lass.

'I know that Mam, but—'

Suddenly, Hannah exclaimed, 'Eee, what about Jessie in all this?'

'Well, Mam, we can't be worrying about that on top of everything else. Anyway, reading between the lines, I think *that* is all but over. And if it wasn't, it certainly will be after this, if I know anything about Jessie Parkin!'

'Oh, what a mess!' Hannah flopped down on the couch. 'She's goin' ter be heartbroken. And where's yer da got himself to?' she asked, as if Jack had no right to be elsewhere at a time like this.

Rene put her hands gently on Hannah's shoulders. 'Don't fret, Mam. He's only outside in the backyard with the others. You sit there, and I'll brew us a nice cup of tea,' she said brightly.

Catching hold of her daughter's hand as Rene passed in front of the couch, Hannah said softly, 'Ay, yer a good lass, our Rene.'

Rene squeezed her hand in response, then pushed the kettle further into the fire. She felt troubled. She could sense both Hannah and Tom were resistant to the whole idea of marrying Madeleine, but she couldn't see how anything would be resolved without that happening. And why didn't either of them want it?

Meanwhile, out in the backyard, Jeannie and her grandda could be heard giggling as they jumped into the itchy bay squares drawn in chalk by Tom. Dominic, fascinated, was waiting his turn when Rene appeared, calling for Jeannie to come and do her homework. Her shout was greeted with a wry '*Aw no!*' all round.

Eyebrows raised, Rene glanced from Jeannie to Tom, then to her da and Dominic. She was about to ask how they could be out playing a child's game when there were life-changing decisions to be made. But then she glanced again at Jeannie, saw the pleasure on her face, and stopped herself. Instead she decided to retain the happy mood for a while longer by saying, 'You older bairns can play a little longer if you want.' Then, after wagging a warning finger, she added in her best mock pit-man's voice, 'But only if yer behave yersels, mind! Else ye'll be back in 'ere with me boot up yer ar— er . . . backsides.'

Jeannie, laughing loudly, ran up to Rene and flung her arms around her waist, hugging her tightly. 'Eee, yer funny when yer talk like that, Mam. Is that how yer used ter talk before yer got all posh?' she asked curiously.

'Yes, it is, pet, and I've worked hard to get rid of that talk. And I'd like you to do the same.'

Seeing Jeannie's disappointed expression, after a moment's thought Rene added, 'If you do, then maybe we can talk like that just for fun sometimes, eh?'

'OK, ah'll try, Mam. But it won't be easy, cause ah keep forgettin', and *nobody*, except you, of course –

and maybe Tom a little bit – talks posh around here.'

Rene took Jeannie's hand and led her back into the house. 'Well, that's the very reason we need to move away, so I can get you in to a better school where you'll have nice new friends.'

'Aw, but, Mam!' Jeannie exclaimed, 'Ah don't want new friends. Ah'm quite 'appy with the ones ah've got, thank you!'

' "Happy", Jeannie,' Rene corrected. 'You see what I mean? We'll *never* improve if we stay here, now, will we?'

'Well, ah'm not comin' with yer!' were Jeannie's words as she rushed off upstairs, slamming the bedroom door behind her.

'Oh dear, what was all that about?' Hannah asked, coming in from the front garden, where she'd been sat on the bench in the cold with her cup of tea.

'Oh, nothing, Mam. I've just told Jeannie that we'll be moving. I didn't mean it to come out the way it did.' Then, close to tears, she added, 'And, needless to say, it was a bit of a shock for her.'

It was Hannah's turn to console Rene now. 'Oh, she'll come round, pet. Just give 'er a bit of time ter get used to the idea. Come and sit next ter me fer a minute,' she said as she patted the cushion next to her on the couch. 'Ah'll pour us another cup of tea, it'll be well stewed be now.'

And there they sat side by side, deep in their own thoughts, listening to the distant sound of three grown men playing itchy bays in the backyard.

Tuesday, 4 December 1945

Next morning, a loud knocking on the front door woke the whole household. Tom came stumbling down the stairs, trying to pull on his trousers while shouting irritably, 'Hang on, for God's sake, will yer!' Who the hell could it be this early? Dishevelled and squinting, he unlocked the front door with one hand while fumbling with the other to get his trousers done up. 'What the hell . . . ?' he said, as a telegram was waved in front of him.

''Ave you got a . . . Dominic Pelletier stayin' 'ere?' the post boy asked, without a glimmer of a smile.

'Yes,' said Tom, as straight-faced as the chap in front of him.

'Well, this 'ere is for 'im,' said the grim-faced messenger. Tom went to take the telegram, and the post boy drew back his hand. 'No, I need to give it to 'im direct,' he said.

Without taking his eyes off the boy, Tom yelled up the stairs, '*Dominic!*'

Dominic came bustling down, coming to an abrupt halt as the telegram was shoved at him.

'From France,' the post boy informed him unnecessarily.

Without speaking, Dominic took the telegram and read it, and Tom watched his face turn ashen.

'*Merci*, Monsieur,' Dominic said to the post boy, who was still standing there.

'That means yer can go!' said Tom, waving the nosey fellow away.

The post boy tutted, clearly unhappy. He'd expected a tip. Tom closed the door in his face and walked slowly towards Dominic, who was slumped on a wooden chair at the table.

'What is it, mate?' he asked cautiously. 'Is someone ill?'

'It's Madeleine,' Dominic answered, staring ahead without blinking.

'Maddie? What about her? Tom asked anxiously, his voice rising along with his heartbeat.

'She's left home,' Dominic answered quietly.

'Left home? What do you mean, left home?'

'Run away, Tom! She's run away!'

'Oh my God! Where to?' Tom flopped down on a stool by the fire, and, picking up the poker, he stirred the previous night's embers as if getting them to flare up was the single most important thing in his life.

'Here, give me that,' Hannah said, coming up behind him and taking the poker.

'Sorry, Madame Hannah. Did we wake you?' Dominic asked in a daze.

'Noo, lad, ah was getting up anyway. Ah heard the commotion from the top of the stairs.'

Looking at Tom now, she said, 'Yer da's gone ter work, and the bairn and our Rene are still fast asleep.' Then, glancing back at Dominic, she asked, 'What yer gonner do, lad?'

'I have to go straight back to France. My parents are frantic, they want me to find her.'

At which Tom, to both Hannah's and Dominic's amazement, and without a second thought, blurted out, 'I'm coming with you.'

And, as Hannah later told Jack: 'From the way he jumped up from that stool you'd'a thought he was leaving right then and there.'

Chapter 18

Marck, France
Sunday, 2 December 1945

Madeleine, unable to get over the news that Dominic had gone to England, immediately thought about running away. She lay on her bed, planning what to do when she left the house. For that's all it was to her now: a house. She didn't think of it as a home any more, because both it and her family had become unrecognizable.

She'd thought – obviously mistakenly – that she and her sisters had grown closer since Martine and Simone had told her what had happened in Boulogne. But where had they been when her parents *and* Dominic had planned this visit to England? *Why* had they allowed it to happen? And *why* had Dominic agreed to go without talking to her first? She couldn't understand why the whole family had taken such a huge decision without involving her.

Yes, she knew they were unhappy, but that wasn't a

good enough reason for them to make plans behind her back. So she decided that it would be better for everyone if she left.

She couldn't remember ever, in her whole life, feeling this miserable and this disappointed in herself. She stared in her bed staring at her little brown valise, which was perched on the top of her wardrobe, begging her to get it down.

Finally, she decided to pack the valise and hide it under her bed until night-time. She'd use Dominic's bike to make her getaway, because he was away, so it wouldn't be missed. She would hide it in the wild fuchsia bushes at the end of the road, where it would be easy to collect. Then she would ride it to the station in Calais, and catch a train to Boulogne.

Once in Boulogne she would find Nicole, who would surely know someone who could help her to get rid of this . . . this . . . she couldn't even say the word. Even the memory of how it had been made, on that fateful day when she and Tom had loved each other so desperately, couldn't make what was growing inside her anything more than a burden. A burden that was going to wreck her life.

How could she have feelings for it, when its father was a liar? She knew now that Tom was never going to write the way he'd promised. She guessed that, once home, he'd go back to the old life he'd had before the war. Probably get back together with a girl who had waited patiently for his return. Huh! No doubt he would marry this girl and live happily ever after! Well, good for you! Madeleine thought fiercely. You just dump this thing into my body, and then go home. Oh, don't you worry, I'll be sick in the mornings for you, I'll take all the shame and humiliation, *and* suffer the pain of childbirth. Just go home and forget all about me, and have a happy life!

But whenever she gave way to negative thoughts like this, they would be accompanied by an unwelcome little tug at her heart, because deep down she knew she was being untrue to her memory of their love affair. There was always that pang that maybe at the time he really had meant every word. Her anger prevented her from trusting her intuition, which sensed that everything between them *had* been sincere.

The last thing she wanted, right now, was to think rationally about Tom. And she certainly wasn't going to accept that she still cared for the person she blamed for her present misfortune, because her anger was making her strong. Strong enough to run away.

And now, here she was standing in the dark, halfway down the stairs, her heart thumping, holding her valise above her head in case it bumped against the banister and alerted the person she could hear moving around.

Hardly daring to breathe, she listened: a familiar sigh came from her parents' room, followed by a loud yawn. *Merde!* It's Papa! He's woken up! Alarm bells rang in her head as she glanced upstairs in panic, not knowing whether to run back up or continue down. But she couldn't move. She was so scared of being caught that she simply froze to the spot, her suitcase poised mid-air. She closed her eyes tightly, waiting for Papa to come out and find her standing there like a statue.

She heard him drag the *petite po* from under the bed, before, to her embarrassment, peeing into it noisily. Still holding her breath, she prayed that he wouldn't come out of the room to empty it. She was so relieved to hear him push it back under the bed, that, unable to hold her breath any longer, she sighed. Luckily, Papa didn't hear it. He yawned loudly and climbed back into his creaky bed, and she silently thanked God for it. Then, still gripping her valise tightly, she crept downstairs in the dark.

At the bottom of the stairs was the heavy oak front door Papa had made. It was Papa's job to bolt the doors at night, after everyone had gone to bed. But, earlier that evening, as he'd been doing his rounds, Madeleine pretended she needed the toilet. 'Don't worry, I'll lock the door when I come back,' she'd called out to him. Since the back garden was completely enclosed there was only one bolt on the door leading to it, unlike the front one, which had *three*. And Papa had continued bolting the front door, responding only with a nod.

After he'd gone upstairs she'd rattled the back door, making a pretence of going out, before rushing to the front of the house, where she'd stared at the ceiling, listening. Finally, she'd heard the rattle of the washstand as Maman poured water from the jugs into two enamel bowls, ready for the nightly toilette. Madeleine had hoped the clattering of jugs and bowls would cover the sound of her wrenching open the three bolts on the front door. Luckily, they had, and she'd crept back upstairs to her bedroom to wait until everyone was asleep. Only, of course, she hadn't planned on Papa getting up to use his *po* in the dark.

She had decided to leave tonight, because Martine was staying with her friend Sophie at Dunkirk, making one less person to worry about. Simone could have been a problem, but she'd gone to her room early with Dominic's wireless, which she was using while he was away. Normally Madeleine would have warned Simone against doing that, knowing how much Dominic treasured it. But, on this occasion, her sister's thoughtlessness was a blessing, because Madeleine knew that once Simone had tuned into the BBC Home Service she would be blissfully unaware of anything else for hours.

Dominic had secretly listened to the BBC all through the occupation, finding it much more accurate than French radio. But no matter how much his older sisters had plagued him about it on their visits home from Boulogne, he'd always refused to let them use it. He'd hidden it away, frightened that otherwise they'd be tempted to tune in when he wasn't around. Heaven knew what might have happened – not just to him but to the whole family – if they'd done that, because even owning a wireless back then had been forbidden.

However, once the war was over, he'd shown all three girls how to work his precious radio, as long as they promised to ask before using it. Simone, in particular, had been hooked ever since. Madeleine knew she'd be dancing around her room right now to the music of Glenn Miller, or pretending to be Marlene Dietrich or Vera Lynn. She was brilliant at impersonating both. Madeleine smiled at the memory, even as she opened the door and prepared to leave her family for ever.

She prayed, eyes squeezed tight, that the hinges wouldn't creak too loudly. Then she opened the door just wide enough to edge through sideways. She picked up her valise and passed it through the opening, trembling so much that she could hardly place it upright on the step outside. Fear nearly overwhelmed her. Then, her knees shaking, and tears filling her eyes, she squeezed through the gap.

She carefully pressed the door shut, her shoulders tensing at the sound of the latch clicking. And then she leaned against it, her heart beating wildly. She couldn't believe she was actually doing this. Maybe it was just a dream, a nightmare. Apart from anything else, she didn't have the courage to be so reckless.

But there was no mistaking the feel of solid wood against her back. The cold night air on her face reminded her, too, that this was not a dream. So she turned and looked up at the house for one last time, feeling that her heart would break. Each intake of breath was a silent sob, hurting her chest. But she fought back the tears. After all, hadn't she cried enough in the last few days to last a lifetime?

She knew it was only a start, but there was no turning back now. This was the only way she could think of to save her family, and herself, from a life of shame and heartache. She also knew that if she didn't act now she never would. Holding on to that thought, she quickly walked away from the house, heading towards the place she'd hidden the bike earlier.

She walked as quietly as possible, and although the houses around her were shrouded in darkness she didn't feel particularly afraid. She'd been much more scared by the blackout in the war. At least tonight there was no chance she'd be confronted by drunken Germans or flying bombs. As she left the last house behind she strained her eyes to see the bushes on the wasteland. She hadn't bargained for it being quite this dark. With a shiver she felt her way along the road, but her sense of direction let her down. She was soon totally disorientated, and couldn't find the fuchsia bushes. Every small sound startled her and she kept turning round anxiously.

Merde alors! she thought. What do I do now? Placing her valise on the ground, she sat on it in despair. She guessed she must have walked too far, because she knew the bushes were near the end of her street. Feeling annoyed with herself now, especially when she felt tears welling up, she told herself not to be so ridiculous. Suddenly, she heard a rumble in the distance, and kept very still, listening carefully. Recognizing the sound as a car, and seeing approaching lights, she crouched down low. The vehicle headed in her direction, and she flattened herself on the ground beside her valise. Then she saw, only a few metres away, glowing in the head-lights, the patch of wild fuchsia bushes.

As the car turned the corner she jumped up and grabbed her valise, almost falling over in her eagerness to get to the bushes before all the light disappeared. She felt around in the bushes, but couldn't find the bike at once, and began to panic. What if the bike had been stolen! *Mon Dieu!* she thought, as she searched the bushes, which were once again enveloped in darkness. Maybe hiding the bike here had been a really bad idea! She'd been in a quandary at the time, anyway.

That afternoon had been unusually sunny for December, and as she'd pushed the bike towards the bushes she'd felt a burst of happiness. How lovely it is here, she'd thought, looking round at the greenery, before remembering what she'd come to do. What if the local children went there to play? she'd suddenly thought. They'd see the bike. But she hadn't been able to think of a better hiding place, so she'd taken the risk, pushing the bike in as far as possible.

She felt her way further into the bushes now, trying not to visualize all the insects that could fall into her hair. She held her valise in front of her like a shield, and there, at last, it was. She felt the back mudguard against her leg, and leaned forward to grasp the handlebars. She'd pushed the bike in so far that it had got wedged in a bush, so she decided to push it out the other side rather than pull it out. Determined not to be defeated, she jammed her valise into the basket on the front, and then shoved the bike with all her might.

Eyes closed tight against the foliage that was brushing against her, and, more than likely, releasing creepy-crawlies on to her head and coat, she forced her way through and out into the open. Itching and shivering with revulsion at what might be running over her, she dropped the bike and danced around in a frenzy, slapping at her clothes and ruffling her hair. Stopping as quickly as she'd started, she prayed that throwing the bike down wouldn't have affected the dynamo, because she wouldn't get anywhere without lights.

She felt for the bike in the darkness, picked it up, and wedged her valise back into the basket. Then, leaning over towards the front wheel, she turned the dynamo until it touched the tyre. Tentatively, she mounted the bike, and pedalled off into the dark, bouncing over the rough terrain, and to her relief the lights flickered on.

Although she was a good rider, she found it difficult to keep the handlebars straight. With a grimace of exasperation, she realized that in her hurry she'd wedged the valise into the basket unevenly. I'll have to stop, she thought. But I'd better wait until I'm further away from home. At this rate, the whole family will be up before I even get to Calais.

But at that moment, she was caught in the headlights of a car approaching from a side street. She rode into a pothole that made the bike judder from side to side, lost control and toppled over. The bike went one way and Madeleine the other. '*Merde alors!*' she whispered, hearing the car stop behind her, and wondering what else would go wrong. She brushed the dirt from her knees and her coat sleeves. Fortunately the grazes on her knees weren't bleeding much, and she was about to rearrange the valise in the basket when the driver called out, 'Are you hurt, Mademoiselle?'

Merde! Merde! Merde! Her immediate instinct was to get on the bike and pedal like fury. But she knew that she'd only fall off again if she didn't straighten the valise, and that would draw even more attention. So, with a carefree smile, she turned to the driver, who had reached her side now, and answered calmly, 'No, monsieur. I am OK, thank you.'

The man, who fortunately she'd never seen before, looked concerned and asked, 'Is there anything I can do? Maybe I can give you a lift somewhere? I am on my way to Calais.'

Madeleine turned to look at his car. The driver's door was open, and the engine running. For a moment she was tempted. But so many things had gone wrong already, and this could be another. After all, she had no idea who the stranger was.

'Oh, no thank you. Er . . . I am going to see a friend, only a few doors away,' she lied. 'I'm staying with her for a few days.' Madeleine pointed to her valise, wondering why she felt she had to explain anything to this stranger.

'OK, if you are sure,' the man said, still sounding troubled. He turned and walked back to his car.

Madeleine waved nervously as he drove past her, heading along the road that she was about to take to Calais. She watched until he had disappeared into the distance, and then mounted the bike. It was much better balanced now, and she pedalled off confidently into the night.

Thankfully there was no other traffic for a while, and she soon found herself riding along beside the high cemetery walls. She slowed down. She remembered climbing them with Tom. But somehow she wasn't frightened of moss-covered tombs any more, even in the dark. She'd outgrown that girlish hysteria: she was experiencing real life – and real fear – tonight. She was so engrossed in thinking about Tom that she had to fight the urge to stop and touch the stretch of wall where they had once laughed and kissed. The memory was suddenly so real that Tom could have been standing in front of her. Involuntarily, she reached out to touch him, lifting her fingers from the handlebar. The bike wobbled so wildly that she only just managed to get it under control before a second car overtook her, hooting.

She cycled on more carefully, angry she'd allowed herself to think about Tom. She had to stop doing it. After all, who was making this dangerous journey in the middle of the night on a never-ending road? Not him! She couldn't allow him to slow her down, because she *had* to get to the station before eleven fifteen. If she missed that train, there wouldn't be another until the morning. Filled with horror at the thought of having to spend the night on a station platform, she cycled faster.

She was so relieved when she finally reached the town hall clock in the centre of Calais. It struck eleven times just as she turned into the road where the station was.

But she still had to reach the far end. *Mon Dieu!* she thought. Am I going to make it?

The traffic lights turned red as she approached, so she jumped off the bike and pushed it on to the footpath, then, quickly jumping back on, pedalled for all she was worth. Outside the station she left the bike in a stand for Dominic to collect later. She'd send him a letter enclosing the padlock key, and telling him where it was. To her horror she realized she'd lost the chain the padlock threaded through. Hurriedly, she hooked the padlock through one of the spokes on the front wheel. She'd just have to hope that would be secure enough.

As she bolted for the ticket office, it crossed her mind that a pregnant woman probably shouldn't be running with a heavy suitcase, let alone cycling at top speed. How stupid I am to worry about that! she thought. It doesn't matter, because I won't be pregnant for much longer, anyway!

Her ticket between her teeth so she could carry her case in one hand and steady herself on hand rails with the other, she realized she had exactly two minutes to get to a platform on the other side of the pedestrian bridge. On previous trips she'd never noticed how many steep steps there were to run up and down. But then she'd never been in such a hurry before.

She reached the platform just as the last door slammed shut and the silhouetted stationmaster, half-visible in the hissing steam, blew the final whistle. 'Oh no! wait!' she called, as the engine clanked into life.

'You are too late, *ma fille*,' the stationmaster said, seeing her.

'Oh no, I'm not!' said Madeleine, as the train jerked and ground, trying to pull away. She pushed her valise at the bewildered stationmaster, then yanked open the first carriage door that came alongside, and jumped in. Then, hanging out of the window, she called to the man, who looked impressed by her daring. 'My case! Please run!' The train began to speed up. 'Give it here! *Quick!*'

The stationmaster sprang into action. He lifted the case above his head and ran level with her. Madeleine grabbed the case with both hands, nearly overbalancing as she hung out of the window. Pressing her knees hard against the inside of the carriage, she managed to hoist it in through the window.

'*Merci*, Monsieur! *Merci!*' she called as the station-master dwindled away into the distance.

With no energy left to lift her case on to the rack, she dropped it to the floor and sank breathlessly into her seat. Once she'd caught her breath she looked around, and, satisfied that no one in the carriage knew her, settled back again. She was pleased the seats facing her were unoccupied. The last thing she wanted right now was to have to talk to anyone. Or even worse, cope with those furtive glances that pass between strangers who aren't speaking.

She tried to relax, but all she could think was: I wonder when they'll discover I've gone? Maybe they know already, and they're out looking for me. She felt a pang, knowing how much she was hurting her parents by running away. But the thought of being packed off to England to live with someone who hadn't even cared enough to write to her . . . No. It was impossible.

Everything still felt so unreal. How can this be happening to me? she thought. I had such a happy childhood. I was born into such a loving family. And look at me now! I don't even know how to fend for myself! Someone else has always looked after me, all my life. I should feel lucky, but right now I just feel desolate.

Travelling so late at night, she was counting on the *boulanger* working into the early hours of the morning, as he often had in the past; no one else could tell her where Nicole lived. If he wasn't there, then she would have nowhere to go until the *boulangerie* was opened at seven thirty the next morning by a bleary-eyed Nicole. So she still didn't know where she'd spend the night. She was worrying about it when suddenly, feeling worn out and weary, she felt her eyes close. She was sleepy, so sleepy . . .

Monday, 3 December 1945

She managed to doze for most of the train journey. And just over an hour later she found herself outside the station in Boulogne trying to hail a taxi, and hoping that she had enough loose change in her purse to cover the fare.

Before she'd left home she'd opened the tin box under her bed where she kept her dressmaking earnings. She'd taken all the notes, but only a handful of franc and centime coins, as she didn't want too much small change cluttering up her purse, and making it bulky and heavy. Now she realized that was a stupid decision, and she should have brought every last centime. She knew that if she didn't find a job, she would only have enough to live on – including bed and breakfast – for four days; and she would have to be very careful to manage even that. All the rest of her money – two hundred francs – was for the abortion.

In the taxi she gave the address of the *boulangerie*. 'You are travelling very late at night, mademoiselle,' the driver commented inquisitively.

'Yes, the *boulanger* is expecting me,' she lied, having decided that the driver was far too slimy for her liking.

'Ah, you work for a *boulanger*!' He seemed to be satisfied with that, so Madeleine made no further comment and they drove on, until, as if suddenly finding the idea preposterous, he broke the silence by saying, 'But it is still very late to be starting work, isn't it?' She didn't like what he was implying, or the suggestive smirk on his face.

'Well, I am a *boulanger* myself, and I *am* going to work,' she answered, guessing what he must imagine she was really going to do. As if it was any of his business! Desperate to change the subject, she asked, 'How much will the fare be?'

'Oh, for you, mademoiselle,' he said with raised eyebrows, 'not too much, probably one franc fifty.' Then, with sudden and obvious concern for himself, he asked, 'You *do* have the money?'

'Yes, of course I do,' she answered becoming more agitated by the minute.

No more was said by either of them until he pulled up at the kerb. 'Here we are, mademoiselle.' The fare was exactly what he'd said, and, pleased to get out, she handed it over, with no apologies for not giving him a tip. She grimaced as he mumbled something unpleasant, before driving off at speed.

Standing there alone with her valise, she looked through the shop window, and felt enormous relief when she saw a glimmer of light seeping under the door to the bakery. She immediately ran round to the back entrance and banged on the door.

'Hello, is anyone there?' she called. When there was no answer she thumped at the wood with her fist. '*Hello!*' she called more loudly, standing on tiptoe to peer through the tiny window at the top of the door.

'Just a minute!' the chubby, red-faced *boulanger* called out impatiently, wiping his floury hands on his apron. '*Mon Dieu!* Is the place on fire?' he complained. He rattled about with the lock, then opened the door a crack. After all, you couldn't be too careful these days, especially in the middle of the night. He was grumbling to himself – but stopped abruptly when he saw a pretty young girl standing in front of him. She looked vaguely familiar, but he couldn't think why.

On seeing his puzzled look, Madeleine explained, 'I am Madeleine, Nicole's friend. Don't you remember me?'

Realization slowly dawning, he said, 'Ah yes, I remember now. Nicole sometimes asked me to bake an extra gateau when she knew that you were coming. Well, she didn't tell me this time.' He frowned. 'No one bothers to tell me anything any more.'

'Nicole doesn't know I am here. It's a surprise, you see.'

She was surprised by her new-found ability to lie at the drop of a hat. 'But I haven't been to where Nicole lives before,' she continued, 'and I'd like you to give me her address.'

He took out his pocket watch and glanced at it, then shook it before glancing at it a second time. 'Well, it's very late,' he said.

On seeing his uncertainty she burst out, 'Oh, please! I'll have nowhere to stay tonight if you don't help me, and I do so want to surprise her . . .'

Looking into her pleading eyes he said, 'At this time of night it *will* be a surprise.'

'*Please!*' she begged.

He took a step back towards the kitchen, and she thought for a moment that he was going to shut the door on her. 'Just let me get these baguettes out of the oven, and I'll take you there. It's not far.'

'Oh!' she said, relieved, 'You don't have to do that. Just the address will be fine.'

He took a pencil out of his apron pocket, and finding a piece of paper by the telephone, he scribbled something, giving verbal instructions at the same time. As he finished Madeleine said, suddenly anxious, 'I hope they won't be angry at being disturbed so late?'

He handed her the paper, and said with a peculiar

chuckle, 'You don't need to worry about that! Her mother won't be asleep, anyway!'

Perplexed by his attitude, she thanked him, picked up her valise, and set off towards the docks as instructed. He'd told her to take the third turning on the left. She glanced at the piece of paper: 58, Rue de la Mer. Pushing it back in her pocket, she looked up at the street sign.

This is it! she thought. But what a strange name for a road that, as far as I can tell, is nowhere near the sea! Suddenly tired and weepy, and her valise feeling as if it was loaded with bricks, she gazed down the length of the road, at an area which, under the two dim street lights, looked to be barely more than rubble. Her spirits sank at the sight. Not just because it was worrying, but because she couldn't help thinking about all the people who had lost their homes and families during the bombing.

Where are they all now? she wondered, walking slowly down the road and fearing she was in the wrong place. But then the baker *had* said that she would see a lot of rubble.

'The remains of a heavy air raid, waiting to be cleared,' he'd complained, as if the French authorities were solely to blame.

She squinted into the distance, where something more solid stuck out from the ruins. Whatever it was, it was well over halfway down the long street. As she got closer she was able to make out four or five fairly large houses, not detached, but all seemingly hanging on to each other. There was even greenery in front of two of them, which, although a bit out of place, helped soften the austere surroundings.

Madeleine had always thought a well-tended garden meant the owners were caring people, and she approached hoping that No. 58 would be one of the two. After all, she had never met Nicole's mother, who might be an ogre for all she knew. Maybe that was why Nicole had never invited her home. Maybe she was ashamed of her mother, Ginette.

Madeleine was suddenly very nervous, and, for the first time since she'd decided to run away, accepted there was a chance she wouldn't be welcomed by Nicole with open arms. She hesitated at the gate of the first house in the block of five, which had No. 58 nailed up on the right of the brightly painted door. It didn't have a garden. But there *were* flowers in the wooden containers on each side of the door. Nicole's maman is probably OK, Madeleine told herself, while trying to summon the courage to lift the huge anchor-shaped door knocker.

She made the first feeble attempt, rat-a-tat-tat . . . and waited. Nothing happened and her nerve began to go. She looked up at the faint glow of light that showed through the gaps of the upstairs shutters, and once again took hold of the metal anchor. Her rat-a-tat-tat was much louder this time. The sound of the metal against wood must have reverberated around the whole street. Still she waited, and no one appeared.

Feeling weak, she sat on the cold stone step and

shivered, not knowing what to do next. And then, from somewhere inside, she heard the sound of footsteps running downstairs. She got up from the step and suddenly found herself face to face with a man who had just let himself out of the front door. 'Well, well, well,' he said with a grin, 'What do we have here?'

Madeleine said haltingly, 'Er, I am Madeleine, a friend of Nicole's.'

'Sure you are,' he answered. 'I had better let you in then.' And he stood to one side. Uncertainly, Madeleine squeezed past him, and was halfway up the stairs when he called, 'Madeleine . . . I will see you next time, eh?'

Madeleine stopped and looked over her shoulder, with no idea what to say in reply. Instead, she shrugged and continued to the top of the stairs. His quiet laugh as he closed the door made her uneasy, and she waited until she heard him run down the stone steps outside, before knocking on the door to her right.

'One minute!' said a voice from the room at the other side of the door. And, with relief, Madeleine recognized it as Nicole's.

'*Oui?*' Nicole enquired, as she opened the door. Then she took a better look and exclaimed in horror . . . 'Madeleine?'

Madeleine, suddenly feeling her knees giving way beneath her, just managed to say, 'Nicole,' before collapsing.

'Oh, *mon Dieu*! What is it, what is wrong?' Nicole said, shaking Madeleine gently. 'Wake up, Madeleine. Wake up!' She called out in panic, 'Maman! Come quickly!'

'What is it?' Ginette said, appearing from an inner room. Seeing Madeleine lying on the floor she said calmly, 'Get her to the divan.'

As Nicole tried to coax her to her feet Madeleine murmured something unintelligible, and Nicole and her mother half-dragged her to the divan.

'Don't talk, Madeleine, just lie still,' Nicole said. Her mother fetched a blanket and a glass of water, and Nicole gently covered up her friend before tilting her head towards the glass.

Madeleine sipped gratefully, then lay back on the cushion, murmuring, 'So sorry, I'm so sorry.'

Nicole glanced at her mother, who beckoned her to the kitchen. 'Who is this girl?' she asked.

'It's Madeleine, Maman! The friend I told you about, who used to call in at the *boulangerie*!'

'What, the one who lives in Calais? Who suddenly disappeared?' Her mother sounded tense.

'Yes, Maman, the one who lives near Calais. And before you say anything else, I'm sure she had a good reason for disappearing like that.'

'*I* can guess why it happened,' Ginette said.

'You think it's because she found out about our life? I think it's more likely her sisters did, and ordered her home without explaining why. I just know she wouldn't have gone without saying goodbye to me. Not if she'd had any choice.'

'I hope you are right. I remember how upset you were when she vanished.'

'She's here now. And she obviously needs our help.'

'Obviously,' Ginette echoed.

Madeleine started to move and Nicole ran over to her. 'Steady, Madeleine, take it easy.' She helped her to sit up.

Madeleine, trembling, looked around. The room was cosy and refined, with a red carpet and antique furniture. It was like something from a magazine, she thought fuzzily. Maybe she was still asleep, and this was all a dream. She slumped back down on the divan.

As she lay there a soft voice that she remembered hearing earlier asked, 'Are you feeling a little better now?'

When Madeleine turned her head slightly she saw a slender, glamorous woman, who had to be Nicole's mother, standing in front of her. Close to tears, Madeleine said, 'I am so sorry to have disturbed you late at night, Madame Jobert, but I had nowhere else to go.' She struggled up from the divan. 'I must leave now, but thank you for your kindness.'

'You will do no such thing,' Nicole scolded. 'You can sleep here tonight,' she added, glancing at her mother for approval.

Her mother nodded. 'OK, we will talk tomorrow. There are a few questions that I'd like to ask you, young lady, before you *disappear* again.'

'*Maman!*' Nicole exclaimed.

Madeleine put her hand on Nicole's arm. ' It's OK. I understand. We do need to talk.'

256

Chapter 19

Tom and Dominic travelled all night. They were so tired when they arrived in Marck that they could have slept leaning on a clothes line. Maman opened the door, and when she saw Tom standing next to Dominic, she perked up immediately, and, taking his hand in both of hers, her voice suddenly full of hope, she said, 'Oh, I can't tell you how pleased I am to see *you*, Tom!'

'I'm so sorry for what's happened, Madame Pelletier . . .' he began, but in answer she just kissed him on the cheeks.

Once she had closed the door firmly behind them, her mood changed again and she said, 'I'd give anything just to know Madeleine is safe.'

Dominic crouched next to the chair she'd sunk into, and took her hand. 'We will find her, Maman, I promise.'

'It's been so long. Where could she be?' Maman gripped Dominic's hand tightly.

'Try not to worry, Maman,' Dominic said. He rose to his feet, concerned at how tired she looked.

He glanced at Tom, who came over and put his hand on Maman's shoulder, and she placed her hand over his before looking up at him. 'We have looked everywhere that we can think of, Tom. Papa, Martine and Simone are out there now talking to her friends, but they don't know anything. They're simply shocked that Madeleine has run away.' She added quickly, 'Of course, we haven't told *anyone* about the circumstances.'

Dominic translated this into English for Tom, who paced around the living room.

'She's taken your bike, Dominic. How far could she go on a bike?' Maman asked, her furrowed brow showing deep lines that he was sure hadn't been there when he'd left home four days ago.

'If she's taken the bike, then she must have been heading further away than we think,' Dominic said.

The door burst open as Maman answered slowly, 'But she knows no one outside the village—'

'But that's it!' Martine interrupted, having caught the tail end of the conversation as she rushed in. 'We've been looking too close to home! She *does* know someone else!' She went over to Maman. 'Oh, why didn't I think of it before?'

She stood up and quickly hugged her brother and Tom, while apologizing for the belated greeting. 'I knew you'd come, Tom,' she said gratefully.

'Where do you think she is?' he asked, trying to fight the guilt, and rising panic, that he felt.

Papa and Simone had just come in through the door. Martine asked Dominic to translate for Tom. 'Madeleine met a girl in Boulogne when she used to visit us there,' she said. 'She told me about her, but I wouldn't allow her to continue the friendship.'

Dominic explained this to Tom, who immediately asked, 'Why, who was she? Where does she live?'

'Slow down, Tom,' begged Dominic. 'One question at a time, eh? *Mon Dieu*, I cannot translate that quickly!'

'OK, Dominic,' Tom said. 'But shouldn't you all have heard something by now if she's gone there?'

Dominic looked at Martine. 'Do you have the name of this girl?'

'Yes. She is called Nicole, and she works in a *boulangerie* near my old flat.'

'So what was the problem with the friendship?' he asked curiously.

Martine glanced warily at Maman before answering. 'Her mother ran a brothel during the war.'

Maman sat bolt upright in her chair. '*A brothel!*' she exclaimed. 'And her daughter, this . . . this Nicole, was she—?'

'No, Maman, I don't think so,' Martine interrupted, 'and Madeleine knew nothing about it at all, as far as I'm aware.'

'You really think she may have gone to find this Nicole?' Maman asked, a glimmer of hope in her tired eyes, because by now she didn't care where Madeleine was – in a brothel or elswhere – just as long as she was safe.

Dominic, knowing his sister the way he did, tried to second-guess what she would have done. He said slowly, 'Yes . . . that makes sense. She'd have used my bike to get to the station in Calais.'

And Tom, who was desperately trying to keep up with what they were saying now that Dominic seemed to have forgotten all about translating, raised his eyebrows enquiringly.

'I will explain later,' Dominic said in answer to Tom's silent question. Then, firmly placing his arm round Tom's shoulder, he said with a decisiveness that he didn't feel, 'Come, Tom, we've work to do!' Everyone else got up from their chairs, as if the matter was resolved.

'Well, I hope you're right, mate,' Tom said, begging Dominic to explain what was happening. He couldn't understand why Madeleine had chosen to go to Boulogne rather than stay with a friend locally, if all she had needed was to get away from the house for a while.

Martine, who was in the middle of writing down the address of the *boulangerie*, stopped and looked up, startled, as if a fresh idea had suddenly hit her. 'Oh, she wouldn't!' she exclaimed in horror. 'She couldn't!'

'Wouldn't, couldn't, what?' Dominic was worried now.

Martine glanced towards Maman, who was now standing at the kitchen table, making a late breakfast for everyone. While she spread her home-made strawberry jam on to thick slices of bread Papa poured coffee. Simone was nowhere to be seen.

Martine whispered urgently to Dominic, 'What if she's trying to get an abortion?'

Dominic, aghast at the suggestion, whispered back, 'She wouldn't do that! She wouldn't know how. And anyway, she's a Catholic!'

'Look, Dominic, I know that you and Madeleine were close, but maybe you don't know her as well as you think any more. She has changed. She's a woman now, and pregnant, with, she thinks, no support from her family, and no husband. Religion would be the last thing on her mind. She'd be more concerned about the shame and embarrassment she's bringing on us all.'

'*Mon Dieu!*' Dominic whispered. 'If you are right we're going to be too late!'

He turned to look at Tom, who had wandered over to the kitchen table, near Maman. He had a slice of bread and jam in one hand, and a tiny coffee cup in the other, and was staring vacantly out of the window.

Papa, who'd said nothing so far, was feeding logs into the top of the range.

Dominic turned back to Martine. 'We've got to leave at once,' he said.

As he headed for the kitchen she gave him the piece of paper with the address of the *boulangerie*. Then she kissed him on both cheeks, and whispered, 'Good luck!'

His mother looked up as he gently gripped her shoulder, but addressed Tom. 'We must go now. I'll explain on the way.'

Tom, perturbed to see Martine looking so distressed, could only nod in response.

Without speaking, Papa gave Dominic a hug. His eyes brimming with tears, he took Tom's hand and said only one word: '*Merci.*'

With a lump in his throat, wishing he had the ability to apologize to – and thank – this wonderful family, Tom picked up the suitcases. Dominic threw back a cup of coffee in a single gulp before reassuring his mother that he would telephone Martine at work when he had some news.

At the front door Tom and Dominic turned and looked back at the Pelletiers, and the expectation in those faces was almost too much for them. They closed the door quietly and set off for Boulogne.

Boulogne, France
Monday, 3 December 1945

Madeleine slept fitfully while Ginette tried to convince her daughter Nicole that if she wanted her friend to stay she had no choice: she had to tell her about the brothel, and her maman's way of life.

'But, Maman, she will be horrified! Now is not the right time!' Nicole exclaimed. 'I can't, I just can't!'

Ginette, feeling her daughter's pain, said sadly, 'I am sorry, *ma fille*, that you are so ashamed of me, but I don't need to remind you how desperate we were when your papa left.'

'Oh, I know all that, Maman! But this is the first time I've ever had a proper friend, and I don't want to embarrass her. Surely you understand that?'

Ginette held her daughter's hands, and said, 'Don't worry, I'll make sure that Madeleine knows you have nothing to do with any of this, and that you don't sell your body like your maman.'

The despair in Nicole's eyes brought tears to Ginette's.

Nicole asked, 'Oh, Maman, why do you continue to do this *awful* job?'

Ginette gestured at the flat. 'Because, *ma fille*, it means we can live like this.' Before Nicole could answer, she added, with a resigned shrug of her shoulders, 'It's as simple as that!'

Nicole realized that as far as her mother was concerned, the conversation was over. She decided to go to bed. 'Goodnight, Maman,' she said, smiling and kissing her on both cheeks.

'Goodnight, *ma fille*.'

Nicole tiptoed over to the divan to check on Madeleine, who, she discovered, was lying there with her eyes open. She hesitated, wondering how much, if any, of the previous conversation she had overheard. But Madeleine only smiled weakly. 'Goodnight, Nicole,' she said.

And Nicole, bringing a second blanket, crouched down in front of her and moved her glass of water within easier reach. Then she asked, 'Would you like something to eat?'

'Oh no, thank you.'

'OK.' Nicole pushed a plate of biscuits towards her,

saying, 'Just in case, eh?' She smiled. 'Goodnight, Madeleine. We'll talk tomorrow.'

'Yes, tomorrow,' Madeleine answered, touching Nicole's hand.

Nicole went off to her room, grateful that Madeleine appeared to have heard nothing.

But Madeleine *had* heard what the two women had said, and felt shaky as she pulled herself up to a sitting position. She had a sip of water, took a biscuit from the selection on the little table in front of her, and stared at the doorway where Nicole's mother had stood earlier.

Everything finally made sense: she understood now why she had only ever met Nicole at the *boulangerie*, and why her friend had never talked much about her mother. But even with these puzzling conditions, she and Nicole had become close. Not exactly in the way Madeleine was close to her school friends, of course, but it was still a loving friendship.

Madeleine was surprised to find she wasn't horrified or shocked by what she'd overheard. On the contrary, she felt strangely at ease, as if she belonged here. The only difference between me and Ginette, she thought grimly, is that she is paid for having sex! But no sooner had this occurred to her than she realized she was being ridiculous. They weren't the same at all.

Her mind worked overtime now. She found herself wondering why all prostitutes weren't constantly pregnant. After all, she herself had done it only once – *one time*, she thought for the umpteenth time – and look at her! If Nicole thinks that I'm in for a shock when she tells me about her mother tomorrow, she thought, she's in for an even bigger one when I tell her my news.

She couldn't help smiling, albeit wryly, at the irony of it all. Here she was, staying with someone who must have come across this problem frequently. Surely it was fate. After all, who would know better than Ginette Jobert where to go and how to put an end to her nightmare?

The reality of what she was planning suddenly dawned on her. She shivered and slid shakily back under the blankets, pulling them up tightly around her neck.

Chapter 20

Boulogne, France
Wednesday, 5 December 1945

The last half hour of the train journey seemed interminable to Tom. Frustrated, and oblivious to the glorious countryside of *la belle France* outside the train window, he reached into his jacket pocket for a cigarette, and absent-mindedly lit it, not giving a second thought to Dominic, who was sitting across from him.

'Oh, sorry, mate,' he said, suddenly realizing what he was doing. He held out a Woodbine to Dominic. He was about to strike a match when it suddenly dawned on him that Maddie had been in Boulogne – alone and unprotected – for two days. 'God Almighty!' he said suddenly, burning his fingers and leaping up from his seat. 'Anything could have happened to her!' He pressed his forehead against the carriage window, willing the train to hurry.

When Dominic tapped him gently on the arm and held up his cigarette, Tom, startled, shook his head.

'Oh, sorry, mate, I was miles away!' he said, giving him the matchbox.

Feeling unbelievably hot, Dominic took out his handkerchief to dab the perspiration from his forehead. The train steamed into a little station, took two passengers on board, and juddered agonizingly slowly into movement again.

'What if she's not even in Boulogne, Dominic? What do we do then?' Tom said, drawing heavily on his cigarette.

'I don't know, Tom. We'll just have to see. I still don't think Madeleine intends to get rid of the baby,' Dominic whispered. 'If she is in Boulogne, her plan is probably to stay there till after the birth.'

'But it doesn't make any sense.' Tom frowned. 'Why would she do that, when she has a family in Marck to take care of her?'

'Oh, Tom, there is much you don't understand. And why should you?' Dominic said. 'We think she has run away to take the shame from her family. I am afraid that our parents were upset at the prospect of a . . . how you say? An illegitimate baby.'

Tom was totally taken aback. 'You mean nobody stood up for her?'

Dominic shook his head sadly. 'Not even me, in the end.'

Tom opened his mouth to speak, wanting to say how desperately sorry he was, and how selfish he'd been not to realize that he *had* to marry Madeleine, but Dominic put a hand up.

'I know what you are going to say, Tom, I know that she always trusted me, and I should have stood by her. I know all that, but I had to think of our parents, also. And, when I came to find you in England, Madeleine did not know I was doing it. Not until I had gone.'

Tom, aghast now, sat rigid on the edge of his seat. 'So she could be running away from *me*, then?'

'She's running from all of us, Tom,' Dominic answered, almost in a whisper.

Tom leaned back in his seat, thinking, yet again, how unforgivably cruel he'd been, not contacting Maddie. Even though, at the time, he'd convinced himself that it was for her good as well as his. But none of his reasons made sense any more.

What did it matter if they didn't speak the same language? They could learn, couldn't they? Maybe, he thought, he could convince her to come back to England with him. But then he realized he was fooling himself. For God's sake, he thought. She's had enough time to turn against me, and who can blame her? She must have gone through hell to end up doing this!

It was some time before he spoke, but when he did he raised his head and looked directly at Dominic, saying quietly, but with total conviction, 'I'm going to put everything right.'

Dominic didn't speak, but with a tight smile he leaned forward and patted Tom's leg. He hoped against hope that they *would* find Madeleine, especially now that Tom had at last been shocked into accepting his responsibilities. It was suddenly obvious that he really *did* care for her after all.

Fifteen minutes later the train finally chuntered into Boulogne station, and Tom, who'd been rummaging through his suitcase for a new pack of cigarettes, snapped the clasps shut and joined Dominic, who had his arm through the carriage window, and was already opening the door.

They stepped down on to the platform, both narrowing their eyes to see through the steam.

'This way,' said Dominic confidently, as he jostled through a group of giggling girls.

'Blimey!' said Tom, joining him after fighting his way through the unruly girls. 'Is there a school outing, or something?'

'Who knows?' Dominic said without much interest. He'd been feeling queasy, and decided it was due to lack of food. 'Before we go any further we will have a coffee and a sandwich,' he stated, in a surprisingly authoritative manner. Seeing Tom's hesitation, he said sharply, 'Come on, Tom! We have to eat something or we will be no good to find Madeleine.'

'OK, but let's be quick. We can't waste any more time. I could have *walked* faster than that bloody train.'

Dominic dived into the first café he saw, ignoring its grubbiness. He ordered two cups of strong coffee, and seeing baguettes filled with meat, two of those as well. He was feeling faint and irritable. In fact, now he thought about it, he realized he hadn't eaten anything –

apart from the bread and jam in Marck – since leaving Tom's house in England.

He carried the tray over to the table and placed it on the sticky surface.

Tom gulped the coffee and almost spat it out. 'This stuff's like dishwater, man!' He took another slurp. 'It's better than nowt, though, I suppose.'

After tasting his, Dominic was ready to take it back. He grumbled, 'I asked her for strong coffee. Can't anybody get anything right?'

'Hey! Hey!' said Tom. 'Calm down! Come on, lad, let's eat and sup up now we're here.' They wolfed the baguettes in no time, and washed them down, grimacing, with the coffee. Ten minutes later they were jumping in a taxi.

Dominic, noticing a look of reluctance on the taxi driver's face when he gave the address of the *boulangerie*, asked, 'Is there a problem?'

'Well, not for you,' the driver answered, with an irritating air of omniscience.

'What do you mean, not for us?' Dominic asked, trying to remain patient.

'Well, they say all the women round there who collaborated with the Germans are going to be rounded up and taken to the market square today. They're going to be taught a lesson.'

Dominic hadn't time to answer before the man continued with undisguised glee, 'And it's anyone's guess what they'll do to them.'

Tom, seeing the colour drain from Dominic's face, exclaimed, 'What did he say?'

As Dominic turned to Tom, the driver added, as if doing them a great favour, 'You can watch if you like. There will be seats in the square and—'

Dominic leapt forward and grabbed the man by the neck. He said fiercely, 'Just shut up and get us there.'

As he released his hold, the driver coughed and spluttered. 'Yes, yes, OK! No need for that, I was only telling you!' There was a distinct shake in his voice.

Tom was astonished, having never *ever* seen Dominic be violent before. He pulled him back into his seat. saying, 'Hey, hey, come on, Dominic, man! What's all this about, anyway?'

'When I tell you, *you* must also stay calm. Otherwise we will have an accident.'

'OK, OK. Just tell me,' said Tom, who was *really* worried now.

Watching how pale Tom's face went, Dominic wasn't surprised when he shouted out, 'But Maddie, man! If she's staying with a prostitute, she's in danger! We all know what they got up to in the war, don't we? Didn't matter to them if the punters were German, Canadian or what, as long as they were paying! Aw, man! But I thought all that vigilante stuff happened just after the war ended,' he continued, his voice raised in disbelief.

'Me also,' said Dominic. 'Perhaps they couldn't get hold of these ones back then. But even so, I can't believe the police would allow it to happen now. Not after all this time!'

'Get a move on!' Tom shouted at the driver, who was looking panicky now, thinking he'd picked up a couple of lunatics. Every gear change grated, and the car bucked and lurched, throwing them around, as he pushed the old Citroën to its limits. He wanted these idiots out of his car as quickly as possible.

Arriving at the patisserie, Tom had the door half-open even before the car had ground to a halt. He jumped out, closely followed by Dominic, who threw some loose change into the front of the car, not even asking what the fare was. There was no way the taxi driver was going to argue: he couldn't get away fast enough, judging by the trail of smoke and dust he left behind.

Boulogne, France
Monday, 3 December 1945

The buzz of the coffee grinder woke Madeleine early, and when she appeared at the kitchen door Nicole looked up in surprise. 'Oh, Madeleine! I'm sorry if I woke you. Are you OK?' She sounded concerned.

'Yes, I'm OK,' Madeleine watched her friend pull out the little drawer at the base of the grinder before emptying the freshly ground coffee into a pot. 'I needed to get up. Where's the toilet?'

'We have to talk, Madeleine, but first things first. It's through here.' Nicole opened a door in the hall.

'Your toilet is *inside* the house?' Madeleine said astonished. She'd expected to be directed downstairs, to a garden at the back.

Nicole smiled widely. 'Ah, your toilet is outside at home, eh?'

Nicole was buttering bread and humming to herself when Madeleine got back to the kitchen. 'That was a real luxury,' Madeleine said. She had watched in awe as water flushed the pan, and revelled in the pretty flowered hand basin and scented soap she'd found in the bathroom next to the toilet.

'Here's your coffee, Madeleine!'

Madeleine glanced around the cheerful room, which, though not quite as big as the kitchen at home, was still spacious. Struck by how uncluttered it was, her gaze fell on a painting hanging below a set of gleaming copper saucepans. It was a seascape – she assumed of somewhere local.

'Lovely, isn't it?' said Nicole, noticing her interest. She added with enthusiasm, 'It was painted by one of Maman's clients.' She immediately wished she hadn't spoken. Desperate to lead the conversation away from any questions about what her mother did for a living, she put in quickly, 'It's the sand dunes at Sangatte, quite a distance north of here, but only a few kilometres south of where you are in the Pas de Calais.'

'I know Sangatte,' Madeleine replied. 'I used to go there before the war. That was when I was young and carefree, of course.'

Her wistful tone caused Nicole to glance at her thoughtfully. 'Madeleine, you sound as if you're carrying the weight of the world on your shoulders. What is it, what's wrong?' she asked, sitting down opposite her friend.

'Oh, where do I start?' Madeleine said.

'Please, just tell me, Madeleine,' Nicole coaxed.

Madeleine looked around self-consciously. 'Where is your maman?'

'She always sleeps late,' Nicole waved dismissively.

'I'm pregnant,' Madeleine blurted out.

Nicole caught the despair in her voice, and her heart went out to her. There was a short silence before she asked calmly, 'And where is the father?'

'In England . . . he lives in England.' Their eyes met as Madeleine looked helplessly at her friend.

'Oh, Madeleine!' Nicole came round to her side of the table and hugged her. 'And he doesn't know?'

'No, he doesn't, and I didn't want him to, but my brother has gone over there to tell him. Can you believe that!' Madeleine's look of outrage made it clear she'd been terribly wounded by this betrayal. She began crying as Nicole pulled her closer.

'Hey, hey, come on,' Nicole said soothingly. 'There's no need to say more. I understand.'

'I want to get rid of it!' Madeleine interrupted, struggling to control her tears. There was another silence before Madeleine went on, 'Don't look at me like that, Nicole. I've made up my mind, and I need your help—'

'Oh, Madeleine! What makes you think I could help?' Nicole said.

'I'm sorry, Nicole, but I overheard your conversation with your maman last night.

'Oh, no!' Nicole's hand flew to her mouth.

'It's all right, Nicole. Please don't look so horrified. It's good, because I understand everything now. You must not be ashamed of your maman. I'm sure she did what she thought was best for—'

But before she could finish Ginette strode into the room, demanding, 'And what do you know about my life? How could you have any idea what it was like when Nicole's father left us with no home, and nothing but the clothes we were standing up in?' She glanced at Nicole before going on, 'A three-year-old baby, and not a centime between us!' She looked round at the flat. 'I worked hard for all this, I had to stay strong for both of us.' Pulling her silk dressing gown around her slim body, she sat down at the table.

'I'm so sorry, Madame Jobert.' Madeleine held her hands to her burning cheeks. 'I didn't mean to offend you.'

'You got it wrong, Maman,' Nicole said. 'Madeleine was not being critical. She needs our help.'

'Help . . . what kind of help?' Ginette took the cup Nicole gave her.

All three sat quietly sipping at their coffee for a moment, unsure who should speak first.

Madeleine was chewing her lower lip anxiously when Ginette broke the silence. 'I'm sorry, Madeleine. Maybe I'm being over-protective of my daughter. You see, you're the first real friend she's ever had, and when you disappeared like that she was heartbroken. She thought you'd discovered her "secret life", and disapproved of it.'

'I'm sure it wasn't like that, Maman,' Nicole butted in. 'And Madeleine can explain it all later, but right now there is something much more important she needs to tell you.' She nodded to Madeleine to go ahead.

'I am pregnant, Madame Jobert,' Madeline said. She added in a whisper, 'And I want an abortion. I've saved some money for it: two hundred francs.'

If Ginette was surprised, she showed no sign. She just asked, 'How many weeks is it?'

'Just over two months,' Madeleine answered hesitantly.

'OK,' Ginette said.

Nicole reached over to place a reassuring hand on Madeleine's, which lay limply on the table.

'What did she mean by "OK"?' Madeleine asked Nicole, when Ginette had gone back to her room to dress.

'Don't worry, Madeleine. Maman has lots of contacts, just give her time to think. It's been a while since she had any girls working for her. Back then, she sometimes had to deal with that sort of thing.' Then, in an effort to make light of things, Nicole added, 'As you can imagine, eh?'

'Where are those girls now?' asked Madeleine.

'Still working. Well, most of them, anyway. But not for Maman.' Nicole said quickly, 'She works alone now – except for her maid, of course.' She thought of the girls who'd been unlucky. Some had been destroyed by the life; others had died because of it. 'Are you sure you want to do this?' she asked, suddenly afraid for Madeleine.

'I don't have any choice,' Madeleine replied, trying to conceal a shiver of fear.

Nicole looked at her watch. 'I have to go to work now. Will you be all right here until I get back?' she asked. And then she added, 'You must tell me if you are not well enough to be left on your own.'

'I'll be fine. I'll rest for a while, then maybe I'll meet you at the *boulangerie*, and we could have a coffee and gateau.' It was odd, but as Madeleine said this, the word 'gateau' actually made her feel nauseous.

'Just like the old days? I'd love that,' said Nicole, jumping up and kissing Madeleine on both cheeks. '*A bientôt alors!*'

'Yes, see you later,' Madeleine called back. But Nicole was already running down the stairs to the front door.

Madeleine poured herself another coffee, and, cupping it in both hands, she wandered over to the divan where she'd slept the night before. She sat there taking in her surroundings.

She was pretty sure that this wasn't a bedroom. It was more like a reception area, she decided, looking at the desk with its ornate telephone. She got up from the divan and reached out tentatively to touch the flowers in the Oriental vase that stood to her left, on an inlaid rosewood table. The table could have been especially designed to display the magnificent bouquet, she thought, stroking one of the white lilies.

'Yes, they are real!' The quiet voice behind her made her jump. It was Ginette. 'I'll be out for a while. Just help yourself to any food in the kitchen,' she said.

'Oh, Madame Jobert, I was just admiring your lovely home.'

'No need to be so nervous, Madeleine. Look around if you like,' Ginette said, gesturing towards the other rooms.

'Well, I . . .'

'It's fine.' Ginette smiled. 'I won't take offence, go ahead.' Her dark eyes flashed. 'I am proud of my home, and it would be good to know what someone else thought about it.' Her mouth took on a mischievous twist. 'Needless to say, my clients,' she raised her eyebrows, 'rarely show an interest in either the decor or the art.'

Madeleine's smile widened into a grin. She decided that she was going to like this woman, with her dry sense of humour.

'*A bientôt!*' Ginette said, as she too ran down the stairs. At the bottom she called out, 'You may call me Ginette. And slam the front door to make sure it is locked when you go out.'

'OK!' Madeleine called back, but Ginette had already gone. Alone now, Madeleine stood in the middle of the room, uncertain what to do next. She walked towards a door leading off the far end of the reception area. The other side was a passageway, and she was immediately struck by how long it was. From where she was standing, she could see three closed doors on the right-hand side. The left-hand side was just a solid wall, although on closer inspection she could make out the faint outline of what must once have been windows.

Perhaps they'd been necessary, she thought, to make the place lighter, before electricity was installed.

Madeleine flicked a switch, and marvelled at the way that the three lights in the corridor came on at the same time. Even though there was electricity at home in Marck, all the lights there hung from the ceiling; she'd never seen lights fixed to a wall before, or ones with such elaborate brass fittings.

As she explored, she could see that, further on, the passage led off to the right. This can't be all one apartment, she thought. She reached the first door, and, unsure what she'd find, took a deep breath as she turned the shiny brass knob.

'Oh lah lah!' she exclaimed, as the door swung open. She was in what she assumed was Nicole's room. She walked to the middle and twirled round, feeling like the ballerina in her musical jewellery box at home.

The room was large and airy, with a double bed in the centre of the far wall, which was painted rich cream, the other three walls being pale lilac. *Mon Dieu*, Nicole, I had no idea you lived like this, Madeleine thought, as she walked over to the pristine white dressing table. There was jewellery laid out there, and as she picked different pieces up she tried to remember if she'd ever noticed Nicole wearing any of them. She couldn't. She's probably never worn these beautiful things, Madeleine thought, as she looked at each item, neatly displayed next to the matching ivory-handled hairbrush, comb and hand mirror.

Sitting down on the cream-cushioned stool, she

looked in the mirror and imagined it wasn't her reflection but Nicole's looking back. She visualized Nicole brushing her long dark hair every night. Lonely, lovely Nicole; how like her mother Ginette she was! They both had the same dark eyes and hair, the same slim bodies – and their mannerisms were almost identical. It was amazing, Madeleine thought, that Nicole hadn't fallen into her mother's way of life; after all, Ginette had obviously done very well out of it. It suddenly became clear to her why Nicole, who she'd always felt could have done so much better, had chosen to work in a *boulangerie*. It must be because, although it was close to home geographically, it was in every other way as different as possible from the life her mother led. It all made sense to Madeleine: Nicole's job was poorly paid, she wore a drab uniform, and she dealt mostly with women – any men who came into the patisserie were mostly old. Nicole had no boyfriend, either. Was that intentional? Madeleine wondered. Or was it simply that she felt too embarrassed to bring anyone home?

She put the brush down and smiled at the two soft toys sitting luxuriously on the beautiful white lace bed-spread, before backing out of the room and gently closing the door. She'd been so fascinated by this glimpse of Nicole's life that for a few minutes she'd completely forgotten her own problems.

When she opened the door next to Nicole's, Madeleine's eyes widened in amazement. This room was even larger. Her eyes focused immediately on the beautiful ornate four-poster bed, which was piled so high with pillows that it was hard to resist the urge to jump on it. The lace pillowcases were beautifully sewn; Madeleine thought they must have come from a very expensive shop.

The walls were lined in a gold and cream wallpaper, and when she touched it she realized the gold pattern was raised. It gave the room an air of taste and luxury. The two slightly open windows, both on the same wall, opened on a vista of rooftops, and beyond them, the open sea. Madeleine took a deep breath, and savoured the freshness of the sea air as it wafted through the dazzling net curtains. Maybe the street did have a right to be called 'Rue de la Mer', after all.

She stood on the polished wooden floor and gazed at the glass chandelier hanging from the high ceiling and swaying and glinting slightly in the sea breeze, and couldn't help revelling in the glamour of the place. This surely isn't where Ginette entertains her clients, she thought. It's too close to where Nicole sleeps. She guessed this was a special haven that Ginette had created for herself, a very private place. And the instant she realized that, she knew she shouldn't stay any longer – and left.

The door of the third room was slightly ajar. Thinking this might be Ginette's workplace, she was almost afraid of what she'd find there. But she reminded herself that Ginette had suggested she look round, so surely there wasn't anything too embarrassing on display. Expecting a carpet and furniture, she pushed the door open firmly. It banged hard on the wall and swung back, and Madeleine realized that it was completely empty, with no curtains, and not even a rug on the floor. It was smaller than the other two rooms, and when Madeleine saw two hairpins and a piece of ribbon on the windowsill she guessed that it had probably been in use recently. Whose was that ribbon? she wondered. Where were they now? Intrigued, she wandered further down the passage and, turning right, came across another door. This was different from the others: it was heavier and panelled, looking more like an exterior door. Beside it there was a heavy red-painted door that appeared to lead straight outside, because there was a tiny window in it through which she could see an iron staircase and a glimpse of the street. She tried the handle, but it was locked. It had to be a fire escape, or, she romanticized, a secret entrance. The panelled door opened on another, shorter passageway. As she walked down it, she saw naked bodies in the paintings on the walls and put her head down, trying not to look at them. But somehow, the display of anonymous breasts and bottoms was irresistible, and she just couldn't stop herself staring. There was a well-worn red chaise longue there, and she flopped gratefully on to it, letting out a long sigh. The paintings in the hallway left her breathless. She was in awe of Ginette for being brave enough to display them. She told herself that perhaps they were art: after all, if Ginette had bought them, they had to be valuable.

There was a room opening off the corridor, and she

dared herself to look into it. It had walls covered in red wallpaper embossed with gold fleurs-de-lis, and two deep red and gold armchairs, one each side of a long low polished oak coffee table. This table had a bowl of sugared almonds on it, and one of mint bonbons. Standing just behind the bowls was an oblong marble cigarette lighter, and an ornate gold box containing cigarettes wrapped in bright pastel-coloured papers.

Madeleine dragged her eyes away from the cigarettes long enough to take in the dresser opposite. On this were four tiny very clean coffee cups and saucers, a coffee pot, some glasses, and alcoholic drinks. There were five paintings in the room, too, showing naked men and women in sexual poses, and there was something faintly cartoonish and humorous about the way they were executed.

Beside her, Madeleine saw double doors, folded back to show a huge bed covered with a gold counterpane. The walls in this smaller inner room were decorated in two shades of red, one much deeper than the other, creating a striped effect, and the curtains were a heavy gold, framed by a red velvet fabric pelmet, and closed against any natural light. She looked down at the floor and moved her foot lightly over the polished wood. Thanks to spending so much time in Papa's workshop, she could tell the floor was oak parquet. It was as beautiful as the floor in Ginette's bedroom, yet this room couldn't be more different. There was no feeling of lightness or airiness here; in fact the place felt claustrophobic.

If it hadn't been for the mirrors, which hung on long chains from the picture rail, it would have been oppressively dark and gloomy. Catching sight of herself in one of these, Madeleine thought she looked disapproving, but that wasn't how she felt. Even though the paintings in this room were seriously explicit, and she felt she should be fleeing them – or at least averting her eyes – she did neither, because in a strange way she found them beautiful.

She sat on the bed. What would Maman and Papa say if they could see me sitting here, in a room like this, where so much must have taken place? she wondered. Well brought up little Madeleine Pelletier, sitting in a brothel *and* content to be there.

Maybe I belong in a place like this now, she thought. Maybe fate brought me here. After all, what I've done isn't that different, is it? Yet again she dismissed this thought the instant it occurred to her, knowing that she was only thinking it to punish herself. She closed her eyes tightly, and tears squeezed their way between and through her lashes. She made no effort to stop them.

Chapter 21

Boulogne, France
Monday, 3 December 1945

Switching off the lights as she went, Madeleine made her way down the passage and back to what she thought of as the reception area of Nicole's apartment. She took some clean underwear and a dress out of her valise and headed for the bathroom she'd seen earlier. The bath looked awfully big compared to the portable aluminium one she used at home, so she used the sink instead, overjoyed to be able to wash and dry her hair and get rid of the smell of coal-dust and dirty steam that still lingered from her train journey.

Finally, feeling revived and fresh in her clean clothes, she placed the old ones in the drawstring laundry bag she'd made especially for going to visit her sisters in Boulogne. Those days seemed a lifetime ago now.

When she'd dried her hair her rumbling stomach reminded her that she'd eaten practically nothing since arriving in Boulogne, so she decided to go and meet

Nicole straight away. She put on her coat and ran down the stairs, not forgetting to slam the hefty outside door to ensure it locked.

Nicole's wide grin as she entered the patisserie lifted her spirits instantly.

'Sit down, Madeleine, I will get us a coffee,' she said, as Madeleine went to their old table in the corner.

Nicole came back to the table with not only the coffee but two half-baguettes with slices of ham on the side, and Madeleine, suddenly ravenous and unable to wait, had already torn her baguette down the middle and stuffed the ham into it by the time Nicole returned carrying the promised gateau.

About to put the baguette into her mouth, she glanced at Nicole, who was watching her curiously. Madeleine apologized, 'Sorry, Nicole, but I'm so hungry.'

'It's OK, Madeleine,' Nicole said, looking concerned. 'Didn't you have any breakfast this morning?'

'Only a slice of bread,' Madeleine answered, biting into her baguette and chewing with gusto.

Nicole filled her own baguette with ham, and, eating quietly, wondered whether this would be a good time to tell Madeleine her news. But she was stopped by Madeleine's sudden sob.

'Nicole, I am so scared, I don't know what to do,' Madeleine said.

'You can take your time, you know,' Nicole said soothingly. 'You don't have to make any decisions until you are ready. Look, Madeleine.' She took hold of her hand. 'If you decide to take a different course about . . . you know . . . the baby,' she whispered, 'you can stay with us as long as you want.'

Madeleine looked questioningly at Nicole.

Nicole smiled. 'Oh, you don't need to worry about Maman,' she said. 'I've cleared it with her.'

Madeleine sniffed and blew her nose. 'But your Maman is going to—'

'Maman has been in to see me already this morning.'

'Oh?' Madeleine looked at her in surprise.

'Look, stay calm, Madeleine, but she has found someone who can help you. That is, well, if you still feel the same about . . .' She stopped and looked around at the three old biddies sitting across from them, before whispering, '. . . going ahead with—' Nicole hesitated.

'Getting rid of the baby,' Madeleine finished for her. Then she added, 'It's against everything I believe in, against my religion, against all that my parents and family have ever believed, and the thought of it terrifies me, but what choice do I have?'

Nicole looked at her friend and felt terrible. Because what she hadn't told Madeleine yet was that when her mother had called by earlier, it had been to let her know that not only had she had found someone willing to help, but had made an appointment for Madeleine to meet them at three o'clock the following afternoon. When Ginette told Nicole the appointment was with Madame Cutto, she'd looked at her mother in disbelief.

'But, Maman, we *can't* send her there, she is *horrible*!'

'I know everyone calls her Madame Cutto, but that

doesn't mean she actually uses a *knife*!' Ginette went on to explain briefly that, because no one had ever known Madame Cutto's real name, girls in trouble during the war had started calling her that, because it sounded like *couteau* – and it had stuck. 'That's *all* it is, a nickname,' Ginette said. Then she'd added, 'She's helped lots of young girls out, you know.'

'But at what cost!' Nicole had exclaimed. 'Some of them died, and others caught terrible infections and could never have babies again.'

'Yes, well, those are the risks of abortion. Everyone knows that. Look, Nicole, no one is forcing Madeleine, and I don't know anyone else who'll do it. They've all vanished into the woodwork since vigilantes started cleaning our streets of "collaborators". Those lunatics think the only girls who had abortions were the ones who slept with Germans. Anyway, if Madeleine decides to do it, I suggest you go with her.' She'd handed Nicole the address, and with a quick peck on each cheek, left.

Madeleine broke the silence. 'When?' she asked listlessly.

'Three o'clock,' Nicole answered.

'What day?'

'Tomorrow.'

'*Tomorrow!*' Madeleine exclaimed in horror.

'Look, I will come with you. And if you don't like it we will leave. OK?'

Madeleine looked down at the uneaten portion of gateau that Nicole had placed in front of her, and pushed the plate away. 'Sorry, Nicole, I can't eat now.'

'Me neither,' said Nicole, putting her fork down.

Suddenly feeling queasy, Madeleine jumped up from her chair and, clutching her stomach, ran for the toilet. A second longer and she wouldn't have made it in time.

Nicole, following closely behind, rushed to Madeleine's side and held her hair back while she retched. When Madeleine finally lifted her swollen, tear-soaked face, Nicole felt her heart would break. To stop herself crying too, she made a big deal of rummaging around in the sleeve of her cardigan, and eventually pulled out a crumpled handkerchief that Madeleine accepted gratefully, before blowing her nose.

She made such a loud noise that under normal circumstances they would have been in fits of giggles about it. Madeleine, aware of this, smiled through her tears. Nicole smiled back and held her close. 'It will be all right, Madeleine. You'll see,' she said.

Squeezing Nicole's hand in response, Madeleine said, 'I don't know what I'd do without you. Thank you so much for taking me into your home.'

'About Maman—' Nicole suddenly felt the need to explain.

'I like your maman. There's no need to explain anything,' Madeleine said.

'Well, now that I can speak freely about our life, I just want you to know that although Maman does . . . that . . . she is not without principles.'

'I know,' Madeleine said gently, still wiping away her tears.

'Please,' Nicole implored, gripping Madeleine's arm, 'I really want you to listen to this.'

'Of course I will.' Madeleine ran the tap so she could wash her face.

'Come through when you're ready,' Nicole told her, 'and I'll tell you.'

Madeleine nodded, then splashed water over her face while Nicole made her way back into the café, walking past the three old biddies, who were sitting there curiously, waiting to see what happened next. One of them whispered, 'Another little whore in trouble!'

'Is there anything else you need before you leave?' Nicole said, staring hard at them and opening the door of the *boulangerie*. They tutted and muttered as they got up from their seats and walked out.

With a shrug of her shoulders Nicole sat down and glanced at Céline, her assistant, who had just appeared behind the counter. Nicole smiled at her, appreciating the way she'd arrived so promptly to take over. Céline nodded back, then began wiping down the glass display case containing bread and sandwiches.

As Madeleine emerged from the toilets, Céline glanced over and asked, 'Would you like another coffee?'

Madeleine smiled and shook her head.

Nicole asked, 'Are you feeling better?'

Madeleine nodded briefly and said, 'What did you want to tell me?'

'Well,' Nicole began, 'as you know, the occupation seemed to last for ever.'

Madeleine didn't need to answer. It was obvious from her expression that she and her family had suffered in the occupation, too.

'Anyway,' Nicole continued, 'at first everyone said they'd spit in the Germans' faces. But when it came down to it, very few did. Anyone who defied them was taken away and tortured or killed, and soon almost everyone else was ready to do whatever they said, just to survive. But I'm sure I don't need to tell you that.' She smiled. 'Unfortunately the Germans were convinced that the French were immoral and decadent. Even officers thought they could do what they liked, especially with women. And, as you know, food, heating and clothing were in short supply. We were eating all kinds of rubbish, and it wasn't long before ordinary decent women – usually housewives and mothers whose husbands were away fighting or locked up as prisoners of war – were prostituting themselves just to eat. Well . . . not all of them did it to survive. Some actually *liked* the Germans, and they were treated well. They had plenty to eat, and beautiful clothes, and went to the cinema, and nightclubs and dances. Needless to say, there were many pregnancies, which in turn led to countless abortionists setting up in business. Some of these had no experience at all, and just saw it as a way of making money out of others' misfortune. And of course, sexual diseases were rife. In fact, one of the few good things the Germans did was to introduce compulsory medical check-ups. But Maman and her girls had always done that anyway . . .'

Nicole suddenly stopped talking, causing Madeleine to ask, 'Are you OK?'

'Yes . . . yes,' she said, as if shaking off an unpleasant memory.

'Even girls my age formed liaisons with the Germans,' she continued, then added wryly. 'They preferred younger women, you know.'

'Yes, I do know that,' said Madeleine quietly.

'Oh, Madeleine, you have your secrets, too! You must tell me.'

'I will, but not today.' She squeezed Nicole's hand and implored, 'Please go on.'

'The reason I'm telling you all this is because never once in all those difficult times did Maman resort to fraternizing with the Germans, and I am so proud of her for that. But they kept coming to our door, and when Maman refused to let them in . . . well, one day they dragged her outside and beat her.'

'*Mon Dieu!*' Madeleine whispered, horrified.

Nicole continued, 'I nursed her with the help of the girls who worked for her at the time. It took a long time for her to recover, and once she was well enough . . . well, that was when the girls left. They were far too afraid to stay after that, and who could blame them?'

Madeleine sat there, stunned, feeling huge admiration for Ginette. Then she leaned towards Nicole. 'I'm so honoured you felt able to tell me all this.'

'One good thing now, is that I think that I've convinced Maman not to do that work any more. She has managed to save quite a bit from her earnings, and

I'm quite capable of earning enough to support us. I only took a job here at the *boulangerie* to be close to her. I'll probably leave soon and look for something better,' she added this last in a whisper, so Céline couldn't hear.

'Maybe it's all turned out for the best, then?' Madeleine said.

'I hope so. But right now we have more pressing things to think about. Are you going to keep that appointment?'

'Yes.'

Nicole was astonished. 'Really?'

'I'm going to see Madame Cutto first, and then I'll make my decision,' Madeleine said, speaking very fast, as if afraid she'd change her mind. Surprised to see the uncertainty on Nicole's face she added, 'It can't do any harm just to meet her . . . can it?'

Without answering the question, Nicole said, 'I'll be with you, anyway.'

Madeleine glanced at her gratefully.

Boulogne, France
Tuesday, 4 December 1945

Madame Cutto lived in a dilapidated end-of-terrace house near the docks. The whole area had been heavily bombed, and they had to scramble over rubble to get to her front door.

The door was answered by a thin, small-boned woman, her hair pulled tightly back from a sharp face.

She wore a plain black dress that looked faintly greasy. She studied them both thoughtfully before leading them through a narrow hallway, and across a well-worn linoleum floor to a back room. It felt unusually cold in there, even though it was a mild and sunny day outside. The room smelled odd, of damp and mustiness covering something disagreeable and faintly feral. But then it was very dirty. Flies buzzed round it, the net curtains were brown and torn, and there were unwashed dishes in a sink at the back. A wooden box stood next to a dusty table, and the only redeeming feature of the place, as far as Nicole was concerned, were the framed photographs nailed to the walls. They showed groups of very solemn, formally dressed people, and Nicole assumed that they must be Madame Cutto's family, and felt reassured. It made the woman seem less chilly, and more human.

'So this is the girl who needs my help?' Madame Cutto asked. She smiled slightly, showing small, grey teeth.

Concerned that Madeleine still hadn't said anything, Nicole glanced at her. She was standing with her arms by her sides, gazing at the box.

'Yes,' Nicole said.

Madame Cutto nodded. She picked up the box and set it on the table. Then she swilled out one of the dishes in the sink and slowly filled it with water from the tap. Then she shook powder into it from a grimy packet.

'And it is eight, nine weeks?' she said, her back turned to them.

'That's right,' Nicole said, since Madeleine didn't answer.

'And you have two hundred francs for me, yes?' Madame Cutto turned round. She set the bowl carefully on the table and rolled up her sleeves.

Nicole noticed that Madeleine was still staring at the box. When Madame Cutto had put it on the table the lid had moved, and something had flopped out of one corner: a length of red rubber tubing, with a bulbous, grimy contraption on the end. Before Nicole could answer Madame Cutto, Madeleine had bolted from the room and down the hallway. She was halfway down the street before Nicole caught up with her.

'I can't, I can't bear it,' Madeleine burst out, her hands curled into fists. 'She was going to do it there and then Nicole!'

'OK! It's OK! No one is forcing you.' Gently she took Madeleine's arm. 'Come on, let's go home.'

They walked in silence, and had nearly reached the flat when they were approached by two very large, dishevelled-looking women. One of them spat repeatedly on the pavement in front of Nicole, and the other looked her up and down in disdain and yelled the vilest obscenities Madeleine had ever heard.

When they'd gone Madeleine, trembling, asked Nicole, 'What was all that about?'

'Oh, ignore it,' Nicole answered, seemingly unconcerned. 'You have too many worries of your own to think about right now.'

Ginette opened the door of the apartment for them. 'Maman, what are you doing home so early?' Nicole asked.

'Is it done? The appointment, I mean,' Ginette asked.

'No, Madam Cutto was preparing to do it straight away!' Nicole answered.

Madeleine rushed to explain. 'I'm so sorry, Ginette, I just didn't realize—'

Ginette gripped Madeleine's arm. 'No need to explain, I understand, but you must make a decision about this baby soon!'

Unexpectedly, Madeleine said, 'I will get it done. I will have the abortion . . .' She swallowed. 'Tomorrow, if possible.'

'Tomorrow!' Nicole exclaimed. 'But we've only just got back from there!'

'I know . . . I know!' Madeleine looked at Ginette. 'That's if you can arrange it again for me, please?'

Ginette looked into Madeleine's eyes, and the hopelessness she saw there brought a lump to her throat. 'Well, I'll try . . . but if you back out again you won't get another chance. Madame Cutto doesn't like being messed around. Do you understand?'

'I understand. It was just such a shock, meeting her, and seeing that room . . . and that box! But I know I have to do it. I know I do.'

'Are you sure?' Nicole asked, before adding tentatively, 'Maybe you should wait a little longer before making up your mind.'

Fighting the panic inside her, Madeleine answered, 'I'm sure. I'm going to do it. I can be brave when I need to be.' Her voice trembled as she said this, and she looked round at them defiantly.

Chapter 22

Boulogne, France
Wednesday, 5 December 1945

Dominic peered in through the window of the *boulangerie* for the umpteenth time, while Tom, drawing heavily on his cigarette, rattled and banged on the door.

A voice across the street called out, 'It's closed.'

They turned around to see an old woman sitting on her doorstep.

'Oh, excuse me, do you know where a girl called Nicole, who works there, lives?' Dominic asked hopefully.

'Oh, that one!' The old woman spat. 'Well, the *boulangerie* is closed now.'

'Yes, we know it is closed. That's why we want to know how to find her.' Dominic forced himself to be patient.

'There's no need to shout! I'm not deaf!' the old woman retorted.

Tom dropped his cigarette to the ground and stamped it out with his foot, before walking over and crouching in front of the old woman, saying very slowly, in English, 'Please, this is very important . . . do you know her address?'

'Ah! An Engleesh man,' she said with a glint in her eye. 'I *like* ze Engleesh man.' She grinned. Then, glancing disapprovingly at Dominic, who had annoyed her by his brusqueness, she asked, 'Why do you want her? Is she in trouble? That one's always in trouble!'

Dominic tried Tom's tactic, and crouched down beside her, explaining as calmly as he could, 'No, Nicole isn't, but I think that my sister may be with her, and she *is* in trouble. Please, if you know where she lives,' he begged, 'tell us.'

'Your sister, you say.' She thought for a moment. 'Well, you need to get her away from there as quickly as possible, before anything worse happens to her.'

'The name of the road, please?' There was a faint edge to Dominic's tone now, which made it clear that he wouldn't take much more of being messed around.

'Rue de la Mer,' the old woman said suddenly, pointing to her right.

'*Merci*,' said Tom, gratefully squeezing her hand.

Dominic impatiently dragged him away. 'Come on, Tom!'

As they broke into a run the old woman's shrill voice shouted from behind them, 'Ask any man who lives round there, and he'll show you where the house is!'

*   *   *

After a restless night, Madeleine, unable to eat, and feeling a desperate need for fresh air, went for a long walk.

Ginette had been to see Madame Cutto the night before, and after a lot of argument, succeeded in bribing her with a few extra francs to give Madeleine another chance. She was to be there at four o'clock sharp.

The day had dragged, and yet already it was time to go.

Once more Madeleine and Nicole were setting off for the docks, but this time, at Madeleine's request, Ginette was going to go with them. At the bottom of the stairs they stopped, took a deep breath, and held hands before Ginette opened the front door.

The scene that greeted them outside was so horrendous that Ginette fell over in panic while trying to push the two girls back in. The seething angry mob had toppled Nicole over in the doorway, making it impossible to shut the door. Madeleine was trying to pull her friend free, when an enormous ruddy-faced woman, who Madeleine recognized as the one who'd spat at her and Nicole the previous day, pushed the door, holding it open against the wall.

Madeleine tried to push her huge hand off the door. But the woman just laughed raucously and put her foot on Nicole – who was now lying with her head inside the doorway and her feet hanging over the top step. Seconds later a pair of rough hands gripped Nicole by the feet, and, to Madeleine's horror, she was dragged down the stone steps, by which time Ginette had already been bound with rope and was being pushed and pulled down the road by two bald, toothless men.

Gasping with terror, Madeleine struggled to get away from the fat woman, who had seized her in a bear hug. Then a hand hit her painfully hard across the mouth. She recoiled, stunned, and two men seized the opportunity to bundle her out of the house and down the steps. She pounded with her fists against the rock-hard chest of one of them, his vile grin revealing his decaying teeth. She screamed, then, and struggled even more desperately, her body debilitated, she fell to the ground. As she was dragged down the street she wondered why this was happening. Surely it was just a nightmare? Or maybe she was delirious . . . yes, that must be it! She would wake up and find herself back at home with Maman and Papa, any minute now. This comforting thought allowed her to endure the indignity as she was buffeted along different streets, half-carried, half-dragged by the nightmarish crowd.

She was only vaguely aware of Ginette and Nicole in the press of people in front of her. Curses and cheers rose from the crowd. The odours of sweat, cigarettes, alcohol, and fried food rose from the people pushing her. She put her hand to her face; it felt wet and slimy. Someone growled, 'Dirty whore!' She heard them clearly, just as another gob of spit landed on her face.

Eventually the crowd came to a standstill and she realized Nicole was next to her. Why was Nicole shaking her? 'Madeleine! Madeleine! Wake up!' Her screeching gave Madeleine a headache. She looked round and everything came into sharp focus. She realized she was in the market square and Ginette was being strapped to a chair while someone stood over her, waving a pair of shears. There were other women she didn't recognize on other chairs. Why was that?

'Madeleine! Tell them! For God's sake, tell them who you are!' Nicole was yelling.

But all that Madeleine wanted at this moment was for Nicole to be quiet.

Nicole, seeing the hopelessness of trying to get through to Madeleine, now pleaded with her captors, 'We are not collaborators, and we never fraternized with the Nazis. My mother was beaten because of it. Surely you heard about that! And this is my friend, Madeleine Pelletier. She came to visit us two days ago. She lives in Marck . . .'

But the group of vigilantes were so full of adrenalin by now that her words meant nothing to them. 'Shut up, you dirty whore, and watch how your mother's hair falls to the ground. It'll be your turn next,' a foul-smelling woman informed her with glee.

Nicole trembled uncontrollably. She wondered at all these people, just standing here, staring, like those ghouls who'd watched the guillotines at work years before. Disgusted and sickened by their morbid curiosity, she barely noticed the pain of her bruised body and cracked ribs.

'We are not collaborators,' she tried again, 'my mother runs a business!' She was shouting, but her words seemed to come out in a whisper.

'Business! Is that what you call it?' a bent old woman with a mole on her cheek spat at Nicole, while the rest of the crowd cheered and clapped.

Hopelessly, Nicole turned away, only to see the almost unrecognizable figure of her mother, her bruised head bleeding round the few remaining jagged tufts of hair, stumble towards her.

'Nicole,' Ginette's voice trembled.

'Maman . . . oh Maman!' Nicole fell to her knees, and was promptly dragged upright and carried to a vacant chair.

As the chair wobbled precariously on the uneven cobbles, her head fell back and she called out, 'You have got this wrong. So wrong!'

Madeleine reached out towards her. 'Don't hurt her, please don't hurt her.'

The savage holding Madeleine tightened his grip, and growled, 'Hurt her? She's lucky not to be executed.'

Madeleine looked around helplessly, unable to believe her own countrymen could behave with such barbarity.

When the woman with the shears approached Nicole, Madeleine tried to turn her head away, but the man with his arms round her had no intention of allowing her to miss the entertainment. He grabbed her by the hair and dragged her head round to face the front. 'You watch,' he grunted.

Madeleine's knees were giving way as she sobbed, 'She is innocent, we are all innocent!' But no one listened. Her knees trembling like jelly, she turned sharply as she felt the pressure of a hand on her shoulder. She found herself looking into Ginette's tear-filled eyes. Her expression of anguish and hopelessness told Madeleine there was no reasoning with these people.

As she felt herself being lifted she heard Ginette call out, 'No! She's pregnant!' It was the worst thing she could have said.

'Pregnant, eh?' One of the women grinned at her skinny little accomplice, whose shrew-like eyes darted from side to side. She shouted, 'Do you hear that, everybody? This one is pregnant! A present left by one of the German bastards, no doubt!'

'The Germans left long ago, how could she be pregnant by one of them, you idiot!'

Ginette was immediately silenced with a forceful slap across the face. 'Shut your mouth, bitch, or we might just decide to cut your tongue out as well.'

Although Ginette reeled from the slap she did not put her hand to her burning face, but stood straight and lifted her head proudly, refusing to show any weakness.

When Madeleine heard Ginette call out, something within her stirred into action; she knew that, no matter what, she must save her baby. She began to struggle fiercely with her captors, one of whom was pushing her into the chair, while another bound the rope around her. She kicked out hitting the man in front of her in the groin. Momentarily he doubled in pain, but when he straightened up he hit Madeleine so hard across the face that the chair she was bound to toppled over onto its side.

'Aah, she's got some grit, this one!' called the woman holding the shears, waving them in the air. The onlookers cheered and called out excitedly, 'Cut off her hair! Cut! Cut! Cut!'

Meantime, Tom had the ominous feeling that something bad was about to happen, though he didn't know what, and was running ahead when he was pulled to a skidding halt by Dominic, who grabbed his sleeve and breathlessly pointed up at a street sign.

Tom read it and said, 'Rue de la Mer. OK, let's go!' He turned abruptly, accidentally knocking a walking stick from the hand of an old man tottering along the footpath. 'Oh, pardon, monsieur!' Tom apologized, picking up the stick and handing it to the flustered old man.

'Young people, always in such a hurry,' the man complained, accepting his stick gratefully.

Dominic, coming up behind Tom, asked the man, 'I don't suppose you know a girl named Nicole, who works in the *boulangerie* down the road? I understand she lives round here with her mother?'

'Oh yes. I know Nicole, a nice little girl, but I'm not so sure about her mother—' the old man said.

'Could you show us where they live?' Dominic interrupted.

'It's the first one in the first block after the rubble. Top floor.' Too unsteady to turn around, the old man pointed his stick over his shoulder.

'Thank you,' they called back, as they ran in that direction.

Arriving at the block of houses, their eyes were drawn straight to the door, which was standing wide open. They glanced at each other without speaking, ran up the porch steps and entered. After taking the inner stairs two at a time they were faced with a shut door. Tom knocked gently, and when there was no answer Dominic thumped with his fist.

'It isn't locked,' said Tom, pressing the handle and finding that it yielded.

Tentatively they walked in. There was no sound, until Dominic suddenly exclaimed, 'Oh, *mon Dieu!*'

'What? What is it? asked Tom, startled.

Dominic pointed to a divan. 'That is Madeleine's valise, I would recognize it anywhere.'

'Well, where the hell is she?' Tom exploded. 'And why was the front door wide open?' he demanded, as if Dominic would have the answer.

'Hello, is anyone there?'

'Hello!' someone answered from downstairs.

Tom stayed at the top while Dominic ran downstairs to be greeted at the bottom by a man whose body seemed to fill the open doorway. 'There will be no business here today,' he said in a bullying tone Dominic disliked.

'What do you mean, no business?'

'The three women have been taken away.'

'What three women?' Dominic asked impatiently.

'The two women who run this place, of course, and another young one I hadn't seen before.'

Dominic quickly translated this to Tom, before asking where they'd been taken and why.

'Why?' the man said. 'Because they collaborated with the Germans, of course. They're being punished in the square with others who escaped the first time. About time, too. It's taken long enough.'

As big as the man was, Dominic grabbed him with both hands and pinned him against the wall. 'You mean to tell me that people are *still* being publicly shamed? The war finished months ago, for God's sake!'

'It's not my fault that they've only just rounded up the last load of whores!'

Tightening his grip, Dominic almost growled, '*Where's the square?*'

'Just down the road.' The man pointed a trembling finger.

Dominic loosened his grip and thrust the man to one side. 'Tom! Hurry!' he urged.

Madeleine lay on her side, still strapped to the chair, screaming to be set free. She thrashed and flailed from side to side, in a paroxysm of fear. The roar of the crowd seemed to fade as she struggled, and for a single instant she felt strangely at one with the earth. She relaxed, and fell face down, and the smell of the damp dirt wedged between the cobbles reached her nostrils. She inhaled deeply, revelling in its pungency.

But then the roar of the crowd came back, and she was aware, again, of the monsters standing round her and jerking her chair upright again. They were laughing, a terrible, sinister sound. It was so loud it felt as if someone had suddenly turned up the volume on a wireless somewhere. The noise, along with the blurred sight of Ginette and Nicole, in their bloodstained clothes, clinging to each other in anguish, was the last thing that she was aware of.

Nicole held a button tightly. She'd picked it up from the cobbles, where it had fallen from Madeleine's dress. She looked over at Madeleine and saw she had collapsed. Her lips had gone so pale they looked blue.

'Oh, Maman!' she cried into her mother's ear. 'If this doesn't make Madeleine lose the baby, then nothing will.' And, unable to control her sobbing, she added in a whisper, 'That's if she's still alive!'

Ginette clutched her sobbing daughter and looked around in disbelief. Surely the gendarmes weren't pretending this wasn't happening? There wasn't a single one to be seen!

Tom and Dominic skidded into the square and were rendered speechless by what they saw.

At first it was difficult to take in exactly what was going on, and then Dominic nudged Tom's arm and pointed. Tom immediately focused on the spot in the middle where a group of dishevelled people were trying to lift an overturned chair. There was an unconscious woman roped into it, her unsupported head flopping backwards at each jerking movement of the chair.

Tom sucked in a huge gasp of air and roared like a wild animal. The veins on his neck swelled. Anger making him fearless and invincible, he hurled himself at the crowd. The look on his face was so terrifying that people scrambled out of his way. He shouldered through, knocking people down, punching them to the ground, kicking them aside. Even the group who'd been trying to lift Madeleine's chair turned to flee at the sight of this lunatic, screaming a war cry and barrelling towards them.

Dominic followed close behind, and got there just as Tom crouched over Madeleine. She was on the ground, still tied to the chair, completely motionless. One of the onlookers tried to help pick up the chair, but Tom punched him on the jaw, sending him reeling back. He turned and faced the crowd, his hands curled into fists, his teeth bared.

'Don't touch her,' he snarled. And even though he spoke in English, the rabble backed away, understanding completely what he meant. There was such fury on his face, and in his tensed muscles, that they flinched. He glared round at their faces and shook his fist at them, before turning back to the chair and lifting it with Dominic's help.

'She's breathing,' Tom said quietly, loosening the ropes.

Madeleine half-opened her eyes. She thought she could see Tom's face leaning over her, and assumed she was hallucinating. She shut them again. Whatever happened to her now didn't matter. Let them do it. They could cut off her hair . . . and then leave her to die . . .

Tom picked her up in his arms, and turned to get out of the square, his heart still thumping furiously, knowing he'd never forget this moment. As he began walking through the dispersing crowd, Dominic by his side, he noticed two pitiful-looking women, bald and bleeding, clinging together and watching him intently. He gave them a curious glance and the younger one came up to him, her eyes dark against a dead-white face, and asked quietly, in English, 'Are you Tom?'

'Yes,' he answered.

'Then follow me,' she said, her tone so reasonable that he complied. Behind him, Dominic put his arm tenderly around the older woman, overwhelmed by pity at her plight, and together they walked out of the square.

There was a tap, tap, tap, on the side of Madeleine's face.

'Maddie!' another light tap. 'Maddie!'

Madeleine's eyes opened reluctantly – and there he was again! Tom! Tom's smiling face, with its deep dimples! Why did he keep appearing like this? She closed her eyes again, and another voice spoke. Why wouldn't they just let her sleep?

'Madeleine! Madeleine!' the voice said. It sounded so familiar, so dear.

She murmured disbelievingly, 'Dominic? Is that you, Dominic?'

'Yes, it's me, little sister.' Dominic held her cold hand in both of his.

She squinted up at him. '*Mon Dieu*,' she squinted again. 'It *is* you . . . ! Oh, Dominic, I've had such a horrific nightmare!'

'I know, I know,' he consoled. 'But you are here now and everything will be fine.'

'And Tom was in it! Why would Tom be in it, Dominic?' she whispered.

'That's because he is here ... with me,' Dominic replied carefully, unsure what her reaction would be.

'What! He is here? Right here?' She tried to lift her head.

'Shh, shh, Madeleine. Stay calm,' Dominic told her. 'Yes, he is here.' He turned to look at Tom and beckoned him forward.

'Tom?'

'Yes, it *is* me, Maddie,' he said cautiously.

'Oh, *mon Dieu*, Tom, why are you here? And where am I?' she said, trying to look around her, totally forgetting that she needed to speak in English to Tom.

Tom put his hand tenderly on her brow. 'Oh, Maddie, Maddie, I'm so sorry, pet. So sorry for everything!'

'Where am I?' she asked more lucidly, now that it was beginning to dawn on her that this might not be a dream after all.

'You're in Nicole's home,' Dominic said.

At this she raised herself from the divan. And, seized by sudden fear, she tried to call out, but her voice was nothing more than a croak. 'Nicole! She is in danger!'

'We arrived too late, Maddie,' Tom said gently. 'Nicole and her maman were already injured when we arrived at the market square. They sheared off their hair.'

As Dominic translated, it all came back to her: the

horror of seeing Nicole and Ginette in such a dreadful state. She lay back down again, and closed her eyes, whispering over and over, '*Non! Oh non!*'

Nicole rushed to her side. 'Don't fret, Madeleine! We're OK. Look,' she said, pointing to the scarf on her head. 'Very chic, don't you think?' Then, seeing Ginette standing in the open kitchen doorway, Nicole beckoned her over. 'See, we match!' Nicole said lightly, pointing to her mother's head. They both wore turquoise silk scarves, knotted at the back, turban style.

Ginette fidgeted nervously. Madeleine was shocked to see such a proud, confident woman looking so crushed. Ginette said haltingly, 'It all happened because of me, Madeleine. I am so sorry, so very sorry.'

Madeleine took her hand. 'It's OK, Ginette, *I* know, and Nicole knows, that you never did any favours for those German bastards. And those idiots, those monsters out there . . .' She pointed towards the door. 'They haven't any idea what special people you both are, and what you risked to avoid doing the very thing you were unjustly accused of. I hope they all rot in hell!'

'Hey, calm down, little sister.' Dominic sat next to her.

'Nicole and Ginette must see a doctor!' Madeleine wasn't ready to quieten down just yet. 'They must have their bruises attended to and—'

'We have seen a doctor, Madeleine,' Nicole interrupted, 'and so have you, although you don't remember it.' Madeleine was about to answer when Nicole continued, 'Anyway, we will talk about all that

311

later. Right now I think you need some time alone with Tom.' She and Ginette retreated to the kitchen, with Dominic following close behind.

Tom sat on the edge of the divan and turned her head to face him, then said gently, 'I know how hard things have been for you, Maddie. And I know I was bad. I was so mean to you. I should have written, and I didn't. Can you forgive me?'

She smiled at him and squeezed his hand.

He went on, 'I know you'll likely say no, and I don't blame you if you do, because I've no right to ask this . . . but . . .' He paused, and swallowed.

Madeleine was looking at him closely, as if lip-reading. There was a tiny wrinkle of concentration on her forehead. He was pretty sure she'd understood everything he'd said so far. He spoke more slowly, just in case she hadn't. 'I love you so much, Maddie. So much. Could you . . . Would you think of . . . coming back with me? Back to England . . . as my wife?'

Maybe it was too soon to ask her this, because she seemed to have some difficulty in responding. But when she did, he was so astonished, so relieved that he felt his heart would burst.

'Yes, Tom, I will.'

'Aw, lass.' His arms were around her now. 'We'll make it work. I think I've learned my lesson.' He bent forward and kissed her gently on the mouth. 'We'll be a family . . . a proper family! You'll see.'

She placed her hand on her stomach, before asking, 'The baby?'

'Yes, we still have our baby,' Tom smiled.

'But will I fit? In England?' she asked, suddenly afraid of what her answer had meant.

'Don't you worry about that, lass, I'll be with you . . . all the way. I love you, and that's all we need. All we'll ever need.'

Chapter 23

''Eee's done *what*!' This wasn't a question, but a statement. Jessie stood, hands on hips, aghast and disbelieving, in the middle of Hannah's living room.

Before Hannah could answer, Jessie spat out her next words. 'And just when did 'ee go, may I ask?'

'A few days back.' Hannah was deliberately being vague.

'And didn't anybody see fit ter let *me* know, like?'

'It was all done in such a hurry, lass. There was no time.' Hannah bent the truth a little, to save Jessie's feelings.

Jessie paced around, saying nothing for a moment.

Hannah added, truthfully this time, 'Ah haven't been able ter believe it meself, yet!'

'And *why*, might I ask, 'as 'ee gone ter France?'

'Look, yer'll 'ave ter talk ter 'im yerself when 'ee gets

314

back, lass. It's not up ter me ter talk ter yer about it,' Hannah said awkwardly.

'It's some lass, isn't it.'

Again this wasn't a question. Jessie stared at Hannah, until Hannah, ashamed, conceded, 'Aye, it's a lass.'

Jessie jumped up. 'Well, *no* wonder 'ee's been such an arse'ole with me, then!'

'Now, now, Jessie. There's no need fer that kind of language.'

'Well, that's nowt ter what 'ee'll get from me when 'ee gets back!' Jessie stood in front of the fire now, one hand resting on the mantelpiece, and when her laugh rang out Hannah visibly jumped. ''Eee's got 'er pregnant!' Jessie said, nodding her head in absolute certainty now, as she started to pace the floor again. 'That's it!' she repeated. ''Ees got 'er pregnant.'

Hannah turned away, her lips pressed tightly together.

Jessie's eyes widened. 'Well, you sayin' nowt says all!' There was a distinct quiver in her voice now as she glared at Hannah's back. And with still no answer from her, Jessie continued her tirade. 'Well, if 'ee's thinkin' of fetchin' 'er back here, yer can be sure ah'll be around ter welcome 'er. There's a thing or two she needs ter know before she gets 'er feet under the table.'

This obvious threat caused Hannah to grip tightly on to the front of her pinny as she answered. 'Ah know me lad hasn't behaved well towards yer, pet, but ah'm askin' yer, please don't cause any trouble when they get here, it'll be difficult enough as it is.'

315

'*Difficult!* Do yer have any idea just how *difficult* this whole *bloody* life is fer me? *Huh!*' Jessie gave a bitter laugh. Then, with a jerk of her head, she rushed from the room, and out of the back door, leaving it wide open.

As Hannah walked over to close it she shivered, even though it wasn't really cold outside, considering it was coming up to Christmas. I wish our Rene would hurry up and get herself home from work, she thought.

Jeannie, oblivious to what had been going on, came wandering down the stairs. 'Gran, can yer sharpen me pencil for uz?' she asked. She held the pencil up while absent-mindedly looking for something suitable to draw on. When there was no answer from Hannah, she walked round in front of her and peered up into her face, asking tentatively, 'Are yer vexed with me, Gran?'

Hannah turned towards her and cleared the lump from her throat before answering softly, 'No, ah'm not vexed with yer, pet.' She patted Jeannie's head affectionately.

'Who are yer vexed with, then?' Jeannie asked.

'Oh pet, ah think ah'm vexed with everything at the moment. Ah still haven't heard anything from our Tom, either.'

Jeannie took hold of her Gran's hand, and said in the most consoling way she could muster, 'Oh, he'll be all right, Gran. Our Tom fought in t' war and managed ter look after 'imself, didn't he? Anyway, it'll be Christmas soon, and he won't want ter miss that now, will he?'

Hannah smiled to herself, realizing just how

grown-up and thoughtful her granddaughter was. She said, 'Yes, pet, yer right. Everybody'll be here by Christmas.'

'Gran?'

'Yes, pet?'

'Yer know that lad what's moved in down the road?'

'The Mortimer lad?'

'Yes, well, his name's Eee-an.'

'Yes, Ian Mortimer. What about him?'

'Well, yer know 'ee talks posh, bein' that 'ee comes from down South, and he's goin' ter be startin' at the grammar school in Bishop?'

'Yes?'

'Well, yer know 'ow we're movin' ter Bishop?'

'Ye-es.'

'Well, ah've told 'im that he'll be able ter come ter visit us, and come for 'is tea an' all sometimes.'

'Well, ah don't know what yer mam'll 'ave ter say about that, lass.'

'Well, see, 'ee doesn't know anybody here, and ah won't know anybody in Bishop, so what ah thought was, that 'ee could learn *me* ter talk posh like 'im, and that'd keep me mam happy. And ah'll learn 'im ter talk like me, and that'll help 'im ter fit in better at 'ees new school, cause 'ee's a bit posh fer round 'ere, like!'

Hannah started laughing hysterically.

'Gran! Gran, what's the matter?' Jeannie yanked at the bottom of Hannah's pinny and pushed it up to her hands. 'Eee, wipe yer face, Gran. Why are yer cryin'?'

Hannah dabbed at her eyes with the crumpled hem of

her pinny. 'Ay, pet! Yer better than any tonic, you are. Come on, let's get tea ready fer when yer mam an' yer grandda get home.'

An hour or so later Rene came rushing in through the back door. 'Look, Mam! A telegram from our Tom!' she shouted, hardly able to contain her excitement. 'I called in to the post office on the way home and they were just going to bring it round!'

Hannah perked up. 'Come on, then, lass. What does it say?'

'It says, "Have found Maddie stop, all is well, stop, be home in next few days, stop, Tom".'

'And that's it?' Hannah said. 'No word about whether or not he's bringin' this lass back with 'im?'

Rene gave Hannah a hug. 'There's only so much you can say in a telegram, Mam,' she explained. 'He's said the main things, that he's all right, and that they've found the girl. So I suppose we'll just have to wait and see what happens next.'

'Aye, yer right, pet. We'll just 'ave ter wait and see,' Hannah said, resigning herself. And after thinking for a few seconds, she added, 'Eee, ah've had a right ter-do with Jessie this afternoon, an' all.'

'Oh well, we knew that there'd be ructions in that quarter, now, didn't we? I'll go down and see her later, because she's not suited about me moving to Bishop, either. It'll be for the best all round, Mam, if we loosen ties with her. She's not good for our Tom, and she and I seem to have outgrown each other as well. She needs to move on. We all do.'

318

'Well, good luck ter yer with that, pet, cause she was spittin' blood when she left here. Mind, ah do feel a bit sorry for 'er. Our Tom could have left 'er a message or something.'

'You know our Tom, Mam. He can only deal with one crisis at a time.'

'Ah know, pet. Like yer said, we'll just have ter wait and see what happens.'

Boulogne, France
Monday, 10 December 1945

Saying goodbye to Nicole and Ginette had been a real ordeal for Madeleine. But she'd been heartened to hear them enthusiastically discussing their future, and how they were going to go on holiday to recuperate and talk about the changes they were going to make to their lives.

Nicole was equally happy to find out that Madeleine was going to marry Tom, and no longer wanted an abortion. She hoped that Madeleine and her family would hold their heads up high, just as she and her mother planned to do. She knew that the people who had assaulted her and Ginette so cruelly would never be punished, but part of her didn't mind, because she sensed that she and her maman, although victims right now, would be the winners in the end. Those monsters had inadvertently changed the course of their lives for the better.

Nicole smiled at the memory of the recent trip into the town centre with her maman. She couldn't remember them ever having spent the whole day shopping together before. And she'd never laughed as much, either. It had been such fun trying on all those scarves, wigs and hats, and searching for the most glamorous possible way to conceal their lack of hair.

When they'd arrived home, they'd had a further fit of the giggles as they'd modelled their purchases for Tom, Dominic and Madeleine. And their small audience had been so touched by their bravery, and the way they were making light of their predicament, that they hadn't known whether to laugh or cry.

But Tom and Dominic had quickly dispelled any hint of sadness by leaping up and modelling the hats and scarves themselves, strutting arrogantly about like mannequins and striking ridiculous poses. Madeleine had laughed so much that if she'd been a few months further into her pregnancy she might have given birth there and then. It was as she was wiping away tears of merriment that she had suddenly pressed her hand to her only slightly rounded stomach and thought: I *do* care about this baby, and I'm going to give it a decent, happy life.

Nicole hoped that she and the lovely Tom would succeed. For, handsome and caring as Tom was, she had no illusions about the huge problems Madeleine would face, once reality set in. Nicole worried that maybe Madeleine had been too hasty in agreeing to live in England with Tom, and that, once everything settled down, she might need to rethink the idea.

Nicole also noticed how carefully Dominic had hidden his dismay when Madeleine had told him she'd decided to go to England. Not wanting to influence her, he'd said nothing, and just hugged her affectionately.

Tom woke from a fitful sleep, and could think of nothing but Madeleine. Nicole had given him and Dominic her bed to sleep in; she was sharing her mother's room. He'd had no qualms about accepting the offer, because he'd realized that Nicole probably wanted an excuse to sleep in her mother's room. Neither she nor Ginette had actually said they were afraid to sleep alone, but they were both still very fragile, and he was sure they wanted to comfort and reassure each other.

He glanced over at Dominic, who was still sleeping soundly. Unable to settle, he jumped out of bed and dressed quickly, before running down the stairs two at a time – the way he always did. He took the key off the hook next to the hefty front door, and carefully unlocked it, then, once outside on the top step, quietly pulled the door to, and gave it a shake to make doubly sure that it was locked. He was taking no chances. He raced down the road and into the *boulangerie*, where he got Céline to help him load up with as many baguettes and pastries as he could carry, sure that the others would be as hungry as he was when they awoke. He was absolutely starving, and he couldn't think clearly about anything without food in his stomach. He *was* changing his whole life, after all, and he was going to need some sustenance to do that!

Marck, France

The journey to Marck went without incident, and when Maman rushed to embrace Madeleine, Papa noticeably held back. After she was released by Maman, uncertain what to do, Madeleine stood there looking nervously at Papa. His eyes suddenly filled with tears, he opened his arms wide, and she ran to him and sobbed.

Tom, who'd stood to one side while all this was going on, noticed that there'd been no formal greeting of a kiss on both cheeks. Just hugs and more hugs from everyone. Martine and Simone were desperate to know what had been happening, and Madeleine didn't keep them waiting. As soon as she'd pulled herself together, she walked over to Tom and held his hand. Then, looking at each member of her family appreciatively, she said, 'Maman, Papa, and my two beautiful sisters . . .'

Simone smiled dazzlingly.

Madeleine bit her lip and gripped Tom's hand tightly before continuing, 'I have decided to go to England with Tom.'

Maman, her lips pressed tightly together, turned away, and there was silence for a moment.

Tom's heart pounded when he saw tears in Martine's eyes, Papa shaking his head sadly, and Simone just gazing at Madeleine with her mouth slightly open. He sensed Maddie's nervousness as, with arms wide, a look of amazement on her face, she asked, 'Why is everyone so shocked? I thought that was what you wanted!' Tears welled up in her eyes, and as she fought them back, Tom put his hand on her shoulder.

Simone was the first to speak. Her gaze was fixed on Madeleine. 'Look, Madeleine, I know I haven't been the best of sisters, but please don't go because you think that *we* . . .' she gestured towards the family, '. . . can't cope with the situation. We have all discussed it, and decided that none of us care any more what other people think or say. We're a family, and that's all that matters.'

Madeleine was astonished by this speech from her sister. Could her attitude have changed that much *in a week*? But then, she thought, look how much I've changed in that time.

Martine proudly took hold of Simone's hand, while Maman said tearfully, 'We really all do feel the same, Madeleine. We did nothing but talk about it all while you were away, and we want you to stay. At least until you have more time to think. That's if you want to, of course.' She looked at her daughter pleadingly.

Papa added, 'Please don't run away from us, *ma fille*.'

Oh, Papa! Madeleine thought, if only you had said this a couple of weeks ago. She turned to Tom, blinking away tears, and he, having got the gist of most of the conversation, took hold of her hand again. He could see how torn she was, and, suddenly angry for her, he

323

squared his shoulders and glanced at her sisters before addressing her parents.

'God Almighty! Why on earth didn't you discuss all this before?' There was an embarrassed silence while Tom went on, 'Yes, I behaved badly. But do you want to know why I didn't write? Believe it or not it was as much for her sake as for mine. I saw no future for us in either of our countries, and I thought that we had to forget and move on with our lives. But the truth is that I couldn't forget her.' He looked down at Maddie. 'And I don't think she forgot about me, either.'

She looked up at him and squeezed his hand.

Dominic was wandering back up the garden from the toilet, reading a letter, when he heard Tom begin his tirade. He pushed the letter into a pocket and ran in at once. Then he stood next to Tom and translated what he was saying for the others.

Tom, calmer now, lowered his head towards Maddie. 'We want to get married.'

Madeleine turned and kissed him hard on the mouth. She held out her hand towards her sisters and parents. 'I do understand why you panicked when I first told you about the baby. Maybe we have all learned something from this, and I am so happy to know that you would have stood by me if I had decided to stay. But I think my place is with Tom now.' She glanced at her maman and smiled, before adding, 'That'll be best for me and the baby. Do you remember, Maman, the conversation we had about telling my baby who it's father was? Well, that won't be a problem any more. So many things will be simpler.'

'You do know your new life won't be easy, don't you, Madeleine?' Maman said anxiously.

'Yes. But I have to do this. Can't you see that?'

Maman hugged her youngest daughter, and whispered, 'I am so proud of you. We will always be here for you, don't forget that.'

'I won't, Maman.'

'Come,' her mother said, 'talk with me in the garden while I pick some herbs for the rabbit stew.'

Tom watched them walk off arm in arm. Then he turned to Dominic and said, 'I still can't believe she's going to be mine. That she said yes.'

'Of course she said yes.' Dominic was surprised that he'd ever thought she wouldn't. 'She's loved you from the day you met at that silly little fair.' He patted Tom on the back. 'Come on, let's open a bottle to celebrate. This needs a proper drink. Besides, I am celebrating, also.'

'Oh?' said Tom.

'Yes, I had a letter from the girl I told you about.'

Tom looked blank for a second. 'Ha! Not the one you met at the station in London?'

'Yes, Yvette! You are obviously not taking me seriously,' Dominic complained.

'Of course I am,' Tom said apologetically, only just beginning to realize how important this must be to Dominic.

'Anyway, she would like to meet to swap stories of our journeys.'

'Well, you'll certainly have plenty to tell her, lad. That's for sure.'

Dominic stopped smiling. 'Yes, I will. And thank God we arrived in time at Boulogne, Tom!' He hardly dared think what might have happened if they hadn't.

'I only wish we'd got there quick enough to stop them hurting those poor lasses, Nicole and Ginette.'

Papa was in the kitchen, cutting bread, and they persuaded him to sit down and share a bottle of wine with them. Dominic began telling him about their adventures in Boulogne, and, unable completely to follow what was being said, Tom glanced out of the window. He saw Madeleine talking animatedly out there in the garden, with her mother and her sisters. She was smiling, but her face shone with tears, too. The other three women were turned towards her, gazing at her with affection, and gesturing with their hands, interrupting each other to speak rapidly. It looked like a passionate debate. He was just thinking what a close family they were, and how lovely it was, when Madeleine glanced up, and caught him watching. She smiled at him, and ran for the kitchen.

'Tom,' she said, bursting in through the door from the *bouanderie*. 'We're talking about the baby, and . . .' she stopped and talked incredibly fast to Dominic.

He turned to Tom. 'She says that she cannot have the baby in England. She knows that she cannot. How can she, if she cannot speak the same language as the doctor?'

'But I'll be there,' Tom said. 'She can talk to me.'

326

'But what if there are . . . how do you say . . . problems, complications? No, it's impossible.' Dominic continued talking, and Tom had the odd feeling he was putting his own point of view, just as much as Madeleine's. 'You must see this, Tom. And you know, when a woman has a baby, she needs her mother to be there. It's a profound connection. To have your baby among strangers, to be without your mother at so vulnerable a time . . . this is insupportable. '

'So what are you saying?' Tom asked, feeling himself grow cold with apprehension. Madeleine stood next to the table, clutching her hands, her huge brown eyes fixed pleadingly on his. Her face was alive, expectant. He thought she'd never looked more beautiful. He knew he couldn't bear to lose her now. He'd agree to anything as long as that didn't happen.

'Madeleine is saying, we are saying, please, can she stay here to have the baby, and *then* come to England to be with you? Will you do that for us, Tom? Will you do that for me? For our friendship?'

Maman bustled in, then. She quickly added a garnish of parsley to the stew before setting it on the table, and asking if anyone was hungry. Madeleine sat next to Tom, and slipped her hand in his, and all the time they ate he felt her glancing at him, begging him to give way about the baby. But really it was not his decision any more. And when they'd all demolished the rich, savoury rabbit stew, cleaning their bowls spotless with thick chunks of bread, Dominic raised his glass and looked at Tom. 'To the future,' he said meaningfully.

'Yes. The future,' Tom responded, and he knew as he did, and as Martine and Simone and Madeleine, and Maman and Papa clinked their glasses to his, that he'd agreed. Madeleine would stay.

Chapter 24

Evenwood, England
Sunday, 9 December 1945

'I thought you'd come,' Hannah smiled, answering the back door.

Norah Atkins from No. 1 bustled into the scullery excitedly. 'Ah've got a message fer yer, lass!'

And before Hannah could even shut the door, Norah said, 'It's from your Tom. 'Eee phoned earlier this mornin', and said yer ter be at my house be five and twenty past eleven, and 'ee'll phone yer with some news at half past!'

'Can ah come too, Gran?' piped up Jeannie, who was on her third attempt to toast a slice of bread on the kitchen fire without setting it alight.

'Well, ah s'ppose so, but 'ee won't have much time ter talk, yer know. It'll cost 'im a fortune as it is, cause ah don't expect that lass in France has got a phone in her house yer know. So ah don't know where he'll be phonin' from.'

329

'Ah promise ah'll just talk to 'im very quick, Gran.'

'All right, pet, we'll see, eh?'

Hannah looked at the grandfather clock, and opened the door at the front to make sure that the chains holding the weights were fully wound up, while Jeannie stood in front swinging her head from side to side with the motion of the pendulum.

'Quarter past ten,' Hannah said anxiously, looking at Norah. 'It's just as well ah thought of giving Tom yer phone number before he went away, Norah, even though 'ee thought he'd never use it.' She was so grateful that there was someone on her street who could afford a telephone in their house.

'Ah wonder what 'ee's got ter tell yer?' Norah asked. Hannah wondered the same. Though she had an inkling he was going to bring that French lass back with him, she couldn't think why he'd want to talk to her about it first.

'Ah'll away back 'ome,' Norah said, 'and get the kettle on. Ah've got a feelin we're goin' ter be needin' a cup of tea after.' She looked sympathetically at Hannah's anxious face. She'd let herself out and was off through the lines of backyard laundry before Hannah had time to move.

Exactly one hour later, Jeannie and Hannah arrived at Norah's house. It was a quarter past eleven on the dot, and they sat there on her over-stuffed settee, barely able to contain their excitement. When the phone finally rang, all three jumped off their cushions. Norah rushed to pick up the bakelite receiver.

'Long-distance call from France to Evenwood 497,' said the operator's shrill, tinny voice, clear enough to be heard by the others.

'Yes ... yes,' Norah replied. Then, suddenly, her voice altered, and Hannah and Jeannie heard her exclaim, 'Eee, Tom, fancy makin' a phone call all the way from France, lad!' He was so far away that she shouted, to make sure he could hear. 'Ah'll hand yer over ter yer ma, then, shall ah?' She listened in case he said anything else, then gave the phone to Hannah.

Both Jeannie and Mrs Atkins watched Hannah intently. Tom's deep voice was only a murmur. They couldn't make out what he was saying. And Hannah, only interspersing the silence with an occasional 'yes', didn't give any clue, either, as to what the conversation might be about. Finally she said, 'All right, lad. If that's how you want it, that's how it'll have ter be. You take care then, and we'll see you soon.'

Jeannie, worried that her gran was going to put the phone down, started jumping up and down in front of her, imploring, 'Let me talk, Gran!' Hannah handed over the receiver, and, without a word, flopped down on to the settee and stared at the fire. Norah pushed the kettle further into the coals, deciding that this was definitely time for that comforting cup of tea. She got out her best china, with the yellow roses on, and after pouring boiling water on the loose leaves, said, 'We'll leave it ter mash fer a minute,' handing a plate of silver-foil-wrapped biscuits to Hannah, who was listening in on Jeannie's rather grown-up conversation with Tom.

'Don't yer realize that yer've had me gran worried sick, our Tom?' she was saying.

Tom was speaking louder now, and Hannah distinctly heard him answer jovially, 'Hey! Who do you think you are, me mam?'

'No, ah don't! But Gran is, and you should 'ave let 'er know what was goin' on.'

'All right, keep your hair on. She knows now, doesn't she?' Tom's voice said. And before Jeannie could ask what he was talking about, he had changed the subject. 'You don't know what you've been missing here, young lass!'

'What? What 'ave ah missed?'

'Oh, it'll keep till ah get home!' he teased.

''Urry up and get back 'ere, then! It's nearly Christmas, fer God's sake!'

'*Jeannie!*' Hannah called out, shocked.

'What?'

'Don't blaspheme like that!'

Jeannie, shaking the phone, asked, 'Why's the phone makin' a buzzin' noise, Gran?'

'You've probably been cut off, lass.'

'But ah hadn't finished with 'im! An' anyway, ah wasn't blast-feemin', Gran, but he does make me vexed, sometimes, our Tom. He's always messin' about.'

'Well, 'ee's not messin' about this time, pet,' she told Jeannie. Then she added, 'No. he's dead serious this time!'

Chapter 25

Evenwood, England
Monday, 10 June 1946

Almost six months had passed since that phone call between Tom and Hannah. Two hectic weeks later, involving a civil marriage ceremony and a blessing in a Catholic church, Tom had come back to England alone.

Hannah had been alarmed and worried by what he'd told her on the phone at Norah Atkins's. Here was her only son, set on marrying a lass none of them had met, *and* a foreigner to boot! What if the new lass didn't fit in? What if she didn't think the house at Glamis Terrace was good enough? How would they even communicate? All these thoughts, jumbling round her head, worried her senseless at first. But, after talking things over with Jack and their Rene, she'd calmed down.

'It's just that ah always thought ah'd be there when our Tom married,' she'd said, wiping a tear from her eye. Rene understood only too well what was going on in her mother's thoughts, because she had the same worries. But she wasn't going to let Hannah know that.

Jeannie, overhearing a bit of all this, piped up, '*Ah'll* be friends with 'er! And *ah'll* look after the new bairn!'

Tom was a changed man. He'd gone straight to the pit, and started work at the bricklaying job he'd been offered the week before, planning to go back over to France and fetch Maddie and the bairn once he got himself established. He knew it was going to take time and dedication, but, he told himself, the bairn wouldn't be born for a while yet, so he had time to prove himself. Also, there'd be a bit more room in the house once their Rene moved to Bishop Auckland.

Rene was absolutely insistent they were going, even though Jeannie kicked up about it. Rene did manage to win Jeannie round a bit by reminding her that she couldn't let her new friend Ian down, now that she'd promised to teach him how to talk like a proper Northerner. So, with permission to invite Ian over for tea on the first Sunday after they'd moved in, Jeannie relented. 'As long as ah can be at me gran's on the day that Tom's new missis and bairn arrive, mind!' She wasn't going to give way on that.

Madeleine sent some photographs of the wedding over to England, and after studying them, the whole family agreed she *looked* nice enough. Madeleine was sure Tom's family would be as curious about her as she was about them. So the photos were a way of introducing herself, and in return she asked Tom to send her some pictures of the Dawsons. He borrowed a camera from his mate Harry, and Jeannie helped him, and they had a lot of fun with it, including pictures of Hannah half-hidden behind a line of drying smalls – and, their favourite – Jack caught unawares, coming in the back gate covered in coal-dust and shaking his fist in mock-annoyance.

Unusually for Hannah, she was sitting down, duster in hand, when she heard Tom whistling as he came in the back door from the yard.

'Eee, pet!' She jumped up. 'Ah was just havin' a bit of a sit-down before you and yer da got in from work. And here you are already. Ah'd lost track of the time.'

'Mam, there's no need to excuse yourself cause you're having a rest. Now, you sit yourself back down.' He led her gently to the couch. 'I've something to tell you.'

'No more shocks, ah hope?' she smiled, flopping down.

He sat opposite her. 'Nah, nowt like that.' He looked across at her from under his brows, and grinned.

'Come on, then, out with it!' She flapped the duster at him impatiently.

'Ooh, it's nowt much. Just that I've been promoted to site manager.'

'Eee, our Tom! *Site manager!* Aw lad, ah'm that pleased for yer! That'll mean a bit more money then, will it?'

'Aye, a bit, but I'll have to prove myself before they give us a decent rise, like.'

'Oh, you'll do it, lad. Ah know yer will.' She patted his arm. 'Eee, two managers in the family!'

'Aye, what will our Rene have to say about that, I wonder?' Tom stuck his jaw out, striking an attitude of mock-superiority. He moved over next to Hannah on the couch. 'Of course, you know what this means now, don't you?' He chose his words carefully.

'Yes, lad, ah do. It means yer can bring that poor lass and the bairn over here sooner than yer thought.'

'I've got to say I'm feeling a bit nervous about it, mind!' Tom confessed.

'Well, imagine what it'll be like fer her. Comin' over here to a country she doesn't know, ter live with folks she's never met and probably won't be able ter talk to very much, none of us having each other's language, like.'

'She knows a bit more English now than she did when I first met her. And I reckon she'll learn quick.'

'Well, ah hope yer right, lad. Otherwise it's goin' ter be very hard for her, what with bein' so far from her mam an' all.'

Tom patted Hannah's arm as he got up to poke the fire. 'Eee, you're such a worrier, Mam! She'll be fine, you'll see.' He wasn't sure who he was trying to convince most: Hannah or himself. Then, suddenly remembering some unfinished business, he said, 'I hope Jessie's not going to be a pain in the arse to her.'

'Well, ah wouldn't expect her ter be friendly,' Hannah answered, equally concerned. 'She took it very badly, yer know, when yer finished with her, like!'

'Aw, Mam, that was months ago, surely she must be used to it by now!'

'Well, ah wouldn't bank on it!' Hannah said with some certainty. 'She might be just biding her time, yer know.'

She'd never forget how Jessie had come barging into the house on the very day Tom had returned from France. Why he'd hardly had chance to draw breath, and there she was in the middle of the living room, hands on hips, yelling her head off. He'd chucked his case down and dragged her out into the backyard.

Hannah hadn't been able to avoid hearing what was said. In the end she'd watched them through the scullery window. She'd felt a pang of sorrow for Jessie. Particularly when the yelling had suddenly stopped, to be replaced by what could only be described as a look of pure horror on Jessie's face, Hannah, knowing that Tom had just told Jessie he was married, had blinked back tears at the sight. Because, for all her gobbiness, she knew that underneath Jessie did have a heart, and was a decent lass. Hannah had always had a soft spot for her, and she'd been like one of the family for years. But, at the same time, she'd had often sensed that the relationship was doomed.

Hannah had watched as Tom tried to take hold of Jessie's hand while he explained what had happened, but Jessie would have none of it, and violently pushed him away before running out of the gate and down the back lane. Worryingly, they hadn't seen hide nor hair of her since. *I hope she's not storing it all up to make a nuisance of herself when the lass and her bairn come over from France*, Hannah thought – and not for the first time, either.

'Penny for them?' Tom asked, wondering what she was worrying about now.

'Oh, it's nowt!' she answered, quickly changing the subject. 'When d'yer think you'll go, lad?' she asked.

'The bairn won't be born for another couple of weeks, so I'll have a word with me boss to give him plenty of warning that I'll be needing a few days off. I reckon it'll be as soon as he can spare me, probably in the next month or so.'

'Ah can get a cot fer the bairn from Mrs Atkins's daughter, because she's moved her bairn into a proper bed now that she's getting bigger,' Hannah offered.

'Oh, aye?' Tom answered, only half paying attention while an idea began to form in his head. Hannah continued, oblivious, 'We'll have to get the beddin' and all that new, though, yer know,' she said, trying to make the point that he was going to have to fork out at least some money. 'This new wife of yours won't be too happy with all second-hand stuff, lad. She'll want new, yer know. You'll have ter take her into Bishop as soon as yer can to buy some proper stuff, our Tom—'

'Ay, Mam,' said Tom, cutting her short as he pulled her up from the couch in his excitement. 'Give it a rest for a minute, will you? I've an idea.'

'Oh aye, and what might that be?' Hannah looked doubtful.

'Well, d'you remember that conversation you had with Mrs Hurd a few weeks back about old Jake, and him dying sudden, like?'

'Yes. What about it?' she asked, puzzled now.

'Well, I wandered past Jake's house after, just being curious, like. Anyway there was a couple of chaps there, clearing the place out, and I asked them what was going to happen to it, and they said it'd probably stand empty till some builder or suchlike came along to do it up.'

'Aye, well, I expect it will. So what about it, anyway?' Hannah asked.

'Think about it, Mam. If that house is standing empty, well, who better to fill it than me, Maddie and the bairn?'

'Well, yes, but—' Hannah suddenly stopped in her tracks. She gave a little laugh. 'Oh, our Tom! You'd never afford a house like that! Why, it's got two bedrooms, if ah remember right, along with a kitchen and livin' room, *and* a proper garden with trees in it!'

'Yes, ah know, Mam. But it's in a hell of a state, so it might be cheap. It'll need doing up an' all that, and I could do the work, couldn't I? But in the meanwhile, I reckon a bit of painting would make it OK. I'll just have ter find a way to get the money . . . Maybe I could rent it – to start with, like!'

He pulled a couple of grainy, yellowed photographs from his inside pocket, and showed them to Hannah. 'Look, I picked these up from a pile of stuff that was being chucked out while ah was there. I didn't know why I wanted them at the time, but I think I do now.'

Was this really *her* son talking? Hannah, dumbfounded, sat on the nearest chair.

Bishop Auckland, England
Sunday, 28 July 1946

'Mam! Mam! Ah've brought Ee-an 'ome for 'is tea!' Jeannie came running through the shop.

'*Jeannie!* What have I told you about running through the shop and shouting like a . . . a fisherwoman?'

'Oh, ah'm sorry, Mam, but there's no customers in on a Sunder, is there?' Jeannie said, crouching down and lifting the curtain of one of the three fitting rooms to peer inside.

The day is "Sunday", Jeannie, not "Sunder". And this is not your "'ome", but your "home".' She gave Jeannie a meaningful look, then, smiling apologetically at Ian, said, 'Oh, just get yourselves upstairs, I'll be up in a minute.' Jeannie's grammar had got even worse since they'd moved to Bishop Auckland, Rene thought.

'Do you think you could finish up in here, Hilda?' she asked her under-manager.

'No problem,' Hilda said, surfacing from under the pile of coats that she'd been unpacking ready for the first day of the sales. 'Una will help me, she's just gone to powder her nose, like. And ah'll tell yer what, ah'm glad we decided to come in today to do all this un-packing. It'd be a right carry-on if we'd left it till Monday, like we were goin' to.'

'You're right there, Hilda. Thanks for coming in. I do appreciate it, you know.'

'Oh, ah know that, Rene. Mind you, ah wouldn't do

340

it fer just anybody, like,' Hilda said. 'But yer a fair boss, and we want ter be fair ter you in return.'

Rene nodded towards her. 'Thanks,' was all she managed after such a compliment.

Before she even turned to go up the stairs she could hear crackling and whistling sounds coming from the wireless. The odd burst of Glenn Miller, interspersed with a comedy show and snatches of the news fading in and out, reminded Rene that it had been a mistake buying a second-hand wireless: she should have bought brand new. But there'd been so many bits and pieces to buy when she'd moved in, that a wireless had been low on her priorities. Had she realized just how much pleasure Jeannie *and* herself, for that matter, would get from it, she would definitely have given it more priority.

She walked into the sitting room and there they both were, Jeannie and Ian, kneeling in front of it each desperately twiddling the knobs. Jeannie looked over her shoulder as her mother came in.

'We're trying ter get the thing ter work, Mam! But the needle thing that goes on the programmes keeps getting stuck,' she exclaimed in frustration. 'Ee-an wants ter listen ter his favourite comedy programme, but the needle won't seem ter stop at t' right place.'

Rene, her arms folded, stopped and observed with a grin, 'Oh girl, what am I going to do with you? Move over, and let's have a look at it.' She crouched down beside them.

'Ah've put the beans in a pan ready ter heat up, and shall ah make some to-ast, Mam?'

'I think you mean "toast", Jeannie,' Rene sighed, in her relentless quest to improve her daughter's speech.

Jeannie understood, and sighed. 'Yes, Mam, ah mean "toast".'

Ian was tipping his prize marbles from a small draw-string bag on to the brightly coloured clippie rug in the middle of the polished wooden floor, and didn't seem to take any notice of the exchanges between Jeannie and her mother.

'Well, shall ah, or shan't ah, do the toast?' Jeannie asked.

'No, you entertain your friend, pet. I'll do it. I don't like you using the grill. It gets a bit too hot.' Rene got up from fixing the wireless. 'Anyway, I thought you two were teaching each other how to speak?'

'We are,' said Jeannie defensively.

'I haven't heard much evidence of it yet,' Rene called from the kitchen.

'Rene! Rene!' A voice called from downstairs. 'Telephone!'

'OK! Just coming, Hilda!' she called, hurriedly dividing the beans and toast between the two plates before calling Jeannie and Ian to the table.

'Who is it?' she called back.

'It's yer mam!' Hilda shouted.

Rene ran downstairs and picked up the receiver. 'Hello, Mam,' she said cautiously, knowing that it must be important, because Hannah had to go all the way to a telephone box, or ask Mrs Atkins at No. 1.

'Hello, pet,' said the voice at the other end. 'Ah

wondered if you and our Jeannie could come over tomorrow, cause our Tom and the lass and the bairn are arriving in the morning. Ah'd like yer ter be here if yer can, fer a bit of moral support, like?'

'Good grief, Mam! Tom only went back over there a couple of days ago. I didn't expect them back so soon! Of course I'll come. That's if I can sort something out here in the shop. I'll ring the school in the morning and get Jeannie the day off.'

'Ay, thanks, pet. Get here as early as yer can, eh?'

'Will do. Bye, Mam, and don't you be worrying on!' Rene instructed, knowing what Hannah was like. She put the receiver down slowly.

'Everything all right?' Hilda asked.

'Yes. Yes, thanks,' Rene answered absent-mindedly. 'Would you mind opening up the shop for me in the morning, Hilda? I've got to go out, maybe even for the whole day.'

'Of course ah will, but—'

'I know. It's the first day of the sales. But Mary is coming in to help out, anyway, so there'll be three of you, and I'll do my best to get back in the afternoon.'

Hilda started to ask what the problem at home was, but Rene, not wanting to explain right then, cut her off gently. 'I'll tell you all about it tomorrow, when I get back. I'd better go up and see to the children now. Thanks again, Hilda.' She smiled. 'I'll see you all right for this.'

'Oh, no bother!' Hilda replied, delighted by the prospect of a bit of extra money.

Evenwood, England
Monday, 29 July 1946

Tom and Madeleine stepped off the train at Ramshaw Station. Baby Francine was fractious and tired, and the stationmaster ran over to help Tom, who was struggling to get two hefty cases down from the train. Tom pushed a sixpenny piece into his hand and thanked him.

'Oh, a tanner! Thanks, mate!' he said gratefully.

Tom, a case in each hand now, led the way, while Maddie had to keep stopping to tuck in Francine's shawl, which seemed to slip down every few steps she took. She tried in vain to keep up with Tom, but guessed that the cases were so heavy he didn't dare slow down.

They had travelled all night, and Maddie was not only tired, but scared and miserable. Leaving her parents this time had been quite different from when she'd left them to run away to Boulogne. This time she felt powerless and dependent. How could she feel otherwise, when she didn't know what sort of place she was going to? And as for the language that she'd heard on the train, well, in no way did it resemble *any* English *she* knew. And, with Tom marching ahead of her now, she suddenly felt lonely.

Tears had streamed down her face for most of the journey, and she certainly wasn't up to meeting Tom's family right now. Tom turned to look at her when she mentioned her swollen face and puffy eyes. 'You look gorgeous, they'll love you,' he encouraged. 'Come on, just under half a mile to go.' He tried to sound positive.

'Half a mile!' she said, horrified. 'Can't we get an autobus?'

'It's too early in the morning for a bus.' He smiled. 'Come on, it won't take long from here.'

Tom had been very kind to her on the journey, but right now she would rather have been anywhere but here, walking along this footpath, beside this cemetery wall. She suddenly realized that this was the wall Tom had described to her, and had told her was like the one between Marck and Calais.

'See?' he said, stopping to rest for a second, and reading her mind. 'What did I tell you? It's like the wall in Marck, eh?'

'*Oui*, it is,' she lied, hardly looking up. To her, this was nothing like the cemetery wall at home. This could never be home, she thought, looking round at her dismal surroundings. *Mon Dieu*, what have I done?

Maman and Papa had been wonderful to her when Francine was born at home in Marck. And afterwards they had taken their new grandchild to their hearts. Madeleine's eyes filled with tears each time she remembered Maman giving Francine one last cuddle before they left. She'd had to avoid thinking about those last goodbyes or she would have spent the whole journey crying even harder.

Instead, she'd thought of Dominic, and how happy he'd been lately, since meeting up again with Yvette. After he'd received that first letter from her he'd written back at once. And at the end of the first day they'd spent together he'd come home filled with joy. Since then,

Yvette had been to visit the family at home, and had fitted in so perfectly that Madeleine had felt they could be good friends. But alas, she'd had to leave all her friends behind. Even though she hadn't seen her school friends much recently, she still mourned their loss, too.

'Madeleine, the quiet and sensible one ... with a baby!' they'd said, taken aback, when they first heard her news. But once they'd come to terms with the idea they'd all been excited. They'd been envious of her starting a new life with the man she loved, in a new world. They thought it incredibly romantic, and she wondered – a little sourly – if any of them would have been brave enough to do the same. There had been promises to write and to meet up, but in her heart Madeleine knew that she would probably never see them again.

'Come on, pet!' Tom's voice broke into her thoughts. 'You're dawdling way behind. Is the bairn all right?'

'*Oui*, she sleeps.' Madeleine quickened her pace.

'We're nearly there,' he said, stopping to rest the suitcases again. 'Aww, just look at her,' he said. 'She's like a little angel when she's asleep.' He gazed at his daughter with pride.

'A heavy angel.' Madeleine hitched the baby up, trying to find a more comfortable carrying position.

Half an hour later they stood in front of the house in Glamis Terrace. Everything was quiet, and there was no one around. Tom looked at his watch. It was seven thirty. He guessed his da must have left for work, and his mam was probably in the scullery having a wash.

'Here we are, pet,' he said, looking very pleased with himself as he lowered the cases to the ground and stretched his back.

Madeleine was so nervous she had to fight the urge to vomit. 'Are they sleeping?' she said. 'We don't wake them.' She started to back away, desperately trying to put off the moment when she'd have to go into the house.

'We can't stand out here now, can we?' Tom put his arm around her. As he rapped on the door Madeleine looked round at the other houses, sure that the whole street must have heard.

When a man's voice called from within, she held her breath.

'Just a minute,' the voice called, and after much rattling, the door was opened by a very startled-looking man.

Francine began to murmur as he spoke.

'Ay, come on in,' he said, glancing at her shyly. 'Yer must have been travellin' all night ter be arrivin' at this hour?'

'Aye, Da, we have,' Tom answered. He brought Madeleine forward. 'Meet my wife, Da. This is Maddie. And Maddie, meet my da.'

Jack held his hand out for a shake. Maddie didn't take it. Instead she leaned forward and kissed him on the cheek.

'Well, well, well,' he said, pleased and flustered. 'And this'll be little Francine, eh?' He smiled at the sleeping bundle in Maddie's arms.

As they stepped inside, Tom saw Hannah standing at the bottom of the stairs, with their Rene close behind. Both looked slightly dishevelled.

'Well, ah didn't expect ter see you here, our Rene,' he said, surprised. He was slightly put out. He'd hoped for a quiet time alone with his little family and his mam and da on the first day.

'Come on, lass,' Jack said to Hannah. 'Get them a cup of tea made, they must be parched after that journey.'

Rene went to do it, while Hannah walked up to Madeleine.

'Eee, pet, yer must be shattered. Come and sit down,' she said, leading her into the sitting room. 'Oh, and look at that poor bairn! She should be in bed!'

'She'll be all right, Mam. We'll take her to bed in a bit,' said Tom, looking at Maddie, who so far hadn't spoken a word.

Rene, still in her nightie, filled the kettle and pushed it into the fire before she came over to Madeleine. 'Hello, Maddie, I'm Rene, Tom's sister,' she said, smiling. 'You'll have to excuse us. We're all a bit shocked. We weren't expecting you so early.'

Maddie spoke at last. 'I 'ope you excuse us also. The afternoon of yesterday was the time of the boat . . .' she was saying, when Jeannie, also in her nightie, appeared at the bottom of the stairs.

'Oh, Mam! She talks just like Dominic,' she said excitedly.

For the first time Madeleine smiled. She said to

Jeannie, 'Dominic, he is my brozer. I am Maddie.' Seeing Jeannie's eyes on the baby she said, 'This is Francine.'

'She's bonny,' said Jeannie, in awe of the little bundle.

Tom had gone off to the toilet by the time Hannah brought the mugs of hot sweet tea, and when Rene offered to take Francine to give Madeleine a chance to get her coat off and drink the tea, Maddie shook her head and held on protectively to her baby. There was no way she was going to hand her over to strangers. She was acutely aware of what seemed to be a roomful of people, all looking at her and smiling, and their awkwardness made her uneasy.

The ticking of the clock dominated the room and she was beginning to feel herself flush with embarrassment, when suddenly Jeannie broke the ice. 'Can ah take the baby out later on? And show her off ter me friends?' she asked.

Tom, who was just coming back, saw the look of horror on Maddie's face. He stepped in quickly, 'Not today, pet, that's for sure. The baby'll need to rest, you see, and get used to the place, don't you think?'

'Well . . .'

Silenced for a second by a meaningful look and shake of the head from Hannah, which she understood as a warning not to say any more, Jeannie whispered quickly, 'Will she wake up in a minute?'

'She'll wake up for her breakfast, I'll bet.' Tom tried to lighten the atmosphere a bit.

'Well, can ah feed 'er, then?' Jeannie asked in a louder whisper.

Rene pulled her on to her lap and tried to explain. 'Look, pet, they've just arrived, and Maddie and the baby are going to need time to get used to us and to the house, without *all* of us hanging around them. So we'll stay for breakfast, then we'll go back home to Bishop.'

Recognizing Jeannie's deep intake of breath as being a prelude to an objection, Rene cut in quickly, 'There'll be plenty more days when you can come over to help with the baby, I'm sure.' She glanced at Madeleine for confirmation.

Maddie nodded and smiled politely.

Tom set about stoking up the fire while Da went out to the coalhouse to fill up the heavy aluminium bucket, and Mam busied herself in the scullery getting breakfast ready. Rene, unsure what to do, said to Tom and Maddie, 'I'll be in the kitchen if you want anything. We'll give you a minute or two to get your breath, eh?' She glanced at Tom, who nodded in appreciation.

When Rene entered the kitchen, Hannah looked up from the eggs she was beating, and said, 'Ah've come in here ter give them a bit of time. Ah don't know what ter say ter the poor lass, she looks terrified.'

'I know,' Rene answered. 'She's probably really tired, and feeling totally lost at the moment.'

Hannah nodded, adding, 'Bye, she's a bonny lass, though!'

'Yes, she is.' Rene smiled in agreement.

'Ah can't wait fer the bairn ter wake up. Yer can't see her properly when her face is turned to her mam like that!'

'Yes, me too, but I came away because Maddie looks so fragile, and I don't know how to get her to relax. She's obviously not going to hand the baby over to anybody at the moment, so there was nothing I could do to help. I thought she might be better with some time to just sit and try to acclimatize herself.'

'Well,' Hannah pointed out, 'it's up ter our Tom ter settle 'er in, really.' She added, 'Ah'm that glad you and our Jeannie came over last night instead of this morning.'

'Yes,' Rene answered, 'so am I, as it's turned out. Although I think as far as Maddie's concerned it's probably been a bit more of a houseful to face than she would have liked. So what I'll do, Mam, is go up and change the sheets while you finish here in the kitchen.'

'OK, pet, that'd be a help,' Hannah replied. Then added as an afterthought, 'And would yer get our Jeannie in here ter get this bread? She could be toastin' it over the fire the while.'

Madeleine sat by the fire, feeling unable to move. Not even when Tom crouched down in front of her, to ask if she wanted to go up to the bedroom to rest, did she move her eyes towards him. She knew that if she did anything she would cry. And she couldn't cry again, because if she did she would never stop.

Tom, at a bit of a loss, not ever having seen Madeleine like this before, offered to take her coat, but her response was to shake her head and pull the coat further around herself.

Not sure how to respond, he said in as light a tone as

he could muster, 'The fire'll be blaring away in a few minutes, and then we'll all feel better for it, eh?'

The corners of her mouth moved up slightly, but she didn't answer, or look at him. Oh, she could see that his family were kind and good people. But they weren't her people. She had left behind the only life she knew and understood, in order to live with the man who was the father of her baby, and, yes, she loved him. But did she love him enough to spend the rest of her life in a world that she neither knew or understood?

Acutely aware of the repetitive ticking of the grandfather clock, she sat there allowing the sound to bore through her head, in this strange, brown-coloured room. She found herself wondering how many times it would have to tick before she could go home to visit her maman and papa.

Rene came back into the room, where, shocked at the misery on Madeleine's face, she whispered urgently to Tom, 'You haven't told her, have you?'

'I was keeping it as a surprise for tomorrow, after she's had time to settle herself in,' he answered.

'Well, looking at her now, I don't think it can wait until tomorrow.'

He glanced over at Madeleine, who was staring at the fire, her eyes swimming with unshed tears.

'Maybe you're right,' he said anxiously. 'Maddie!' he shook her arm lightly, causing her to look up vacantly. 'Maddie! I've got something to show you. Just sit there and I'll be back in a second.'

Racing upstairs, he grabbed an envelope from his

bedside table, and, after quickly checking the contents, he ran back down the stairs, and, coming to rest at Madeleine's side, he crouched down beside her and handed it to her.

A deep frown formed on her forehead. 'What is it?' she asked.

'Open it and see,' he prompted with a smile.

From the envelope she pulled out two photographs. One showed the front of a little cottage with a man peering through the doorway, and the other a garden with trees in it, and a group of people sitting under one of the tallest ones.

'I don't understand,' she said. 'Who are this people?'

'No, no, not the people. Forget the people. What do you see?' Tom urged.

'A house, and a garden?' Madeleine answered, confused by his question.

'It's yours, pet. Well, what I mean is, it's ours,' he corrected.

'Ours . . . ? The house? You mean this house is for you and me?' she exclaimed.

Tom nodded, looking mightily pleased with himself.

'Oh, *mon Dieu!*' She clapped her hand over her mouth, then asked, 'Why did you not tell me, Tom?'

'I planned to take you there tomorrow, as a surprise, but you looked so sad that I had to tell you now.'

Madeleine sat there, saying nothing, but her mind was working very fast. How could she have doubted whether she loved this man enough? This man who had done this thing for her, this huge thing, which she knew must be well beyond his means. She had no idea how he'd done it, but he had, and she had no doubt that he'd have to work long hours to afford it. But he'd done it for her.

Tom, concerned about Madeleine's continuing silence, tried to encourage her by saying, 'Ah know it's a bit run down, but it will be lovely when we've finished decorating it. I thought we could do it together, bit by bit, and Mam is happy for us to stay with her until it's done. Come on, pet, we'll manage till then, and we'll have fun choosing the wallpaper and all that, won't we?'

Madeleine knew then that, no matter what lay ahead, if this husband of hers, who she loved more than ever before, had found a way, against all the odds, to make this huge gesture to her, then *she* was damned well going to find a way to make a new life here in England with him.

She looked up at the family. Rene and Jack stood side by side, Jeannie and Hannah held hands, waiting and wondering.

As an answer, Maddie stood up, gently handed Francine to Rene, and threw her arms around Tom, before, unashamedly, kissing him hard on the mouth. The only sound in the room was Jeannie's embarrassed exclamation, 'Eee, Gran!'

Author's Note

Although *Northern Girl* is a work of fiction, it was inspired by the true story of how my parents met, and created a life together . . .

'I was dancing with an officer when I first saw Tom [my mother, Madeleine, recounts]. He was making fun of me while he was with other girls, some even sitting on his knee. After a while, he managed to ask me to dance, and it all started from there.

Over the next few months we had a lovely time, and he came to see me every day. Sometimes he would go to a shop in the market place, where there was another girl. But I guess he must have preferred me.

Some months later after he was moved to Belgium I discovered that I was pregnant, and that was a terrible thing to happen in those days. It was such a worry for my family, as well as for me. (My sister Martine told me of the shocked and urgent whispers going around the village: "*Have you heard about Madeleine Pelletier?*")

We had no idea how to contact Tom. Eventually Martine went to Lille to meet an officer of his detachment, a very nice man. But when Tom was contacted from Lille, he said that the baby couldn't be his.

Sometime after that he was demobilized and he returned to England, where, I heard later, he was given a big, hero-style welcome-home party.

After Francine was born, my family and I managed to get Tom's home address and we contacted him, to let him know that he had a lovely little girl. It must have been a huge shock for his family.

He then started to write, and eventually, when he saw his daughter, any doubts he'd had were dispelled. She was his, and in his heart he'd always known it. But what could a man who was just out of the army with no proper job give to a woman and a child who lived in France? The initial denial of his child had been a result of nothing more than poverty and fear.

Tom and I married in France. Before I went to live in England (the only option we had) Dominic, my brother, insisted on going before me, to check on where I would be living, and to meet Tom's parents. When he arrived in Bishop Auckland he took the bus to Evenwood. By amazing coincidence he recognized two little criss-cross lines on the back of the neck of the person sitting in front of him. It was Tom.

After an emotional reunion, Tom and Dominic continued the five-mile bus journey together. It was a huge surprise for the family when they walked into Tom's house but they couldn't do enough for Dominic. Anyone who knew the Dawson family will know exactly what I mean. They were very warm and caring people.

I remember the day Francine and I arrived in Evenwood. It was very early in the morning, and the whole family had got out of bed very quickly. Rene, Jeannie, one of their aunties (Hilda), Hannah and Jack, all looking at us.

As I remember it now, the whole family seemed to be standing there just smiling at us. But I was too sad to smile.

Tom did not understand how hard it was for me when I arrived in England. I knew no one, and I couldn't speak the language. We also had a little girl to look after and she was only one year old at the time. What if she fell ill? How would I speak to the doctor? How would I speak to anyone about anything? But Tom was young, and he didn't realize what I had given up.

Little Jeannie wanted to take Francine to show her off to her friends, but I was afraid and reluctant to let my little girl go away from me. Everything was so new and so different here, and it took me a *very, very* long time to get used to this difficult way of life.'

*

After many years of heartache and almost unbearable homesickness Madeleine did get used to this way of life. And by looking at newspapers, listening to the radio and to people conversing, amazingly she conquered the language barrier.

Her yearly visits home to France, although very necessary to her, could also be detrimental, as she suffered such heart-wrenching pain each time she left her family to make the tearful journey back to the north-east of England. However, aware that without the warmth of Tom's family she might not have coped at all, bit by bit she began to allow herself to embrace the cultural differences.

Two years after the birth of Francine, Madeleine found herself pregnant again, and returned to France. After the birth of their son, she journeyed back to the north-east of England, where she and Tom continued to bring up their two children until the early 1960s when, due to lack of building work in the north-east, she and her family moved south.

At eighty-three years old, Madeleine, who still retains her very attractive French accent, enjoys the loving affection of her children, grandchildren, great-grandchildren, and, of course, the friends she has made over the years. And most surprisingly, she's more at home now in this once alien country of England than in her homeland.

Sadly, Tom died some years ago.